Also available from Julia London and HQN

A Royal Match

Last Duke Standing

A Royal Wedding

The Princess Plan
A Royal Kiss & Tell
A Princess by Christmas

The Cabot Sisters

The Trouble with Honor
The Devil Takes a Bride
The Scoundrel and the Debutante

The Highland Grooms

Wild Wicked Scot
Sinful Scottish Laird
Hard-Hearted Highlander
Devil in Tartan
Tempting the Laird
Seduced by a Scot

For additional books by Julia London,
visit her website, julialondon.com.

LAST DUKE
STANDING

JULIA LONDON

HQN

ISBN-13: 978-1-335-63986-8

Last Duke Standing

Copyright © 2022 by Dinah Dinwiddie

Recycling programs
for this product may
not exist in your area.

This edition published by arrangement with Harlequin Books S.A.

For questions and comments about the quality of this book,
please contact us at CustomerService@Harlequin.com.

HQN
22 Adelaide St. West, 41st Floor
Toronto, Ontario M5H 4E3, Canada
www.Harlequin.com

Printed and bound in Barcelona, Spain by CPI Black Print

"I love you," Buttercup said. "I know this must come as something of a surprise to you, since all I've ever done is scorn you and degrade you and taunt you, but I have loved you for several hours now, and every second, more."

—William Goldman, *The Princess Bride*

LAST DUKE STANDING

PROLOGUE

1844

WHEN JUSTINE WAS FOURTEEN, her father took her to the mountainous north country of Wesloria. He said he was to meet with coal barons because they were restless and in need of appeasing. Why? Justine had wondered.

"Because coal barons are always restless and in need of appeasing, darling," he'd said, as if everyone knew that.

She'd imagined large, heavily cloaked men, faces covered in soot, pacing their hearths and muttering their grievances. But the coal barons were, in fact, like all well-dressed Weslorian gentlemen with clean faces.

They peered at her with expressions that ranged from disgust to indifference to curiosity.

"Don't mind them," her father had said. "They are not modern men."

Justine and her father were housed at Astasia Castle. It was a fortress that jutted out forebodingly from a rocky outcropping so high on the mountain that the horses labored to pull the royal coach up the steep drive. It was purported to be the best of all the accommodations in the area, afforded to Justine and her father by virtue of the fact Justine's father was the king of Wesloria, and she was the crown princess, the invested heir to the throne.

Justine said the castle looked scary. Her father explained

that castles were built in this manner so that armies and marauders could be seen advancing from miles away, and runaway brides could be seen fleeing for miles.

"Runaway brides?" Justine had been enthralled by the idea of something so romantic gone so horribly awry.

"Petr the Mad watched his bride run away with his best knight, and then watched his men chase them for miles before they got away. He was so angry he burned down half the village." Her father did not elaborate further, as the gates had opened, and the castellan had come rushing forward, eager to show the king and his heir the old royal castle he proudly kept.

Sir Corin wore a dusty blue waistcoat that hung to his thighs, the last four buttons undone to allow for his paunch. His hair, scraggly and gray, had been pulled into an old-fashioned queue at his nape. He kept a ring of keys attached to his waist that clanked with each step he took.

He was a student of history, he'd said, and could answer any question they might have about Astasia Castle, and proceeded to exhibit his detailed knowledge of the dank, drafty place with narrow halls and low ceilings. A young Russian prince had died in this room. An ancient queen had lost her life giving birth to her tenth child in that room.

Sir Corin showed them to the throne room. "More than one monarch's held court here."

Justine was accustomed to the opulence of the palace in Wesloria's capital of St. Edys. This looked more like a common room of a public house—it was small and dark, the king and queen's thrones wooden, and the tapestries faded by time and smoke.

Another room, Sir Corin pointed out, was where King Maksim had accepted the surrender of the feudal King

Igor, thereby uniting all Weslorians under one rule after generations of strife.

"My namesake," her father said proudly, forgetting, perhaps, that King Maksim had slaughtered King Igor's forces to unite them all.

They came upon a small inner courtyard. Stone walls rose up on three sides of it, but the outer wall was a battlement. Sir Corin pointed to a door at one end of the battlement that led into a keep with narrow windows. "We use it for storage now, but they kept the prisoners there in the old days. Worse than any dungeon your young eyes have ever seen, Your Royal Highness."

Justine had never seen a dungeon.

"Is this not where Lord Rabat was beheaded?" her father asked casually. To Justine, he said, "That would have been your great-great-uncle Rabat."

"*Je*, Your Majesty, the block is still here." Sir Corin pointed to a large wooden block that stood alone, about two feet high and two feet wide. It looked to have been weathered by years of sitting in hard sun and wretched winters.

"Oh, how *terrible*," Justine said, crinkling her nose.

"Quite," her father agreed, and explained, with far too much enthusiasm, how a person was made to kneel before the block and lay their neck upon it. "A good executioner could make clean work of it with a single stroke. *Whap*, and the head would tumble into a basket."

"If I may, Your Majesty, a good executioner was hard to come by. More miners in these parts than men good with broadswords. Fact is, it took *three* strikes of the sword to sever Rabat's head completely." Sir Corin felt it necessary to demonstrate the three strikes with his arm.

"Ah…" Justine swallowed down a swell of nausea.

"*Three* whacks?" her father repeated, rapt. "Couldn't get it done in one?"

Sir Corin shook his head. "Just goes to prove how important it is to keep the broadsword sharp."

"And to keep someone close who knows how to wield it," her father added. The two men laughed roundly.

Justine looked around for someplace to sit so that she could put her head between her legs and gulp some air. Alas, the only place to sit was the block.

"Steady there, my girl. I've not told you who ordered the beheading," her father said.

Sir Corin clasped his hands together in anticipation, clearly trying to contain his glee.

"Your great-great-aunt Queen Elena!"

Queen Elena had beheaded Lord Rabat? "Her *husband*?"

"Worse. Her *brother*."

Justine gasped. "But why?"

"Because Rabat meant to behead her first. Whoever survived the battle here would be crowned the sovereign."

"Ooh, a bloody battle it was, too," Sir Corin said eagerly. "Four thousand souls lost, many of them falling right off the battlement."

Justine backed up a step. A quake was beginning somewhere deep inside her, making her a little short of breath. Her knees felt as if they might buckle, and her skin crawled with anxiety, imagining the loss of so many. "Could she not have banished him?"

"And have him slither back like a snake?" Her father draped his arm around her shoulders before she could back up all the way to St. Edys. "She did the right thing. Why, minutes before, she was on the block herself."

"Dear *God*," Justine whispered.

"But at the last minute the people here saved her," her

father said. "She sentenced her brother to die immediately for his insurrection and stood right where we are now to watch his traitorous head roll."

"Well," Sir Corin said. "I wouldn't say it *rolled*, precisely."

The two men laughed again.

"Don't close your eyes, darling," her father said, squeezing her into his side. "Look at that block. Elena was only seventeen years old, but she was very clever. She knew what she had to do to hold power and rule the kingdom. And she ruled a very long time."

"Forty-three years, all told," Sir Corin said proudly.

"Queen Elena learned what every sovereign must—be decisive and act quickly. Do you understand?"

"I don't…think so?" Justine was starting to feel a bit like she was spinning.

"You will." Her father dropped his arm. He wandered over to the block to inspect it. "We almost named you Elena after her. But they called her Elena the Bi—Witch," he said. "And your mother feared they might call you the same."

"You said she was a good queen."

"She was an excellent queen. But sometimes it is difficult to do the things that must be done and keep the admiration of your people at the same time."

The spinning was getting worse. She gripped her father's arm. "Why?"

"Because people expect a woman to behave like a woman. But a good queen must sometimes behave more like a king for the good of the kingdom. People don't care for it." He shrugged. "No king or queen can make all their subjects happy all the time." He suddenly smiled. "You look a bit like Queen Elena."

"The very image," Sir Corin piped up.

Later that day Justine saw a portrait of Queen Elena. She wasn't smiling, but she didn't appear completely unpleasant. She simply looked…determined. And her dress was elegantly pretty, with lots of pearls sewn into it.

Later still, when her father and his men had retired to smoke cigars and talk about coal or some such, Justine returned to the courtyard alone. No one was there, no sentry looking out for marauders or runaway brides. She looked up at the tops of pines bending in a relentless wind, appearing to scrape a dull gray sky. She walked up the steps to the battlement and gazed out over the mountain valley below the castle. She spread her arms wide, closed her eyes and turned her face to the heavens.

That was the first time she truly felt it—the pull from somewhere deep, the energy of all the kings and queens who had come before her, rising up to the crown of her head, anchoring her to this earth. She felt the centuries of warfare and struggle, of the people her family had ruled. She felt the enormous responsibilities they'd all carried, the work they'd done to carve a road to the future.

Her father had often said that he could feel the weight of his crown on his shoulders. But Justine felt something entirely different. She didn't feel as if it was weighing her down, but more like it was lifting her off her feet and holding her here. She didn't believe this was a conceit on her part, but a tether to her past. She would be a queen. She knew that she would, and standing there, she felt like she should be. She felt born to it.

A gust of wind very nearly sent her flying, so she came down from the battlement. She paused just before the block and tried to imagine herself on her knees, knowing her death was imminent. She imagined how she would look.

She hoped she would appear strong and noble with no hint of her fear of the pain or the unknown.

Being queen was her destiny. She knew it would come. But she hadn't known then it would come so soon.

CHAPTER ONE

1855
In the capital city of St. Edys
Wesloria

THE CROWN PRINCESS JUSTINE MARIE EDDA IVANOSEN took one hesitant step from behind the curtain and glanced at the podium in the center of the stage. She slid the palm of her hand down the side of her skirt and—

"Non, non, non, non." A wiry gentleman with very blond hair threw up his hands in despair.

The princess groaned to the ceiling. *"Now* what have I done?"

The inimitable Monsieur DuPree, an instructor of elocution and comportment on loan to Wesloria from Empress Eugénie of France, clasped his hands together and pleadingly said, "Your Royal Highness, *s'il vous plaît."* He leaped onto the stage and strode across to instruct her again.

From his royal box seat beside Her Majesty Queen Agnes, Weslorian Prime Minister Dante Robuchard swallowed a sigh. The princess suffered from terrible nerves at the mere thought of public speaking, which was a conundrum for a future queen, as *public speaking* was high on the list of requirements. The citizens of Wesloria would need a queen who spoke firmly and elegantly, who exuded confidence and command of her kingdom. Not one who shook the moment she took a stage. Even now the shake in the hem of her gown betrayed her nerves and exuded the opposite of confidence.

"You must not hesitate," Monsieur DuPree insisted.

"I beg your pardon, but this is my first time seeing the completed hall," the princess said.

It was indeed a grand stage. The new Prince Vasilly Hall—with its domed ceiling depicting Joan of Arc, boxes festooned in velvet and gold ropes above the general seating, huge crystal chandeliers, each sporting one hundred gaslights, and its seats for five hundred souls—dwarfed the princess. Only in Paris and Rome and London would you find a stage as grand as this. Not in Wesloria. Not until he'd become Prime Minister.

At least, he mused, if there was one good thing that could be said of Princess Justine—and little good was said of her, frankly—it was that she had the carriage and fine looks of a queen. She was a bit taller than average, like her mother, and possessed a fine figure, also like her mother. But where the queen's eyes were blue, the daughter's eyes were bright and curious and a warm shade of honey, and they tended to lock with yours when she was speaking to you.

Ministers—most of them old men whose libido had been lost decades ago—would forgive many faults if they resided in an attractive young woman, and the princess was certainly that. She had long, dark brown hair gathered in an artful array of braided loops and knots at her nape as was the Weslorian fashion. The streak of white in her hair, a slender tress that refused any color—a trait peculiar to the Ivanosen family—looked almost like it had been dyed white on purpose. She wore a gown of gold silk patterned with starbursts and styled in the manner of French and English fashion—a full tiered skirt, voluminous sleeves—and ending just at her ankles, so that her embroidered kid-leather-and-silk shoes could be seen.

The gown had been hotly debated between himself and the queen. The Weslorian style of women's clothing was typically worn close to the body with a long, embroidered train, which the queen thought important for the future queen to wear. But Dante had argued that people feared what they did not understand, and as the princess was a commodity in an international marriage mart, in public she ought to dress as noble women did in Paris and London.

He'd won that battle, at least.

The princess and Monsieur DuPree disappeared behind the stage curtain again.

Princess Justine was here today to rehearse the speech she would give for the grand opening of the hall. The event would mark the start of the annual Carlarian arts fair, for which people would flock to St. Edys from all over the world. The grand opening ceremony was generally presided over by the king, but his precarious health prevented it this year. The king suffered from consumption. He was declining; there was no dispute. Privately, the royal physicians had said he might not last the year.

The king knew how poor his health was and had expressed to Dante his fervent wish that Princess Justine be prepared in earnest for the throne and that, if at all possible, a prince consort be decided. "They'll eat her alive without a husband at her side," he'd said one night.

The king was right about that, and Dante would certainly be counted among their ranks. He was the prime minister, after all. He needed to be able to steer that young woman in any direction he needed.

He looked at the princess now, she of the slender shoulders and youthful head, and tried to imagine how she would carry the burdens of an entire country without her father to help her. She was not prepared for the throne in his humble opinion, and the queen clearly shared that opinion, based on the number of sighs she emitted when her daughter was near. He understood her impatience—he himself had spent an awful lot of time thinking about Princess Justine when more pressing matters required his attention.

He glanced at the queen from the corner of his eye and noted her sour expression as she contemplated her older daughter. It was only the two of them in the box, as this was only a rehearsal. In fact, Dante had believed the two of them would be the only ones in attendance, but below was a smattering of onlookers. Courtiers, mostly. But also in attendance, without explanation, was Princess Amelia, the next in line to the throne. She was in the company of her three constant companions. Dante viewed those girls like so many rabbits, a little warren of them always hopping around and getting into things that didn't concern them. He'd recently suggested to the queen that perhaps Princess Amelia might study art in Switzerland as many grown daughters of royalty and nobility were wont to do. The queen wouldn't hear of it.

Dante had won a hard-fought battle for his office only a year ago. He understood early on that he must tread lightly around the topic of the princesses. Amelia was her mother's favorite, and Justine…well, Justine was not. Perhaps she had been at some point early on, but recent events had tarnished the young woman's halo. Nevertheless, she would be queen, and as he intended to keep a grip on power for many years, *she* was the princess who concerned him most.

He was determined to take the poor economy that had plagued Wesloria for centuries into prosperity and modernity. Under King Maksim, the country had made significant progress, but there was so much more to do. Given the king's advancing consumption, he needed Princess Justine as malleable as possible. Therein lay the rub.

Below them, Monsieur DuPree finished his consultation. He hurried to the edge of the stage, leaped to the floor and took his seat among the courtiers.

Dante's first mistake had been in assuming that a young woman of Princess Justine's age—she'd be five and twenty in a couple of weeks—could be easily influenced. But she simply did not behave in ways he could predict or find logical. This had perplexed him for many months until one day he realized that what he needed her to be was a man. To think and walk and talk like a man. And as she could not be that, the next best thing was to marry her to one. *Posthaste*. Get her a consort as the king had suggested; someone who would guide her with Dante's considerable influence.

"Yes, then, begin again!" Monsieur DuPree bellowed.

Princess Justine stepped out from behind the curtain, and this time strode purposefully across the stage to the podium as the onlookers rose to their feet. She gestured in a queenly manner that they should sit. For the next few moments she stood at the podium, looking very much like the intelligent young woman who had been tutored by the best educators in Wesloria. She looked fit and athletic, too, which Dante certainly appreciated but never said so, because the queen had made it abundantly clear she did not approve of athleticism in a princess, and particularly fencing, at which, Dante had heard, the princess excelled.

The point was that she had all the necessary ingredients to be a good queen and a good wife and would be a fine catch for the right sort of man…

The *right* sort of man.

And therein lay yet another rub. Dante didn't trust the

princess to choose the right sort, especially given recent events. He still grimaced when thinking of how his first year in office had been consumed with the princess's wretched involvement with Duke Gustav's son, the degenerate libertine, Aldabert.

Princess Justine placed her hands on either side of the podium. She looked up at the small audience and said, "Good evening."

"I beg your pardon, Your Royal Highness, but you must speak louder," Monsieur DuPree urged her.

The princess bowed her head a moment to gather herself. *Aldabert Gustav.* What delight had filled Dante when that lying scoundrel had been banished from the country. He was a spoiled brat who valued carnal pleasure over duty, the trophy of a young princess's virtue over the national scandal it could cause. He had nothing to recommend him and had boldly lied to gain the princess's favor and God only knew what liberties. And still, when presented with the evidence of his perfidy, Princess Justine had stubbornly refused to believe him rotten to the core.

The whole sordid affair had become a royal fiasco and had required a rather large payment from the king's personal coffers to the estate of Lord Gustav to see his profligate son married to a German heiress at once and booted from the country.

The princess lifted her head again. Her cheeks were now entirely devoid of color and caused her to appear unwell. Was it really so very painful to address a few? It was so odd to Dante—she could be *quite* self-assured in private, but when pressed to speak publicly, she lost all confidence.

She cleared her throat. She picked up the paper on which her speech had been penned, and even from this distance Dante could see how it shook.

"If only she would speak," the queen whispered loudly. "I think it would be better if Amelia made the speech. She's much livelier."

Princess Justine lowered the paper and looked up at the royal box. "I would be just as happy for Amelia to make the speech, Mama."

"Oh! I beg your pardon, darling. Don't pay us any heed. You're doing very well, dear!" the queen tittered.

The princess looked at the paper again.

Dante disagreed with the queen's opinion. Princess Amelia reminded him of an unruly child whereas Princess Justine was elegant.

"Good evening!" the princess said again, much louder. She absently wiped her palm along the side of her skirt again, and the queen clucked her tongue with annoyance. *"Bonem owen,"* the princess continued, wishing everyone a good evening in Weslorian. And then she began to speak in Weslorian, her voice quaking, the words halting. She spoke as if the words made no sense to her, which was absurd. While it was true that the princesses had been born to a mother whose native tongue was German and a father whose native tongue was Weslorian, and who together spoke the common language between them—English—the princess spoke Weslorian fluently.

"Ledia et harrad." Ladies and gentlemen. That was better, then. "Welcome," she said again in English, forgetting which language she ought to speak for a moment. And then she continued in Weslorian often broken with English. *"En honra e...*independence..." She paused to squint at the paper. "We...co..."

"Non!" Monsieur DuPree said, coming to his feet. "Again, please, Your Royal Highness."

"I beg your pardon, sir, but I can't read without my eye-glasses."

"We had quite a row about them yesterday," the queen whispered to Dante. "But I will not have her looking like a bluestocking." As if there was something wrong with a daughter who might appear to be educated and well-read.

"Perhaps it is the Weslorian?" Dante wondered aloud. "It is not her preferred language."

The queen bristled. "But it is her native language. She should have applied herself to the study of it more fully."

That was rich, seeing as how the queen had never learned to speak Weslorian.

"Par de...candidates?" the princess said below. She squinted at the paper. "Oh, I beg your pardon. *Candreda*," she said.

The princess moved the paper farther from her face. Below her, her sister and her friends giggled. The small crowd of courtiers grew restless, and the princess turned even paler. *"Par de candreda,"* she said.

Monsieur DuPree stood slowly. With his hands clasped behind his back, he deliberately walked up the steps and onto the stage to consult with her again. The princess turned to face him almost as if she expected a blow.

"I often wonder why couldn't Amelia have been first-born?" the queen mused on a sigh, and settled back in her chair. "She's so gregarious. A natural at this sort of thing, and—"

"Mama!" Princess Justine said sharply. "I can *hear* you."

"I beg your pardon, my darling. Carry on!" The queen folded her arms. "What are we going to do, Robuchard?" she whispered. "She's *hopeless*."

Princess Justine wasn't hopeless in the least, but that was neither here nor there. This was the moment Dante had long been seeking, the opportunity to suggest his well-studied plan to the queen without appearing to be impertinent. "I do have one suggestion, if you please, Your Majesty."

"What is it?"

He leaned as close as he could without drawing attention. He spoke in a whisper as Monsieur DuPree went behind the princess, put his hands on her waist and positioned her before the podium. "I would suggest that we send Her Royal Highness to London to apprentice with a woman who herself was once a young queen. Victoria assumed the throne at the age of eighteen and I think she could offer invaluable advice."

Monsieur DuPree's arms waved toward the audience as he explained something to the princess.

"And, if I may add, it would also be advantageous to have her and Princess Amelia out of the country until... events are all but forgotten?"

The queen slanted a dark look at him. "Meaning the Gustavs."

Dante was very careful to keep his expression neutral. "We might catch two fish with one net. If we are to send her to London to apprentice, we could also see to it that our preferred list of potential suitors are presented there. Think of it—she might return with someone she wishes to marry."

"Are you mad, Robuchard? *Suitors?*" The queen looked at her daughter on the stage, leaned toward Dante and whispered, "After all that has happened? Without me there to keep watch over her? I can't leave my husband."

Dante had expected her to leap at the chance to put distance behind what the newspapers had dubbed The Great Princess Predicament. Was it possible the queen was more maternal than he'd given her credit for being?

No, not possible. Actually, so far from the realm of possibility as to be laughable.

"Would you not agree that it is preferable to have the princess married than not? Particularly if it becomes necessary to revisit abdication."

The queen stiffened. The subject had been broached with her and the king before, but only in theory…the theory being that if the king's health declined to the point he could no longer effectively carry out his duties, for the sake of the nation and the stability of the monarchy, it might become necessary to abdicate in favor of Princess Justine.

"Naturally, I would not suggest this were I not assured that *all* proper precautions will be taken. She would be advised and supervised by a master of the chamber, Lord Bardaline, and his wife as lady-in-waiting."

The queen pondered this. "Lady Bardaline is clever."

Of course she was, or Dante wouldn't have suggested her. She was the queen's close friend, but she was a lady who knew to keep all windows open, so to speak, and frequently whispered in his ear. "I would also suggest that if you and the king allow, we might retain the services of Lady Lila Aleksander of Denmark."

The queen's eyes widened with surprise. She leaned back and looked him up and down. "I beg your pardon?"

"Lady Aleksander is a matchmaker—"

"I know who she is, Robuchard."

"She is the best in all of Europe," Dante calmly continued. "She has made matches for the most difficult subjects. The German prince, Heinz Jäger, who everyone says is a half-wit, was brought to a successful match by her ladyship. If he can be matched, imagine what could be done with her highness—"

"Are you suggesting my daughter is a difficult match?"

"Not at all," he said quickly, raising a hand, kicking himself mentally. "But she is a *challenging* match given that she will be queen. Her future husband must be the right man if we are to have any hope of her ruling effectively. We know the few candidates we would entertain," he said, making it sound as if it was the queen's thinking and not his, "but what we need is an opportunity for the princess to meet them and form an attachment with one."

"We can't have a *matchmaker*, Robuchard!" the queen whispered hotly. "What will people think? They will think something is wrong with my daughter!"

"That's why I suggest you proceed with Lady Aleksander's impeccable service while the princess is in England. She will see to it that when the princess returns to Wesloria, it will be with a formal engagement to an excellent man who might lead her. Everyone wins."

Queen Agnes gaped at him. But then she closed her mouth and looked at the stage, where Monsieur DuPree was leaning so close to Princess Justine that she was leaning back. "Amelia, too?"

Yes, of course, *Amelia, too*, that little troublemaker. "Princess Amelia is her sister's truest companion and would likewise benefit from the tutelage."

Monsieur DuPree, having delivered his instruction, leaped off the stage once more, and the princess stood with her head high.

"Their father might not survive the summer, you realize," the queen whispered.

"All the more reason to move with due haste, Your Majesty. The crown princess will need a husband to lean on through grief and coronation and the assumption of all the sovereign's duties. The people of Wesloria will appreciate a man's steady hand behind the throne."

She snorted. "You have greatly overestimated the value of any man's hand, sir, but I do see your point. You are wise to suggest it, I think. How do we approach Victoria?"

Dante almost leaped from his seat with a victorious shout. "It's already done, Your Majesty."

Her eyes narrowed. "Is it?" she drawled. "And what guarantee do we have that Lady Aleksander will act in the direction we want?"

The guarantee was that Robuchard was never without his royal ducks neatly in a row. He was working through every part of his plan, including the engagement of Lady Aleksander's services and installing a spy who would report solely to him. "The compensation for a successful conclusion to this particular task is motivation enough, I assure you. But there are telegraphs, and I have eyes in England. We will be aware of everything that happens, down to the amount of milk her highness drinks each day."

The queen chewed her bottom lip as she stared at her daughter on the stage, who had walked out from behind the podium to appeal to Monsieur DuPree. "Really, monsieur, I think this problem would be solved if I had my eyeglasses."

"I beg your pardon, Highness, they are not recommended," Monsieur DuPree said smoothly.

"I beg to differ. They are very *much* recommended in order that I may read," the princess insisted, not unreasonably.

"Perhaps you might commit the speech to memory. It will provide you the opportunity to practice your enunciation."

Princess Justine groaned heavenward. "What is *wrong* with needing eyeglasses to read?"

Princess Amelia and her little rabbits giggled into their hands.

"*Je*," Queen Agnes said pertly. "*Je*, Robuchard, I think your plan is a good one."

CHAPTER TWO

Four months later
London, England

LAST NIGHT'S SUPPER had turned into a bloody bacchanal, and William was feeling the effects of it. *Beck*, damn him. Ten years ago William would have imbibed with abandon, but he'd long ceased being willing or able to pass the hours with drink. Ten years ago he would have bounced back to form like Indian rubber, but today every part of him ached.

This seemed to happen every time he was in London. It was his own rotten fault. He'd believed that because his old friend, Beckett Hawke, the Earl of Iddesleigh, was a husband and a father now, there would be none of the debauchery of yore. What a bloody fool he'd been to think it.

He'd intended to get plenty of rest before a day he knew he'd need all his wits about him. He'd assumed, *quite* incorrectly, that supper on Upper Brook Street would come to an early conclusion given that Beck's four young daughters were being reared without any sort of proper discipline and required a near army of parents and servants to corral them into bed.

But Beck's wife, the ginger-haired, plump Blythe Northcote Hawke, had taken the children to the old Honeycutt House where their bachelor uncle Donovan generally resided. Donovan would keep them for the night and, she reported with glee, would tell them ghost stories and frighten them out of their wits. Her happiness stemmed not from the fact that her children would likely refuse to sleep in their own beds for a fortnight, but from the fact that for one night, she and Beck could behave indiscriminately.

For the occasion they'd included Beck's good-for-nothing friends, Lord Montford and Sir Martin.

William should have sensed the minute he was shown into the drawing room that trouble was afoot. He should have begged off the minute Beck introduced "very fine Scotch whisky" that might have been obtained "from a smuggler's den." But he hadn't, and the next thing he knew, his valet, Ewan MacDuff, had come to fetch him at four in the morning.

That was how he'd come to be staring bleary-eyed at the imposing, three-story facade of Prescott Hall. He hated mornings like this. The ride from his house in Mayfair had jostled every bone in his body and had only worsened his wretched headache.

He removed his gloves, and then his hat, and shoved his fingers through his hair. He did not miss Ewan's grimace—the man took great pride in his work, and even though he had not personally combed William's hair, he considered it part of the overall effect of his sartorial work.

William turned from his valet's judgmental countenance, and his gaze landed on a young groom, come to take the horses. William meant to dismount, but he blinked at the house again. More than a house, really. A sprawling edifice practically bulging at the seams with opulence, one of the many homes owned by the Duke of Beauford and one of the few grand enough to house a royal princess and her entourage. He understood the gardens were extraordinary. He would like to take a look at them—how pleasing it would be to meander about while the sun burned the fog from his brain. But alas, there was no time for that. William intended to pay his call and depart for his house on Arlington Street as quickly as possible, have Ewan draw him a scorching-hot bath, then contemplate how, in a universe as vast as this, he kept ending up in these untenable situations.

One would think that William Douglas of Scotland, the Marquess of Douglas and Clydesdale, the future Duke of Hamilton and Brandon, might have a wee bit more control of his own life at the ripe age of three and thirty, and yet, nothing could be further from the truth. The older he became, the less things seemed in his control. His sister Susan was right—he ought to have been wed by now and have children of his own. He ought to have become one of those tinkering country gentlemen with a painting hobby who demanded reports on the number of sheep in the fields and read poetry to his wife. But no, he was a bachelor, who had been abroad as much of the past ten years as possible, and had been asked—no, *commanded*—to mollycoddle a bloody European princess.

The groom kept sliding looks at Ewan, his brows clearly asking his unspoken question of what the devil was going on here. Ewan straightened his vest, pulled his cuffs from the sleeves of his coat and returned a look that clearly conveyed he didn't rightly know.

"Fine," William said to them both. He slid off his horse and nodded at the impatient groom to take the reins, then nodded at Ewan, indicating he should go ahead and announce his presence.

As Ewan was the sort of man who liked to have a mission, he immediately began to stride for the entry. He was a very large man, six inches taller and broader than William, and when he jogged up the steps to the double doors, one half expected the ground to tremble. He rapped so loud that William could hear it on the drive.

William pulled on his gloves, but he did not reseat his hat. He turned his face to the afternoon sun. Lord, he could use a cup of tea and a nap. *One last toast*, indeed.

He shifted his gaze to the park spread before him. The grounds were perfectly manicured, including a field before the house where sheep were grazing, and stately trees lining the drive. Chestnut trees, he thought. They looked like the dozens upon dozens his father had planted at Hamilton Palace in Scotland several years ago.

Father. He was the one who'd put William up to this. Just a month ago he'd called William home from Paris with an urgent telegraph—*come at once.* Naturally, William had feared that his father was ill and was holding off the Grim Reaper. And then he feared his father would die and saddle him with massive debt and the monstrosity they called Hamilton Palace, and he'd be a duke and the surviving descendent of the Scottish throne—if his father's claims were to be believed—and stuck in Lanarkshire, far from the sort of society he enjoyed.

But it turned out his father was very much alive and very pleased to see him. Clad in a dressing gown at two in the afternoon, he'd hugged William tightly, patted him on the back, said William looked fatter since the last he saw him.

His father chatted about the new ewes he'd personally bought at market, about the chicken pie the cook had made for supper. He eagerly showed William the new rooms he was adding to the house. He reported that William's mother had gone to visit her sister, and that Susan had brought the children around last week, and poor little Arthur had gotten lost in the house and they'd searched the better part of a day for him before they found him crying in the blue drawing room.

Oh aye, William's father was very well, thank you. The emergency for which he'd summoned his heir home was that he was in desperate financial straits.

Again.

William loved his father. He enjoyed his company—the old man could always be depended upon for a laugh. He'd been the best father one could hope for. Though he was prone to excess, he really did care about things like the Hamilton seat. His father had one great flaw. Well, two, really—William and Susan agreed that the duke's oft-made claim of being the true and rightful heir to the Scottish throne due to the tracing he'd done on the family tree was suspect at best. But his greatest flaw was that he was horrible with money. Utterly and thoroughly awful. He hadn't the least bit of financial sense and would not listen to reason. He'd come close to ruining the storied Hamilton family more than once.

One had only to look at the sumptuous and obscenely large palace his father had spent his entire life adding to. The huge monolith rivaled Buckingham and required extraordinary sums to maintain. Even now his father was adding more rooms! This house was the reason the coffers were bleeding. The duke had even forced William to sell the ship he'd purchased with his earnings from high-stakes gambling, and had used the funds to pay off some of the debt.

Naturally, *everyone* in Britain thought William was the profligate, the spendthrift, the foolish man soon to be parted with his money. But in truth, he was the sensible one.

A movement caught his eye, and William turned his head. In a patch of garden at one end of the house, two figures were dressed in white fencing attire with masks covering their faces and necks. Interested, he moved closer to see them better.

The green was just off a terrace where three gentlemen stood, observing the bout. The opponents were not evenly matched in terms of size—one was broader and taller than the other—but the smaller of the two was the more aggressive, pushing his opponent back with some hard advances. William winced as the larger opponent was pushed off balance, onto his heels. William was no fencer, but he knew sluggish footwork when he saw it.

He turned his face to the sun again. What had he been thinking? Ah, yes. His father's latest debacle.

In spite of William's strong recommendation that he not do so, his father had apparently gone ahead and invested in the Weslorian coal industry. His father had been enticed by the new Weslorian Prime Minister, Dante Robuchard, a vague acquaintance of the family. When one possessed a title and a fortune, one tended to end up in the same salons with like titles and fortunes.

William knew Robuchard to be ambitious. So ambitious that he'd convinced a wealthy Scottish duke to invest a considerable amount, which, William suspected, was Robuchard's way of shoring up the Weslorian economy. And now, his father had explained, there were suddenly currents of concern with the investment and the continued prosperity in Wesloria. The king was dying and the young crown princess had been involved in a scandalous incident with a bounder. It looked as if the princess would assume the throne within months, and Robuchard feared a rebellion might result if she ascended without a husband. "I understand she hasn't the brain of a bloody hare," William's father had declared. "Our investment could be lost."

William had to bite his tongue to keep from reminding his father that it was not *our* investment.

That Princess Justine Ivanosen was involved in a *scandalous incident* did not surprise William in the least. He certainly hadn't forgotten his own *scandalous incident* with her in London eight years ago. When he asked his father what her current predicament had to do with him, his father had smiled in that way he did when he meant to ask for something and knew he shouldn't. Over the next weeks, he'd said, the princess would be in London meeting potential matches. He needed William to go and keep an eye on things and just…let Robuchard know every week how things were progressing. A small favor, he said. A simple task.

At first, William had been struck mute. He couldn't make sense of those words. Go and keep an eye on things?

So his father had explained it all to him again. It was *imperative*, he said, that someone keep Robuchard in the loop.

"No," William had said flatly to that outrageous request. "I'll no' do it, Father. I'm no' a nursemaid, aye?" He knew how these things worked—many people had to be consulted and appeased on such a match. What did he have to do with it? Wouldn't the Weslorians have scores of people to report back?

As evidenced by the fact that he was here, in London, calling on the princess, he'd lost the debate. When it was clear his father would not yield, William had groaned and asked, "How long?"

His father had put aside the lamb shank he'd been eating and wiped his hands on a linen napkin embroidered with an H in the corners. "Until the lass is engaged."

"Diah!" William had exploded. "That could be weeks! Months!"

"Months," his father had scoffed. "She'll be in Wesloria before the year ends. The king hasna long to live."

"I won't do it," William had said with conviction.

"Need I remind you," his father asked as he pulled a piece of meat from the bone of the shank, "of the favor I've done you?"

William groaned again, but this time, in pain. "*No*, you need no' remind me."

Unfortunately for the Hamiltons, William's father wasn't the only one who made unwise decisions. William's had been an act of honest concern for a woman… And of course, because his decision was unwise, it had turned into a financial burden. This was what he got for trying to help someone—he was to be a bloody nursemaid.

Ewan startled him by suddenly popping up in front of him. "For God's sake, Ewan," he said, and yanked at the ends of his waistcoat. "Well, then?"

"You are invited in, milord."

"Invited in. What does that mean? What of the princess?"

"The gent said he would inform Her Royal Highness you'd arrived."

William sighed. "Did you tell him that it was the Marquess of Doug—"

"Aye, milord," Ewan said.

William studied Ewan. "Do they understand that I—"

"Aye, I believe they do, milord."

William frowned. "Very well." She had better see him after he'd come all this way. He turned, and when he did, he caught sight of the fencers again. The larger one was on the ground with an épée at his throat, courtesy of the smaller one standing over him. That had escalated quickly.

He turned fully toward the entrance of Prescott Hall and

set his mind to meeting Princess Justine again, eight years since the last time. He remembered a young, vain and ill-behaved princess. He thought she might have been pretty, but with no curves to speak of. Ah, and the strange white streak in her hair that marked the royal family of Wesloria. They all had it somewhere on their head—a streak or forelock of pure white that would not accept color. Odd.

How old had she been then? Sixteen years? Maybe seventeen? Old enough that she'd accompanied her parents to London. Young enough that he recalled she'd said when she was queen, she would host a ball every weekend. That was what one could expect when children ascended to thrones—they thought of nothing but the number of ponies and balls they would have.

He would have this over and done. William set off with verve, striding toward the mansion's entrance so abruptly he caused Ewan to stumble in his haste to catch up.

He'd first met the princess at a ball. He'd danced twice with her, two dances one right after the other, which had been scandal in and of itself. She'd decreed that she wanted two dances, and he'd not declined, as that would have been impolite. He'd been a bit amused by it, really, that girl telling him what to do. She'd worn a pale blue gown, cut in the body-hugging style of Alucia and Wesloria, which he found to be a very pleasing style on grown women, but on her girlish frame, too heavy.

He'd met her again at another soiree, this one at the same Upper Brook Street house where William had sallied forth into debauchery just last night. Beck had reminded him of the incident, a bit of a contretemps over a game of Chairs at a Christmas party. William was blamed for it, of course, and it might have been all his doing, but in his defense, his memory was made hazy by the absinthe he'd drunk. He'd brought the drink from France as a gift to his host, and it had flowed freely, and chaos had ensued with a delightful vengeance.

The game consisted of ten adults trooping in a circle around nine chairs as music played, and once the musicians stopped, everyone had to grab a seat. The person left without a chair was eliminated. A chair was taken away, and the procession begun again.

The dispute occurred during a round that had come down to William, the princess and one other person he couldn't recall now. The princess had said some very insolent things in the course of the game, and he, in turn, had bumped her with his hip out of the way to win a seat in the final round. She had shrieked with indignation, and he had remarked that it sounded much like he imagined the cry of the banshee. Someone had to explain to the little foreigner what a banshee was, and then she'd turned a lovely little face full of murderous rage on him and they'd argued, and all right, all *right*, it was badly done. But he didn't think Beck had to toss him out on his ear like he'd done.

William reached the steps and took them two at a time, each stride bringing him that much closer to the child. The sooner he had this over and done, the sooner he could retreat to his bath.

Ewan, who had struggled to keep up the entire way, probably because he was ten years older and five stone heavier, was still breathless from the exertion of chasing his employer up the steps. He reached around William and knocked on the door again. A liveried footman answered it. "His Lordship...the Marquess...of Douglas," Ewan panted.

"Please," the footman said, stepping back into the vast entry hall.

William stepped inside and handed his hat and gloves to

the footman. Another one appeared and indicated that William should follow him down the long entry hall to a salon. The room was pink and white, with pink velvet curtains tied back with cheerful gold ropes. The palette reminded him a little of a marzipan cake.

A settee and two armchairs were centered in the room, covered with floral brocade. The carpet, he noted as he walked deeper into the room, was thick and a grassy shade of green. He looked up at the painting over a hearth that was taller than he was. It was a woman in a black-and-white gown, smiling coyly over her shoulder while a pair of spaniels romped at her feet.

A noise outside caught his attention, and he walked to a pair of French doors that were opened onto the terrace and green where he'd seen the fencers earlier. The observers had gone, and now the two fencers were on the terrace, the larger one clearly instructing the smaller one.

Another sound, this one in the room. William looked to his right and very clearly saw someone or something disappear behind the drapes on the east wall. What tomfoolery was this? He walked over and pulled the drapes aside, starting at the sight of a woman looking back at him. She looked familiar…but she didn't have the golden eyes of Princess Justine. And her hair was gold whereas the princess's had been dark brown. He frowned with confusion. "I beg your pardon." Was it possible he had misremembered her completely?

The young woman rose up on her toes, uncomfortably close to him, tilted her head back and smiled coquettishly. "You don't remember me?" she accused in a slightly accented voice.

He did not remember her *precisely* like this, and was,

in fact, baffled that his memory could betray him so thoroughly. "I do, of course. But I—"

"My lord."

William turned; a man had stepped through the French doors. He was a Weslorian gentleman, judging by the long coat and the small patch of green on his lapel. It was a curious habit of the Weslorians to always wear a patch of forest green, much like a Scotsman often wore plaid.

"You *don't* remember me." The young woman sounded perturbed, and spoke as if the man had not entered, and William reflexively turned back to her.

"We met when I was in London last. Do you recall me now?" She coyly lifted her lashes, her brown-eyed gaze meeting his.

"I think—"

"My lord!" the man said again, and this time when William turned his head, he was startled to see one of the fencers step into the room. And after a moment of hesitation, the fencer was suddenly advancing on him, and William braced himself, feeling as if he ought to prepare to defend his person.

But something stirred in a nether region of his brain, distracting him. It had to do with the fencer's attire. Or rather, the curves in that attire. Or rather still, the figure he *imagined* in that attire. The trousers fit loosely, but when the fencer moved, he could see the shape of a woman's body. Hips that curved into slender legs. The jacket, fuller in the chest, narrowed at a trim waist. The épée bouncing against a shapely calf.

This person, this alluring figure, was…was the one he'd seen with an épée at the throat of the bigger opponent.

"If I may," the gentleman said to the fencer, "Lord

William Douglas of Hamilton, Marquess of Douglas and Clydesdale."

The fencer, in response, removed the mask. A thick, dark brown braid of hair tumbled down the front of the fencing jacket. The streak of white—he would never forget it—was still as prominent as ever. But her hair looked thicker and more luxurious than he recalled. This was not the teenage girl who lived in the attic of his memories. This was a grown woman, with curves and swells and lips and dark brows that arched above her eyes with surprise, and Lord, something bothersome and distracting was fluttering in his chest.

That it was, in fact, Princess Justine in the fencing attire, caused him to smile from the sheer absurdity of it. A bit lopsidedly, to be fair, but a smile nonetheless. Look at how well she had turned out. Oh aye, that was Her Royal Highness—William would know her anywhere.

She said pertly to the gentleman, "I know who he is, thank you." And she handed the gentleman her mask with such force that William heard an *oof* of breath escape him.

William bowed. "Your Royal Highness, welcome to England."

The woman he'd found behind the drapes sauntered around him to stand by Princess Justine. The two of them blinked back at him. How could he ever have mistaken the other one for Princess Justine? The woman with fair hair was obviously the younger sister, Princess Amelia.

"You're much grown now," William said, the thought hopping onto his tongue before his head had even registered it.

The two women exchanged a look that was almost identical. "And you are...thicker," Princess Justine said.

Thicker? He'd just had this suit of clothing tailored and the gentleman had proclaimed him perfectly trim.

"He doesn't remember me," Princess Amelia said, and folded her arms. Like her sister, she was slightly taller than average. She had a streak of white in her hair, too, but as her hair was golden, it looked more like a bit of blond.

"I beg your pardon, Your Royal Highness. It has been many years."

Princess Amelia sniffed disdainfully.

"If I may, I am the master of Her Royal Highness's chamber, Lord Bardaline, at your service." The gentleman bowed, and the two princesses rolled their eyes in almost perfect unison.

"How do you do?" William was very much aware that Princess Justine's gaze was moving over him, taking him in.

"Have you come alone?" Princess Amelia asked. "Or did you bring your friends?"

"Pardon?"

Princess Justine put her hand on her sister's arm to silence her. "A better question is, *why* have you come?"

Princess Amelia sighed, clasped her hands behind her back and slunk away to the far end of the room to look at the painting. Bardaline's eyes followed her every step.

But Princess Justine kept her gaze fixed on William, one dark brow arching above the other. She seemed bemused by him. But why? Surely, she knew he was coming. Or had there been some mistake? Perhaps she'd expected him another day? Or, hopefully, his father had it all wrong and he was not expected to be her nursemaid, after all—stranger mistakes had been made at Hamilton Palace. But as often was the case, William proved to be his own worst enemy and said, "Am I no' expected?"

Both of her brows sank into a vee. "Certainly not by *me*, my lord."

What the devil? Had no one *told* her?

"Your Royal Highness?" Bardaline stepped forward with a smile so forced and pained that William thought he should have hid it altogether. "Perhaps you might prefer to receive Lord Douglas at tea?"

William almost choked—he had no intention of staying for tea. Tea was *hours* away. What about his scalding hot bath? He meant only to come and greet her and say whatever he must and leave. "Thank you, but I'd no' take—"

"Je," she said before he could finish his thought. "I should like to change." And with that, she turned and walked out of the room, without inquiring if that would suit him, without any polite discourse at all, no asking after his health, no how-do-you-do after all these years. The épée bounced against her calf as she went, her hips moving in a manner so distinctly female that William had to swallow.

Princess Amelia scampered after her.

William looked at Bardaline, who, he noted, did not seem terribly surprised by her abrupt departure, but merely chagrined. He gestured lamely to the door. "If you will please come with me, sir." He stepped into the hall.

William hesitated—he had the sinking sensation that he was about to walk off a plank into an untenable situation. And yet, instead of thinking of all the excuses he might make here and now, his mind's eye was fixated on the image of Princess Justine walking away.

He followed Lord Bardaline like a milk cow headed to the barn.

CHAPTER THREE

AMELIA WAS INSULTED that Douglas hadn't immediately recalled who she was. In Amelia's world, to be unremarkable was worse than being dead and forgotten. She carried on in disbelief as she jogged up the grand staircase in pursuit of the quicker Justine. "Why should he not *remember* me? Does he go about meeting princesses every day?"

Justine didn't remind Amelia she'd been a girl when they'd last been in London and had since changed considerably, because she herself was so incandescently angry that she thought she might explode. *Bardaline, that snake*, had come to fetch her from her fencing practice to tell her she had a caller, one who had come at the personal request of Robuchard. Well, *that* had immediately raised her suspicions, *and* her hackles, because Robuchard was also a snake, and even from hundreds of miles away, he was intruding on her life.

But then when she'd seen *who* had come to call at the *personal request* of Robuchard, she had very nearly choked on her fury.

Bardaline could have warned her. *Someone* could have warned her. But no, they had surprised her with it, which meant she couldn't beg off before being forced to reacquaint herself with that man. There was something underfoot, and damn them, she would not play this game, because *she* remembered Douglas *very* well and with not the least bit of fondness.

But now her mind was racing ahead of her feet. *Why* had Robuchard sent him? Why *him*? For what purpose?

"Justine! You're not even listening!" Amelia pouted as they strode through the carpeted hallway to Justine's suite of rooms. A maid scurried out of their path and curtsied as they passed. Not that the princesses noticed. Justine was plotting the fiery, spectacular death of Lord Bardaline, the *master* of her *chamber*, he'd said, in an obvious attempt to make his actual role as zookeeper sound more important than it was.

She flung open the door to her dressing room and called for Seviana, her maid. The young woman came running from the adjoining room at such a pace her lace cap bounced right out of one of the pins that anchored it to her hair.

"Your Royal Highness, how may I be of service?"

"I must dress." Justine began to unbutton her fencing jacket. "Something… I don't know what, but something *quite* dazzling. Do I have something dazzling, Sevie?"

"*Je*, ma'am, you have several dazzling things."

"Dazzling!" Amelia laughed as she fell in a *whoosh* of silk onto a chaise. "It's only tea."

"May I suggest the blue and white?" Seviana asked.

"Yes!" Justine loved that gown. It had come from Paris. "That suits me very well. Thank you, Sevie."

She shrugged out of her fencing jacket and tossed it onto the back of a settee as Seviana went to fetch the gown. She caught sight of herself in the mirror at her vanity. "Lord save me, my hair!"

"What is the matter with you? Why are you behaving like you're about to meet someone loftier than the Queen of England?"

"Loftier!" Justine snorted. "No one could possibly be lower in my estimation. I am dressing in my best because I hate him, Amelia." Hate may seem an odd reason to want to look her best, but there it was, the very word tossed down between them as evidence.

"That makes no sense," Amelia said, giving voice to what Justine was thinking.

"It makes *all* the sense," a female voice intoned.

And like clockwork, here she came, the venerable and reviled—by Justine and Amelia, anyway—Lady Bardaline. Justine's lady-in-waiting. At least that was the title her mother had given her. To Justine, she was merely a nuisance not to be trusted. Justine and Amelia didn't always see eye to eye, but on the subject of the Bardalines, they did.

Lady Bardaline had been sent to accompany Justine to England by her mother, the queen. She was here, her mother had said, to advise Justine and guard her virtue. Justine had argued that at her age, she didn't need anyone to guard her virtue; she was perfectly capable of doing it herself. Alas, she'd made a terrible mistake with one man, and it seemed she would be forever held to account for it. Now an entire kingdom watched her virtue as if she were a nun in a convent.

Nevertheless, Justine knew the true reason for Lady Bardaline's presence was to report back to the queen every little thing she and Amelia said or did. Justine received a telegraph from her parents once a week, and every week, without fail, her mother mentioned events that happened, words that were said…things only someone in close proximity to Justine could possibly know. It was entirely possible the informant was her *master of the chamber*, that officious bloated ego, or any number of Weslorian servants who swept in and out of her days with various tasks…but

Justine would bet her future throne it was Lady Barda-line. She and Amelia had been making a game of it lately, saying things just to see what came back to them in their mother's letters.

"May I ask who it is we hate?" Lady Bardaline asked, as if she were a friend and had just caught the bit of conversation that was meant for the three of them.

"No one, really," Justine said airily.

Amelia caught Justine's eye and flashed a hint of a smile. "We don't *hate* Lord Douglas, but he did indeed call here today."

"Who?"

"Lord William, the Marquess of Douglas," Justine said. She could still remember how he'd introduced himself years ago. *I am a marquess. The son of a duke.*

"Oh." Lady Bardaline frowned lightly, as if trying to recall him.

"We met the gentleman when we were in London before," Amelia explained. "At a supper or a ball—oh, who can remember? It was so long ago I hardly recall him at all." Apparently, Amelia had decided that if he didn't remember her, then she would certainly not remember him.

But Justine remembered him with crystal clarity. They had been in each other's company several times. At suppers, at soirees, at a ball or two and, of course, that wretched Christmas party. "I didn't care for him," she said, and caught Amelia's eye in the mirror and winked. "How could I? He was so *terribly* rude to Mama." That, of course, was a total fabrication. But when her mother heard this bit of talk, she would spend all her days trying to recall who was rude to her.

Seviana returned, the blue-and-white-striped gown in her arms.

Justine loved the off-shoulder sleeves and the dark blue silk bow at the bodice. She stepped behind a tri-fold screen and quickly shed her fencing attire.

"If I may, Highness, why not invite the gentleman to dine?" Lady Bardaline suggested. "Then you might have all the time you need to reacquaint yourself."

Justine rolled her eyes. "I don't need time with the gentleman at all. I would have saved him the call had I known he was coming." She popped her head out from behind the screen. "I wonder, Lady Bardaline, why no one told me he was coming."

Lady Bardaline blinked quite innocently. But the color in her cheeks proclaimed her guilt. At least that was what Justine wanted to believe. "*I* certainly have no knowledge of who calls on you, Your Royal Highness."

"Really? None whatsoever?"

Lady Bardaline's hand fluttered to her chest. *"No,"* she said, as if mortally offended Justine would ask.

Justine moved back behind the screen. Why had he come? Why had no one told her? How did he know she was here? Sometimes it felt as if she had nothing but her gut instincts to guide her. Her father had told her once that no one, save Amelia, could be considered a true friend, and even Amelia could be persuaded to turn against her under the right circumstances.

"Amelia would never, Papa!" Justine had said firmly, incensed on her sister's behalf.

"No?" One of his thick brows had risen. "Have you forgotten Queen Elena so soon?"

Well, *that* was a sobering reminder, chopping block and all, but still, Justine didn't believe for a moment Amelia would ever turn on her. And there was no danger of her ever trusting Lady Bardaline. She liked to think that she and the lady had come to an unspoken understanding—Lady Bardaline would not ask *too* many questions, and Justine would allow her to stay.

For now.

"Well, *I* won't take tea with him," Amelia sniffed. "And besides, I am to Holland House this evening. Are you sure you won't come, Jussie?"

Justine put her hands to her waist as Seviana laced her corset. "I can't possibly, Amelia. I am to leave for Windsor at first light to call on Queen Victoria."

Not to mention she was not allowed to attend a supper so casually with people she scarcely knew. To arrive at Holland House without all the necessary king's men around her would be a terrible breach of etiquette, according to her mother and Lord Bardaline. Honestly, it felt like anything Justine ever desired fell into the category of terrible breaches, whereas life was a lark for Amelia. She could come and go as she pleased as long as she kept her reputation above reproach.

Justine envied Amelia's freedom. And she hated how everything that *she* did was studied and remarked upon and scrutinized for cracks and weaknesses. She hated that unlike Amelia, who basked in the attention of crowds, she felt so uncomfortable in the midst of strangers. Her breath would grow shallow and her palms go damp.

"Who will accompany you to Holland House?" Justine asked Amelia.

"Lady Holland."

"Lady Holland?" Lady Bardaline repeated as Justine stepped into a petticoat.

"Yes, Lady Holland," Amelia said with a bit of iciness in her voice. And then, because she could never help herself, could never be coy, she blurted, "Why *not* Lady Holland?"

"No reason at all, Your Highness," Lady Bardaline said smoothly. But the insinuation was evident in the twinge of disapproval in her voice. In a few days Amelia would receive a letter from their mother admonishing her for being seen with people who were so wildly political in their dealings, which the Hollands notoriously were, and exhorting her to remain above and beyond the fray. Justine could practically write the missive herself.

And Amelia, who always chafed at having her movements questioned, would then find every reason she could to call on Holland House. "I like her, very much," Amelia said to Lady Bardaline, as if to prove Justine's thought. "I'm bored with this. I'll look in on you tomorrow, Jussie," she said, and Justine heard her go out the door.

She finished dressing with Seviana's help and stepped out from behind the screen. Lady Bardaline had taken a seat on the chaise and had picked up a fashion magazine Justine had left there. It was such a trifling thing, but Justine chafed—sometimes, the lady made herself very much at home in Justine's rooms. She wondered if when she was queen people would sit on her chaise and look at her fashion magazines. She would issue a decree against it if they did, knowing full well her mother would admonish her for being rude. Sometimes it seemed to Justine that her mother didn't appreciate at all the responsibility her daughter would have as queen, but cared more for appearances.

Lady Bardaline looked up from her study of the latest in fashion and smiled. "That gown suits you very well, ma'am."

"Thank you."

"Might I be of assistance?"

Well… Seviana had helped her dress, so unless Lady Bardaline wanted to brush her hair, she couldn't see how.

"Actually…" Justine sat at her vanity and signaled to Seviana to begin work on her hair. "You may take your leave." The moment she said it, she held her breath. She was never quite certain if a command would be obeyed, and she watched Lady Bardaline in the mirror at her vanity, expecting her to pull a disapproving face, to even challenge her. But the lady smiled sweetly and stood. "As you wish." She curtsied and disappeared into the adjoining room.

And in moments like this, Justine wondered if she had it all wrong—maybe Lady Bardaline really did want only to help. And maybe she would be taken seriously as a queen, and not just her mother's puppet.

Seviana brushed her hair to a sheen and knotted it at her nape. The white streak that had mortified Justine when she was a girl looked a bit like someone had painted a white line into her hair. She didn't mind it so much now, especially since it matched the white in her father's hair.

She stood up and examined her appearance in a full-length mirror. Yes, this gown would do. She looked worldly, she decided, which was precisely what she wanted. The last time she'd seen Douglas, he'd treated her like a child. In fairness, she'd been little more than a child, having turned seventeen on the voyage over, but still, he might have shown her a little more deference.

She glanced at the clock. She'd kept Lord Douglas waiting only an hour, and that wasn't long enough. "Thank you, Seviana."

Seviana curtsied and took Justine's fencing clothes into the adjoining dressing room.

Douglas. What was she supposed to say to him? *So good to see you?* She didn't even want to look at him. Not because he repulsed her—far from it. Because he'd stood before her with that hint of an amused smile. And she'd been struck with how his looks had somehow improved, which her teenage eyes would have thought impossible. Oh, but she'd been enamored with his handsome face then, hadn't she? He was the most attractive man she'd ever seen.

Eight years later he was attractive but also, more…seasoned. Broader in the shoulder and more muscular. There were a few new lines around his eyes, and his sideburns grew into a full beard. And his hair…well, it appeared too soft and too long and was indescribably enticing in its tousled state. Why *did* gentlemen put so much pomade in their hair? His was infinitely better without it.

Also, she couldn't help but notice the slight hint of leather and clove as she'd come closer to him, a scent that seemed strangely at odds with the fine clothes he wore, when, in fact, it was the perfect combination.

And then there were his eyes. Ah, yes, his eyes… She suppressed a sigh. The exact color of a winter sky, at times blue, at times gray.

Damn him. Why in heaven must it be him to appear from nowhere, even more handsome than before? Well, it hardly mattered—he was still a scoundrel. Scoundrels never changed their stripes, and she'd learned that very much the hard way.

She walked to the window and braced her hands on the sill, rising up on her toes to have a look at the lovely pastoral view in front of the house. In the beginning she had not been pleased with her banishment to London—her mother insisted it was not a banishment, but Justine understood quite clearly that it was. However, she did think Prescott Hall was quite beautiful. The grounds were bucolic, and it soothed her. She was prone to feelings of anxiousness, and nothing could calm her quite like a walk in the country or a view such as this. She gazed idly at a shepherd moving his flock from a field. His two dogs raced back and forth behind them, forcing the sheep into a river of wool, moving them steadily into a narrow country road. The sheep moved along the road, pushed together like so many loaves of bread.

She thought as she watched them that she would tell Douglas she was terribly busy, there were many matters that were before her, and if he was calling on her socially, perhaps he could come at a more convenient time.

Or she could say she was unwell. Except that he'd not believe it, given how well she'd dressed just to refuse to see him.

She supposed whatever she would say, she ought to do it so that she could prepare for another evening with the insufferable Bardalines, making small talk, all the while wishing she could crawl into bed and read a book.

She sighed and began to turn from the window, but when she did, she happened to catch sight of someone at the end of the lane where the shepherd was herding his sheep. She paused and leaned forward, squinting out the thick-paned window. While her eyesight for things near was abysmal, her eyesight for things in the distance was quite good, and that was Douglas. He'd walked out onto the road for God knew what reason, and was strolling along, his gaze on the surroundings. He looked bored. He held his hat in his hand and tapped it against his leg as he ambled along.

Did he have something to say to her? Some news to impart? Or was he one of the many gentlemen who had tried to insinuate themselves into her presence? Being an unmarried princess made one quite popular in society.

She began to realize that Douglas hadn't noticed the sheep. He paused at the stone fence and propped one foot on it, then leaned forward to gaze into the landscape.

The sheep had turned the corner. They filled the lane, pressed together, scraping against the stone fence on either side, rushing forward to get away from the dogs. Douglas *still* had not seen them, and Justine mewled with alarm. The flock would run him over if he wasn't careful.

Then Douglas heard them. He brought his foot down from the fence and stared at the approaching onslaught of wool a moment too long. He looked back at the road he'd come from, and seeing there was no escape, at the last possible moment he leaped over the stone fence, stumbling on the other side and catching himself with a hand to the ground before tumbling onto his bum. He managed to gain his feet as the sheep rushed by, and looked down at his empty hand. He'd lost his hat.

Justine laughed out loud. She laughed so loud that Seviana came into the room. Justine waved her away. "It's nothing, Sevie. Once a fool, always a fool, that's all."

She supposed she'd kept his lordship waiting long enough.

CHAPTER FOUR

WILLIAM WAS STILL brushing off the dust and dirt of the fence he'd hurdled and the ground he'd encountered after his disastrous ramble when the door at the far end of the salon opened. He hastily ran a hand through his hair and managed to arrange himself just as Princess Justine walked into the salon.

She paused to stare at him. She had changed into a blue-and-white-striped gown, styled in the English fashion with a wide skirt and tight bodice. While he had long admired the body-hugging gowns of the Alucia-Wesloria regions, he would be the first to say this gown was very flattering. Quite different from the fencing attire, obviously, but just as appealing in a different sort of way.

She began to move, gliding forward with the confidence of someone who might have built this house, brick by brick.

William clasped his hands at his back and bowed when she came to a halt a few feet away from him. When he rose, her gaze raked down the front of him and up again. "My lord," she said prettily, "it is very kind of you to call after all these years. But I won't keep you—my duties of state require my attention and I should think surely you have something to do as well."

Did she just imply that he had nothing to do with his time? And why did that bit of speech sound as if she'd rehearsed in front of a mirror? William arched one dubious brow. "I see."

"Good." She lifted her chin a smidge higher.

William didn't move. *He* was the one who was inconvenienced by this meeting, not she. But if he had one fault... All right, he had many, too many to count. But if he was to *rank* his faults, he would have to put his inability to let a woman best him at the very top.

The irony of his indignation very nearly poked him in the eye. Not fifteen minutes ago he'd concocted a reason to leave at once, but she'd beat him to it. Which made him now intent on staying. Oh aye, he could be childish along with the best of them. He said, "And what duties are those?"

He saw only the tiniest bit of a wobble in her. "I beg your pardon?"

"You said you had duties of state. I wonder what those duties might be." He shrugged lightly, as if it was a trifling thing to ask, like asking after the weather or her health.

Her eyes rounded to the size of small tea saucers and shone with utter disbelief at his gall. "I beg your pardon, Lord Douglas, but my duties are none of your concern. And certainly nothing you would *ever* hope to understand."

The inquiry rattled her, as he knew it would, because people didn't go about questioning princesses. It was terribly ill-mannered to question *any* acquaintance, but nevertheless, he'd done it, and he would bet all of Hamilton Palace that the princess didn't have a convincing answer for him. "*Ever?* You might be surprised, aye?" He smiled.

She frowned. "I would *not* be surprised, and furthermore, I see this," she said, fluttering slender fingers at him, "for what it is. Make no mistake."

"*This* is an invitation to tea. Extended to me by you."

"It was extended by Bardaline, not *me*, and this is an

ambush. I know you won't take your leave until you've told me whatever it is you think I cannot *possibly* bear to not know. Very well, Lord Douglas. You may have your moment." She gestured with a grand swirl of her hand that he should sit at a small tea table. The moment she did, footmen leaped into action, practically leapfrogging over each other and bustling around Princess Justine with dishes and tiny china cups while one of them trundled in a cart with the tea.

William looked at her delicate, authoritarian hand and bowed again. "Please, madam. After you."

"At least do me the courtesy of addressing me as *Your Royal Highness*," she said as she sat.

Well, then. It looked as if William and the princess would pick up where they'd last left off.

One of the footmen was at Princess Justine's side before her perfect derriere had touched the silk-covered seat. He removed a linen napkin from the plate before her and whipped it open with such flourish that a curl of her hair flew up. "Oh," she said, surprised by the drama.

The footman laid the napkin in her lap. When William sat, the footman did the same with his napkin, but with much less flair. Another footman placed a platter on the table, removed the domed covering and with two fingers, indicated the delicacies to them. Cucumber sandwiches. Scots salmon on bread. Teacakes. A third footman poured the tea into cups. Was it really necessary to have three footmen serve two people tea? William thought they might have managed well enough on their own, but such was the life of *Your Royal Highness*, he supposed. *He* would find such overattention insufferable.

When the tea was poured, the footmen returned to their posts around the room. William slid them a look from the corner of his eye. "Can you no' dismiss them?"

She sniffed and leaned forward to examine the food, and in doing so, afforded William a view of her bosom that most definitely confirmed she was entirely grown now. "Lord Bardaline prefers I be attended at all times. Unfortunately, some things are quite beyond my control." She selected a teacake and put it on a small plate painted with bluebirds.

"You have me fooled, *Your Royal Highness*, for you looked very much in control earlier today."

She slid him a suspicious look. "Pardon?"

"I saw you toss your fencing opponent onto his arse. Very nearly impaled him with your épée by the look of it."

She nibbled the cake and then lowered it to her plate. "You know nothing, my lord. For one, I was wielding a foil, not an épée, and two, the mere suggestion I would *impale* him would run contrary to the sport. The fact of the matter is he tripped, because he is not very good with his footwork, and then he fell as a lark, pretending to be felled, and I merely played along."

"Your instructor has poor footwork? I should think a princess could retain the best."

"A princess *can* retain the best. My instructor is the captain of the palace guard and is currently guarding the palace in St. Edys. My fencing partner was not my instructor."

"Ah. Who was your friend, then?"

"I didn't say he was a friend. And why do you want to know?" she asked, looking curiously at the contents of her teacup.

"No reason. Perhaps I know him."

"You don't."

"I know many people in London."

She sipped her tea. "His name is Lord Mawbley and he kindly offered to be my fencing partner."

Mawbley. A smile slowly spread across William's lips.

A reprobate always recognized a fellow reprobate, and William and Mawbley had recognized each other years ago. In the not too distant past, a rumor had gone round that Mawbley had impregnated one of his chambermaids and had been disinherited for it. Whether or not that was true, William certainly didn't know or really care, but it would explain Mawbley's sudden interest in this particular princess's hobby sport. "I was no' aware that Mawbley's talents extended to fencing."

Princess Justine smiled wryly. "I assure you they do not."

William laughed. She seemed to relax a bit when he did.

"You look very well, Your Royal Highness. In all regards."

"Thank you." Her response was perfunctory—and she didn't bother to spare him as much as a glance with it. She pretended to examine the food again and William stubbornly waited a beat or two, thinking she might return the favor and comment on his appearance.

When she offered no such compliment, it vexed him to realize that it vexed him.

At last, she looked up, and he smiled at her so that she would know he understood she had deliberately remained silent. She may be a princess, but he'd flirted and teased many women in more sitting rooms than she would ever know, and he knew how to play this game.

"Will you not try the tea?" She nodded at his untouched cup.

He picked up the cup and saucer before him, then brought the cup to his lips. He locked his eyes with hers. She held his gaze. Ah, but she was willful...and he liked it. He decided to try a different tack.

"How did you find the journey from Wesloria, then?"

Princess Justine gave a half-suppressed laugh and picked up her teacup again. "Do you really care?"

He did not. But he left her in suspense for a moment and allowed his eyes to wander over her. Slowly. Appreciatively. And then said, "No. But I thought it polite to inquire."

She could not completely suppress her smile. "Still honest to a fault, I see. You first—how did you find your drive to Prescott Hall?"

"Aggravating." Another deadly honest answer.

"Oh? I thought the roads were quite good."

"It was no' the roads that have me aggrieved, aye?"

"Mmm. Well, *I* certainly didn't summon you." She sipped her tea again.

Oddly enough, William was enjoying this exchange. He was accustomed to talking to ladies about weather and how much they'd enjoyed the vicar's sermon. He liked a healthy bit of sparring. "I, too, appreciate honesty."

"Good." The princess put down her tea with conviction this time, then folded her hands tightly in her lap. "*If* we are being honest—*why* are you here?"

He didn't think she would appreciate his honesty quite so completely in this. He put aside his tea, too. "Pity you've nothing stronger." He glanced around the room, hoping that something stronger would magically appear.

The princess ignored him. "I can't imagine why you've come. The last I saw you, you'd been banished from a home for conduct unbecoming a gentleman. After that display, I rather imagined I would never see you again."

William gave a bark of surprised laughter. "Your memory is faulty—you *shouted* at me. You called me dishonorable before God and all that were gathered."

"You were! You pushed me aside to win a silly game."

"*I* pushed—" He drew a breath. "Funny, is it no', that before I won, you seemed to think that silly game was a matter of life or death. I did no' *push* you, madam. I *bested* you. It was a contest. And you could no' bear to lose. Admit it."

She gaped at him. A bit of color rose in her cheeks. "Fine. I will freely admit I don't care to lose," she said with a shrug of her fair shoulders. "Show me a single person who can bear to lose. But that is not the point. I didn't *shout*. I *said* that you had behaved dishonorably, and you called me a spoiled child!"

"Aye, that I did, because you were acting the part of spoiled princess to all who witnessed that night."

She gasped. "I had scarcely turned seventeen years old! And I had drunk that terrible punch! Better you turn your critique to yourself, sir, as you were acting like a child and you were what, thirty years old?"

"Thirty! I was the very age you are now!" He suddenly laughed, thinking back to that night. The entire party had drunk the absinthe punch, and all were as pissed as a passel of codgers on homemade gin. "I concede that it is entirely possible I might have been a wee bit childish—I was a bit in my cups."

"A bit? Lord Iddesleigh threw you out of his house."

"And you were a bit in yours, too, ma'am. Besides, I went very graciously even though you were clearly at fault."

She blinked innocently and pressed her hand to her chest as if she were a saint. "If I were at fault, then why did you apologize for arguing?"

"I did no' apologize for arguing. I apologized for arguing with a mere lass who was half in love with me."

"I was not! And even if I had been, all affection would have ceased the moment you took that poor woman, whom you clearly did not know, and kissed her under the mistletoe in front of us all."

He smiled a little lopsidedly. "Aye, and she kissed me back. Were you jealous?"

"Mein Gott!" she exclaimed. And then she picked up her tea and drank it like she was tossing back a tot of whisky before putting it down again.

William chuckled. He was enjoying this lively trip into the past. Princess Justine refused to smile back at him, and her eyes were shining with what he was certain was ire. But the way they shone reminded him of another night he'd been in her company. Another soiree, but at this one, they'd danced.

Her eyes had a different sort of glint that evening. He knew at the time that she was enamored of him. He'd enjoyed dancing with her—she'd made him laugh. But then he'd been pulled away by the hostess, Lady Bishop, and lectured for taking two dances *in a row* with a princess whose dance card was apparently *quite crowded.* "Everyone will think she esteems you," Lady Bishop had hissed at him.

He'd said, "Does she no'?"

Lady Bishop had huffed, "I don't know how things are in Scotland, my lord, but I find you incorrigible!"

"You are no' alone in your opinion," he'd said breezily. He'd been an incorrigible man for many years.

But he was a different man now. He'd had to become one, because of his father. Unfortunately, he wasn't sure what sort of man he was.

"Now that you've made it clear you are not here to apologize for that night," the princess said primly, "please do enlighten me as to why you have come."

"Let us nab two fish with one net, aye? Firstly, I apologize, Your *Royal* Highness," he said with a grin, and pressed the palm of his hand to his heart. "If I insulted you or injured you in any way, I am truly and irrevocably remorseful." He meant that sincerely.

"Well, you didn't," she retorted. "I didn't care enough to be insulted or injured."

He laughed. "A proper cut."

The color in her cheeks deepened a little. "For heaven's sake," she said, "can we please get on with it? It hardly matters what happened eight years ago. I want to know why you're here *now*."

William contemplated his response. He could tell her he was here to mollycoddle her because clearly, no one in Wesloria trusted her to be left to her own devices. Judging by the number of footmen standing about, he was certain of it. But he didn't care to injure her feelings. He leaned forward, braced an arm against his knee and said quietly, "Your prime minister has asked me to introduce you to mutual friends of ours so that you might—" he gestured with his hand, wishing he didn't have to say it aloud "—make friends."

She stared at him. He couldn't tell if she was angry or hurt or—

She burst into laughter. *"You?"* She laughed again, and rather heartily at that, one hand going to her stomach as if to contain the peals of laughter, then falling back in her seat, chortling to the ceiling.

"Why no' me?" William asked, feeling a bit offended.

"Robuchard asked *you*, a known scoundrel, to keep watch over *me*?"

"I'm perfectly capable of introducing you to the *haute ton*."

"*Je*, but…" Her laughter died down. She was still smiling when she said, "You are hardly the first person I should think he'd ask to look over me."

She was no fool, this one. "Nevertheless...here I am."

"How dare he! Or you. Or whoever is behind this. Let me be clear, Lord Douglas—I don't *need* a keeper. Your... *offer* is declined."

He winced. "It's no' precisely an *offer*—"

"I don't care what it is. Not for a moment do I require your help."

"Agreed," he said, holding up a hand in surrender. "For what it is worth, I was as surprised as you. I agreed only to make myself as useful as you might allow. I hope you will consider it a friendly gesture, one made in the spirit of forgiveness."

"That would be lovely, but there is a slight flaw to you thinking—I am the one who should forgive *you*."

"Well," he said, and rubbed his knee a little. "One could argue it both ways."

"One can argue it all day long and I still do not require any help from you."

"Excellent," William said. "Saves me that trouble, does it no'? Aye, but I do wonder, then, who will tour you about London?"

"Anyone else," she said, and popped the rest of an uneaten teacake into her mouth.

"I shall endeavor no' to be offended by the idea that *anyone* else would suit you."

"*No* one suits me."

"Hmm. It would appear that someone has lost all her jolly."

She rolled her eyes and picked up another teacake, this one with her fingers, dispensing with all table manners. "I never had any jolly. I was not allowed to *be* jolly. You would have lost yours, too, if you'd been sent to England against your will, held prisoner at an estate with nothing to occupy you, only to discover your nemesis is to be your jailer." She took a healthy bite.

"Now you've insulted me. I'm no' your nemesis, and I am sincerely attempting to be your friend. From what you've said, perhaps the only one you've got."

The princess snorted.

William glanced at the footmen, who stared straight ahead. He leaned forward and spoke softly again. "You are no' a prisoner here. Robuchard has asked me to introduce you to *friends*. People who will make your stay easier. Why no' allow me to show you London? There is much to see. And, if I may…you might want an ally when suitors begin to call. Word has it that there will be many."

"Is *that* what word has?" Her gaze turned dark, and she pinned him in his chair with it.

"Ah…"

"The number of suitors I may or may not have does not answer the question of why Robuchard would suddenly go to such pains to ensure I had *friends*. Can you explain that?"

William was fairly certain he didn't have to explain— she seemed to understand her prime minister. Or at least understood enough not to trust him. He scratched the side of his nose and thought about the many excuses and lies he could offer. But like her, he appreciated honesty. "In truth, I donna know if he cares at all if you have friends in London. But he would like to know about the suitors."

Princess Justine blinked. "What would you possibly have to do with it?"

"I know some of the gentlemen that your family has in mind. And I am a neutral observer."

"Neutral," she repeated dubiously.

"You are considered one of the most desirable matches in all of Europe, and out from under the prime minister's watchful eye, you might be enticed to no good by gentle-men such as Mawbley."

"Mawbley!"

The conversation was beginning to make him uncom-fortable. It was none of his concern who she might wed one day. And he didn't want to be the one to tell her how wretched the male sex could be when it came to the pos-sibility of wealth and power. "Have you no' guessed what Mawbley is about?"

She looked away from him, which suggested that she had indeed guessed.

"I think Robuchard thought it might be useful to you to have someone about who is acquainted with those who will come calling."

"Useful?" She lifted her gaze. "I'm surrounded at every moment of the day. Do you and Robuchard think I don't have enough advice on what I should say or think or do at any moment? Do you and Robuchard think I haven't any sense at all?"

William had wondered the same thing. "Perhaps because you have only Weslorian advice?" he posed. "Perhaps Wes-lorians will no' always tell you the truth, aye? But me?" He spread his arms wide. "I've nothing to gain. I've got all the time in the world to watch you be courted."

"I don't want to be courted. I'm completely *against* any sort of courting."

He shrugged. "It hardly matters to me what you do— I've nothing to prove to you. But I have given my word to a friend."

She looked at him sharply. "Robuchard is your friend?"

That was a misstep. "A better term is a powerful ac-quaintance."

Princess Justine leaned back in her seat, her gaze intent.

Curious and studious. Her eyes, he thought, were enchanting. They were so amber in color that from a distance, they looked a little like spun gold. Princess eyes.

She suddenly leaned forward. "What were your terms?"

"My *terms*?"

She inched forward on her seat and leaned closer, her eyes glistening. "What did you agree to do for him? What information does Robuchard want from you?"

"To be your friend—"

She waved her hand, dismissing the notion before he could prevaricate. "I may be young...but you will at least agree I am not new to the appetite of men for political maneuvering."

"True."

"How often are you to escort me about like a child?"

"You're no' a child, quite obviously—"

"How often?"

"That...that would be determined by, ah..." How in hell should he know how often? That was Beck's fault, too—one could not think through a delicate situation like this when one was captured and forced to drink whisky the night before.

She clucked her tongue at his ignorance and failure to have thought this entirely through. "Let's start simply. What precisely has he asked you to do?"

"From time to time, he would like to have word on your happiness...or lack thereof, depending."

She snorted. "You may report immediately that my happiness is waning with his tricks. If you are to escort me about to make *friends*, then we must have an understanding."

Now they were getting somewhere. He imagined they

would agree to certain hours, a frequency of events. "All right."

"To begin, you will recognize that I am to be queen soon and you are not at liberty to tell me what to do, under any circumstance."

His eyes widened with surprise. "Now, there's a winning scheme if ever I heard one—befriend others by beaning them on the head with your scepter."

She ignored him and carried on. "You are not to have or offer an opinion on any would-be suitors."

William laughed. "I will have an opinion. It's human nature to have an opinion. But you mistake me for someone who cares who you shackle yourself to for all eternity. I will have an opinion, and I will escort you about London so you are properly tended, but I hardly care who the lucky fellow is."

"Then kindly don't give me your opinion unless I specifically ask for it."

He held up both hands. "Fair. Are we agreed?"

"No. When you are not escorting me in an official capacity, you are to keep to yourself. I am none of your business."

This was beginning to sound a bit like a dressing down. "I'll no' agree to that," he said, holding up a finger. "You must admit you are a *wee* bit of my business, as I have agreed with your prime minister, who has the consent of your mother the queen as I understand it, to escort you about. And if you donna mind me saying, I've heard you are your own worst enemy. And lastly, but certainly no' the least of it, I am good company."

"I'm sure you believe that is true," she said smartly. "And I am *not* my own worst enemy. I am my own best counsel! Why is it that men can never see that the villains are always the men? Why do gentlemen always believe that they have some divine understanding of a woman that is better than a woman's own understanding? And by the bye, you are to address me as Your Royal Highness."

"Huh." He sat a little straighter. "You do excel at keeping the mincing of words to a minimum, and for that, I must commend you. In answer to your...*complaint*, gentlemen generally know better than ladies because ladies are emotional and gentlemen are practical."

She snorted. "A ridiculous lie men tell themselves."

"And I will address you as you prefer when we are in public, but I donna intend to scrape my knuckles on your floor every time I cast my eyes on you, *Your Royal Highness*."

A corner of her mouth tipped up. "That seems a rather emotional response, no?"

He suppressed his strange desire to smile. "What will you have me call you in private?" he stubbornly insisted.

"Highness." She lifted her chin ever so slightly.

"Aye, you've already tried to decree it. But as you are not my sovereign I have declined the offer. We are old friends, so I shall call you Justine and you may call me William."

She gave a small laugh of incredulity. "We are not old friends. We are not even *friends*."

"We are indeed friends, even if you have forgotten our earlier acquaintance." He stood up, and the footmen began to cartwheel around him in their haste to pull his chair away and carry off his napkin, held on a tray, like it was soaked in blood. William bowed to Justine. "A fellow Scot, the Duke of Sutherland, is opening his picture gallery for viewing to a small group of acquaintances at Stafford House. I should like to extend an invitation to you and Princess Amelia to attend as my guests."

Justine stood up, too. "You may give the details to the

master of my chamber. He will send word if we accept the invitation."

His eyes narrowed. "I think you might accept for yourself as I am, at this very moment, presenting you with the invitation. That is, if you are so inclined."

Her eyes narrowed, too. "I think it beyond your simple comprehension that a princess of my standing might have a calendar that is a bit complicated."

He took a small step forward, closing the gap between them. "Complicated? Or persnickety?"

She lifted her chin and shifted closer to him, too. "I don't know what that means."

He glared down at her. "It means that I believe you intend to make this situation," he said, wagging his forefinger back and forth between them, "as difficult as possible."

She shifted even closer and smiled devilishly. "I will make our situation whatever I want to make it, for I am a *royal princess*."

William shifted so close that his legs were engulfed in her skirts and she had to tilt her head back to glare up at him. "A piece of friendly advice, *Justine*, aye? Perhaps you need no' mention you are a royal princess at every conceivable opportunity."

"Oh! *Thank* you for advice I specifically asked you not to offer me! Now, here is a piece of advice for you, *William*. Perhaps you ought to remember that I *am* a royal princess, and not a debutante to be blinded by your charms. I suggest you not even try. Shall I have a footman fetch your hat?"

Her eyes were glittering with something that looked a bit like mirth and ire. Mirthful ire. Was there such a thing? Worse, William knew that by some sorcery, she knew that his hat had been trampled by sheep. "I will speak to Bardaline on my way out." He stepped back and bowed very low. "Your *Royal Highness*."

She put her hands on her waist. "My Lord Douglas."

William strode out.

He marched through the corridor to the front door. He'd known there would be issues between them, and that she would resist…but he hadn't expected to be so bloody attracted to her resistance.

And now he was stuck. He was stuck with a very attractive, glittery-eyed *princess* who was going to be a queen and meant to remind him of it every moment she was in his company.

"Ewan!" he croaked as he strode out the door.

Ewan was just outside, and tried to hand him a muddied, crumpled hat. William batted it aside. "Leave it as a souvenir for *Her Royal Highness*," he said crossly, and walked down to the drive to await his horse. He was already composing his telegraph to Mr. Robuchard in his head. *I've been received by Her Royal Highness and find her as willful and prideful as ever.* He would leave out any mention of finding her far more attractive than he'd anticipated. That was just a bothersome bit of business he'd tamp down.

He was fully confident of it.

CHAPTER FIVE

Truelson Stot, Elsinor, Denmark

THE MORNING SUN dappled the path before Lila Aleksander. She loved summer mornings and long walks alike, and would rise early, dressing in a plain skirt and her husband's heavy coat. Her hair was braided and she'd stuffed a hat on her head in the event a stray cloud rained on her. She used a walking stick, marking the time with a steady jab to the earth.

Her mind wandered to all the little, mundane things that married life brought to one's mind. The supper party in a few days. What they needed from the market. Her husband's birthday soon, his fiftieth, and what she might do to mark it.

She reached the small woodland lake nestled in the middle of the park that surrounded her home. She went around, and started up the expansive park lawn to the house ahead of her. It was white and long, its many windows like a pattern of dark squares. *Truelson Stot*, her home these past fifteen years.

And they said she'd be forever ruined.

As she approached the house, she could see her beloved Valentin seated at a table on the terrace. He was still in his dressing gown and nightshirt. He was reading a letter, his legs stretched out long before him. Lila walked to his chair, leaned over and kissed the top of his head. *"God Morgen."*

He caught her hand and pulled her onto his lap. "Where have you been? I missed you when I woke."

"Walking."

"You walk so much you'll need new leather boots before long."

Lila stretched out her leg and pulled up her skirt and they both had a look at the fine leather boots he'd brought her from Rome. "They've many miles left in them."

She looked at the plate on the table before them. It was heaped with eggs and cheese, and on another plate, *aebleskiver*, a pastry Lila had come to love. She picked one off his plate and popped it into her mouth. Karla, the kitchen maid, appeared to pour coffee.

Valentin's attention had returned to the letter. "Ah, look, will you? Herre Johansson has agreed to the terms for the sale of our little ship." He beamed up at her, then brought her hand to his lips and kissed it. He'd endeavored to sell that ship for more than a year now, as he preferred his two bigger, faster ships, built by the best Danish shipbuilders.

"A letter has come for you as well, darling."

"For me? My mother?"

He shook his head. "It appears to be official."

Lila spotted it and leaned forward to pick it up.

"*Och*, you're hurting my knee," Valentin said, and gave her a gentle push off his lap.

Lila placed the letter on the table and settled into a chair. She helped herself to another pastry and turned her face up to the sun, feeling the warmth of it seep into her skin this beautiful morning. So still, she could hear the sea in the distance.

"Who so desperately needs you now, my love?" Valentin put aside his letter. He picked up his fork and began eating his eggs.

Lila lifted the letter and broke the seal. She scanned to the signature on the bottom of the page. "Ah, of course. It's my old friend Dante Robuchard."

Valentin paused. "Robuchard. The prime minister of Wesloria?"

"The very one."

He sipped his coffee. "I've met him, have I? At the..." He paused, squinting skyward.

"Prince Heinrich's wedding."

"Ah, yes, yes, of course." He nodded. Then looked at her again. "Small man?"

"Average."

"Middle-aged," he said.

"I beg your pardon. He is only a year or two older than me."

"Astonishingly young, then," he said with a grin. "Gray hair?"

Lila laughed. "Very brown. He has a serious disposition and is never far from Queen Agnes."

Valentin swallowed another forkful of eggs. "That's it. I remember him now. Where is the king?"

"In St. Edys. He's quite ill."

"Yes, that's right," Valentin said. "The weakest king of Europe, isn't it said?"

"Perhaps the sickest," Lila said. She read the letter from Robuchard.

"Well?" Valentin asked as he polished off his eggs. "Who is it this time?"

Who was the most important unmarried person in all of Europe just now. Lila looked up at her husband. "Princess Justine. The crown princess of Wesloria."

"She had a bit of trouble, didn't she?" He shook his head. "She ought to have been married before now."

"Valentin!" Lila laughed. "You know such arrangements are made with much study. She is in London, under the tutelage of Queen Victoria. Robuchard says the king's health is dire and the princess will be queen very soon, perhaps before the year's end."

"Oh dear. Then she *must* be married straightaway," Valentin said gravely, then winked playfully.

Lila smiled. She loved his thick, dark hair, salted with gray, his neatly trimmed beard, his wide chest...and other parts of him, too. She just loved him.

"This will be the match of the decade," Valentin offered, although he knew nothing of matches and matchmaking.

"Possibly."

"And the retainer?" he asked.

Lila held up the letter and pointed to the figure Robuchard had suggested as a fee for her matchmaking services. Valentin's brows rose. "Oh. He must want a match very badly. I suppose you'll accept?"

She was most intrigued. A successful match with a crown princess would be a boon for her business. She lowered the letter. "Do you want me to stay here?"

"Of course I want you to stay here, with me." He took her hand and tugged on it, forcing her to stand and come to his lap again. She laughed as he kissed her mouth, her chest through the vee of her shirt. "Of course I want you to stay, Lila. You know I can't bear to be away from you. London, you say? Maybe I'll come with you. How long will you be gone?"

She thought about it—matchmaking required a certain finesse. Sometimes it could be done in a matter of weeks. Sometimes it took much longer to convince two people they were perfect for each other. "A month. Maybe two. Will you really come?"

"I really will the moment I begin to miss you so desperately I can't breathe." He moved his mouth lower, pulling her shirt open to press his lips against the tops of her breasts. "You taste like salt."

"It's rather warm today."

"You need a bath."

"I do."

"Ah, my English rose. I am the one to give it to you." He lifted his head. "Karla!" he called. "Karla, come and clear this away. My wife must have her bath." He suddenly stood up, taking Lila with him, and walked toward the house, carrying her in his arms. He kissed her as she laughed and told him to watch where he was going when he banged her head into the door frame.

CHAPTER SIX

London

SOMEONE HAD PREPARED a lunch for Justine that she had not requested and did not want, given her late breakfast. But it arrived in the drawing room along with the day's post, which included a letter from her mother.

Justine preferred to receive letters from her mother in private, and generally near a good, blazing hearth into which she could toss the pages in the event she disagreed with her mother's words, as the physical distance between them prevented Justine from arguing her point. But sometimes watching her mother's words go up in flames was just as satisfying.

This afternoon, lamentably, Justine was not alone—because Lady Bardaline was looping Amelia's braids over her ears in the fashion English ladies arranged their hair. Lady Bardaline wore a new afternoon dress. It was quite becoming on her, but then again, she was a small, attractive woman, with very dark hair and clear blue eyes. Justine took particular note of the dress, because she thought it meant her lady-in-waiting believed she would accompany Justine to Windsor.

"Is that from Mama?" Amelia asked, pointing at the letter Justine held in her hand. The elaborate state seal of the Weslorian monarchy could be seen from clear across the room.

"It is," Justine confirmed.

"What does she write?"

Justine broke the seal of the letter and scanned the contents. She could almost write the letters herself these days, as her mother's admonishments were consistently and frequently given. "Mostly that you are spending far too much."

Amelia gasped so loudly that Lady Bardaline jumped.

"And that you should not frequent Holland House, because it is *ungehörig* to be perceived as favoring one political party over the other." Sometimes their mother couldn't think quickly of the English word and substituted her native German. Particularly when she was displeased.

"What does that mean?" Amelia asked.

"Umm...unseemly, I think."

"Unseemly! How can it be unseemly? How can she possibly expect me to know which political party the Hollands prefer? I don't even know what political parties there are to choose from."

Justine laughed at her sister. She often wondered if Amelia was terribly clever or truly daft. "How can you not know that all your new friends are Whigs, Amelia?"

"What are you talking about?"

Lady Bardaline said soothingly, "The Hollands host many prominent members of the Whig party in their salon."

"Do they?" Amelia asked and sounded, at least, entirely innocent. "How do *you* know who they host in their salon, madam? You've not been there, have you? I certainly hadn't noticed and even if I had, I hardly care. What can Mama possibly mean, I am spending too much? It's not possible! I am very careful with my purchases."

Yes, Amelia was very careful with her purchases—care-

ful to ensure that every new gown was properly acces-
sorized. Here she sat now, in a new gown, with matching
new slippers and a new shawl. She and Lady Holland had
returned from Bond Street just yesterday with more boxes
and wrapped packages than Justine had ever seen, filled
with kid leather gloves and ribbon-trimmed hats and silk
undergarments. Justine scarcely left Prescott Hall at all.
Lord Bardaline wouldn't allow it without at least two guards
to accompany her.

"She means that she has seen the outrageous receipts for
your many purchases and finds them costly," Justine said.

Amelia abruptly stood up, even though she had two
braids that had not been looped and pinned. She marched
across the room and held out her hand for the letter, her
fingers wiggling in a manner that suggested Justine ought
to hand it over. Justine was more than happy to oblige her
sister and even pointed out the paragraph.

Amelia read the sentence, *I have seen the outrageous
receipts.* She thrust the letter back at Justine. "She didn't
say they were too costly, just that she'd seen them. And it's
not even true!"

When Amelia insisted that something wasn't true, it
generally meant that it was.

Her sister marched back to her chair and sat, and Lady
Bardaline continued her task of pinning the braids. "Any
word of Papa?" she asked sweetly, clearly wanting to change
the subject.

Yes, there was word of their father, and it roiled Justine's
stomach. She despaired she would never see him again—
perhaps because he'd all but told her, as she was preparing to leave for England, that it was entirely possible they
would not meet again in this life.

Justine refused to accept that. She wanted to believe she

would see him again and would tell him what a good king and better father he was. "Mama writes that his health has not improved, but that he does enjoy sitting in the garden in the afternoons when the sun is warm."

No one said anything until Lady Bardaline broke the silence by proclaiming Amelia's braids done. She put her hands on Amelia's shoulders and leaned over the top of her head, as if Amelia was her niece or daughter. "You look very appealing."

"I do, don't I?" Amelia asked, examining her reflection.

Justine was saved from retching at that little exchange when her master of chamber appeared at the door of the drawing room and bowed to Justine. "Your Royal Highness, if you are ready?"

"I am, thank you."

Bardaline glanced at his wife, who gestured impatiently for Seviana to carry off the mirror and pins and began to smooth her gown. Justine stood up and put her back to her lady-in-waiting and walked to the door. "Shall we?"

"Your Royal Highness, my wife—"

"No, thank you," Justine interjected pleasantly. "I will go on my own." She walked to the door, aware that Bardaline did not follow her straightaway, and mentally braced herself before looking back. She pasted a smile on her face and turned. "Is something the matter, my lord?"

"If I may, Your Royal Highness, it is appropriate for you to have an escort."

"Oh, that." She laughed airily. "It's just as appropriate if I don't."

"But I—"

"I didn't understand from my mother that her ladyship was to learn from the feet of Queen Victoria alongside me. I thought that was to be all for me, as I am the only one here who will be queen one day. Well. Amelia might be, if something were to happen to me, but that seems unlikely."

She heard Amelia's sound of surprise, and honestly, she might as well have made it—she rarely spoke like this to Bardaline. Or to anyone, for that matter. Maybe she was a tiny bit afraid of him or afraid of what he could do if he were of a mind. And even now she was quaking just a very little bit on the inside. Frankly, she didn't know what she would do if he disagreed with her. All she knew was that she was sick of being watched all the time and told what to do and treated like a prisoner.

An uncomfortable moment passed.

Justine almost laughed with relief when it became clear that Lord Bardaline did not intend to disagree or disobey. He exchanged a look with his suddenly sour-looking wife and reluctantly followed Justine out the door.

"Good day, dear sister!" Amelia cheerfully called after her.

Justine walked down the hall, her head high, refusing to look back, to give any hint of her uncertainty. She imagined herself to be Queen Elena of Astasia Castle, walking out to meet her subjects after she'd been crowned queen. She wondered how Elena had felt or what she'd done when she sensed those around her were trying to control her. Had she been as uncertain as Justine sometimes felt? She rather imagined not.

She was determined to be more like Elena.

JUSTINE HAD MADE Queen Victoria's acquaintance previously. She'd been formally introduced when she'd first arrived in London, and she and the Weslorian Ambassador had presented the queen with a small onyx sculpture of a ballerina. It was a gift from her mother as a thank-you for her "tutelage" of her daughter. The ambassador's speech, which Justine suspected was delivered after one too many glasses of wine, had droned on—she swore she saw Queen Victoria briefly nod off.

The second time she'd met the queen had been at a small reception the queen had held in honor of Justine and Amelia. Her Majesty's ministers, her husband, her older children and an excess of courtiers had attended, surrounding the queen and clamoring for her attention. Justine had spent most of the reception trying to appear demure and regal as her mother and Monsieur DuPree always insisted she appear, her stomach in knots, and her nerves fraying as she watched Amelia flirt shamelessly with various English gentlemen. The older she became—and especially after the debacle with Aldabert—the more uncomfortably conspicuous she felt in crowds. But at least she'd managed to resist the urge to press herself against a wall and make herself small.

Today, however, would be the first time she was to have tea with the queen alone. As it was a private meeting, none of the nerves she felt about large groups had been able to gain a footing in her. She was actually quite excited—she had so many questions!

When Justine arrived at Windsor, she was escorted to a red drawing room. She was briefly left alone, and she took the opportunity to gawk at the surroundings. The soaring ceiling had been plastered with gilded medallions, and from the center of them dropped the most massive crystal chandeliers Justine had ever seen. One might think that if a woman grew up inside palace walls herself, she would not be easily impressed. But Rohalan Palace in St. Edys was not as grand as this. At Rohalan, the ceilings were lower, designed to keep the heat in the interior, as the climate was colder than this. The furnishings were sturdy and practical—a lot

of hardwood and leather as opposed to the lush, red upholstered furnishings here. And the art in any given room was
almost entirely of generals and kings and nobles in military
regalia. Even the drawing room in which she and Amelia
had spent many hours as children had so many portraits of
male dignitaries that she'd felt surrounded by men. In this
room, however, the portraits included women and children.
The colors were softer, the faces smiling.

She was admiring the view of the countryside out the
window when a door at the end of the room opened. "Good
afternoon!" The voice was high, almost childlike. Indeed,
from across the room, Queen Victoria almost looked like
a child, she was so small, not even five feet tall. Justine
sank into a graceful curtsy…and kept sinking to get her
head below the queen's. She'd gone so low that she had to
use every muscle in her body to rise up without the aid of
a chair. But she managed it, and she smiled with triumph,
and the queen greeted her sunnily. That was when Justine
noticed the girl. And the dog. A small brown dachshund.

"My daughter, Victoria. She will join us, if you please,"
the queen said. "And Boy. Isn't he lovely? I told him he was
not to come but he disobeyed me. You're a naughty boy,
aren't you, Boy?"

The dog sat and looked up at the queen adoringly, his
tail madly sweeping the rug behind him.

Justine didn't please. She wanted the queen's attention
all to herself. But she smiled warmly and said, "I would
be delighted."

The princess royal wasn't even as tall as her mother.
She curtsied to Justine and welcomed her to Windsor. Justine thanked her, then bent down to greet the dog. Boy
accepted her greeting, then scampered ahead of them to
greet the footmen.

"Please, be seated," the queen offered, gesturing to a table in the middle of the room. It was inlaid with jade and sported a gold candelabra fashioned to look like a tree with many branches. As the day was sunny and bright, the drapes had been drawn back to allow in the light, and two of the windows had been opened to air the room.

A footman came forward to hold a chair for the queen. When she was seated, two more appeared to seat the princess royal and Justine. There was a fourth chair that a footman whisked away, as if the very sight of it was offensive. If the queen seemed curious to know why Justine had come without a governess, escort, spy or zookeeper, she didn't ask. She remarked the fine weather as they took their seats.

"I've asked for my favorite cake to be served," the queen said, and a footman dutifully removed a dome from a cake platter to reveal a sponge cake covered in raspberries. "It is divinely light." She gestured to the butler, and while he set about pouring the tea, the queen picked up the dachshund and allowed it to lick her face before setting him down again. The dog disappeared under the table, and a moment later Justine felt his weight against her foot as he settled in.

Queen Victoria took the tea the footman had served and poured it into another cup. She looked at Justine, who had yet to pick up her own tea. "You'll want to do the same," she advised. "It cools the tea."

The princess royal copied her mother, and therein doing solved the mystery of why there were so many cups and saucers on the table. It seemed odd, but Justine did as the queen did, too. She was not here to question how Queen Victoria took her tea.

The queen said she was pleased that Justine had come to tea, that Vicky, as she called the princess royal, was fifteen, and that just a month ago she'd announced her daughter's engagement to Prince Frederick of Prussia. "You might have read about it?" the queen asked.

"I have—" Justine was going to say she had not, but another thing she was swiftly learning about Queen Victoria was that she liked to do the talking.

"Her father and I agreed to the engagement but will not allow Vicky to wed until she is seventeen. Fifteen is far too young, don't you think?"

Vicky blushed and cast her gaze to her cup.

"I, ah…"

"Have you met him? Fine young man, he is."

"No, I've not had—"

"Why haven't *you* been betrothed, my dear?" the queen asked bluntly.

Justine blinked. She was still forming her opinion of being engaged at fifteen, or searching her memory to see if she'd ever been introduced to Frederick of Prussia. She was not ready to discuss her failure to have secured a husband.

"These things should be decided long before you become of age. I was the exception, I suppose, but I didn't *want* to be married. I truly didn't. But then I met Albert and I changed my mind. You would have, too, had you seen him. So handsome." She eyed Justine curiously. "You're quite up in years not to have it all sorted out, are you not? And your sister, too, I should think. She has no prospect, either?"

"Umm…" Justine picked up the tea she had transferred to a new cup and noticed, to her horror, that she'd not made clean work of it and a bit remained in the saucer. "My father's illness has kept me close." That was partly true— she'd spent some time in her father's company, watching him review the piles of letters and petitions and state business that came to him every day. Watching him cough and grimace with pain.

"But surely, there have been *discussions*," the queen persisted.

Of course there had been discussions. *Scores* of them. It was as if all of Wesloria was on tenterhooks to see when she might take a husband, and who it might be. There was nothing quite like having people all around you talk about your future husband as if finding one was something you were incapable of doing on your own, and as you were practically a worthless human without a husband, you were not allowed to have a public opinion on the matter. "Yes, ma'am. I believe I am to meet potential consorts while I am in England."

"And you've all the necessary people around you to assess them, have you? You really ought to have your parents, but I understand that is impossible at present. Who do you have?"

"Well…" She couldn't bring herself to say Lord and Lady Bardaline. "My sister has—"

"You can't rely on your sister!" the queen insisted loudly as a footman put a very large piece of cake before the queen. "She'll want what you want, someone who is handsome and kind. *You*, however, must look at these gentlemen in terms of the monarchy, my dear. Who can best serve your country?"

Justine would like for at least a *little* of it to be about who was handsome and kind.

The footman served two smaller pieces to Justine and Vicky. The queen picked up a fork and began to eat the cake. And then suddenly dropped her fork. "Oh no, this will not do. Take it. It's all wrong."

Justine was holding her fork when the footman whisked the piece of cake out from under her.

"But I'm sure you'll sort it all out," the queen said breezily, apparently unconcerned that the footman had just taken Justine's cake. "I suppose things must happen differently when one's father is so ill." She turned in her chair to address one of the footmen. "The cake served yesterday was perfection. I don't see why this one is not as good as that." She looked back at Justine. "Would you not agree?"

Justine was still reeling from the loss of cake. "I didn't taste it."

"I mean, it is different for you because your father is so ill."

"Ah, yes. Regrettably, it is true, Your Majesty."

"My sincere condolences," the queen said. She picked up her teacup and sipped, her gaze on Justine. She put the cup down and said, "I understand your dilemma quite well, really. My late uncle, King William, was ill. It seemed to me he lasted an age before he finally succumbed. And all that time, there I was, waiting for my turn on the throne."

Justine nearly choked on her tea. She was *not* waiting for her turn. Did Her Majesty not understand that for her to be queen meant her father would be dead? She would much rather have her father than be queen, and that was the honest truth. She couldn't imagine doing it without him, her one true ally, the only one who could possibly understand the burden that awaited her. She was destined to be queen; she knew that—but how could she *want* that? She suddenly wished she were in St. Edys with him.

"William once said he hoped to survive until I turned eighteen years, and he did, passing one month after my eighteenth birthday. Can you imagine?"

"Why, Mama?" Vicky asked.

"Oh, well, he was very much against my mother as regent, and, I will admit, so was I."

Justine thought she spoke in jest, but the queen looked at her, frowning slightly. "Will your mother act as regent?"

"No, ma'am. I am five and twenty. I've been…" She tried to think of the right word for the urgency with which her father had taught her the business of the throne.

But it turned out she didn't need a word, because the queen said, "Very good. Regents are generally hungry for power, you know. They'll stop at nothing." She paused and seemed to consider her words. "But I'm certain Her Majesty Queen Agnes would *never* plot against you. I didn't mean that at all." She smiled sympathetically. "I think that perhaps your father is willing himself to live until you have taken a husband. I have no doubt he understands it will be easier for you with a helpmate. Assuming you can find one."

Justine had to concentrate to keep from squirming in her seat. "I think he is willing himself to simply live." She sounded as if she was being contrary, and she could almost hear DuPree *non non non*-ing somewhere on the continent.

"Well. We pray for his continued health. But as he cannot always be with you, you must have someone at your side whom you can trust when your time comes to sit the throne. Have you someone like that?"

"My sister," Justine said, without reservation.

"I am referring to someone who might know a thing or two about ruling. I had Lord Melbourne, of course, my prime minister. I trusted him completely and when the Tories came to power and they tried to replace him, I would not hear of it. What of your prime minister? Could he be depended upon to offer sound advice?"

Oh, Justine imagined Robuchard would like nothing better than to offer all the advice in the world to her—but not to help her. To control her. "I think he is…an honorable man," she said carefully.

The queen smiled slyly. "You did not answer my question. But you needn't bother—I can see that you have a good head on your shoulders." She leaned forward. "You have a sense about him, do you? Then don't bother with him. That's my advice. Get someone you *know* you can trust. Get yourself a Melbourne!"

"But how will she do that?" the princess royal asked for Justine.

"Well, she'll just have to meet with her privy council and assess them. But that is the reason it is so important you find someone to marry," the queen continued, addressing Justine now. "Someone you may trust as you trust your sister. Someone who will help you with the burden of the crown, like my Albert. I do not mean to be indelicate when I say that time is of the essence for you, my dear. You *must* have someone on whom you can depend. On whom the country can depend. If you don't, the courtiers will eat you alive."

Justine made a sound of disbelief. Here they were again, returned to her glaring lack of a husband and her inability, apparently, to be queen in her own right.

The queen leaned back and pushed her teacup away as she shrewdly studied Justine. A footman was there at once to refill it. "Do not misunderstand me, dear, please. You are perfectly capable of being a queen, and I daresay, a good one. But the world wants a king. As you can't give them that in a sovereign, you can give them a consort to admire."

The queen took the tea the footman had poured, and poured that into another cup. She now had three discarded cups. "Now. What names have you considered for a husband?"

The princess royal looked up from her tea, eager to hear the answer.

"I, ah… I haven't, actually. My mother has, umm…retained the services of someone to help me, ah…put together a list, so to speak."

"Yes, but who has been put forth for the list?" A footman stepped in and cleared away the empty cups.

"I don't rightly know," Justine said apologetically. "But I know many have been suggested."

"Of course many have!" the queen declared. "You're young and comely, and you appear to have a figure suitable for providing the next heir. You'll make a fine catch for a man with ambition, won't you? Are you particular? You've every right to be. The wrong man will take your throne if you're not careful."

Once again, Justine's surprise nearly caused her to choke on her tea. "Pardon?"

"Men like to control things. Albert was a bit like that when we first met, wanting to tell me what to do."

Her daughter laughed.

"But I married him because he was so very handsome, and there is no one dearer to me than my family."

That would argue that Victoria had not followed the advice she was offering, but had married based on looks alone.

A footman appeared with a plate of scones. He set them on the table along with small tubs of clotted cream and honey. They looked delicious, and Justine's belly might have given a slight rumble.

"I don't want them," the queen said. "I had my mind set on cake. Take it," she said, and the footman deftly removed the scones. "You've nearly finished your tea," she said to Justine. "Have more." The queen lifted her hand to signal the butler.

"I wouldn't want to trouble—"

"Of course you must. A pity the cake wasn't baked properly. It is most excellent. You'll have to take my word for it."

The footman poured tea into Justine's cup, and with the eyes of the queen and princess royal on her, she carefully transferred the contents to yet another cup. As she worked to cool her tea, the queen continued to offer her advice. "There will always be men who think they know what's best for you, but no one will ever know what's best for you as well as you know it yourself. You must trust your instincts. Do you hear me? And your ladies-in-waiting! Oh, but you must be *very* careful there. Have at least two, if not three. Choose ladies who don't always agree with each other. If they don't agree with each other, one of them will be whispering in your ear about the other, and you'll never miss a thing. Heed me, dear. If you don't decide who you want for your ladies *straightaway*, your prime minister will install ladies for whom you have no camaraderie and therefore, cannot trust."

Justine thought at once of Lady Bardaline. This warning was not new to her—her father had said the same, and really, it was not something she needed to be told, particularly when people as august as the queen and her father spoke of it like it was a matter of life and death. It certainly was for her father—there had been an attempt to poison him eight years ago when they'd been in London.

But Justine's problem was a little different. It wasn't as if people were telling her untruths or she was listening to the wrong advice. People didn't tell her anything at all. As if they thought she was easier to manipulate if she was kept in the dark. Well…with the exception of Douglas, who was determined to be honest in a way she didn't care for.

She didn't need a minder, either, and that was precisely what they'd asked Douglas to be. It was humiliating! She knew exactly what he'd been asked to do, not because any-one had *told* her—because they never *told* her—but be-cause she knew Robuchard. There was a man who liked his power. He had her mother's ear, and while Justine didn't know what the two of them had sorted out as far as Doug-las was concerned, she was quite sure it had nothing to do with her happiness. She was not daft. And she intended to nip this wrinkle in the bud.

The tea was concluded when no pastry would meet with the queen's approval. Justine was disappointed—she'd hardly managed to say a word, and there were so many questions she had not had the opportunity to ask. Fortu-nately, the queen extended another invitation.

"The Duchess of Wellington has invited the mistresses of the robe and ladies of the bedchamber together to knit socks for our soldiers in the Crimea. We'll have a lunch—perhaps you and your sister would care to lend your con-siderable talents to the endeavor?"

Neither one of them had considerable talents with knit-ting needles, but of course Justine had accepted the invi-tation, pleased to have something to look forward to in the near future.

She was escorted out of the castle, to where her coach and her Weslorian guards were waiting. She climbed in-side and looked straight ahead as the coachman closed the door behind her. When she was alone, she leaned her head back against the silk squabs and stared blankly at the bro-cade pleats in the ceiling.

She dreaded going back to Prescott Hall, to spending hours in the company of the Bardalines. They would be so eager to hear every word the queen uttered today, and Jus-tine couldn't put them off entirely.

She thought of the invitation Douglas had extended to

see the Duke of Sutherland's picture gallery. She'd had no intention of accepting it and hadn't even mentioned it to Bardaline. But as London rolled by her window, she wondered if perhaps she was missing an opportunity to be free of her English prison because she was vexed. She still thought Douglas a scoundrel of the first water, but he might be a way out from under the watchful eye of the Bardalines. There were far worse options, she supposed, and at least he was pleasing to look at.

Yes, she decided as the coach picked up speed, rocking along the road, she would tell Bardaline to accept Douglas's invitation to Stafford House.

CHAPTER SEVEN

WILLIAM WAS DEAD ASLEEP when Ewan made a terrible decision to draw open the drapes and did so with a godawful racket, which he capped by then tripping over the rug. A very large man made a very large noise.

William was facedown on the bed, buried in a valley of pillows. He was fairly certain he had on the same clothes he'd worn the night before. Either that, or someone had tied a noose around his neck. He opened one eye and glared at his valet. "Damn Beckett Hawke, then, Ewan. Do you hear me? Damn him all the way to hell."

"Aye, milord." Ewan advanced carefully toward the bed as if he intended to cage a wild animal and expected it to attack. William managed to dig his arm out from under him—scraping past buttons and wool on its way to freedom—and felt the bit of silk around his neck. Neck cloth. Not a noose, then.

He'd happened upon Beck at Brook's Gentlemen's Club on St. James Street last night. Beck had been playing cards and had invited William to sit in a game of whist. He'd enticed him by announcing he'd discovered a new drink. It was called a *Ladies' Blush*, and had come to him by way of America, although how it had come to him all the way from America, Beck failed to illuminate. All William remembered was that the drink was sweet and made of gin, and then someone he didn't know, but whom Beck had enthusiastically recommended, brought him home. William vaguely remembered arguing with Ewan about removing his clothes.

He held up a single finger in the direction of Ewan, whom he could no longer see, what with his face returned to his pillow. "Lord Iddesleigh is not to be admitted to this house. He is not allowed to as much as darken the threshold. Shoot him if he lifts his arm to knock."

"Aye, milord."

William dropped his hand. He waited to hear Ewan retreat, but there was only silence. "Why are you still here?" he demanded into his pillow.

"A letter has come, milord. A right proper one, by the look of it."

"A right proper letter." William pushed himself up and swiped away a thick lock of hair that had fallen over his eyes. "What does that mean, Ewan? Are no' all letters right and proper simply by virtue of *being* a letter?"

"That I donna know, milord."

"How can you no' know, MacDuff? You donna know if letters are letters merely by being letters, but yet, you know that it requires my immediate attention at this ungodly hour."

"It is half past one, milord."

"Bloody hell, why did you no' wake me, then?" William groused. He sighed and rolled onto his back. "I'll have tea, if you please. No—make it coffee. The Turkish sort. Aye, I'll have coffee—and a side of beef if you can manage it."

"Aye, milord."

And yet, Ewan did not move, still held out the blasted letter on his little silver tray. "Holy hell," William muttered and pushed himself up to sitting, his back against the headboard. He dragged his fingers through his hair. "I mean what I say, then, Ewan. Iddesleigh is no' welcome here. When he talks, I can no' seem to say no." He could only marginally be blamed for his current state—Beck could be very persuasive when he was of a mind.

William rubbed his face with his hands, then looked at Ewan. The man was determined to hand that letter to him. He stretched out his arm and wiggled his fingers. "All right. Give it to me."

Ewan gingerly placed the letter onto William's palm. William squinted at it. He didn't recognize the handwriting, so he turned it over to look at the wax seal. The letter had come from Prescott Hall. He groaned. "Of all the days to have this to bother with," he complained, then broke the seal and unfolded the letter.

My Lord Douglas,
Greetings and salutations from HRH Princess Justine. She bids me accept your gracious invitation to view the picture gallery at Stafford House. She and HRH Princess Amelia look forward to your escort Thursday at three o'clock. If you cannot provide the necessary conveyance for the princesses, one will be provided for you.
Sincerely,
Gregor Bardaline, Earl of Talin, Master of the Chamber, duly appointed to serve *HRH Princess Justine*

William crumpled the letter in his fist and glared in the direction of the window. Tomorrow was Thursday.

He didn't want to go. He regretted ever making the offer. He was in a foul mood, and the thought of interacting with the duke and his cloying minions made his stomach roil worse than drink. He knew the sort of people that would attend—the sort to throng the princesses and press for introductions. Which meant he'd have to remain upright and alert as her escort. He would much prefer to remain here, with his feet propped on a stool and nothing more than a newspaper to burden him. But that stubborn princess had changed her wee mind and wanted to see the picture gallery.

William's head throbbed.

He flung the letter toward Ewan and watched it fall to the ground between them. "God save me, MacDuff. I've a picture gallery reception to attend tomorrow. Bring the coffee, will you?"

"Aye, milord," Ewan said. He retrieved the letter and went out. William sank back into his bed with a groan.

He'd managed to forget Her Royally Smug Highness in the days since his visit to Prescott Hall. Or rather, he'd forgotten her as much as a man could forget meeting a princess on the verge of becoming queen. But when he didn't hear a word from her, no yay or nay to his invitation, he'd convinced himself he'd acquitted his duty. But here she was, creeping back into his thoughts with her last-minute acceptance of his invitation.

It was annoying…but maybe after a cup of coffee or two, it wouldn't seem entirely awful.

SUTHERLAND HAPPENED TO BE a neighbor to William, a short walk down the street or through Green Park as the spirit moved you. So William called on his fellow Scotsman to inform him he'd be escorting the princesses to the picture gallery viewing. "If you donna mind," he said.

"Mind?" Sutherland was beside himself with joy. "Argyll will certainly take note, will he no'?" he'd said gleefully, referring to another Scottish duke with whom he had a rivalry.

William supposed everyone would take note. They

would wonder how a bachelor like William Douglas—
"notoriously unmarried," as his sister described him—
had come to be in the company of the two princesses, one
of whom would soon be a queen. And then there would be
those gentlemen who would congratulate him with crude
gestures to indicate what they thought he was after.

He could do without all of that.

He'd sent a message to Prescott Hall that he would
"happily" fetch the princesses as instructed—Ewan had
added that, without William's approval—and that he had a
carriage, thank you. It was not as big and grand as a royal
one, but it had managed to cart his father, a duke, around
town, so he thought it would do well enough. Ewan had
rewritten the note without the last part.

William dressed as one might on the way to meet their
maker, in a stiff collar, ironed trousers and a superfine coat.
He had his horses groomed, the carriage readied and the
coachmen assembled. When Ewan had assured him that
all was ready, William set out for Prescott Hall with all the
pomp and circumstance two princesses apparently required.

At the hall a butler showed him into a small receiving
room. There was only one painting in this close room, a
portrait of a man who looked to be about sixty years. He
had florid cheeks and a very round belly that in William's
experience appeared after years of too much drink. He put
a hand to his waist and was surreptitiously feeling his girth
when he heard someone at the door. He turned around.

Princess Amelia smiled as she sailed into the room and
right over to him, her eyes moving over his body. "Good
afternoon, my lord."

"Your Royal Highness." He bowed.

Her smile turned sultry and she came so close to him that
her skirts brushed against his leg. Her gaze moved down

his chest, lingering on the button of his waistcoat. "Do you recall me *now*, Lord Douglas?"

What a little coquette she was. What he recalled about her was that she'd been a mouse, a mere shadow in his memory. "Aye, that I do. You are Her Royal Highness Princess Amelia of Wesloria. Is your sister coming?"

"Of course Jussie is coming," she said, and flounced away from him—but only a foot or two before pivoting about. "She asked that I keep you company while you wait."

One of William's brows rose. "Did she?"

"Je."

"I donna believe you."

Princess Amelia gasped. *"You* should have a care, my lord."

"As should you, Amelia. We don't yet know his lordship's intent."

Neither of them had seen Justine enter the room, and the pair of them started like guilty lovers. William instantly bowed low. "Good afternoon, Your Royal Highness."

"My lord," she said breezily. She was wearing a gown of russet velvet and pink silk, a bit of the Weslorian green pinned to her sleeve, and her breasts, he could not help noticing, were two perfect, creamy mounds that looked like they might spill out of that bodice at any moment. It was his observation, born of many years of study, that the most difficult women were always the most alluring.

"He accused me of flirting with him," Princess Amelia said.

"That's absurd!" Justine said brightly. "He's old enough to be your father."

"What?" William sputtered. "I'm no' as old as that."

"Older?" She smiled, because she was a dastardly thing.

"Well, Douglas, here we are," she said and spread her arms wide. "All of us dressed for a picture gallery viewing."

"And if I may say, the effect is quite pleasing."

Her gaze flicked over him uncertainly. She held out one arm, palm up, and said, "Torrin?"

A footman appeared instantly with a silk wrap. Justine presented her back to the man so that he could drape it over her shoulders, all while keeping her gaze locked on William's. "We'll need our bonnets, too."

Bardaline must have been waiting for the request in the wings, because he suddenly appeared with two elaborately decorated bonnets, one gold, the other green and white. He gave William a thin, weaselly smile, and William decided then and there that he didn't care for Bardaline, *master of the chamber*, on principle. He noticed the way Justine leaned slightly away from the man when he bent to whisper something in her ear.

"Thank you," she said. She took her hat and put it on her head, expertly tying the ribbon beneath her chin in a matter of seconds. Amelia took her bonnet, too, but skipped over to a large mirror on the opposite wall from the windows to admire herself in it.

"We thank you for your kind invitation," Justine said, all graciousness.

"Do you? You didn't seem to think it kind the last we spoke."

"Didn't I? Well, my sister and I are looking forward to seeing the art."

"The Duke of Sutherland is quite eager for you to see his art. I've a coach."

"Excellent. Then shall we?"

"Please." He gestured toward the door. She turned to go, and Amelia, who was still admiring herself, let out a small squeal. "I'm not ready!" But she rushed after her sister nonetheless. And Bardaline, well…he trotted alongside Justine like a pony, speaking so low that William, who apparently was left to bring up the rear, couldn't hear a word he said.

Out on the drive Amelia squinted at the double brougham, emblazoned with the Hamilton crest on the door. "Is this it? It's not very big, is it? The coaches are much bigger in Wesloria."

"You're thinking of the royal coaches," Justine said. "This is not a *royal* coach."

William looked at his coach. They tended to be a standard size, made so that horses could pull them around. Any bigger than this, he'd need a team of six to cart these two in fancy bonnets to St. James.

Two Weslorian guards trotted out on horses and took a position behind the coach.

One of William's coachmen leaped to the ground from the back runner. He opened the door and pulled down a step for the ladies. Amelia immediately stepped forward and allowed the young man to hand her up. Justine was next, stepping elegantly into the interior. When she was seated, she leaned forward and looked out the door at William. "Are you riding with us?"

Well, yes. He'd invited them, had provided the coach. "Would you prefer I ride up top?" He meant it quite sarcastically.

But a devilish smile appeared on Princess Justine's lips. "Whatever suits you, my lord. I rather thought you'd want to take the opportunity to offer your advice on any number of subjects."

Her eyes were sparkling like gold at the end of the proverbial rainbow. "I thought you did no' care for or need my advice."

"I don't!" she cheerfully confirmed. "I assumed you'd be eager to provide it all the same."

He bowed again, then put his hat on his head. "I find I am better at offering advice in the moment."

She laughed. "Well, *that* should be diverting."

"Are we going?" Princess Amelia called from inside the coach.

Princess Justine continued to smile at him with far too much satisfaction. Now, there was a piece of advice he could offer—stop smiling at him like that. It made him feel…unsteady.

Justine leaned back, disappearing into the interior of the coach.

This afternoon had all the signs of being interminable. He strode to the front of the coach. But he did not climb up.

He wished his father would stop spending all the family money and forcing him into situations like this. And he wished that he could stop seeing Justine's pert smile, and the absolute pleasure of having chased him off shining in her eyes. He abruptly pivoted around and strode to the door of the coach, yanked it open and climbed into the interior.

There was an immediate problem that left him bent over in a crouch just inside the door. The two of them were sitting across from each other and there was no place for him.

"What are you doing?" Princess Amelia complained, clearly unwilling to move. "There's not enough room."

"Amelia. Come over here," Justine said and patted the bench beside her, shifting over to make room. Her younger sister huffed but did as she was bid. The two of them sat there with their skirts filling all the available space.

William settled on the bench facing the rear of the coach.

Princess Amelia clucked her tongue and glared at his long legs. "You're mashing my skirt."

He desperately wanted to point out that her bloody skirt filled the interior and there was no way to avoid it. But he said, "I beg your pardon," and angled his long legs away from her as best he could. The result was to mash Justine's skirts. She sighed loudly.

As the coach began to move, he tried not to mash anything, but it was impossible in that cramped space. Justine continued to watch him, clearly amused. She obviously sensed his discomfit and he didn't like it. When the coach turned a corner and he nearly fell off the bench in his effort to keep from touching their skirts, a smile of delight appeared on her face.

"You're rather chipper, Your Royal Highness," he groused.

"What does that mean, *chipper*?"

"Cheerful."

"Ah! Yes, I suppose I am. I am away from Prescott Hall, after all."

"They keep her there," Amelia said gravely.

"Who?" he asked, confused.

"The *watchers*," Justine added ominously, and she and her sister laughed. "They keep me there under their watchful eyes with little to occupy me. Not even a dog."

"*I* keep you company, Jussie," Princess Amelia said.

"Yes, but you're gone quite a lot, darling. I really should have insisted they allow me to bring Bear."

"I *told* you," Princess Amelia said. "But you were right. The journey would have been hard for him."

"Bear?" William asked.

"One of my dogs," Justine said. She sighed. "It really doesn't matter now." She cocked her head to one side and looked William up and down. "Do you enjoy art?"

"Me? Aye, very much."

"How much?" Princess Amelia asked him, eyeing him dubiously.

"I donna know how to answer that precisely. But I've procured paintings for my family's estate."

The sisters glanced at each other. Princess Amelia rolled her eyes.

These two were impossible to please. "I once spent a full day at the Grande Galerie in the Louvre, trying to take it all in." It had been a cold, wet day, and he'd been awed by the talent he'd seen in the paintings. How did one manage to capture the way the sun lit a woman's face?

"Oh," Justine said dreamily. "I've long wanted to visit Paris and the museums there. Was it magnificent?"

"Quite. Perhaps when you are queen," he said. "A state visit. Curators will be delighted to show you about. It would be well worth your while if you are an admirer of the masters."

"I can't imagine anything more boring," Princess Amelia said wearily.

"Do you paint, my lord?" Justine asked.

"Badly. I'm rather hopeless."

"Well, there's something you share with Justine," Princess Amelia offered. "She paints very badly."

"I beg your pardon?" Justine asked with a laugh of surprise.

"It's awful, Jussie! You can't see a blessed thing!"

Justine laughed, but a bit of color rose in her cheeks. She gave a slight shrug of her perfect shoulders. "It's true. My eyesight is very poor up close." She patted her reticule. "I've a pair of eyeglasses in the event of an emergency, but I am under strict instructions not to wear them and ruin any and all prospects for a match." She and her sister giggled.

William didn't know about the eyeglasses or what she meant about not being allowed to wear them. What he knew was that she was very pretty when she laughed. She looked…adorable.

"If painting is not your talent, my lord, then what is?" Justine asked.

His *talent*? He liked to think his talents were best displayed in bedrooms and in gaming hells, but even in that, he wasn't entirely certain. "None that are obvious." Perhaps his best talent at this stage of his life was keeping his father from ruin.

But the princess clucked her tongue. "You must be good at *something*."

"I am good at many things," he said with a pointed look. "What do *you* enjoy?"

"Fencing! When I was a girl, I wanted very much to be a warrior queen like my ancestor, Queen Elena."

He didn't think she could be a warrior queen with an épée. Pardon—*foil*.

"All right, then, I've answered, now you must."

"All right. I have a talent for training sheepdogs."

Justine and her sister blinked at him. Princess Amelia laughed. "That's ridiculous."

"It is no'," he said defensively. "I think there is nothing more bucolic than sheep dotting a field, and nothing more artistic than a dog herding them. The sheepdogs, they are born to it, aye, but they need a bit of finessing. When I was a wee lad, I spent as much time as I could with the shepherds and learned how to train them properly." Frankly, William's fondest memories were of a simpler time. He'd never been as happy as he had been at twelve years old with four sheepdogs to train. He'd continued to train them up until he left for the continent the first time.

"I wish I had as much enthusiasm for a task as a sheep-dog," Justine said wistfully.

"They are amazing in their tenacity," he agreed. "You enjoy dogs, then?"

"*Adore* them. Rohalan Palace is full of them. If you love dogs and sheep, why do you always seem to be in salons? Should you not be wandering around Scotland, herding your sheep?"

"Ah, would that I was, but it's no' so easy as that, is it? There comes a few burdens with it."

"With being a shepherd?" Princess Amelia scoffed.

"With being the sort of shepherd I would have to be. There comes with it estate duties and family with differing opinions and whatno', aye?"

"*Je,*" Princess Justine said instantly. She looked at him for a long moment, as if working something out. "I understand a bit about that."

"Aye, I've no doubt that you do. Far better than me."

"It seems there are always so many complications and people who must be considered."

They weren't talking about sheepdogs anymore, he gathered. "Aye, it can be very taxing on one's good humor. One wants only to do what is just, but justice can have so many dimensions."

"*Je!*" She seemed surprised. "That is precisely it." She looked as if she meant to say something more, but Princess Amelia suddenly cried out with delight.

"Look at all the people! What is this place?"

Justine jerked toward the window. William looked out, too. "Aye, that would be Stafford House." There were many people milling about on the expansive lawn.

Justine suddenly surged toward the window, pushing her

sister out of the way. When she'd seen it, she fell back and glared at William. "You said a small reception."

"It was supposed to be that, aye."

"What *happened*?"

She sounded a bit frantic. It was a remarkable turn from the easy conversation they'd just been having moments ago. "I rather think *you* happened, Your Royal Highness. Many of these people have never seen their own queen, much less a foreign one in search of a king—"

"Not a *king*, a prince consort!"

One of his brows rose. "I beg your pardon." He would have laughed, but she seemed almost beside herself and he didn't know what to make of it. "Are you surprised to be the object of interest? Sutherland will call them distinguished guests. I will call them gawpers, all of them eager for the sight of two young, unmarried, handsome princesses."

"Gawper? What does that mean?" Princess Amelia asked.

"He means onlookers," Justine said. She swallowed, then drew a shallow breath. "God knows how many more inside."

"I hope there are squads of them," Princess Amelia said eagerly as the coach swung through the gates.

"Oh *no*," Justine muttered.

Her behavior was mildly alarming. "Is something wrong?" William asked.

"Didn't anyone tell you?" Amelia asked lightly as the coach came to the gate. "She goes *mad* in crowds."

William looked at Justine. All the color had drained from her face.

"I don't go *mad*," Justine said, swallowing again and looking as if she was attempting to find her breath. "I don't care for crowds, that's all. They're stifling. Could we open a window? I need air."

William stared at her in disbelief. He did not see how it was possible for a woman who seemed so bloody sure of herself at Prescott Hall to suddenly seem as if she was about to faint.

And then she did.

CHAPTER EIGHT

JUSTINE DIDN'T FAINT—she was desperately trying to breathe deeply as Monsieur DuPree had advised her, and found it was easier to do when her head was lolling against the squabs and her eyes were closed.

"Your Royal Highness!" William said sharply. "Justine!"

She felt his hand on her cheek and opened her eyes to see him looming over her, peering closely, his gray eyes filled with concern she didn't want from him. "Stop that!" She batted his hand away.

He sank back, looking startled. "I thought—"

"I told you she went mad," Amelia said from her spot in front of the window.

Justine drew a steadying breath. "Stop saying that, Amelia. I'm *fine*."

She wasn't mad—she was a ball of anxiety. She abhorred moments like the one she was apparently about to face, when crowds of people would draw close to see her, to study her, sometimes even touch her. A shiver coursed down her spine.

The first time she'd come undone had been when she was eight or nine years old. She'd accompanied her father out of the palace and into the streets of St. Edys. The onlookers wanting a glimpse of her had gotten so thick that they'd begun to push. The wave of humanity got close enough to touch her, to stroke her hair and her face. She couldn't remember much but the terror she'd felt, the screams that had erupted from her throat, the guards whisking her away to safety.

For weeks afterward she was plagued by nightmares of being snatched. It didn't help in the least to know that her father had had another child before her, a son, who'd been stolen from his cradle in an attempted palace coup before his first year, never to be seen again.

Now that she was an adult, she didn't fear being snatched...but she couldn't shake her nerves in large crowds on those occasions she was outside palace walls. She felt entirely conspicuous, a zoo animal. It felt as if they could all but see through her clothing and her skin to her spine. They whispered. They smiled and laughed, or glared, or called out to her, begging for alms. Some still tried to touch her.

That fervid attention stoked her insecurities. What did they see in her? Did they see someone as confident as Queen Elena? Or did they see a sniveling young woman with no fortitude for the throne?

"I rather think they are looking at Amelia," her mother had once said when Justine had complained of the attention. "Fair-haired ladies are always preferred." She'd said it quite matter-of-factly, and Justine hadn't taken offense— she thought it was true enough. And fair-haired Amelia liked that sort of attention. It invigorated her.

The breathing helped to fill Justine's lungs again and she settled somewhat from her surprise at seeing so many people gathered. She slowly realized that Douglas was still watching her with concern. Blast it, now her mortification was taking root. "Please...don't mind me." She refused to meet his gaze, annoyed he was there to see her like this. She hadn't really wanted him in the coach, hadn't wanted to look at his smug face. But curiously, she'd wanted him to *want* to be in the coach.

Well, she was confused about what exactly she'd wanted, but she certainly hadn't wanted *this*.

"The footmen are coming," Amelia announced excitedly.

Justine sat up and smoothed the side of her hair. In spite of the tremor she still felt inside her, her hands seemed steady enough. She didn't look at Douglas, knowing that the striking, self-assured man before her in his black frock coat, his patterned waistcoat, his gray top hat, had witnessed her panic. For heaven's sake, she was going to be *queen*! She could do or be whatever she wanted! Except leave Prescott Hall when she liked, or dance too often, or smile too broadly in public, or cry too deeply in private lest she get circles under her eyes, or go out in public without escort for fear that she might fall in love with another bounder.

Oh yes, she could do whatever she liked, couldn't she? Queen Elena she was not.

The door suddenly swung open. Both sisters sat back. Douglas glanced uncertainly at Justine, then exited the coach. A moment later a gloved hand, attached to a black sleeve of superfine wool, extended across the opening, palm up.

Amelia didn't hesitate—she grabbed that free-floating hand and launched through the door, disappearing from Justine's sight.

Justine drew another breath. "It's like every public appearance you've made in the last ten years. Don't be such a ninny," she muttered under her breath. She gathered her skirts and moved toward the opening. At the threshold she caught sight of Amelia standing a few feet away and waving. *Waving.* As if they were all friends.

The hand appeared again, and Justine slipped hers into

it. The thumb of that hand wrapped across her knuckles, holding firmly as she stepped down. When she had both feet on the ground, she tried to pull her hand free, but William squeezed her fingers and forced her to look up at him from beneath the rim of her bonnet. "Better?"

"Fine." She pulled her hand free and pretended that the little tingle that went up her spine when he'd squeezed her hand hadn't happened. And then all thoughts of little tingles quickly disappeared when she looked up at the house and saw the windows had been opened and scores of people were crowding into them to see her.

She hadn't expected the house to be *this* grand, but there it was, three stories, as long and square as the two palaces it was situated between—Buckingham to the south, St. James to the north. The entrance was supported by Greek columns so large they dwarfed the people who were spilling out onto the portico. And built on the edge of Green Park as it was, it looked almost to be in the country. "Does *everyone* live in a palace here?" Justine murmured.

"Oh, *je*, they live like kings and queens in *le bon ton* here," Amelia responded. "Every house seems bigger than the last."

"That is Sutherland, aye?" William said. "The tall one."

A man had appeared on the portico who was a head taller than anyone around him. He paused at the top of a long flight of stairs to the drive and seemed to be arranging a retinue of gentlemen and ladies behind him. *"Aug,"* Justine said, because her mind couldn't seem to think of any real words to say. Behind her she heard the coach roll away, and with it, her hope for an escape.

"Shall we proceed?" William asked. "Or would you prefer to stand on the drive and be met like the royalty you are?"

"Actually, I should like to return to Prescott Hall."

"Don't be silly! This will be so diverting," Amelia said with a confidence Justine did not feel and would never feel, even if she lived to be one hundred years old.

"I suggest we carry on. It will only grow worse the longer you contemplate it." William offered his arm to Justine. "The trick, as they say, is to sally forth."

"You're an expert in reticence, are you?" Justine snapped. Not that she meant to—it just happened when she felt so at sea.

He took that in stride. "No. But I am absolutely brimming with common sense. Take my arm before Sutherland throws himself down the steps to take your hand."

She grasped his arm stiffly, and too tightly. She cleared her throat and lifted her chin. "You realize, don't you, that people might infer something that is most assuredly not true now that I've taken your arm."

"Horror of *horrors*. But it would be a wee bit awkward for you to strike off on your own as if you are marching into battle."

"For heaven's sake, take a breath," Amelia chided her. "Offer me your arm as well, Douglas, and we'll all go together, a happy trio, and no one will think anything of it, *rendben*?" She slipped her hand into the crook of William's other elbow, taking his arm as she would take the arm of their father, or a close male acquaintance, leaning into him for support.

Justine wished she could be so relaxed.

"Ladies," William said and began to escort them toward the stairs. Sutherland, having arranged his welcome party, had begun to descend the stairs, but paused halfway down to rearrange them all again.

"It is no' necessary to appear so disgusted with my arm,"

William murmured as they waited for Sutherland to direct his guests.

"Neither is it necessary to appear smug with princesses on either arm," she murmured back.

"You think this is a look of smugness? No, madam, the look you see on my face is the discomforting pain of being put upon to attend a picture gallery viewing under these circumstances. And if I may, *my* pained expression is only surpassed by *your* pained expression. You might at least appear as if you were no' dragged here by force."

"Lord help me, you're not to tell me what to do, have you forgotten?" But she made herself smile as he suggested.

"Oh, I've no' forgotten a word you've said, on my word, and I swear on the graves of all my ancestors, I never will. Good afternoon, Sutherland," he said loudly.

Sutherland whirled around on his step. "Welcome, welcome!" he called. He began to descend the rest of the steps so eagerly that he looked as if he might suddenly curl into a ball and bounce all the way to their feet.

"Why does he look so gleeful?" Justine whispered. "Did you tell him I'm a devotee of art? Or that I'm without a match and ripe for the plucking?"

William snorted. "There is no' a titled man in London who doesn't know you're without a match and ripe for the plucking. Why do you think they've all come? I know Sutherland, and he will seek to astonish you with all that he has and who he knows."

Justine's breath was growing shallow again.

"Stop complaining," Amelia whispered. "I'm quite excited to meet all these interesting people."

All these...people had Justine's heart climbing into her throat. She was so fixated on those crowding the windows above that she almost missed Sutherland bouncing onto the last step of the staircase before her.

"My Lord Douglas!" Sutherland said loudly as his flock closed in behind him. The boom of his voice startled Justine and quite possibly knocked a few leaves from the trees. He bowed theatrically over one extended leg. When he lifted, he beamed at Justine. "Your Royal Highness, you do us the *greatest* honor with your *presence*."

"You are too kind," Justine said. She was very pleased that her voice didn't shake in the slightest. "Thank you for your gracious invitation. May I introduce my sister, Princess Amelia?"

Amelia put herself in front of William, ready to consume the attention. "Your Grace," she said charmingly, and extended her hand, bowing her head, almost as if she thought Sutherland could be a potential suitor. Justine did not expect that she and William would exchange a look at Amelia's coquettishness, but they did, surprising them both.

Sutherland surged forward so quickly and with so much energy that Amelia reflexively took a tiny step back. Her mother would have pinched her had she been here, and Justine made a note to remind Amelia of that later so they might laugh about it. *An Ivanosen stands as a mountain in the face of a challenge.* They used to play a game where one of them would stand as a mountain while the other did her best to knock her over.

Sutherland looked as if he indeed might knock Amelia over—he eagerly took her hand and bent over it, welcomed her to his house, then promptly dropped her hand and stepped to one side, to better see Justine.

"Oh." Justine, too, fought the urge to take a tiny step back.

"Your Royal Highness, how *pleased* we are you have

come to see the *picture* gallery," Sutherland crowed. He had a curious habit of swaying forward with certain words, as if to emphasize them, coming terribly close to her person when he did. Twice, he forced Justine to lean backward for fear that his thin lips might land on hers. "You will find we have one of the *finest* art collections in all of *London*. May I introduce my daughter," he said, gesturing to air. When no one appeared, he smiled and called, *"Constance!"*

A young woman was trying to step through the crowd at his back and managed to make it just when Sutherland turned sharply in search of her and caught her shoulder with his elbow.

"Ow," she said, touching a hand to her shoulder, and with a grimace, sank into a curtsy.

"My *daughter*, Lady Constance," Sutherland said with a proud sway, gesturing to Lady Constance as if she was one of his works of art.

"Please," Justine said, indicating the woman should rise.

Lady Constance smiled graciously. "We are so very honored." She was dark haired and quite small, and looked a few years younger than Justine and Amelia.

"My daughter should very *much* like to show Princess Amelia *inside*, if you please," Sutherland said, swaying at Justine again. She couldn't help it—she leaned to one side and bumped against William. "Many of her friends have gathered and we thought Her *Highness* might enjoy making their *acquaintance*." He smiled expectantly, waiting for Justine to agree.

Amelia hopped forward. "I'd be delighted."

"Wonderful!" Sutherland said, his gaze still on Justine. "Constance?" He gestured in the air for his daughter, and just like that, Amelia and Lady Constance were walking up the steps. Justine watched them be swallowed up by

Sutherland's crowd. It made her feel strangely hot not to be able to see Amelia. Knowing her sister was close by helped her keep her nerve, and without her, that same nerve seemed to flare.

Sutherland suddenly surged back into Justine's line of sight, his eyes shining with eagerness. It had been her experience that anyone *so* eager should probably be avoided, because eagerness often made a person rather suffocating. "If you will allow, Your Royal Highness, I'll escort you inside. You'll find a bit of a throng, I'm afraid—there is much *curiosity* about the crown princess of Wesloria."

"What?" Justine's heart began to pound. "Not a *throng*." It was more a plea than anything else, but Sutherland laughed as if he thought she was jesting.

She was not jesting.

"You are an esteemed guest, to be sure," he said jovially. "I had the whole of London requesting an *invitation*." He laughed again, as if they should all be gaily amused by how many people wanted an invitation to gawk at her.

Justine wished the gentleman would have ignored those requests if for no other reason than the comfort of his esteemed guest. But as these things so often went for her, the more, the merrier for everyone but her. "I…"

"Yes?" he asked, swaying at her, eager to hear what she might have to say.

"I wonder if you might have some wine or champagne." She practically blurted the words.

"Indeed!"

She was alarmed when he moved as if he meant to displace William and offer his arm, but thankfully, William parried. "If you donna mind, old friend, I'll see the princess in, aye?"

This time when William held out his arm to her, she

took it without hesitation. If she couldn't have Amelia, he was the next best thing.

Sutherland was not deterred. He simply moved to her other side and walked beside her as they began to climb the steps, nattering about the house and grounds, his arms making sweeping gestures as he pointed at this or that. One of those sweeping arms came so dangerously close to the brim of her bonnet that she instinctively ducked her head and in doing so, knocked into William's shoulder.

When they reached the top of the steps, Sutherland jogged ahead to the door to clear some of the people from it. "Make room, make room!" he shouted at them.

William leaned in and murmured, "Should I interpret that bump as a wee bit of flirtation, or a signal of distress? I should like to know the difference in case it happens again."

"*Flirtation?* Why did God give all gentlemen the confidence of fools and goats?" she whispered back. "That man may very well blacken my eye before the afternoon is done."

William chuckled, and she found the sound of it oddly comforting. She didn't want to feel any affinity for him, entirely on principle. But when she glanced at him and his strong profile, she couldn't help but feel a little affinity. And the tiniest bit safe. Perhaps more than a tiny bit. How the devil had it come to this? "Thank you," she made herself say.

"Pardon?"

"I said *thank* you."

"I did no' quite—"

She managed to pinch his arm through the fabric of his frock coat. He put his hand on hers and squeezed it. "You are welcome," he said and removed his hand from hers. "I should have warned you."

"This way!" Sutherland said eagerly, gesturing them forward.

William guided her toward the door.

"Why didn't you warn me?" she murmured.

"Oh, I donna know, really. I do enjoy watching the countless expressions that sail across your face."

"Here, madam, *this* way," Sutherland said eagerly and turned down a wide corridor.

Justine and Douglas followed him. "Impossible," Justine whispered. "I don't allow my feelings to be seen. I've been trained to be a sovereign, William. One must keep one's emotions from showing at all times."

"Ah, how delightful my given name sounds when said with such a lovely Weslorian accent. I rather like it. I would imagine you feel the same delight when you hear *Justine* said by a Scot."

"*Mein Gott.*" She meant to tell him she did not, but in truth there was something about the lilt of his Scottish brogue that sent a tiny trickle of delight down her spine.

"Has anyone ever told you that you have a surprisingly strong grip, *Justine*?"

Justine looked down at her hand clutching his arm and saw that she'd dug her gloved fingers into his sleeve.

"Here we are!" Sutherland said loudly from the door of the gallery. He swayed forward to announce, "Your Royal *Highness*, Princess *Justine*, may I introduce my *wife*, Lady Sutherland."

And Justine was forced to let go of William's arm to be swept into a crowded foyer, where many, *many* introductions were made. Without his arm to cling to, she began to worry a thin gold bracelet on her wrist, twisting it around. She was surrounded by so many curious onlookers, with so many names and so many words said to her. She felt a little dizzy what with all the smiling and agreeing that the weather was pleasant, or that she did very well, thank you, or yes, she'd had the pleasure of visiting London before. Someone took her bonnet, but she never saw who. It felt as if the foyer was shrinking in size, the walls and people closing in on her, all of them vying for her attention. Did she learn English in Wesloria? How did her father and mother fare? Did she recall meeting this or that one in London eight years ago? The people and questions became a sea, growing and pressing in on her.

Someone put champagne in her hand. She could hardly feel the glass, as she seemed to have lost the feeling in her fingers. And yet, she still managed to sip more than was advisable on an empty stomach. When a woman wearing a red-and-white-striped dress that reminded Justine of the candy sticks she coveted as a girl said loudly that they were all *waiting* and that this entrance was *taking far too long*, Sutherland invited Justine to join him as they moved around the gallery. His guests ambled alongside her as if they were one giant organism, blocking any meaningful view of the art. Justine made quick work of the champagne in her glass and looked around for another.

A gloved hand appeared in her line of sight, palm up. She placed the glass in it and said, "More, please."

"You do no' exaggerate your discomfort." It was William, of course, and he frowned down at her. "If you donna mind me saying, you're looking a wee bit wild-eyed. Perhaps more champagne is no' the best idea?"

"Why are you speaking to me as if you are my mother? *Please* get me more." She couldn't wait for him to agree, as the river was suddenly moving along again. But she kept checking over her shoulder to see if William was still close by.

He was.

And if she doubted it, she felt his hand on the small of her back a time or two. Hardly a touch at all, but to keep her from bumping into someone, or to let her know he was there. And then, thankfully, the glass of champagne she had requested appeared. She smiled at him with sincere gratitude.

He clucked his tongue, and with his chin, indicated the doors from the gallery to the park had been flung open. "I deliver this only because I fear you might explode into bits. But I am no' a servant."

"I asked nicely."

"There was a wee hint of expectation."

"And *that*, Your Royal Highness, is the picture *gallery*!" Sutherland announced grandly as they completed their circle of the room large enough to host a grand ball. "What do you think?"

She thought that she had hardly seen a single work of art. "Mmm," she said, nodding, and took a good, fortifying sip of the champagne, resisted the urge to wipe the back of her hand across her mouth and looked up at the painted ceiling that soared high overhead, and the view through the French doors to the lawn and Green Park beyond. "It's magnificent, Your Grace."

"It is, it *is*," he enthusiastically agreed. "Your Royal Highness, if you please, will you stand just here? This spot affords the best *view* of the gallery." He gestured to a star inlaid into the floor in the center of the room. But people were standing on it, so he began to urge them all to move away, to allow the princess room to view the work.

William stayed beside her while Sutherland herded his guests. He clasped his hands at his back, turned his attention to a painting and said softly, "Sutherland fancies himself a broker."

She was almost out of champagne. Her hands were shaking slightly as she lifted the glass to her lips, and she saw that William had noticed. "Of art?"

"Probably that, too." He slid a look at her.

Justine hastily swallowed the bit of champagne she'd just sipped. "Do you mean...?"

"I mean he would be most delighted to be involved in any future marriage agreement you might make."

That was so stunning and so none-of-Sutherland's-business that Justine was pressed to down the rest of her champagne.

"Your Royal Highness? Just here," Sutherland called again, gesturing to the best spot in the room, cleared of any onlookers.

"If you get the opportunity, have a look at the Rubens on the south wall. I believe it is a painting of one of your distant ancestors. And do have a care, Justine," William murmured, glancing back at their host. "As your friend, I must warn you no' to trust a gentleman on the mere basis of a compliment prettily given."

Justine gaped at him, but William had strolled a few feet away from her, his gaze on a Biblical scene.

Sutherland, apparently having grown impatient for her to join him, was suddenly at her side, swaying into her person again. "The view of the gallery is *perfect* from the star," he said, pointing.

Justine didn't think the view could possibly be any better than where she was standing, but she went along with her host, and stood in a circle of people who were staring at her more than they took in the art. She tried to listen to Sutherland; she really did. She wanted nothing more than to be a model guest. But the champagne had given fizz to her nerves, and her thoughts were racing wildly around her conversation with William Douglas. How *dare* he imply that he knew anything about her at all, much less what she *thought* of any gentleman? He couldn't possibly know how many gentlemen she met in any given week, of all stripes, or how she received them.

But what really vexed her was that he was probably right, that she did like compliments "prettily given." It infuriated her so completely, that had she not drunk all her champagne, she might have been tempted to fling it at him and demand satisfaction.

That was another thing she remembered about him from before—he was so sure of himself, so full of conceit, and yet, at the tender age of seventeen, she'd believed he seemed to know her in ways she had not known herself. Perhaps more maddening, now that she was the wizened age of twenty five, it would appear that he still did.

She helped herself to another glass of champagne from a footman and continued to stew and sip as Sutherland pointed out this painting and that. She tried to see the Rubens, but the crowd was too thick. She agreed that everything was masterful and captured the essence of the subject, but she couldn't really think or appreciate the beauty of it. She felt hot in her gown, and all the champagne was mixing sourly with her nerves. She thought it was a tragedy she wasn't afforded the opportunity to simply walk through his gallery and absorb it all on her own. To see the Rubens! She did truly love art when she was allowed to look at it without having to seem a connoisseur, or be careful not to commend one over another, or even use her eyeglasses to take a closer look.

Where was Amelia? She'd lost sight of her sister, which

was never good. But then she heard Amelia's tinkling laugh somewhere in the throng. At least she hadn't absconded with an Englishman. Yet.

At various intervals Sutherland expected a response to his speech and, she suspected, some recognition that she saw him for the art scholar he clearly wanted to be. Worse yet, the people gathered around them leaned in to hear every word she spoke, then fluttered like small birds behind their fans, whispering to each other. Did they agree? Disagree? Did they find her childish or urbane? Uneducated or sophisticated in her tastes?

Sutherland continued to talk, his gangly arms swinging in all directions as he spoke, his body swaying dangerously close and then away, until he paused to introduce her to "dear, close" friends. She was close to finishing an uncharacteristic third glass of champagne—oh, she knew better; she certainly did. Wasn't this exactly what had happened the night of the infamous Christmas party in Mayfair?—when he introduced her to the Earl of Rotham.

Earl Rotham. Justine could feel a smile stretching across her lips. Perhaps the champagne had dulled her nerves, but she suddenly felt the fizziness in her bubble up a notch. Dear Lord, what a pleasing sight *he* was. He was young, with a fine figure. He had an easy, sympathetic smile, curly gold locks and very blue eyes. "A pleasure, my lord." She chirped those words like Amelia might have done, and it startled her.

"Ah, *Rotham.* You've returned to London."

With that rumble of a deep voice, Justine was reminded that William Douglas was her keeper, and felt a flash of irritation. Did he mean to thwart any compliment "prettily given"?

"Douglas," the earl said tersely, then quickly focused

on Justine, taking the gloved hand that she hadn't realized she'd offered, and bending over it, his eyes on hers as he touched his lips to her knuckles. "I beg your forgiveness for saying so, Your Royal Highness, but you are the most beautiful princess I have ever had the pleasure to meet." He let go of her hand.

Justine felt herself bloom and her laughter trilled. Behind her she heard William mutter beneath his breath. "How very kind of you to say, my lord," she said and imagined that she sounded gracious and queenly. "But surely you've not met many princesses?"

"On the contrary, I am certain I have met scores of them, and they are all forgotten in the light of your smile."

"For the love of God," William muttered.

Justine stepped away from him before she kicked him, and brought herself closer to Rotham, her smile beaming. He was indeed a beautiful man. Oh, she knew words like his were meant to ingratiate—she'd obviously learned that in the most unfortunate way by falling in love with Alda-bert Gustav—but she was pleased to hear them all the same. Who didn't like to be admired for her looks? Particularly someone who had spent her whole life being compared to Amelia? Her mother had always said Amelia was the beauty, and Justine would have the throne, as if those two things were somehow equivalent. So no, she would never tire of receiving a few compliments here and there, and she very much wanted to turn and explain this to Douglas. But she decided that she'd rather continue to gaze upon the very handsome face of Lord Rotham.

The earl knew he was being admired; she could tell by the way his own smile played at the corners of his lips. "If I may, Your Royal Highness? I don't know if you've yet viewed the ceiling." He shifted closer to her and turned his gaze upward.

Justine looked up, too.

"It's Cupid," he said, gesturing to a cherub with a bow and arrow hovering in the north corner. "And Venus." He pointed to another figure. He spoke softly, as if he was sharing a secret with her. They viewed the elaborate allegorical painting together, Rotham pointing out some of the smaller details, such as the pair of hunting dogs in one corner, hidden behind a shadow, and in another part of the ceiling, a benevolent face in the cloud.

"My lord, pardon?"

A pair of women who had come up on Rotham's right. The older one glanced anxiously at Justine and curtsied. But she quickly turned her attention to Rotham again.

He seemed unbothered by the intrusion. He smiled at Justine and said, "If you will excuse me, ma'am?" He bowed and stepped away, his head bent as he listened to the older woman speak.

Justine returned her gaze to the ceiling. She wanted to down the last of her champagne but felt too many eyes on her.

"How it gladdens my old, battered heart to see Rotham taking your art education in hand."

William. She kept her gaze on the ceiling.

"You should know that he and Sutherland are in the business of steel and are looking for new places to build rail lines," he said quite low. "You take my meaning, aye?"

Justine did not take her gaze from the ceiling. "I speak English, my lord, and understood every single word. And what I surmise from your words is that you are dangerously close to forming an opinion I forbid you from sharing." She lowered her gaze and looked at him. "Was there a *point* to the opinion you're not allowed to offer?"

"Aye, there is. Wesloria would be a bonny land for new rail lines."

She leaned slightly forward, as his eyes seemed to have developed a particular shine. "Are you implying that the only *possible* interest the gentleman would have in speaking to me would be to gain access to build a rail?"

William's shining gray gaze flicked to her mouth. "That is obviously no' the only *possible* interest he would have in speaking to you, Justine. Even a blind man would want to speak to you. You're as bonny as a rose, as elegant as a swan. But it is nonetheless a possible interest that you should no' ignore." He smiled, as if he had just graced her with superior knowledge that he reserved for only his brightest students.

"You are so...*bothersome*," she said, exasperated. "And you are standing so close I can scarcely breathe. Incidentally, I have revised my opinion and I do like the way you say my name."

"I know."

She tried to take a deep breath, but her corset was too tight. Or something. She just couldn't breathe properly. She looked at Rotham, who was still smiling charmingly at the women who had called him away. She noticed that when he looked at the younger of the two women, his smile was very similar to the one he had shown to her. "Who is that he's speaking to?"

William glanced in that direction. "Lady Worth and her daughter, Lady Ellen. I would guess that Lady Worth is frantic with worry that he will somehow win your hand, leaving her daughter without the match she has pursued with great vigor. But he'll have no cause to mourn if you decide against him, as Lady Ellen is a superb match. Her fortune is no' as large as yours, naturally, and her title no' as illustrious. But it is enough for a man like him."

A man like him. Of course Justine knew about *men like him*. She'd been warned about *men like him* all her life. William might be right about Rotham, but it wasn't as if he was some extraordinary judge of character. "The same truth could be said of all the men crowded into this gallery. Including you."

One of his brows arched. "I beg to differ."

"Please. Men marry for advantage and women marry for wealth. Do you think I'm not aware what sort of match I present to someone like him?"

"I think you'd have to be dead no' to know it."

"Exactly. And for all I know, you're as hungry for advantage as Rotham. Should I trust you?"

The other brow shot up to meet the other. *"Yes,"* he said emphatically. "How can you even ask it? We've been round this, have we no'? Your fortune and your throne hold no interest for me."

She shrugged insouciantly. "So you say."

"I *do* say." He appeared to be squaring off to argue. "Have I been anything less than honest with you? Have I no' offered my thoughts even if they are unflattering? And really, have you any other choice than to trust me?"

True, he had been nothing but completely honest. And he did seem unreasonably determined to tell her what he thought, just as he'd said. She didn't *want* to believe him… but for some reason her fizzy thoughts couldn't sort out just now, she did. "I have very little choice in most things. Isn't that a wonderful bit of irony? I am to be queen, and I have the least bit of choice of anyone here." She sipped more of the champagne to hide her displeasure from the many onlookers.

An awkward moment passed, the two of them standing like a married couple in the middle of a row. He said, finally, "You have a choice. I'll no' interfere." He took her by the elbow and steered her from Rotham's view. "I give you my word to be honest at every turn. Spend the entire afternoon in Rotham's company if you like. Bring him home with you. Keep him in your rooms and naked in your bed."

Justine choked on another sip of champagne.

"Pardon—did I shock your tender sensibilities?"

"Hardly. I'm not as naive as you seem determined to believe."

"Ah," he said, holding up a finger. "You're no' even a wee bit naive. That's why I feel quite at ease to bluntly advise you, especially about Rotham. Now, look up."

Justine looked up. They were standing before a portrait of a woman, and Justine knew her instantly. "Anna of Austria," she whispered in awe.

"Know her?"

"Je."

"Remarkable, is it no'?" William said. "Look at the way she smiles."

It was a portrait of her mother's ancestor, who had become the French queen two hundred or so years ago. Justine had seen reproductions, but William was right, the original painting was remarkable. She wore a blue velvet gown, encrusted with pearls. Her lips were cherubic, her smile knowing, her blue eyes shrewd.

"Ah, the Rubens." Justine turned her head and smiled at Rotham. "Your Royal Highness, please do forgive the interruption. If I may turn your attention to the ceiling? There was one last thing I wanted to draw to your attention. You might notice a bit of a surprise in the scene painted on the ceiling in the far corner of the room, if I may show you?"

"You may!" she said brightly. "I'd like just one very quick word with Lord Douglas before we view it."

Rotham bowed and stepped away, putting his back to them. Sutherland took the opportunity to confer with him.

Justine turned to William and pushed her now empty glass into his chest, forcing him to take it. "You needn't worry about me. And now, here is some advice for *you*."

"At last," he said, catching the glass and her fingers with it for a moment. "I await with bated breath."

"Lady Ellen can't take her eyes off you. But you really must be aware that a young woman who seeks you out is most assuredly looking for a fortune."

"Pardon?" He turned his head to look, of course he did, and in that moment Justine stepped away and moved forward to greet Rotham again.

She did not look back to see if William watched her. She knew that he did.

Or at least she hoped that he did.

CHAPTER NINE

AS PRINCESSES WENT—or rather, how William assumed princesses went, as he didn't have any firsthand knowledge—Justine Ivanosen was a confounding one. There was simply no other word that he could think of to properly describe her. In her salon, with the footmen stacked against the walls like toy soldiers, she was assured and regal. In the coach he'd been convinced she had the upper hand with him. But here at Stafford House she seemed on the verge of coming out of her skin. In one hand she gripped the side of her gown, and in the other she gripped a crystal flute with enough champagne to launch a fleet. If someone said something to her that she found amusing, she laughed. But not politely as young women were taught—as a general rule, he was suspicious of women who didn't truly laugh—but as if she'd just heard the funniest anecdote in twenty-five years of living. Then in the next moment she would lean forward, her brow furrowed, with an expression that made him fear she might cry.

The future queen of Wesloria was crowd shy. Remarkable! Of all the women in the world to be afflicted with nerves, it would be the one who would be queen and as such, never really free of crowds.

It was remarkable, too, that he hadn't sensed it when she'd been in London eight years ago. It might have helped to explain her behavior the night of Chairs—the house had been packed to the rafters with guests. But then again, she'd been seventeen years old, and everything she did had seemed a direct result of inexperience.

He idly wondered just how much champagne she'd drunk thus far. He considered himself something of an expert and if the lovely flush in her cheeks and the thick strand of dark hair that had come undone and curled enticingly over one eye were any indication, she was pissed. Not that he was the sort to count another's cups, but today he felt intolerably responsible for her, having brought her here to begin with.

Bloody hell, Sutherland. He doubted there would be this many gawkers at her coronation. He'd decided, as he'd watched Rotham flirting with her, that it was too late to save her, and maybe what he ought to do is shield her so that no one would guess her state of inebriation. He could imagine the talk that would spread like fire through London. *Princess Justine, drunk and stumbling at Stafford House.*

First things first. He had to get the lass some air. He suggested repairing to the lawn for a stroll. There was a small pond, a lovely fountain and the flowers were in full bloom.

Sutherland thought it a grand idea and Rotham, sensing an opportunity, had surely strained himself in his mad rush to be the one to escort her through the French doors onto the terrace. As William suspected, Justine was desperate to be outside, and practically hurdled over her would-be suitor to get out of the crowded room.

But the outdoors had not accomplished what he'd hoped, for everyone poured out after the crown princess, surrounding her in hooped skirts and dark coats. William had never seen so many people trip over themselves in his life.

He made the mistake of not moving quickly enough and now Rotham, damn him, had very craftily positioned himself as protector to the future queen. Several more gentlemen, most of them unmarried and available and eager for attention, jogged down the steps behind her from the terrace to a landing like a litter of puppies with tails high.

On the landing Justine took a fan someone had offered her and was waving a gale force wind at her face. William had the dreaded sense that things were on the verge of going awry, and he had visions of the entire afternoon unraveling like a ball of yarn, picking up speed as it went. He was debating how to extract her from that crowded landing when Princess Amelia suddenly appeared beside him with an unusual glow about her. He didn't see how she'd reached him and eyed her with suspicion—that sort of glow came from good food, good drink or good sex, and he dared not guess which one. "Where have you been?" he asked, looking over the top of her head.

She clucked her tongue at him. "You're not my father."

"And we're both grateful for it, aye?" He offered his arm to Princess Amelia. "Take it."

"What?" She looked at his arm, held aloft. "Why? Where are we going?" And yet, she took it, because this was a woman who was naturally inclined toward the male arm.

"We must rescue your sister."

Princess Amelia groaned. *"Again?"* As if she was often asked to save her sister. "Why? What's she done?"

"She's had a wee bit of champagne. A bucket more to the point. And she's in a crowd of admiring young gentlemen."

"Where?" She craned her neck to see Justine in the crowd, surrounded by people clearly eager to speak to her. The party hadn't even made it to the lawn. "You're right. We must stay close." She glanced at her hand on his arm. "What are you waiting for?"

What was he waiting for? For just one of these Weslorian princesses to behave in a manner he could at least anticipate, that was what. But he and Princess Amelia marched down the steps to catch up with the mob. When they reached the landing, he led Princess Amelia to skirt around to intercept the princess and her escort before they descended any further. Justine noticed; she eyed him and her sister suspiciously.

And then Rotham turned to see what had caught her eye. When he saw Princess Amelia, he suddenly beamed. He was a little pig in slop, his hidden curly tail probably wagging with furious abandon.

"There you are, sister!" Princess Amelia said grandly. The crowd parted to allow her to join Justine. Princess Amelia exclaimed with delight to one and all that today was a beautiful day for a walk about the gardens, and she was so happy to see her dear sister enjoying herself.

"Je," Justine said. She looked as if she was tilting a smidge to the right. Lord, she wasn't about to topple, was she? "May I introduce Lord Rotham and—" Justine glanced at the men who were edging forward to have a look at Princess Amelia, and flicked her wrist in their direction "—his many friends. My sister, Princess Amelia."

"Your Royal Highness," Rotham said, bowing low. "It is my great honor to make your acquaintance." He took a long step forward, beating out any other gentleman who had in mind to reach her first. Amelia let go of William's arm and moved toward Rotham, her hand charmingly outstretched.

Rotham took it, and as he gushed about all the pleasure he was having in making her acquaintance, William sidled next to Justine. She looked a bit clammy. "All right?" he asked.

"Je. Why wouldn't I be?" Her words came out in a rush.

Princess Amelia was gesturing to the small lake below, where several geese were gliding serenely across the surface. Rotham offered his arm, and then, just like that, Princess Amelia and the merry band of gentlemen began to jog down the steps to the lawn and the lake.

"You're as pale as a sheet and gripping the champagne flute like a croquet mallet," he said as they watched them go.

Justine looked at her hand as if she wasn't aware she held a flute, and seeing it, tossed what remained down her throat before handing the glass to William.

He took the glass and held it away from his person until a footman took it.

"Would you like to join your sister and the others? Or would you like a reprieve from the crowd?" He winged his arm for her.

"Thank you, but I don't need a reprieve from my duty and I never will."

"There's a boast that's likely to come back like a bad cold."

At that moment Rotham seemed to remember he'd been in the midst of charming the crown princess and jerked around, as if he'd forgotten and left his child in the middle of a market stall. "Your Royal Highness!" he called and began striding up the steps again. "I do beg your pardon, I thought you'd come along with us."

"Coming!" she said brightly, then muttered, *"God help me."*

Rotham was halfway up the steps to her when a cry went up from the crowd he'd just left, and he stopped, turning back to see what had happened.

What had happened was that Princess Amelia had apparently carried on to the water's edge, then squatted down, offering an empty hand to a goose. Now all the geese had come up on the lawn and were flapping and surging forward, quacking with anticipation, hoping to share in what they assumed was bounty. When the lot of them realized there was no bounty, they began to squawk and run furiously at the people gathered. Suddenly, people were shrieking and geese were squawking and a melee unfolded before them in the blink of an eye. One of the gentlemen took Princess Amelia by the hand and pulled her safely out of the path of a goose as she laughed with delight.

Everyone was trying to escape the agitated geese who, with surprising speed and agility, were snapping at arses, catching fabric in some cases. William watched one gentleman grab the top of his leg where a goose had nicked him.

"My God!" Rotham exclaimed. "Douglas, will you help me?" he cried as he hurried down the steps to quell the disturbance.

"Afraid I can no'. Bad back," William said to Rotham's departing figure.

"There is nothing wrong with your back," Justine said.

"No," he said. "And nothing wrong with my pride, either. I intend to keep it that way."

Justine actually smiled.

He was right to assume this would be a disaster, as the geese were chasing everyone now, their wings spread to enormous width, honking and taking a particular liking to the ladies' bottoms, as they were covered in colorful fabric and about beak height. The more ladies shrieked and ran, the more enraged the geese seemed to become. Princess Amelia and her savior had disappeared into the hedgerow, and the other gentlemen assembled were trying to usher the geese back into their pond before they caused any more harm. More than one brave gentleman was forced to flee from an attacker, however.

Justine and William stood shoulder to shoulder on the landing, watching the melee.

Now Sutherland had appeared with his groundsmen, all of whom were doing a great deal of shouting. One groundsman had brought a gun and pointed it skyward, firing it. The result was a collective scream from everyone. People collided with each other and the geese in their frantic escapes. Some of them fell into the shrubbery.

"My goodness," Justine said. "It's pandemonium."

"A wee bit diverting, is it no'?"

"The most entertaining thing I've seen in weeks." She looked up at him and grinned.

William grinned back.

He watched Rotham realize that both princesses had gotten away from him, turning this way and that, looking for them. He decided to rush into the maze to find Princess Amelia, and no doubt would be slinking back up the stairs to Justine before it was all said and done.

"What do you think? Should I go in search of Amelia?" Justine asked. She shifted, bumping into his shoulder.

"No."

She glanced up at him, still swaying a little. "Do you mean to say, as you *wish*?" she asked, and poked his shoulder with one long finger.

Aye, Justine was as stewed as a sailor his first day back on shore, and William couldn't help but smile. "I would do as *you wish* in a heartbeat if I thought you could manage the stairs, madam. Word to the wise—if you continue to drink champagne in such a swarthy manner, you may draw the attention you so diligently work to avoid."

It might have been the glint of the sun, but Justine's eyes took on the sheen of gold. "Why are you so confoundingly concerned about me? Lady Ellen has not taken her eyes from you since you spoke to her inside. You think you know how the game is played, and yet, you don't even recognize the players."

William looked over his shoulder and instantly caught the eye of Lady Ellen. She was not watching the efforts to corral the geese—she was watching him. She smiled.

He smiled, too, and turned back. "Now, there is a well-reared young woman who has a kind word for everyone she meets. You could learn a thing or two from her."

"Ha. Let her be princess for a day and see how kind she is. She would be forced to attend gatherings such as this so that people could stare at her and wait for her to falter."

"Is that what you think they are doing? Waiting for you to falter?"

"Why else would they never take their eyes from me?"

Because she was pretty? Because she would be a queen? Because she was interesting?

Another blast of a shotgun caused them both to crouch. But it seemed to have done the trick—the geese were flying back into the water and sailing away, all while managing to look like the offended parties. People slowly began to pick themselves up and assess the damage.

"I'd say this soiree is done in," William mused.

"I certainly hope so," Justine muttered. "Does it seem unusually hot to you?"

That was the moment Princess Amelia emerged from the maze, her arm linked through Lady Constance's arm, a half dozen young men trailing behind them, moving toward the steps.

And then came Sutherland, jogging up the steps, and behind him, Earl Rotham.

Justine sighed deeply.

"Had enough of this outing, have you?" William asked hopefully.

"Is it obvious?"

"No' to anyone else," he answered honestly.

Just as Sutherland and Princess Amelia and Rotham reached the landing, William took a step away from Justine and said loudly, "If I may, Your Royal Highness, the hour grows late. I am at fault for no' being more mindful of your appointments. I believe you are expected elsewhere. Shall I have the coach brought round?"

His suggestion was instantly met with cries of protest and entreaties for her to stay. Justine was wrong about one thing—these people had not come to see her falter; they had come to gawk, to curry favor. To see for themselves just how unmatched she was and pray for a small miracle for their sons.

"But you're still here on the landing!" Princess Amelia exclaimed. "You've not even come down to the lawn."

"So soon!" Sutherland echoed. "You must not fear the geese, Your Royal Highness. As you can see, they have swum to the other side—"

"Your Royal Highness, I had hoped to have a word with you before you go," Rotham said quickly.

"You can't think to leave," Princess Amelia begged her. "Lady Constance has invited us to dine."

Justine looked flummoxed. Her gaze moved from Lady Constance to Princess Amelia and to all the gentlemen behind the two young women. "You stay, Amelia. I have so many things to attend," she said and gave a flick of her wrist in the directions of the vague things she had to attend.

Princess Amelia's countenance instantly brightened. "Do you mind terribly?"

"We'll see her safely home, ma'am," Sutherland said

helpfully. "I'll send an army of footmen along with her. Have no fear."

"Then it's settled." Amelia clapped her hands with delight and turned to Lady Constance with a smile, reaching for the hand of her new friend. The two of them scooted off, the gentlemen on their trail.

"Are you certain you won't stay, Your Royal Highness?" Rotham asked pitifully.

All eyes were on her, and Justine's breath seemed to grow a little short. "I'm afraid I cannot." Her smile was wobbly. To Sutherland, she said, "Thank you for your kind invitation to my sister. And for the tour of your picture gallery. It was indeed a wonder to behold. I shall add it to my list of favorite sites."

Sutherland gushed his return of thanks for coming to his "humble" home and gracing them all with her *exalted* presence. The more effusively he talked, the more Justine seemed to shrink. She was such a curious creature, this woman. William noticed how her gaze flicked between Sutherland and the people pressing closer to hear what he was saying. When the duke turned away for a moment to address someone who had posed a question, Justine touched William's hand to gain his attention.

It was odd how well he understood what she needed from him without even a word. The crowd had grown in number, everyone jockeying for a glimpse of the princess before she escaped, some of them calling out invitations of their own. "Thank you again, my lord," he said firmly to Sutherland. He took Justine's elbow and escorted her back up the stairs, through the French doors, through the picture gallery and to the foyer, where a butler was waiting with his hat and her bonnet.

He escorted her down the front stairs to the drive with

Sutherland bouncing alongside, carrying on about a ball he thought he was considering, and how delighted he would be if Her Royal Highness might attend. The Weslorian guards were already assembled behind his coach. William reached the door before the coachman and helped Justine inside. He shut the door, then turned back to Sutherland and his never-ending grin.

"Sutherland, old friend," he said, and patted him on the chest. "If anything were to happen this evening that would give a single person a reason to cast aspersions on Princess Amelia, I will personally remove your bollocks with my sheep shears, aye?" He smiled.

Sutherland blinked. "Of course, Douglas. Of course."

"Good lad." And with that, he opened the door of the coach and climbed inside.

CHAPTER TEN

INSIDE THE COACH Justine leaned back against the velvet squabs, her legs sprawled before her, and rested one hand across a ridiculously tight corset, anticipating the moment she would remove the offending thing from her body. She closed her eyes and drew several deep breaths. She was tired, she'd had *far* too much champagne—not that she would ever admit it to one Scottish marquess—and she wanted only a bath.

It was always the same after a crowded event like this— she felt emotionally and physically drained. The press of people, the scrutiny, her bloody raw nerves. She wished she could be like Amelia, who basked in the attention, but she wilted like a dandelion.

But now it was over and she needed to eat something after having drunk so much. She was imagining what that might be when the door suddenly opened again. She scrambled upright and watched with consternation as William Douglas climbed into the coach and sat directly across from her. "Thank you, William, but I should like to be alone."

"It would be rude to send you home without company."

"No." She reached across and managed to push the door ajar. "I am perfectly at ease and quite accustomed to a lack of company. Off you go."

A footman or someone closed the door from the outside.

"What sort of gentleman would I be if I allowed it?" He

smiled and removed his hat, placing it next to him on the bench. The coach lurched forward, almost spilling her out of her seat and making her stomach roil. "And it's too late," he added cheerfully.

With a groan she tossed her wrap and bonnet aside and looked out the window as the coach moved on from Stafford House. She was aware of William's eyes on her and turned her head to look at him. He was studying her, all right. "What is it?"

He shrugged. "I was observing how regal you looked just now, with the afternoon light on your face."

She blinked with surprise. "Why are you speaking to me in that way?"

"What way?"

"Like you're a suitor. Not a half hour ago you said I was swarthy."

"I did no'," he said, holding up a finger. "I said your drinking of champagne was swarthy."

"It's my prerogative to drink as much as I like without comment from you."

"So you made perfectly clear." He nudged her foot with his. "I donna care if you drink a barrel of it, Justine."

"*Thank* you, *William*, Chamberlain of the Champagne, for your permission."

He smiled. When he smiled like that, it made her feel a little dizzy. Oh yes, she'd had far too much champagne.

"I do wonder, however."

She didn't want to ask; she *didn't want to ask*. She asked. "Wonder what?"

"Why do you shake so?"

She could feel the blush rise in her cheeks. "No one would like to know the answer to that more than me. But thank you for asking." She sat a little straighter in her seat and turned her gaze to the window and watched a plain building that looked like an asylum disappear from view as they rolled past. Seemed an odd location for one.

"Did you think I didna notice it?"

Her blush deepened. She hadn't been so ridiculous to think that, but she'd certainly hoped it. "I don't care if you did." She turned her gaze back to him. "The only reason you noticed is because you have the awful habit of standing too close and staring at me. No one said you must shadow my every move."

He laughed. "I'm to keep you under my watch. What is it, then?" he asked curiously. "A malady?"

"A *malady*?" She shook her head. "I don't know why, but if I did, I would employ all remedy necessary if only to avoid my mother's priest, who believes I might be cured if only I pray harder." She shuddered to think of the time in her life when she was required to meet with Lord Reverend Pontifo every morning at five for Matins prayers. She sighed and began to yank the gloves from her hands. Every part of her needed air. "It's nerves. When I was a girl I had a terrible experience in a crowd. That's the first time I can remember experiencing the sensation of being unable to breathe. Unfortunately, it seems to have gotten worse the older I've become, and I think because the crowds around me have gotten bigger. When there is a large group of people very close to me, it happens."

She tossed her gloves onto the pile with her bonnet and wrap and folded her arms across her middle. "I've been told by *everyone* that my nerves are vexing. But I can't help that my heart races and I feel a little ill. And the champagne… it soothes me. So there you have it, William. I am all bad nerves and soothed only by drink."

"No, lass. I saw what you did to Mawbley—you canna

be all bad nerves and command a match as you did. I would imagine it unbearable to be in the thick of a crowd with so many people vying for your attention."

She was a little astonished that he wasn't saying the things she usually heard—that she was so fortunate to be in her position, that she had to swallow her fears and present herself as queen, that she was being foolish. "It is," she agreed softly. She didn't like talking about it—it made her realize how truly vulnerable she was. Her father said she must project strength and calm in public. Never fear.

"Something similar happened to me," William said.

She laughed. "Someone tried to snatch you in a crowd when you were a girl?"

"No. But when I was a wee lad, my father wanted to teach me to fence."

"Oh?" She sat a little straighter. "Why didn't you tell me you were a fencer?"

"Because I'm no' a fencer," he said, smiling easily. "In that particular lesson, my father was teaching me to feint, but he was no' very skilled, and cut me, right here," he said. He pointed to his face, turning his head slightly. She could just make out the scar that ran from his cheek and into his sideburns. "I have no' picked up an épée since. Canna go near them."

How intriguing. She'd never known any man to admit a weakness, with the exception of her father, and his weakness—consumption—was there for everyone to see. Moreover, she'd never known a man who ever tried to help her feel better about things. She appreciated his effort more than he knew. Blast it, she was blushing again. "I will have a care not to issue a challenge to you, then."

"That would be most kind." He smiled softly.

That smile again! It made her feel…a bit slushy. "May I ask you something?"

"Anything, aye."

"Why don't you care for Lady Ellen?"

He laughed a little.

"She couldn't take her eyes from you! She's quite pretty. Why don't you like her?"

"Who said I didna like her?"

"You scarcely looked at her." She suddenly thought of something and sat up. "You were being coy!"

"I am incapable of being coy," he scoffed. "I never looked at her because I was looking at someone else. Someone far more attractive in my eyes."

Justine's eyes widened. "Lady Constance."

"No' Lady Constance." He looked pointedly at her.

Justine felt a stirring in her chest as the blood rose in her cheeks again. That light-headed feeling one had when they suspected they were about to be surprised. "Not *Amelia*—"

"Och, no, no' Amelia. *You*, Justine."

She was taken aback. "Me?"

"Aye, you. Your beauty has no' gone unnoticed by me."

"My…" What was happening in this moment? Why was he paying her this compliment? It seemed all wrong. Amelia was the comely one and she was the studious one. She rubbed her neck and tried to think of what to say. "I'm… surprised."

Now he looked baffled. "Why? I'm a man and I appreciate a fine female form and a lovelier face." He shrugged. "'Tis no' my fault that you have an outrageously tempting mouth."

Justine gaped at him. She wanted to laugh at him. She wanted to say something pithy and clever and flirty. But she could never think of those things to say. "Are you at-tempting to ingratiate yourself to me?"

He snorted. "If I meant to ingratiate myself, I'd be a damn sight better at it than this. I am merely telling you what I see, and it's the truth. *Sutherland*, now there is a man to ingratiate himself. And Rotham." He nudged her foot with his again. "Go on."

"What?"

"Go on, then, admit I was right."

"Is that so important to you, really?"

"Aye," he said, grinning. "Very."

She rolled her eyes. "Fine. You were right, William. But you really don't need to tell me things that are painfully obvious. I can see these things with my own eyes."

William suddenly surged forward, planting his hands on either side of her skirt and pinning her to the squabs. "Would you like to know what I think, Justine Ivanosen?"

"*No*, I would not! But you are obviously desperate to tell me, so go on, then."

"I think you like my company. I think you like it very much."

She was not prepared to admit that to herself, much less to him. She gave him a lopsided smile and leaned for-ward, too, so close that she could see the bits of blue and green floating in all the gray of his eyes. "You know what *I* think? I think you are very much in love with yourself."

His gaze moved to her lips. "Perhaps that's the very rea-son you enjoy my company as much as you do—I may be the only man in your acquaintance who doesna drool over the possibility of you."

"I never said I enjoyed your company. And you are cer-tainly the only man in my acquaintance who thinks he has leave to say such outlandish things to me."

"Which makes me good for you, too." His gaze moved down to her chest.

Her skin began to heat under his gaze. "You're a scoundrel."

He smiled and slowly lifted his gaze. "Aye, it's been said."

"I've had enough of scoundrels. One almost ruined me."

"Then you're in luck. I'm no' a scoundrel. No,' anymore."

"Oh, I'm sure *not*."

"I've enough to keep me occupied with my family and the Hamilton estate—it leaves very little time for scoundreling."

"Hmm," she said dubiously. "Does Lady Ellen know you've abandoned your role as scoundrel? Perhaps that would account for her interest in you."

"Whatever interest Lady Ellen holds for me has been dictated by her mother."

"Poor thing." Justine smiled.

So did William. His gaze flicked to her lips once more, and for a moment she thought he meant to kiss her. She hoped he meant to kiss her. She would act properly offended, but she really hoped he would.

Alas, the man sighed and settled back against the squabs.

They rode along, their gazes locked, neither of them speaking, and yet, Justine could hear an entire conversation in her head. She was mesmerized, and she was fairly certain it wasn't the champagne any longer. That had all fizzed out of her. She was also fairly certain she hadn't felt this way since…well, since Aladabert.

The coach made the turn into the drive at Prescott Hall, bouncing along the tree-lined lane to the entrance. "Would you care to make a wee wager, Your Royal Highness?" William asked.

"It depends on the wager."

"As I am the only man in your acquaintance who is no' held in thrall by your presence, I can plainly offer my advice on your suitors."

"I don't want your advice."

"And yet, you need it."

She eyed him speculatively. "What sort of advice would you offer?"

"Whether or no' the gentleman is a good match for you."

She laughed. "How can you possibly know who is a good match for me?"

"Perhaps I will better know who is *no'* a good match for you. I have a fine head for these things."

"Really?" She couldn't stop giggling, appalled and amused by how confident he was. "A pity you did not offer to do the matchmaking yourself. Very well, what is your wager?"

"If I'm right, and the gentleman is no' a good match... I win a kiss from you."

Justine's mouth dropped open. He was ridiculous! "Spoken like a true scoundrel."

"Reformed scoundrel. I'd no' have wagered a kiss before I was unscoundreled. I would have taken it the first moment I felt your sentiments toward me soften."

She imagined him taking her in his arms and kissing her. An alarming little shiver shot down her spine. "My guards would have hauled you away and put you in chains."

"Risks are meant to be taken."

Justine didn't want to squirm in her seat but she couldn't help it. "And if I win?"

"You may be as smug as you like and lord it over me at every opportunity, and I'll no' complain."

She smiled instantly. "I would *love* that."

"I thought you might. Do we have a deal, then?"

She looked at his mouth and imagined all sorts of kissing. Desperate, passionate kissing. She was such a fool. "You are so presumptuous."

"It's a fair bet. And where is the harm in making this odious matchmaking process a wee bit more diverting?"

He had a point. She pondered it as the coach rolled to a stop in front of the hall. "Just a kiss?"

He held up his right hand. "On my honor, just a kiss."

She imagined the expressions of Lady Bardaline and her mother if they were to hear of this entirely inappropriate wager. Perhaps that was what made her suddenly put out her hand to seal the wager. "Agreed."

Something sparked in his eyes, and Justine realized he hadn't expected her to agree—he'd expected her to decline, probably demurely, like a proper princess would do. Well, maybe she wasn't a proper princess. He took her hand and lifted it to his lips, lingering there. She could feel the heat of his lips, and her entire body tingled with anticipation. "I look forward to the challenge, Your Royal Highness."

"Don't look too far forward or you'll strain your neck, my Lord Douglas. I fully intend to win."

He smiled in a way that sent white-hot flames shooting through her. He smiled as if he knew he'd already won and was humoring her.

The door swung open and a footman put down the step. William went out first and held up his hand to help Justine out. When she came out of the coach, she had forgotten her things. He reached inside for them and handed them to her. She took the wrap and gloves in one hand, reached for the brim of the bonnet with the other. But William didn't let go of it right away. He caressed one of her fingers with his thumb.

Justine lifted her gaze to his. "What are you doing?"

"Imagining."

"Stop imagining."

"Impossible. I found the afternoon to be surprisingly diverting, despite you draining all of the champagne from Sutherland's wine cellars."

"And I found the afternoon intolerable, in spite of draining all the champagne from Sutherland's cellars. Isn't it odd how a single event can be viewed so differently by two people?" She heard the sound of a coach turn onto the drive.

"If you found the day so truly wretched, I will make it up to you."

She laughed and yanked her bonnet from his hand. "How?"

The coach drew closer. "Another invitation, perhaps. A smaller crowd. *Much* smaller."

She laughed. This man was making her laugh, and there was hardly a person who had done that since Aldabert. She recalled that he'd made her laugh the last time she was in London, too. She couldn't remember why, exactly, but remembered laughing often at the suppers and soirees.

She didn't know what to make of the way she was feeling.

"I'll arrange something and send word, aye?"

She smiled coyly. "Send all the words you like. To me, to Robuchard, even to Bardaline. Oh, and if you please, you mustn't forget to tell the prime minister that in my first outing, I managed to avoid starting a war or ruining my prospects. He will be—"

"Your Royal Highness, I beg your pardon."

Funny, Justine would later think, how neither she nor William saw or heard Bardaline approach. It was as if they were standing in their own private little patch of sunlight. But there he suddenly was, tall and thin and pointed chin, looking entirely too pleased for anything that could possibly be happening at Prescott Hall. Justine realized only then that the coach she'd heard had come to a halt behind William's.

"Je?" Justine asked.

"Lady Aleksander has arrived."

Just then the door on the second coach opened, and an attractive woman who looked to be around forty years or so, stepped out of the coach. She put her hands behind her and bent backward. *"Lord!* My back can scarcely stand the long coach rides anymore. I should rather walk, I think."

"Who?" William whispered at the same time as Justine muttered, "She's *here*?"

They watched as Bardaline hurried forward and the woman tried to listen to him while at the same time instructing the coachman to be careful with her bags.

Justine gave William a *God-help-me* look. "It's the matchmaker."

CHAPTER ELEVEN

LILA HAD ARRIVED after an unremarkable crossing of the English Channel and a quick trip up from Dover to London. She was effusively greeted by Lord Bardaline, whose unrelenting demand for attention made itself immediately known as a pair of footmen ushered the crown princess into the house while Lila stood on the drive.

Lila knew very well that the young woman was Princess Justine—she'd been sent several copies of portraits done of the princess over the years. While giving his remarks, Bardaline noticed Lila looking past him and hastened to assure her that once the princess was settled, there would be an audience. And wouldn't she like to "freshen" before she made Her Royal Highness's acquaintance? He then enlisted the aid of his wife, and the two of them hurried Lila inside. Was there anything she needed, anything at all? Perhaps some tea or wine or port?

The Bardalines, both of them, were insufferably eager to please. Lila was always suspicious of people who were *too* eager to please—one couldn't help but feel that at some point, something would be demanded in return after all that eager pleasing.

She was shown to a suite of rooms that she would occupy in her time here. There was a small, but well-appointed bedroom, a smaller sitting area and a dressing room. The walls were done in bright yellow floral wallpapering, and the view from the tall windows faced the drive and the park beyond.

She unpacked her own bags. The task gave her hands something to do while her mind floated over many thoughts and questions about what she needed to do here, about Valentin—she already missed him terribly—about the things she had learned about Wesloria in her journey here, about the young Italian prince who would arrive on the morrow. And perhaps most urgently, she wondered who was the gentleman who'd been standing with the princess on the drive? He was quite handsome—that was the first thing she'd noticed. But then she had slowly realized that she must know him. From where or when was the mystery, but there was something indeterminately familiar about him.

The two of them had been standing beside a grand coach, pulled by a team of four, with showy red feather plumes at each corner. They'd been standing close, speaking so intently that neither of them seemed to notice her coach pull in behind them. Whoever the gentleman was, the spread of warmth across Lila's nape had told her that her eyes were not lying—those two were having a moment. They were having such a private moment, in fact, that neither of them saw Bardaline barreling out the door, charging at them like a ram.

"Well, well, well, Your Royal Highness," Lila murmured. "Who is your acquaintance? Have you done my job for me?"

When she finished unpacking, she had still not been summoned to meet the princess. She decided to stroll the grounds of Prescott Hall and see the gardens for which it was renowned. She discovered them to be as spectacular as reported, full of vibrant color and very much to her liking. She would enjoy her morning walks here.

The sun was sinking toward the horizon and it was well past the time for a proper English tea. She wondered if Princess Justine had any intention of receiving her this evening. She returned to her suite to try and read while she awaited some word, but she'd only just picked up the book when she heard a knock at the door. "Enter."

A maid stepped inside and curtsied. "Lady Bardaline bids me tell you that Her Royal Highness will receive you in the green drawing room."

About time. "Lovely!" Lila picked up her shawl, wrapped it around her shoulders and headed downstairs.

Lord Bardaline was on hand to greet her at the bottom of the stairs. "There you are," he said, that silly beaming smile returned to him. He gestured to a closed door across the grand foyer, and started in that direction.

"If I may inquire, my lord," Lila asked as she kept pace with him, "who was the gentleman who accompanied Her Royal Highness home?"

"The Marquess of Douglas."

Lila blinked. Of *course*. No wonder he'd seemed familiar to her—she *had* met him before. Not that they were close acquaintances by any means, but she knew *of* him, knew he was a Scottish noble who roamed the continent and cropped up at some of the best houses for a weekend shoot or a ball. She recalled she'd met him a few years ago, at the marriage of Princess Charlotte of Prussia to Prince Georg of Saxe-Meiningen. What she couldn't recall was if he'd attended in the company of someone or had come alone. "Is he a suitor?" she asked as they reached the double doors into the salon.

"What?" Bardaline looked startled and appalled by the question. "Certainly not. He is an acquaintance of Robuchard, as I understand it, and has agreed to accompany Her

Royal Highness in and around London so that she might take in some of the sights."

Aha. Lila didn't know Douglas, but she knew Robuchard, and there was only one reason Robuchard would send an *acquaintance* to show the princess *some of the sights*, and that was to know how things were progressing. Which meant Douglas was a spy. That was information she would keep in mind and use to her advantage should the situation arise.

Bardaline opened the doors and announced her.

Princess Justine was standing in the middle of the room, her hands clasped loosely at her waist. Lila's first thought was that she was tall and slender and quite lovely. She strode across the room with a smile and curtsied, very low, because queens and princesses could be a bit judgmental about the depth of a woman's curtsy. "Your Royal Highness, how good of you to receive me."

"*Je*, of course."

Lila rose from her curtsy. Princess Justine had a pretty face and a fine figure. But her truly remarkable feature was not the streak of white in her hair—that was just an odd little thing that seemed to run in the Ivanosen family—but her unusual gold amber eyes. Just like her father's. And just like her father, she didn't seem to smile easily. She was studying Lila, taking her measure, until she seemed to remember herself. "Welcome, Lady Aleksander." She gestured to a chair as if it was an afterthought.

Lila doubted a colder reception could be had, but she was not daunted. "Thank you." She perched on the edge of the chair the princess had indicated. The princess likewise took a seat across from her and folded her hands in her lap.

Princess Justine was stiff. Lila understood why that was probably so—the princess did not want to be matched. Who could blame her? There was nothing drier or less romantic than a match made at the highest levels of society. Her Royal Highness would not be the first reluctant or aloof young woman she'd been hired to match, and she would not be the last.

"I didn't think you'd come so soon," the princess said.

Lila tilted her head to one side. "No? I understood Prime Minister Robuchard had sent word to you."

The princess glanced down at her lap and pretended to address a loose thread or piece of lint. "I don't read every communiqué from the prime minister."

Lila almost laughed. "I don't suppose I would, either, if I were to be bartered to the highest bidder like a broodmare."

That certainly brought the young woman's head up. She looked positively horrified, those lovely gold eyes round as crowns. "I beg your pardon?"

"Oh dear, I've shocked you. My husband tells me I am too open with people I've only just met. I suppose I ought to pretty things up, but you're an intelligent young woman and I suspect you appreciate honesty. If I may be so bold... I suggest that we dispense with the nonsense of pretending and acknowledge that you will be matched to someone who can bring the right sort of connections to Wesloria, and for whom you can provide something to their circumstance in return. Do you agree?"

The princess's face was pinkening. "I, ah... I—"

"And that is hardly the stuff of marital dreams, is it?" Lila pressed on. "My guess is that you think the best you can hope for is a match that might develop into love, while at the same time fervently hoping whoever he may be is at least pleasing to the eye and isn't cruel."

Princess Justine stared at Lila as if she'd just suggested they overthrow the throne—a mix of horror and fascination and acute curiosity. She cleared her throat. "That's hardly the most encouraging thing anyone has ever said about my marrying."

"I've no doubt that's true," Lila said breezily. "You must think that when they called me to assist, all was lost. But I am here to tell you that the Lord shined His countenance on you the day your mother decided to retain my services."

The princess smiled wryly. "*Did* He?"

"Yes, ma'am. Because I will make certain that you are matched to someone who is as compatible to you, the woman, as he is to your future throne. No one else will do that for you."

The princess regarded Lila coolly. "Are you saying these things to make me agreeable?"

Intelligent *and* cynical. How delightful! Lila rather liked the challenge this young woman represented. "Not in the least. I don't expect you to agree or disagree with anything I might say. But whatever I say will be the truth."

The princess looked down, but she made a sound that Lila was fairly certain was a snort of dubiousness.

"It may surprise you to know that I was once like you," Lila said. "Not like *you*, precisely—heaven knows that I should never have endured the weight of a crown. But I narrowly avoided being forced into a loveless marriage when my father fell from grace."

Princess Justine looked up, interested again.

"My father was a shipbuilder. An important one, too. He built the sort of big ships that nations purchase for war and merchant fleets."

The princess said nothing, but kept her gaze fixed on Lila.

"My prospects were very bright," she continued. "We had wealth, and so many British aristocrats need wealth to maintain estates that have been entailed for generations.

My father fancied himself the future father-in-law to a ti-tled man. Someone who would give him entry to the high-est reaches of society. You understand the sort of man I mean, I suspect."

The princess gave a barely perceptible nod.

"He put together a list of gentlemen who would make him proud. He never once asked for my opinion in the mat-ter and I think truly didn't care if I found any of the gentle-men compatible or not. The connection was the thing. He said that you married for advantage, and love came later. Although, quite honestly, I can't say that he ever really came to love my mother. Or she him." She paused a moment, re-membering her parents' separate lives. She supposed there were worse things. "Anyway," she said, pushing away the memory, "what my father wanted was access. Power."

"My father is not like that," Princess Justine said defen-sively. "My *parents* are not like that."

"Oh, I suspect not. Your father seems very kind and de-voted to your mother."

"He is."

"Nevertheless, my situation was somewhat similar to yours now, wouldn't you say?"

She appeared to mull over the question. "Somewhat," she admitted stiffly. "Did you marry one of them?"

Lila shook her head. She was so happy with Valentin that she rarely thought about those years. "They were not all terrible matches. Some were agreeable. But my father was corrupt, may God rest his soul. It was revealed that he'd been bribing members of Parliament to put forward his name for ship-building engagements to the exclusion of other shipbuilders. He was charged with it and absolutely ruined. And then, so were my prospects."

"Oh." The princess's dubious expression softened. "How terrible for you and your family."

"Ghastly," Lila agreed.

"So ghastly that now you exact your revenge on people like me?"

Lila laughed, and the princess actually smiled a little. "I *help* people like you, Your Royal Highness. Just like I helped myself."

"What do you mean?"

"Well, I was a bit incorrigible as, I think, every woman is. When I realized I was ruined, and would not have the sort of marriage I always believed I would have, I was despondent. What was I to do? Toil away as a spinster governess for the rest of my life? That might have been well and good for another woman, but it was not for me. But with no one to help me, I had to take matters into my own hands."

Princess Justine's amber gaze fixed on hers. "And how did you do that?"

"I matched myself!" she said gaily. "I created my own list of candidates and set out to arrange a marriage."

The princess gasped. Then she laughed. "You must be joking."

Lila shook her head. "I matched myself to a Danish baron, set the wheels in motion and have been very happily married to my Valentin for sixteen years."

Princess Justine slowly leaned forward, clearly intrigued. "How did you do that?"

"By trial and error, I suppose. I started with my father's list." She laughed. "He always aimed quite high, and Valentin was on the list. I learned all that I could about the gentlemen, ruled out some on the basis of compatibility, then contrived ways to make the acquaintance of those I had not had the pleasure of meeting."

"But you were ruined, as you said. How could you possibly have done so?"

"Oh, well, I had to finesse the invitations, to be sure, and I was not always successful. Some on the list were put off by my overtures. Some were curious, as you seem to be. And two of them were men of character who did not hold me responsible for my father's crimes. One of those two fell in love with me." She smiled again, remembering the night she'd first met Valentin. It had been at a soiree at the home of one of the few friends she'd managed to keep after the scandal. She could still remember the moment she had looked at him across the room and their eyes had met. Lila had never felt such a furious fluttering in her veins. It still happened when their eyes met. "It only takes one."

"I would say you are very lucky, then," the princess said. "But what has any of that to do with me?"

"Everything. I learned how to make a successful match, and out of ruins, I created happiness for myself. When an acquaintance realized what I had done for myself, she wondered if I might help her son, who had likewise suffered a public scandal. Could I take the same steps and find *him* a match that would make him happy?"

"Men brag about their scandals," the princess scoffed. "Didn't he have any money?"

Lila smiled at her cynicism. "Yes, as it happens, and quite a lot of it. Unfortunately, he did not have a handsome face."

"Ah." The princess nodded knowingly.

"*Fortunately* for him, not every woman desires a handsome face. Some desire to be provided for above all else. Some desire to be cherished above all else. In hindsight, I believe his was one of the easier matches I made because he desired nothing more than to have a wife to cherish. I've had much harder matches through the years. And now?" She casually flicked her hand. "My services are in high demand."

"My life is not in ruins, Lady Aleksander. Quite the contrary—I will be queen before long." She stiffened slightly, as if the admission of it made her uncomfortable. "You may be disappointed by how easily you complete your task."

"I am very happy that your life is not in ruins, Your Royal Highness. But perhaps your prospects are not as great as they might have been before your unfortunate association?"

Princess Justine's face instantly mottled with a bruising blush. "Ah. It would appear that the prime minister didn't leave out a single detail."

"I think he was wise to reveal it. It might come up."

"Why would it come up?"

"Some candidates might have questions about…your purity? But regardless of the answer to that question, this is not an insurmountable issue."

Princess Justine laughed darkly. "Wonderful! My mistake at having trusted someone is not insurmountable! And here I had worried so needlessly." She stood up.

So did Lila. She hadn't meant to insult her, but true to her word, she would be honest with this young woman.

"It's been quite a long day, Lady Aleksander."

"Of course." Lila curtsied deeply. "Thank you for receiving me."

The princess said nothing to that. She gave Lila one last curious look then walked out, her hand on the nape of her neck.

"Good evening, Your Royal Highness," Lila added.

The princess did not look back or acknowledge her.

"Oh. I neglected to mention…"

The princess came to a reluctant halt and turned around to look at her.

"Your first potential match will come to call on the morrow."

"What?"

"It so happens he was in London before me. The Italian Principe Gaetano di Aggiani. He has a vast fortune."

Princess Justine stared at her for a long moment, then turned and walked out the door a footman opened for her and disappeared into the hall.

Lila remained standing after the princess had gone, staring at the open door while the footman patiently waited.

Princess Justine would be a challenge. She was smart enough to hate this process, but unfortunate enough to be in a situation bad enough that she couldn't refuse it.

Gaetano was no match for this princess. He was a decoy, someone who would show Lila what she had to work with in the princess. She thought of her book upstairs, filled with the names and particulars about eligible gentlemen across Europe. She would delight in going through them this evening and refining her list.

And she would need to know more about William Douglas.

CHAPTER TWELVE

A LIGHT KNOCK at her door brought Justine up with a start—but it was only Seviana, who did her best to tiptoe across the floor to open the drapes. With a moan, Justine rolled onto her back and blinked up at the dark red canopy above her. "What time is it?"

"Good morning, ma'am," Seviana said as she pulled the drapes. "Half past eight." She went out. She'd be back again soon enough, with tea and toast, like every morning.

Justine debated rising at all. What was there to do but worry about Amelia? She yawned, stretching her arms overhead.

She'd dreamt she was trying to catch Amelia in the gardens at Stafford House, but Amelia kept getting farther and farther away from her, and Justine's feet had seemed mired in mud. She'd become aware of someone close by and when she turned to see who, William Douglas was standing against the hedgerow, his arms crossed. "What are you doing?" he'd asked, looking at her feet. "You'll never catch her like that."

Seviana had interrupted the retort Justine surely would have made.

She sat up and pushed her hair from her eyes. The man was haunting her dreams now, telling her what to do, his gray eyes shining with that irritating mix of amusement and smugness or whatever it was that was always twinkling back at her. And now she couldn't stop thinking about his wager. Who in blazes did that man think he was? And as for her, well…she needed to cut a wide berth around champagne, apparently, because she was the bigger fool for having agreed to it.

Seviana came back in with toast and tea. "Lady Bardaline asked me to tell you that Lady Aleksander will have breakfast at half past ten if you care to join her."

Lord, she'd all but forgotten about that one. "I care to sleep, Seviana."

Seviana handed Justine her tea, and Justine carefully settled back against the pillows to sip it. "May I at least dine in a dressing gown, or does Lady Bardaline think it important that I dress for the occasion?"

"If it pleases Your Royal Highness, I'll ask—"

"Lord, no, Sevie, don't you dare. She would delight in writing that to my mother." She sipped more of her tea. "It was a jest. But if I had my way, I wouldn't go to breakfast at all. I didn't invite the woman to Prescott Hall, did I? But since I must go, *obviously*, lest I start an international incident, I'll wear the pale yellow with the green trim."

Seviana curtsied and practically sprinted to the dressing room, probably delirious with joy to have something to do other than listen to her mistress complain. Justine was terrible like that, always a bit crotchety in the mornings, especially when her dreams of William Douglas had been interrupted.

Seviana returned with Justine's clothes and the things she would need to dress her hair. With a groan Justine made herself crawl out of bed. As she was dressing, Seviana opened the drapes even wider. "Oh my," she said. "You ought to see the flowers, ma'am."

"I've seen them," Justine said.

"There must be five wagons full."

Five wagons? Justine walked to the window and peered out.

Seviana was not talking about the gardens. There were five wagons on the drive, each nearly bursting with flowers, a riot of red and gold and pink and yellow, looking very cheerful on this sun-washed day. Justine had never seen so many flowers in her life. "What are they for?" she asked as she returned to her dressing.

"I couldn't say, ma'am."

The tea, the sunshine and the flowers had helped to improve Justine's mood somewhat by the time she made her way downstairs to breakfast.

There were more flowers on the ground floor, the foyer filled with them in crates and vases. The scent was overpowering. Footmen were carrying still more to the back terrace. Justine paused to have a look at all the flowers being carried outside, and with a shrug, entered the breakfast room.

Lady Aleksander was there as promised, bent over the buffet to examine the offerings. She stopped only to curtsy when Justine entered. "Good morning, Your Royal Highness! You are looking well indeed."

Liar. She looked pale and had circles from a lack of sleep shadowing her eyes. "Thank you."

Lady Aleksander stepped away from the buffet, smiling, waiting for Justine to take a plate and go ahead of her. Protocol could be so beastly inconvenient at times. "Please carry on," Justine said and looked around for the house butler. "Carlton? Might I have coffee?"

"Oh, what a wonderful idea! I should like some too, please," Lady Aleksander said to Carlton.

Justine nodded at the butler, who in turn nodded to one

of the footmen. She walked to the table, and yet another footman pounced at her chair to pull it out for her. Sometimes she almost expected four men and a litter to appear just to ferry her across a room.

Carlton deftly removed the plate from her setting and leaned over her shoulder, asking softly if she cared to sample the buffet or if there was something in particular she desired. "Just some toast, please," Justine said. She was too interested in what Lady Aleksander was doing to think about her own choices.

At present, Lady Aleksander was questioning the footman about the ingredients of one of the dishes. Apparently, she didn't care for too much spice.

Eventually, Lady Aleksander made her way to the table, setting down a plate heaped high with breakfast food before taking her seat. Justine was amazed by it, really.

Lady Aleksander picked up her fork. "Did you sleep well, ma'am?"

"I slept horribly, thank you," Justine said. "And you?"

"*Very* well! Terribly relaxing here, I must say."

A footman entered the room with a letter on a tray. He came to Justine's side and bowed. She took the message as Lady Aleksander took a large bite of black pudding.

Justine fumbled in her pocket for her eyeglasses. She didn't recognize the handwriting and when she opened it, she found the note written sloppily. One large ink splatter adorned the edge of the paper. It was signed by Lord Sutherland. She wondered how drunk he'd been when he'd written it. She adjusted her eyeglasses and read.

YRH, last evening, HRH Princess Amelia, Lady Constance and my wife and I concluded that it was best if HRH remained for the night, as the roads were too

*dangerous to traverse at such a late hour. We will be
delighted to see her safely to you today.*

"He must be joking," Justine muttered. She removed her
eyeglasses and squeezed the bridge of her nose between
two fingers a moment.

"Is everything all right?" Lady Aleksander asked.

"Amelia is having a lark," she said and put aside the note
and her eyeglasses. "It would seem that at the last possible
moment she decided to stay the night at Stafford House."

"Oh, how lovely," Lady Aleksander said without the
slightest hesitation. She took another bite of black pudding,
then pointed her fork at it. "This is *delicious*." She turned
around to the footman. "You must tell the cook that the
breakfast is very good, and the black pudding spectacular."

The footman looked startled, as if he didn't know if
he was to hurry off and do it now. Poor man. No one ever
spoke *to* the footmen here. More like…at them. If at all.
This one finally bowed his head in acknowledgment but remained standing exactly where he was. He wouldn't move
until Justine required him to.

"Aren't you alarmed by my sister's behavior?" Justine
asked, wanting company in her pique.

Lady Aleksander's head swiveled back to her like an
owl. "Not at all, Your Royal Highness."

Of course not. "There are others in this hall who are. Not
me, of course. As I have said on many occasions, Amelia
is perfectly capable of taking care of herself."

"I've no doubt of it! Ma'am, you *must* try these eggs.
Expertly done. My husband would be in ecstasy."

As if on cue, Carlton set a plate of toast before Justine.

"By the bye, I had opportunity to review my list of suitors last night." Lady Aleksander announced this as if it was

perfectly appropriate to broach the subject of Justine's arranged marriage at breakfast when they had only just met.

Justine didn't want to hear it. She didn't want to *think* about it. She wanted to avoid the whole wretched business. "Hmm," she said. She began to eat quickly, shoveling in her toast, thinking if she could just get something down her, she could get out of this room, maybe take a long walk and avoid the topic altogether. She wasn't fool enough to think she could avoid it forever, but she could at least avoid it today.

"And I've had word from Prince Aggiani. He will call today." She looked up from her plate. "I asked Lord Bardaline to help with your schedule."

Justine gulped down her coffee. "Well. A prince. How... fitting. Carlton? You may take this."

"What?" Lady Aleksander looked with surprise at her plate. "But you've hardly touched your plate."

"I ate a piece of toast. You are right. The food is very good. You, sir," she said, gesturing to the footman, "may add my compliments to Lady Aleksander's when you speak to the cook."

Lady Aleksander quickly dabbed at her mouth with her napkin. "Why the rush?"

"Oh. Ah." There was a question that posed a bit of a dilemma, as there was nothing to rush off to when one did nothing but await her next audience with Queen Victoria. "I mean to fetch Amelia," Justine said, seizing on the idea. "That was badly done on her part."

"Wonderful! Mind if I join you?" Lady Aleksander scrambled to her feet, leaning over her plate to take one more bite of eggs.

A small swell of panic seized Justine. "Why?"

"To see London, of course. I haven't been here in ages.

It's been what…ten years? No, eleven, I think. Well," she said, waving a hand, "ten or eleven. I'll just fetch my—"

The dining room doors suddenly swung open and Bardaline sprinted inside. "Your Royal Highness," he said breathlessly, bowing low, "you should—"

"I'm *famished*," Amelia announced, sweeping in behind Bardaline. She handed her cloak to him as if he was a footman and proceeded into the middle of the room. She was wearing a dress Justine had not seen before, which made her wonder if Amelia had purchased it. Or borrowed it.

Her sister went to the buffet, her hair bound in a loose knot at her nape. She didn't seem to notice Lady Aleksander until she almost collided with her. She startled and bounced back a step. "Who are you?"

"Amelia, you have the pleasure of meeting Lady Aleksander," Justine said.

Amelia gasped. "The *matchmaker*?"

Lady Aleksander curtsied to Amelia. "It is my great pleasure to make your acquaintance, Your Royal Highness."

"But when did you come?" Amelia asked. "Why weren't we informed? We weren't informed, were we?" she asked Justine, just to make sure her indignation was warranted.

Bardaline, perhaps sensing a line of questioning he did not care to answer, chose that moment to exit the room with Amelia's cloak.

"We weren't informed the *precise* moment her ladyship would arrive," Justine said. "And I would have told you straightaway the moment I learned of it…but you were having a lark at Stafford House, weren't you? Really, Amelia, what were you thinking? Can you imagine the sort of talk that could spark?"

"Why shouldn't I stay with Lady Constance? She's quite a lot of fun."

Justine was gearing up to tell her sister that it didn't matter how much fun Lady Constance was, that it was the *appearance* of things that mattered, and God help her, it felt almost as if her mother was living in her head, because she never would have said such things before her own little scandal.

"Good morning," a deep voice rumbled.

Justine and Lady Aleksander turned toward the door at the same moment. Amelia did not.

William Douglas casually strolled into the room as if he lived here and had just come in from his morning constitutional. He did pause to bow—a generous interpretation of the slight dip of his head—and then he straightened and smiled directly at Justine with the expression of one who'd happened upon a theatrical street performance and was delighted by it.

"What are you doing here?" Justine demanded. "Where is Bardaline?"

"The last I saw him he was in the cloak closet mumbling to himself."

"You walked in without announcing yourself to anyone?"

"I wouldn't say that, no." He glanced at Amelia, whose attention was solidly on the buffet. "I am returning your sister to you, as you see. I was very clear with your butler about that. And the groom who came to tend the horses. And, of course, Her Royal Highness herself. But I think all of them are a bit undone by all the flowers. I pray no one has died."

"I didn't want to go with him. His escort was decidedly against my wishes," Amelia said at the buffet. She suddenly gasped. "*Did* someone die? Was it—"

"No," Justine said firmly. "I would have come to fetch you and tell you myself if that had happened."

"Oh. Of course. Then why *are* there so many flowers?"

"They are the gift of an admirer," Lady Aleksander said.

"What?" Justine asked at the same time Amelia whirled from the buffet, her face illuminated with pleasure. "For who?"

"Her Royal Highness, Princess Justine," Lady Aleksander said.

Amelia made a sound of disapproval and turned back to the buffet.

An admirer? What admirer? And what about William sauntering in here? There was suddenly too much to absorb.

She decided to absorb William first. "*You* were at Stafford House all night?"

He laughed. "I most certainly was no'. I called on the duke this morning and found the entire family engaged in a discussion of how best to deliver Her Royal Highness to Prescott Hall. I volunteered."

This made no sense to Justine. Why would he call on Sutherland this morning? He must have known somehow that Amelia would still be there and had gone to see her. She looked at Amelia, who was picking through a selection of cheeses. Her sister was beautiful. And that was not false praise—she was perhaps the most attractive Ivanosen to have ever lived. And Justine was…handsome? Passably pleasing? She didn't know what she was, and it hardly mattered. All her life, gentlemen had been attracted to Amelia, and it would not surprise her to know William was, too. But had she imagined the moment between them yesterday? What of the things he'd said about her? What of their wager?

She turned back to William, cross with him now. "What, you just happened to be walking by Stafford House?"

"I reside very close by."

"The big red house," Amelia offered helpfully. "You know, the one at the top of the street."

Justine did indeed remember the big red building. "The big and plain red building? I saw only an asylum or sanitarium matching that description."

"It is no' an asylum, for heaven's sake, and it is most assuredly mine."

"It's a *house*?" Justine's face felt a little hot. "You didn't say that was your house."

"You didna ask."

"Why would I ask if that…house belonged to you?"

"She didn't mention it because she was halfway in her cups and muddled," Amelia offered and took her plate to the table. "She's always muddled after being in a crowd. Justine, you haven't introduced our guest."

"Nerves and muddled are not the same thing and I was just about to do that, Amelia, thank you." She sucked in a breath and puffed it out, rubbed her forehead a moment, then dropped her hand. "Lady Aleksander, may I introduce Lord Douglas of Hamilton?" she said, and gestured loosely in his direction.

Lady Aleksander smiled and curtsied. "A pleasure to see you again, my lord."

"Again? Surely no', madam. I'd remember making your lovely acquaintance, that I would."

"Lord," Justine murmured impatiently under her breath.

But William was looking at Lady Aleksander as if he thought maybe he had met her and couldn't recall when or where.

"At the wedding of Princess Charlotte and—"

"Prince Georg! Of course," he finished for her. "How could I possibly have forgotten?"

"It's been an age," Lady Aleksander said kindly.

"Aye, that it has."

He strode across the room to greet her properly. "It is a pleasure to see you again, madam. You are well? Your husband?"

"Oh, exceedingly, both of us, thank you. And you? How does your father do?"

Justine watched them smile at each other as their recognition came back to them. They were reminiscing about the wedding, laughing at something that had happened there, and she felt left out.

"Well!" she said loudly, to remind them all that she was still standing there. "Now that your friendship has been renewed, I shall leave the two of you to reminisce." She started for the door, surprised by her own irritation. It really wasn't like her—she was used to being disappointed.

"Your Royal Highness, if I may?" Lady Aleksander called after her.

No, she may not. But Justine paused, clenched her jaw and forced herself to turn around. "*Je*, Lady Aleksander?"

"It's such a perfect morning, I thought perhaps we might all walk in the garden."

"Not me," Amelia said over her breakfast. "I danced so much last night that my feet are killing me."

"Thank you," Justine said. "But I have quite a full calendar today."

"I understand it is terribly crowded. But I thought perhaps now that your calendar has opened up to a bit of sunlight this morning, as Lord Douglas has brought your sister to you, that you might enjoy the air."

Amelia looked up from her plate. "What is she talking about?"

"Her Royal Highness was just on her way out to fetch you, but Lord Douglas has saved her the trouble."

"I'm not *trouble*." At least Amelia had the decency to sound a little uncertain.

Justine stared at the smiling Lady Aleksander, who seemed completely at ease rearranging Justine's day. Not that there was truly much to be rearranged, but nevertheless, Justine had the sense that the lady enjoyed doing it. And Bardaline, who had returned to the room, did not seem to mind that she did any rearranging, for he remained silent. The very same man who had held such tight control of her daily schedule, it was a wonder that he could unclamp his fingers from the leather-bound calendar every night. She wondered what these two were up to, what plots and schemes they'd hatched.

"It is a bonny day," William mused.

Justine glared at him. "This?" she said, gesturing between herself and Lady Aleksander, "is precisely the sort of thing I told you was not your affair."

"Then I beg forgiveness," he said easily. "Perhaps you and Lady Aleksander can go one way, and I can go the other and we all might take our private air."

"Nonsense! We'll go together!" Lady Aleksander piped up.

What was Justine supposed to say? Should she announce to all assembled that she was the crown princess and would decide what they did? Decline altogether because she didn't like yielding to the matchmaker, and if she started yielding with something as inconsequential as a walk, the next thing would be a match?

But it seemed unduly petulant to stomp her foot and refuse to walk. In truth, she *liked* to walk—she just didn't like feeling trapped into it. Was this the sort of thing she should expect when she was queen? People maneuvering her into whatever corner they liked all because she couldn't quickly think what to say?

Even now they were all looking at her, awaiting her decree, as she tried valiantly to sort through her many feelings on the subject. *"Auugh,"* she said heavenward. "Fine, all right! But a very *short* walk. I have my business, after all." She looked at Bardaline.

He was studying a spot on the carpet and didn't pick up her not so subtle suggestion immediately. "Oh. *Je,* Your Royal Highness. The business of the crown, certainly. Quite a lot of it. Meetings and such."

"What business?" Amelia demanded from the table. "Why has no one ever any business for me?"

Justine started for the door. She could feel Lady Aleksander on her heels before she reached it.

"Wait for me," Amelia cried, and her poor, aching feet forgotten, bounced up from the table, hurrying past Bardaline to join the others.

Justine kept walking purposefully down the long hall to the terrace, brushing past pots of flowers. Footmen hurried ahead of them to open the doors; to remove any stray leaf that might have fallen carelessly onto the terrace; to tell the groundskeepers to put themselves out of sight; to push the pots and stands of flowers aside so by the time Justine walked out onto the terrace, there was nothing but a serene and stunning view of gardens bursting with color below her, and the sweet scent of the floral bouquets that now littered the terrace.

"All of these flowers are for Justine?" Amelia asked. "Who has sent them? Why are there so many?"

Justine didn't care who they were from. She paused at the top of the steps and drew a breath as she took in the gardens.

William paused, too.

She looked at him. He looked at her. She felt herself on the verge of a smile he did not deserve, or a pithy remark on the tip of her tongue she was not known for making, but before any smile or words could come forth, Lady Aleksander suddenly appeared between them, her hand on her belly. "This walk is sorely needed, on my word! I must have eaten my weight at breakfast. There is something about sea travel that always whets my appetite."

Justine turned her gaze back to the gardens and suppressed the same sigh she'd been suppressing for a few weeks now.

CHAPTER THIRTEEN

WAS THERE NO ONE else who saw what Lila saw so plainly before her?

She glanced at Princess Amelia, but that one had not stopped talking, recalling every moment of her grand time at Stafford House. She strolled alongside Lila, her fingers trailing over bushes and vines, so lost in her own little world that she scarcely even looked up to see if Lila was listening, much less to notice her sister and the marquess in front of them.

Lila was certain Bardaline had failed to see it, judging by how dismissive of Douglas he'd been when she'd inquired yesterday.

Well, *she'd* noticed that something was brewing between the princess and the marquess. She did not miss how their fingers accidentally brushed together when they paused so that he might toss a coin into the fountain. He said he wished she would find a match as quickly as possible. She said his wish was better spent on a match for himself.

Nor did Lila miss the way the princess kept looking at the marquess from the corner of her eye, a charmingly pert smile on her lips. Of the way he looked at her—utterly attentive and striving not to appear enchanted.

Lila wondered if the two of them had even noticed. It was her experience that mutual regard is not always mutually recognized. When it came to affairs of the heart, the heart had a way of making a person question everything he or she thought they knew, confusing even the most pragmatic outlook on life.

She decided to test them. She quickened her step to catch up to them. Princess Amelia, sensing she was about to lose her captive audience, hurried to catch up, too.

"Splendid day, isn't it?" Lila asked cheerfully as she stepped in between Douglas and Princess Justine, looping her arms through both of theirs.

"Aye, that it is," Douglas agreed.

"One could not ask for a better day to receive a special guest."

"Who is our guest?" Princess Amelia asked with delight.

"A gentleman who should very much like to meet Her Royal Highness, Princess Justine. A *prince*."

"Only her? Why only her? There are *two* royal princesses presently at Prescott Hall, in case everyone has forgotten."

"No one has forgotten, Amelia," Princess Justine said. "It is rather impossible to forget with the daily reminders. But I'm the one who needs a match."

"Well, now, I could no' be more delighted for you, Your Royal Highness," said Douglas. "I can scarcely wait to see the gentleman who might win your hand. Although if you ask me—"

"Which I did not—"

"But if you had, I would have advised you to hold out for a king. You could unite nations in your bed…among other things."

Lila and Princess Amelia laughed.

"You clearly don't understand how these things work," said Princess Justine through a smile.

"Oh, but I understand it all too well," said Douglas.

"Perhaps *you* ought to engage the services of Lady Aleksander if you understand it so well. Her services come highly recommended."

"How kind of you to say, ma'am," Lila trilled. "I would indeed be happy to assist you, my lord."

"Thank you, but that will no' be necessary. I am perfectly capable of doing it all on my own."

"So you say," Princess Justine said cheerfully. "And yet, here you are, on the cusp of middle age—"

"Hardly—"

"And without any visible prospects." She leaned around Lila to smile at Douglas, and the effect, Lila thought, was very pleasing. Princess Justine really was a very pretty woman. It was a quiet beauty—it didn't strike you straightaway like Princess Amelia's looks, but built every time one laid eyes on her.

Amelia pushed her way into the group. "Well, *I* understand how these things work. Who is coming?"

"Principe Gaetano di Aggiani," Lila said.

"Pardon?" Douglas jerked his gaze to Lila. "Did you say Aggiani?"

"Oh, are you acquainted? Why, that's marvelous! You can be on hand when he arrives. There is nothing as helpful as a familiar face in the crowd for our foreign visitors."

"Please, Lady Aleksander, I can think of nothing more disturbing than finding Lord Douglas's familiar face in my crowd," said Princess Justine.

And with that feigned protestation, Lila understood the attraction was stronger than she knew, and she was positively filled with glee. It was entirely possible that the marquess and the princess were meant for each other. At the moment it was only a feeling she had, but as Valentin often said, there was nothing more accurate than her intuition. She didn't know how she divined such things; she only knew she was awfully good at it, and she knew what these two didn't know.

Yet.

Lila clasped her hands behind her back. "How are you are acquainted with Prince Gaetano, my lord?"

"We've met a time or two. A hunting party once. And then I had occasion to see him at the home of a mutual friend."

"Wonderful! Then perhaps you can vouch what an excellent match the prince would be for Her Royal Highness."

"No need for him to vouch," the princess chimed in. "The gentleman is not a king, but he's a prince! What more does one need to know?"

"I should think there would be one or two things you might want to know," Princess Amelia said. "Is he handsome? Is he rich?"

"That goes right to the heart of it, does it no'?" William asked with a chuckle. "Aye, he is handsome."

"And he is rich," Lila confirmed.

"Then *I* can scarcely wait to meet him," Princess Amelia said. "If Jussie doesn't want him, perhaps I will."

"Amelia," Princess Justine said.

"What?"

"He's not a doll to be passed between sisters."

Lila surreptitiously studied Lord Douglas as Princess Amelia argued that her question was a fair one, as all Weslorian princesses must eventually find a match.

Lila suspected Douglas would meet Robuchard's financial criteria for a match with the princess—meaning that surely as the heir to the Hamilton duchy, he had a fortune in his own right and would not drain the state coffers for his amusement.

But there was something else about him; something niggling at her. A shadow of a rumor, a bit of information she'd tucked away that was making her suspect he had a scandalous reputation. What was it that she was trying to recall? Whatever it was, she needed to know if it was something that would remove him from consideration.

Not that she cared, particularly. Reputations and scandals were things she was skilled at finessing. What she cared about was the spark in Princess Justine's eye when she looked at Lord Douglas, and the way he couldn't take his eyes off her. These two believed they were at odds, which simply delighted her. A man and woman who believed they were enemies made the most remarkable couples, ruled by passion. All she had to do was get them to see it…and then make them think it was their idea all along.

She was so exhilarated by this development that she almost skipped along.

"Madam? Lady Aleksander!"

They all stopped walking and turned around to see Bardaline striding down the path toward them. He was waving what looked like a calling card in his hand. When he reached Princess Justine, he bowed and held out the card to her.

The princess took it. She squinted. Held it out as far from her as she could until Princess Amelia snatched it from her hand and read it. "It's the prince!" she said excitedly.

"Wonderful!" Lila said. "Lord Bardaline, might we trouble you for tea? I think introductions on the terrace among all the lovely flowers would be perfect."

Bardaline bowed and started up the path. Princess Amelia hurried after him, probably to get a peek at the prince.

"Well, then," Douglas said. "The time has come for me to take my leave."

"Not at all, my lord! You must come and greet your friend," Lila insisted.

"I would no' call him friend. I've scarcely made his acquaintance."

He wouldn't be any closer to being Douglas's friend after today, either. Lila looped her arm through the marquess's. "He would be disappointed to miss you. Do at least come and greet him."

"I'll do as Her Royal Highness desires," Douglas said, his gaze on Justine.

"Do as you like," she said and began walking ahead of them.

He scowled after her, then turned a smile to Lila. "Then I'll come and greet him."

CHAPTER FOURTEEN

WILLIAM SNEEZED.

He shook it off, because sneezing interrupted his view, and he couldn't believe what he was witnessing. Justine was laughing and batting her eyes and leaning in to hear the simp Aggiani speak of nothing. Gone were any signs of nerves. She had turned into her sister, who was also batting and giggling and leaning in to the gentleman when he spoke. It was enough to make a grown man want to put his fist through an Italian.

Justine couldn't possibly be as enamored with this man as she was pretending to be. Was she doing it to goad him? To win the bloody bet he'd so foolishly made?

Really, what had he been thinking? What was he doing to himself? His goal, he reminded himself as he trailed after the lovers, was to be done with this task as quickly as possible, to return to his life of stopping his father from depleting the family wealth. He had given up his rakish ways...but Justine had looked so charmingly disheveled in the coach after leaving Stafford House that his cock had developed a mind of its own. He had desperately wanted to kiss her in that moment. He still did.

When he'd understood that Gaetano di Aggiani would be the first potential suitor, he'd almost laughed out loud. He'd managed not to, thankfully, but had begun at once to compose his missive to Robuchard in his head. *My Lord*

Robuchard, I should hope the Weslorian crown has not spent an exorbitant amount on the services of a match-maker, for her first potential suitor was quite possibly the worst candidate in all of Europe! A witch might have con-jured a slightly better man using a few gnomes and some mushrooms!

Or something to that effect.

William knew something of Gaetano di Aggiani, if any-one was interested in his opinion. It appeared no one was. But he knew Aggiani to be an insincere lothario when it came to women, and furthermore, he suspected he cheated at cards. Not that he'd ever played cards with him, but he seemed the type. William meant to pull Lady Aleksander aside as soon as possible and tell her so.

He began to suspect the matchmaker hadn't a clue what she was doing, and ought to be sent on her way. Why, he'd even volunteer to see her to the nearest port.

William sneezed again. He'd been sneezing since the in-troductions were made and they'd been forced to wander about the terrace, looking at the many displays of massive floral sprays. The smell was overwhelming him, sweet and sickly. His nose felt the size of an apple.

He sneezed again.

"*Felicita*, Douglas," Aggiani called cheerfully over his shoulder.

William scowled at the back of the man with the curly black hair and the sienna skin until he turned around.

"Unfortunately, there must be a particular variety some-where in the mix that does not agree with you. One does not know what one is getting when one buys all of what Covent Garden had to offer." He slid his gaze to Justine, making certain she'd heard him.

"*All* of Covent Garden?" Princess Amelia asked, successfully drawing his attention back to her. "Really?"

"Every last one. Five wagons in all, each one filled to the gills. It was quite the journey to Prescott Hall. The fine citizens of London came out of their houses to have a look, for they are *magnifici*, no?"

"They are *quite* spectacular," Princess Amelia agreed.

Aggiani looked slyly at Justine.

"*Je*, they are indeed," she agreed.

William sneezed again, then watched Aggiani offer his arms to both sisters so that he could lead them through the displays and they could study each and every bloom, as seemed to be his intent. He reluctantly followed. Lady Aleksander stayed back to walk with him. "I thought you said you were only vaguely acquainted with the prince, and yet, he greeted you so warmly."

"We are only vaguely acquainted." Aggiani had greeted him with false sincerity, and he was surprised Lady Aleksander hadn't understood it. Aggiani said it had been too long since their last meeting, and William said he couldn't recall when that was. Aggiani confessed he couldn't, either.

The trio disappeared into a copse of floral stands, and the sound of Justine's laugh rose, floating above the flowers. It startled William—he hadn't heard her laugh so gaily.

"I'm so *pleased* that Her Royal Highness seems to esteem him!" Lady Aleksander said.

William snorted. "Were I you, I'd no' be so certain that she thinks anything at all of him."

"Really? She appears to be enjoying herself," Lady Aleksander said with far more cheer than the situation warranted.

As if to prove it, they heard the laughter of both sisters. William and Lady Aleksander stepped around a particularly big spray just in time to see Justine put her hand lightly on Aggiani's shoulder as they bent to examine a flower.

William erupted into a bout of sneezing. He whipped his handkerchief out and dabbed at his eyes.

"I think she likes him very much," Lady Aleksander whispered as the trio moved on.

"Because she laughed? People laugh when they are angry or bored."

"Oh, but surely most people laugh when they are gay." Lady Aleksander smiled pertly at him and glided away. "Your Royal Highness, the tea has come. Shall we take it?" she called, one arm sweeping in the direction of the table that had been set with linen and silver, porcelain plates engraved with tiny red roses around the rims.

"*Je*, thank you," Justine said and walked with Aggiani to the table.

William stuffed his handkerchief into his pocket and reluctantly made his way to the table, too.

"No one appreciates the flowers quite like the Italians," Aggiani was saying as he helped Justine into a chair. "It is in our blood. Beautiful women, beautiful flowers, beautiful wine, beautiful food...all *Italiano*," he said and kissed the tips of his fingers and pretended to fling the kiss in the air.

"So ridiculous," William muttered.

"Pardon?" Aggiani asked.

"I said that your Italian blood has nothing to do with any of that."

Aggiani laughed. "My English, it is not perfected," he said in perfected English. "I mean that we Italians live for beauty. Alas, you did not see the faces of the merchants,

Your Royal Highness," he said to Justine. "I said to them, nothing but the best for the future queen of Wesloria."

"They are beautiful," Justine said again. She touched her fingers to the petals of a rose in the massive bouquet on the table, and William sneezed.

"Si." Aggiani glanced around the terrace, admiring his handiwork.

Princess Amelia frowned at William, as if he was sneezing purposefully to annoy her. "Your eyes are getting fat, my lord. Perhaps you ought to have a lie down."

William ignored her.

"I shall tell you a secret," Aggiani said and leaned forward, beckoning with his finger. Justine and Amelia leaned forward, too.

As Aggiani whispered into Justine's ear, Lady Aleksander whispered to William. "You can't deny that they make a lovely couple. Can you imagine the beautiful children they would bring into the world?"

He gave her a startled look. "That's putting the cart before the horse, aye?" From where he was sitting, the peacock Aggiani was the worst possible match for Justine. "I think, madam, that you do no' know my old friend as well as you think."

"Really? Tell me *everything* about the man you are not really acquainted with, but whom you refer to as your old friend."

William gave her a withering look, which lost its intended impact when the butler leaned between them and poured tea. William sneezed again. His eyes were watering, and his nose felt even larger. He had a decision to make—he could sit here and watch Aggiani charm his way into a crown, or he could remove himself before he couldn't breathe at all.

He could do without breath for a few more minutes.

"Have you ever smelled anything as fragrant?" Aggiani asked, gesturing limply to the flowers at the center of the table.

"I'm certain I have not," Justine said. She closed her eyes and inhaled the scent of what were supposedly the most perfect flowers ever to have been grown.

Princess Amelia sat forward in her seat to smell them, too. "The scent is *divine*." She smiled at Aggiani, and Aggiani smiled back.

"No one has ever come bearing so many flowers, have they?" Aggiani asked.

Justine drummed her fingers lightly on the table, and William perked up. Her smile seemed a bit tighter. "No one ever has."

Aha! She was tiring of this one already, and not a moment too soon. William sneezed again, and quite violently at that. But it was a triumphant sneeze, however, because of course he'd been right—Aggiani was not suitable for her.

The butler placed the scones onto plates and set them on the table. Aggiani shifted in his seat, and William couldn't see him because of those damn flowers, but he could bloody well hear him—he dominated the conversation. He talked about himself and his country, his family's palace. How fond he was of Wesloria. He again mentioned the flowers.

Princess Amelia listened intently with her chin on her hand to everything Aggiani said. She asked what his family's palace was like. Aggiani said it was built on a cliff and looked out over the ocean and the floors were marble and the ceilings gilded with gold. And that the vineyards were among the oldest in Italy and produced some of the finest wine in the world. That the flowers grown there were as fine as any you'd ever see at Covent Garden.

Princess Amelia was enthralled, clearly, but William couldn't read Justine. The laughter they'd heard earlier had disappeared. But she was listening, and every time Aggiani leaned forward, fixing his dark brown eyes and treacly smile on her, William sneezed.

At last, at long last, Lady Aleksander suggested they once again stroll the gardens. Naturally, William was relegated to bystander, made to trail behind the princesses with the matchmaker again. But he kept his eyes open, looking for the opportunity to speak to his charge.

Well. Not his charge, really, but his...responsibility. Except not a responsibility so much as a...well, something like that—charge, responsibility. Friend.

His moment came when Bardaline sought out Lady Aleksander. A messenger had come for her and she departed the group and left the rest of them to carry on to the small garden maze. The two ever-present footmen or guards or whatever they were positioned themselves at the entrance, so that no one could enter the maze while the princesses were rambling about.

His sneezing had stopped, thank the saints, and William was grumpily meandering along behind them when suddenly, Princess Amelia reached up and snatched the hat from Aggiani's head. With a shriek of laughter, she ran ahead with it.

Aggiani did, too, laughingly warning her that she ought not to toy with him.

William seized the moment to catch up with Justine, who watched her sister and Aggiani disappear around the next turn. "Well," he said.

"Well, what?"

"We can make quick work of this one if you will allow some friendly advice."

"No, thank you. Are you all right? Your eyes are nearly swollen shut and your nose is so *red*."

"I'm fine. Are you really swayed by a sea of flowers?"

She sighed. "Don't be daft. He's *supposed* to woo me."

"Oh aye, and that he will. That will be the thing you most esteem about him, mark me. He'll be charming and solicitous and far too admiring of himself."

She squinted at him. "What are you talking about?"

He was going about this all wrong. "How many times have you been forced to thank him for the flowers?"

Justine considered it a moment. She held up a finger. "I grant you, he is very pleased with his gift."

"Pleased! He practically begged you to genuflect in your praise of them."

"No, he didn't." She picked up her pace a little. "He seems very kind. And he's *very* handsome. Not enough attention is paid to fine looks in these things, if you ask me."

William snorted his opinion of that. "Is that what you want? Someone who is kind and handsome?"

Justine laughed. "Should I prefer someone who is cross and does not bring me flowers and is plain?"

"Should you no' want someone who is compatible with your person and is charming with only *one* bouquet? One is manageable. Five wagons full present a bit of a problem. This man is unsuitable to you as a lifelong companion. He'd probably drink your wine cellar dry, Justine. You're too—" he struggled to find an appropriate word. She was too *everything* for him "—soft for him."

She looked up at him with surprise. *"Soft?"*

"Soft."

Her brows dipped. "What makes you think I'm soft?"

"You may be a princess, aye, but you're a woman, and no' so different from the rest of your sex."

Her brows dipped even lower. "And what, pray tell, does *that* mean?"

"It means that women, on the whole, are easily conquered by men."

Her lovely mouth gaped open. "Not only is that not even remotely true, it's the most absurd thing you've said yet!"

"You have no' answered my question. Do you want a husband who requires praise at every turn? And once he's grown accustomed to extracting that from you, what will be next? To sit on your throne? To take your meetings with ministers?"

She stopped and stared at him with astonishment. "You went from too many flowers to complete usurpation?"

He groaned. Yes, he had, but only to make a point. "I'm only trying to say that this will be far less painful for you if you take my advice. I donna mean to boast, but I will say again, I've a good head for these things."

"Well, *I* have a good head for the true character of a person. And why shouldn't I admire a man's assertiveness in asking for what he wants? No matter what you think of it, no one can change the fact that *I* will be queen—not him."

William put his hands on his waist. "Mark my words, Justine. You will regret the day you met him."

"You are so *arrogant*." She lifted her chin. "I think he seems perfect."

"You do no' think that. You say so only to vex me, and in that, you have succeeded. I am trying to help you."

"William. My mother has engaged the expertise of Lady Aleksander for what I am sure is an outrageous sum. *You* don't know anything."

Wasn't it interesting how just a few words, strung together in a certain order, could highly motivate a man? Particularly when the person to utter the words was so bloody attractive and so bloody stubborn. "I will have great empathy for whoever ends up at your side, for you can be quite imperious."

She gave a bark of laughter. "That is truly the pot calling the kettle black!" She began striding toward the corner her sister and Aggiani had turned, marching away from him. William started after her. But when she reached that corner, she came to such an abrupt halt that he accidentally plowed into her, and had to catch her shoulders to keep from knocking her over. Not that she seemed to notice.

He looked over her head to see what had stopped her.

He was shocked into silence that one man could be so bloody stupid. And yet, in the corner, there he was, the dumbest man to inhabit the earth and Princess Amelia against the hedge. Their arms were wrapped around each other in a fierce embrace and they were kissing like long-separated lovers.

"Amelia!"

The kissing pair flew apart. Aggiani's face turned white as snow. "Your Royal Highness, I can explain." He stepped away from Princess Amelia and said, "She kissed me."

Princess Amelia gasped loudly. Her face turned crimson. "That is not true!" She looked to her sister for help.

"Amelia, come away from there," Justine said calmly, and held out her hand.

Princess Amelia glared at the Italian and hurried forward, taking her sister's hand. Justine put her arm around her sister's waist and off they marched, two women in a temper for very different reasons.

When they turned the corner of the maze, William looked back at Aggiani. The Italian prince looked as if he would be ill. "Well, then. You've gone and stepped in shite, have you no'?"

Aggiani sighed. "Do you blame me? The younger one, she's the beauty of the two."

William squinted at the man. In the first place, he was quite wrong. Princess Amelia was pretty, but Princess Justine was beautiful. In the second place, "Are you out of your fool mind?"

"It would appear," Aggiani said morosely.

The two of them began to make their way out of the maze, Aggiani sighing several times, the weight of his folly sinking in with each new step. As they neared the hall, he said, "'Twas a waste of money for the flowers. Did you see them? You won't see finer."

William didn't respond to his lament—his mind had wandered to the bet and how precisely he would go about collecting it.

CHAPTER FIFTEEN

AMELIA FLED TO her suite of rooms, embarrassed for what she'd done, incensed that Aggiani had blamed her for the kiss and proclaiming utter humiliation to her reputation. Justine wasn't certain how Amelia figured any humiliation when *she* was the injured party. Her sister seemed to have forgotten that Aggiani was to have been *her* suitor.

Not that she wanted him, God forfend. But it stung that he obviously didn't want her, either.

Justine had demanded—no, *commanded*—that Lady Aleksander send Aggiani away at once. Of course she'd had to explain to the matchmaker what had happened, as she had not been present, all while Aggiani talked over her, insisting that it had been a misunderstanding and that Amelia was the one who had kissed *him*.

His cowardly protests made Justine hate him even more.

Lady Aleksander had said of *course* he'd be sent *straight* away, then had ushered Aggiani into the small receiving room just off the entry for a word.

Justine had stared in astonishment at the closed door, stunned that Aggiani hadn't been tossed out on his ear. She looked at Bardaline, who avoided her gaze.

Did she have a say in *anything*?

She needed air.

She whirled around and started for the front door, barking at the guards not to follow her, but of course they did.

She strode across the drive, her skirt billowing out behind her. When she reached the stone fence, she whirled around. "Do *not* follow me under threat of death, do you hear?"

The two guards looked at each other as if silently debating death versus duty.

Justine picked up her hem and ran through the gate and into the estate's park in front of the house, running as fast as she could, wishing she could run from Prescott Hall and all the trappings of her birth. But she couldn't escape, and really, she couldn't run very far, either, not without collapsing for want of air.

She bent over, her hands on her knees, dragging air into her lungs. She glanced back and saw she'd hardly gained any ground at all. She straightened up and began to walk, her hand pressed to her corseted abdomen, still trying to catch her breath.

She thought of her parents, and how appalled they would have been had they witnessed what had happened. Robuchard would have called the ministers together to discuss. Her mother would have been so infuriated with Amelia that she probably would have forgotten Justine altogether. But her father...

Her father would tell her that she was fortunate to have seen the character of the man so soon. He would say that as the reprobate had kissed Amelia, he was certainly not worthy of her. And then he would add something about Amelia's impetuosity and how it would be incumbent on Justine to keep her close until she was properly married to save herself trouble and scandal.

Justine kept walking deeper into the park and through a flock of sheep that hardly spared her a glance. There was a small lake at the outer reaches of the park, and she headed for that, knowing there were a pair of benches near the shore.

The walk was restoring her, dousing her anger and shame and turning her numb. When she reached the lake, she put her hands on her waist and took several deep breaths before tilting her head to the late-afternoon sun.

As a girl, she'd never expected that disappointment would become such a constant in her life. She had assumed, naively, that as a future sovereign, everyone around her would want nothing more than to please her. Now she knew that disappointment *would* be a constant part of her life, whether she liked it or not. She would never be able to trust the motives of anyone who was not very close to her. She would never know if someone was seeking approval or favor or time from her.

How would she ever be at ease with so much distrust running through her?

She sat on a bench and leaned forward, covering her face for a few moments.

It does no good to anyone to mope. Her father's words. He'd said that every moment spent moping was a moment lost to the kingdom's good. "Quite easy to say it," Justine muttered. But she lifted her head. He was right—there truly was no point in moping. What was done was done, and it hardly mattered, really, because she had no desire for Aggiani. She'd been caught up in his fine looks, excited that someone handsome and royal might want her. She hadn't been harmed, and but for the humiliation of once again seeing a gentleman's interest turn to Amelia, she was glad to be rid of him.

But she would have a word with Lady Aleksander. If that was the sort of gentleman the lady intended to introduce to her, Justine would dismiss her.

She stood up, straightened her skirts, took another deep breath, then turned around, prepared to go back to the hall. But she had a fright, as she saw William leaning against a tree several feet away.

"How long have you been standing there?"

"A moment."

She looked past him, expecting to see others.

"If you're looking for your guards, they've been called away."

"I don't believe you." They were always nearby. "Why?"

"Because your sister has chosen the moment to confront her accuser."

"Oh." She winced, imagining how that might unfold. Amelia could be volatile. "Was it very bad?"

"If you consider a lot of shouting and tears to be bad, then, aye."

She sighed. "I'm not sorry to have missed it."

William pushed away from the tree. "How are you, Princess?"

"I should ask *you*. You look far less puffy than you did earlier. But still a bit red."

"How kind of you to notice. And you?"

"I'm fine." She absently rubbed her earlobe. Maybe not perfectly well, but well enough.

He tilted his head to one side. "A wee bit angry, perhaps?"

"What could have possibly given you that idea?" she drawled.

"Oh, I donna know—I suppose the way you sprinted away from Prescott Hall. You're faster than I would have guessed."

"Wouldn't *you* be angry?"

"Angry? No." He strolled toward her. "I'd be murderous. It must be maddening for you."

"What must be?"

He paused a couple of feet from her and shrugged. "All of it, I'd reckon."

How strange—it was almost as if William was in her head.

He took a step closer. "Meaning, the responsibility of your birth and what will come when you assume the throne. The pressing need for a husband that will be followed by a more urgent need for an heir. This process seems…unnatural to the true course of marital felicity. But perhaps necessary, given your birth."

She could not think of another time someone had commiserated or understood her position in this life. Everyone seemed to believe she was incredibly lucky to have been born into it. "Do you really believe that? Or are you saying it only to appease me?"

He laughed. "Have I yet said anything to appease you?"

"No."

He reached up and removed something from her hair. He held it out—a fragile petal of a flower bloom. "I'm no' unfamiliar with this sort of courtship—my sister suffered similarly to you."

Justine winced. "A matchmaker?"

"Worse. My mother. She was desperate to see Susan properly married, to someone whom she deemed appropriate for the daughter of the Duke of Hamilton. There was a parade of rich Scotsmen until she determined which would suit her. I always thought it was a bit like choosing a new milk cow."

In spite of herself, Justine laughed. "And what about you, Lord Douglas? Surely, your mother is just as desperate to see you properly married. You'll provide the heirs, after all."

"It is mentioned frequently," he said with a smile.

"Then why haven't you married? I seem to recall everyone talking about your supposed interests when I was in London before. I saw with my own eyes the number of young ladies interested in you."

"Did you?" He looked pleased by that. "Canna say I recall."

The self-confidence of gentlemen never ceased to amaze her. "Why haven't you married?"

"Och," he said congenially. "There are issues that complicate a marriage for me, lass. I am the heir, like you."

Meaning, she thought, that the woman who would bear his offspring and hopefully produce a future duke would have to meet all the necessary requirements for mergers of powerful families.

"No one has ever caught your eye?"

He smiled lopsidedly. "I didna say that. There was one, many years ago. Alas, someone else had caught her eye. And you? Is there a certain gentleman who has your heart?"

She immediately thought of Aldabert, and the painful memory pierced her heart. How easily and quickly she'd fallen in love. How she'd believed him, trusted him. Amelia said it was because no man had ever paid attention to her in that way, and she was inexperienced. "There was someone who held it in his hands," she said truthfully. "But he smashed it."

William's brows knit. "It pains me to hear that."

Justine waved a hand to dismiss it. "It's done. Perhaps now you understand why my mother insisted on a matchmaker. She doesn't trust me."

"Sounds a wee bit like my mother," he said. "Perhaps you and I are more alike than we know?"

"Oh, I don't think so," she said, but she was smiling. "For example, you are bothersome and I am not."

"Aye, I canna deny it. But I should like to at least be considered a friend."

"Hmm… I'll think about it."

"Donna trust me?"

She laughed. "Not in the *least*."

He grinned. "Nevertheless, there is something else we should address."

"Is there?"

"It is the small matter of a wager fairly made."

In the chaos, she'd forgotten about her ridiculous bet. William hadn't, and he obviously liked the surprise on her face, because his grin turned into a smile that made her feel a little warm.

"I didn't…" Her voice trailed away. She honored her word, and she'd meant that bet in the heat of the moment, of course…but she'd assumed she'd win. Handily.

"You seem confused, Your Royal Highness. You made a wager and I would like to collect."

"You can't just demand it."

"I'm no' demanding it. I am reminding you. Aggiani was unsuitable—do you disagree?"

"No! He was unsuitable in every possible way."

"Then if you concede that I was *right*, and you were *wrong*, you should honor your bet."

His gray eyes were sparkling with merriment and a bit of heat, and Justine felt that sparkle sizzle all the way down to her belly. "There you go again, telling me what to do. And I don't really care for the way you emphasize *right* and *wrong*."

"Mmm. I think perhaps you fear the consequence of your wager."

"Certainly not." She wasn't *afraid*, for God's sake. But his sheer masculinity made her nervous. Aldabert had been less…virile.

"Well, then?"

It didn't help that his smile was so alluring. She cleared her throat. She rubbed her cheek in the spot where her skin was tingling for no apparent reason. She clasped her hands behind her back and lifted her face. "All right. Carry on."

He looked confused. "What are you doing?"

"Presenting my face."

His brows sank. "I donna accept."

She gaped at him. "I'm honoring my bet! Why would you not accept?"

"Because it is *your* debt to pay, no' mine. And you're stiff as a log. You donna present your *face* for a kiss."

"There are rules now?" Justine was many things, but she was not *stiff*. She stepped forward, put her hands on his arms, then rose up on her toes and touched her lips to his, lingering for a beat or two, then sinking back down on her heels.

The feel of his lips confirmed her expectations—they were soft and firm at once, and she wasn't supposed to feel anything but a *peck*. And yet, she felt suddenly hot. But she'd done it. She all but dusted her hands of the task. "There you are. My debt is paid."

William was staring at her quizzically. Then his hands found his hips. "Was that some sort of jest?"

"No!"

He scraped his fingers through his hair. "*That* wasn't a kiss, Justine."

She had the sudden fear that kissing in Scotland was

something quite different than what she had experienced and no one had told her. It would be her second humiliation of the day if that was true. "It was!"

He shook his head. He reached up and touched her face, his fingers as light as air, and the tingling feeling in her cheek began to spread like liquid over her. He shifted forward. She felt his arm go around her waist. "That was no kiss," he said quietly. He moved his hand, his palm against her neck, his thumb touching the corner of her mouth. His hand was warm against her skin, and the scent of him musk and clove. He looked at her lips, then at her eyes and then he lowered his head to hers.

Whatever Justine thought about kissing was drowned by William's kiss. She opened her mouth to his, felt his tongue slide in between her teeth and tangle with hers. He cupped her face, angling her head slightly, nipping at her lips.

Her heart pounded a frantic rhythm—that kiss was full of pleasure, full of craving and anticipation, full of a thirst that could not be slaked in this park, on this day...but oh, how her thoughts raced ahead to when and where and how that thirst might be quenched. She was pressed against his hard chest, her breath and pulse dangerously erratic—

And then, William ended it. He let go of her waist and drew back from her. With the tip of his little finger he swiped his bottom lip, as if he'd had a nibble of a morsel. But his eyes said something different. His eyes were the gray of storm clouds. "*Now* your debt is paid, madam."

Once, her father told her that she must always be careful to understand the stakes in any negotiation. She had clearly not understood the consequences of this wager—she felt as if she was bobbing along on a stream with no control over anything. "Very well, then. Good." She touched her nape, uncertain how to proceed.

His smile suggested that he understood she had miscalculated, that he knew the effect he had on her and that he enjoyed it. "Shall we return to the hall?"

"Right. The hall and the disturbance there."

William offered his arm.

She took it. They began to walk as if that kiss had not happened. From the corner of her eye, she stole a look at him. His smile had settled into a look of perfect satisfaction. "This doesn't mean you may advise me. I will keep my own counsel."

"I wouldna dream of it."

"And you should not think it is an invitation to tell me what to do."

"Never, as you will be queen, high priestess of all."

She could feel a smile on her lips. "Exactly so. You were lucky this time."

"Aye, sheer luck. So much luck, in fact, that I could have been blind and still known he was not for you."

"*Je*, well, I would discourage you from assuming that you will be so lucky again."

"I would never," he said and put his hand on hers and gave it a bit of a squeeze. "I would be a fool to question your counsel of yourself." He winked at her.

And Justine's heart fluttered madly.

CHAPTER SIXTEEN

PRINCESS JUSTINE RETURNED to the hall looking a bit wind-blown. She'd left Lord Douglas on the drive, Lila noticed, looking a bit windblown himself as he waited for a foot-man to bring him his hat and riding cloak.

But Lila had other things to think about in that moment: the princesses were furious.

Princess Amelia declared herself a victim of Aggiani's advances, her honor stained. She stubbornly refused to en-tertain Justine's idea that perhaps she had helped to stain it. Princess Amelia was so adamant that she had done nothing wrong that she flounced from the room, loudly proclaim-ing that no one ever cared what she thought.

Princess Justine was just as displeased, but for very dif-ferent reasons. The moment her sister left the room, she turned gold eyes dark as honey to Lila. "Why did you not dismiss him straightaway as I asked?"

"I beg your pardon, Your Royal Highness, but it took a bit of negotiation."

"Negotiation! What possible negotiation would he be entitled to?"

"He was concerned what might be said to his father about the incident."

The princess stared at Lila. But her gaze slid to Lady Bardaline, who was very close to them, her ears practically pointed at the princess like a shepherd's dog. Lila could tell the princess didn't want to speak in front of her lady's maid, which she found curious, because she certainly had no qualms about speaking her mind all day long in front of Lord Douglas.

"Lady Bardaline...could you see after the supper arrangements?" Lila asked.

Lady Bardaline jerked her gaze to Lila. "Ah..." She obviously did not want to be dismissed, but appeared to weigh her options. She at last gave a curt nod. "Of course." She quit the room, leaving Lila alone with Princess Justine.

But she did not close the door as she exited, so Lila did it for her. When she turned back, the princess was glaring at her. "Your Royal Highness—"

"Before you utter a word," Princess Justine said, "you should know that what happened here today was a calamity of the highest order. It was wretched in every *possible* way."

"It was indeed," Lila agreed and bowed her head apologetically. "He was a true reprobate."

The princess's brows rose. "Then why did you invite him here?"

"Shall we sit?"

"No! Tell me why."

"Very well." Lila had to proceed carefully here. Of course she had no way of knowing that Aggiani would present himself to be an ass. She hadn't expected the princess to care for him, but she hadn't expected he would be caught with her sister, either, for heaven's sake. Valentin would laugh when he heard this tale. But she needed to get the princess past Aggiani's terrible mistake if she was to have any hope of making the match she had planned for the princess. "There is a method to proper matchmaking that may be difficult for the layperson to understand. But sometimes it's helpful to have someone who might test compatibility with a subject in a variety of ways."

The princess's dark brows knitted. *"What?"*

"It's the way I go about finding a perfect match for you, ma'am. I never expected you to think Principe di Aggiani was anything other than a gentleman with too many flowers. I didn't believe he would suit you for more than a pleasant afternoon."

The princess glared at her. "Are you *trifling* with me, Lady Aleksander?"

"I am not. I can confidently say now that I've seen a few things—"

"What *things*?"

"Well, for example, I didn't know for certain if infidelity was something that would concern you."

As she expected, the princess gaped at her. "Are you *mad*?"

Lila clasped her hands tightly at her waist. "I certainly hope not." The princess's frown deepened. "Some people in your position care only for the strength of national alliances in a potential mate, and not conjugal compatibility. Particularly."

Princess Justine's eyes were wide with disbelief now. Lila hardly believed herself. "And I wasn't certain if you… would you say you are one of those people?"

"No, I am not one of those people," the princess said angrily. "Could you not simply have asked me this *thing*? Compatibility in all its forms is very important to me. You said you would find someone compatible to me!"

"And that's exactly what I intend to do. I beg your pardon that I didn't explain precisely how I would go about it. I'm learning about you, too, you understand."

"No, I don't understand, madam. This is madness! What

am I to think? What of the next one? Is he to be some sort of test, too?"

"Of course not."

"Of course not," the princess scoffed. "Who *is* the next one?"

Lila had someone traveling to London as they spoke. A good candidate, someone she thought might be suitable for the princess in the event her instincts were wrong about Douglas. But she wasn't certain if he would be the next one. She had some work to do, and the longer she stood here apologizing for Aggiani, the less time she had to think. "I am reluctant to say as I should like to review a few things to make certain he is someone who could make you happy."

"I sincerely hope for both our sakes that your next introduction is more compatible than this one."

"Rest assured he will be," Lila said with all the bravado that came from years of assuring skittish clients when she hardly knew herself. "Shall I have the flowers removed?"

"I think that would be appropriate," the princess snapped, and strode from the room.

As soon as the door closed behind her, Lila sank onto the nearest chair, laid her head back and closed her eyes. What a terrible disaster this day had been. She didn't know which was the worst of it—that Aggiani was a true reprobate with no more sense than a rock? That Princess Amelia had come close to losing her reputation and may have already lost her royal bearing? Or that Princess Justine hated her?

All of it.

Lila opened her eyes and sat up. There was at least one thing she'd gotten quite right—the spark between the crown princess and Lord Douglas was undeniable. She needed a little more information about him. And she knew just the person to give it to her.

CHAPTER SEVENTEEN

BECKETT HAWKE, LORD IDDESLEIGH, otherwise known as Beck to most in London, greeted Lila at the door. "Lila!" he bellowed. He was holding a small girl child who had been napping on his shoulder, but who was startled awake and began to cry. Beck seemed not to hear the girl's cries, grabbed Lila into a one-armed hug she was not expecting and pulled her into the entry of his house on Upper Brook Street in Mayfair. "It's so good to see you after all these years. Kept out of trouble, have you?" He laughed.

Lila smiled. "That was ages ago, Beck."

"Scandal never ages, darling. Come in, come in! You've not met my wife."

Lila had grown up around the corner from Beckett Hawke and his sister, Caroline. When they were children, they'd often been in each other's company. When Beck was sent off to university, he would bring them both trinkets when he visited home. Once, Caroline tried to match Lila to Beck, but when Beck discovered it, he'd scolded his sister and said that Lila was like a cousin to him, and besides, he had no intention of ever marrying, anyway.

Lila followed him into a large salon with pale green silk walls and yellow upholstered furnishings. At a table in the center of the room, she noticed straightaway an *incredibly* handsome man was reading a broadsheet. One rarely saw such male beauty in one man. Two young girls were beneath the table where he was seated, playing with dolls. Their hair looked as if they'd been running, falling out of ribbons. Another small girl was pulling a red toy carriage by a string around and around the table.

"May I introduce the governess, Mr. Donovan," Beck said. "Donovan, my dear friend, allow me to present Lady Aleksander."

Mr. Donovan put down his paper and stood. "I prefer governor." He stepped over the girls without even looking and sauntered forward with a charming smile. "Lady Aleksander. The pleasure is most assuredly mine." He bowed over her hand, his eyes meeting hers as he kissed her knuckles. But then he promptly dropped her hand and turned away. "Children, come and meet your papa's guest."

The two older girls looked up as if they'd just noticed Lila. They leaped to their feet and raced forward, more blond and brown curls bouncing out of their ribbons. The smaller of the two threw her arms around Lila's legs, almost knocking her off balance. "Oh!"

Mr. Donovan reached for the girl's collar and dragged her back. "A little less enthusiasm, Maren."

"Beg your pardon," Beck said, and put the one he was holding on the floor. She crawled away. "That one is a bit of a hellion," he said, pointing at Maren.

"I'm not, Papa!" She giggled.

"What am I, Papa?" The bigger girl asked.

"Mathilda, my love, you are a rapscallion."

"Me, Papa!" The girl with the red carriage flew across the room, knocking into her older sister.

"Maisie, you are a potato."

The smallest girl looked to her sisters for assurance that was good.

"She's not a potato!" Maren said, laughing.

"And what is Meg?" Mathilda asked.

Beck looked at the baby crawling across the floor. "Meg is an angel as she doesn't yet talk."

All three of the girls giggled.

Mr. Donovan bent down and picked up the one with the wagon, holding her upside down. "Come along, then, all of you. It's teatime." He walked across the room with the one girl hanging upside down and squealing with laughter, and bent down to pick up the baby. At the far end of the large room was a child's table, set with a child's play tea service.

It was a remarkable scene of domesticity that Lila had never in the wildest of dreams imagined she would see in Beck's house. The last she'd seen him, he'd preferred the gentlemen's clubs and ladies' salons to home.

"So good to see you, Lila," Beck said. "And how does Valentin do?"

"He is very well, thank you. He'll join me soon."

Beck gestured to a settee and the two of them sat. "I was delighted to receive your note. I told Blythe—that's my wife, formerly Blythe Northcote—I said, you will like Lila very much. She was the only one who could ever convince Caro to do anything she didn't want to do."

Lila laughed. "As I recall it, Eliza Tricklebank could talk her into anything that her sister Hollis couldn't. I was a mere bystander."

"You were all incorrigible."

Just then, a plump, broad-shouldered woman with thick ringlets of ginger hair entered the room. She was quite obviously pregnant. She walked up behind Beck, and with her hands on his shoulders, she leaned over and kissed his cheek. "Is this the incomparable Lila Aleksander?"

Incomparable?

"Lady Iddesleigh, allow me to introduce my friend, Lady Aleksander."

Lila stood. Lady Iddesleigh came around the settee and looked her up and down, a smile on her face. "How well you look! Darling, you didn't tell me she was pretty. You're *very* pretty, Lady Aleksander."

"Ah…thank you."

"Lila and I were childhood friends," Beck said.

"Then why have I never made your acquaintance?" his wife asked.

"I live in Denmark with my husband now."

"Oh, how lovely!"

"She was forced to leave London because of a dreadful scandal," Beck added.

Lila's eyes flew wide with surprise.

His wife settled into a chair and leaned forward, all ears, her eyes shining with eagerness. "What *sort* of scandal?"

"I'll tell you later," Beck said.

The child Maisie had escaped the pretend tea service and climbed over the back of the settee where Beck was sitting, then began to make her way down his body, head-first, covering Beck's face in skirts and petticoats. He batted the fabric away with one hand. "You must tell us what brings you here," he said.

"Maisie? The tea is served," Mr. Donovan announced. The girl rolled over the arm of the settee and landed…well, Lila didn't know how she landed, as she couldn't see her. But in the next moment the girl was up and running across the room. She watched with fascination as Mr. Donovan draped a towel over one arm and stood back as the two oldest girls began to argue who was going to pour. Maisie, having arrived too late to be considered for pouring, yanked a lock of hair of one of the older girls.

The howling that commenced was enough to almost launch Lila from her seat.

The girls' parents seemed not to notice or pretended to ignore the caterwauling at the other end of the salon.

Lila tried to do the same. "How is Caroline? Is she well?"

"Exceedingly," Beck said. "She's a gardener now, of all things. She's married to a prince, as you know. She's coming to London in the next week or so, so you must come round and see her! How long will you be in town?"

"A few weeks, I think."

"Yes, yes, and as to that, what *are* you doing in London, darling?"

"I have come to offer my services to the young Weslorian princess." To Lady Iddesleigh, she added, "I am a matchmaker."

"Ah, yes, I've heard all about the fair princess," said Beck.

"You have?" Lila asked.

"We all have!" his wife said cheerfully. "Everyone knows she is here and in search of a king."

"A prince consort," Lila corrected her.

"All the same," Lady Iddesleigh said agreeably.

But it wasn't at all the same—one was a ruler, and the other a spouse of a ruler.

"That's it, that's why you're here!" Beck said suddenly. "You're looking for someone to match to the princess. I've got it. The young chap from Birmingham. What was his name, darling? A viscount who has just come into a large inheritance."

"Edward," Lady Iddesleigh said, her brow knitting. "Edward, Edward…"

"Northrup," Mr. Donovan supplied from across the room.

"Northrup!" the Iddesleighs shouted at the same time.

Lila smiled serenely. "I shall keep him in mind. But I've quite a few of my own. I've come about one name in particular, whom I think you know rather well. I should like to inquire…discreetly of course—"

"Of course," Beck hastened to assure her.

"We are the soul of discretion," Lady Iddesleigh chirped. "Who is it?"

"Lord Douglas, Marquess of Hamilton," Lila said.

The room stilled. She had the attention of all three adults and at least one of the girls.

"William Douglas," Beck repeated, sounding amazed.

"Yes?" She looked around at their shared surprise. "Is something wrong?"

Beck looked at his wife, then burst out laughing. Donovan laughed, too. Even the girls began to laugh, although it was quite clear they didn't know why. But the laughter excited them. They got up from their miniature tea table and one of them began to turn cartwheels.

"William Douglas!" Beck said again through a wheeze. "Of all people!"

"Why?" Lila asked again.

"Oh dear," Beck said and tried to contain himself. "Got off on the wrong foot a few years ago. Doesn't care for the princess."

Lila frowned with bewilderment. Had they confused the Douglas she meant with someone else? "Doesn't he?"

"Darling, you don't know what you're saying," Lady Iddesleigh said to her husband, still giggling. "Sometimes a gentleman appears not to care for a woman when, in fact, he cares for her quite a lot."

"That makes no sense, love," Beck said.

"Aye, she's right about that," offered Donovan.

"Lady Aleksander, what would you like to know about Lord Douglas?" Lady Iddesleigh asked.

"I must speak confidentially," Lila said again.

"Yes, yes," Lady Iddesleigh said, gesturing for her to continue.

"Papa, what does confachly mean?" the oldest girl asked as she climbed onto his lap.

"It means not for your ears, darling."

Maren climbed up, too, then pushed Mathilda off Beck's lap. Mathilda shrieked.

"Come here, Mathilda," Beck's wife said. The girl who had tumbled to the floor hopped up and ran sobbing to her mother.

Beck set the other one down. "Off you go, Maren. All of you, off you go. And of course, Lila, whatever you say will not leave these four walls."

"Umm…" Lila wasn't very certain about that. She glanced around at them all, the adults attentive, the children involved in some sort of contretemps under the larger table now.

Beck looked around, too. "Yes, I see your concern," he said. "Donovan?"

"Right." The handsome Mr. Donovan stood. "Aye, come along, lassies, it's time to pet the pony."

"The pony! Me first!" shouted Maren.

"No, me!" shouted Mathilda.

"Me!" shouted Maisie.

Donovan picked up the baby, and with a smile for Lila, he led the gaggle of girls out of the room.

"I do hope the next one is a boy," Beck said wistfully as he watched them go. "All right, Lila."

Lila could suddenly think much more clearly with the girls gone. She sat up. "I think that Lord Douglas would make Her Royal Highness a very fine match. But I need to know if there is anything I should be aware about him."

Husband and wife stared at her. "You don't say," Lady Iddesleigh said, her voice full of wonder. Then husband and wife looked at each other.

They seemed alarmingly incredulous. "What is it?" Lila asked.

A butler rolled in with a real tea service and began to hand cups around. Lila said, "It seems as if there is something you think I ought to know."

"No, no, we don't know very much at all, do we, darling?" Beck said. "I mean, how could we possibly? We are chained to our salon by the presence of four young souls." He accepted a cup from the butler. "But I *have* heard it said that his father the duke is financially incompetent and has made some questionable decisions."

"Yes, darling, but remember, we believe that Douglas has his own funds," Lady Iddesleigh said.

Remember? So they had discussed this before.

"I'm certain he does," Beck said as if it was fact.

Lila accepted a cup of tea. "Is that the only cause for concern?" She did not miss the exchange of looks between husband and wife, or how pink Lady Iddesleigh's complexion turned.

"Well," Lady Iddesleigh said as she studied her tea. "There has been a rumor."

Lila couldn't help but laugh. "There is always a rumor."

"Yes, but this…" Lady Iddesleigh shook her head.

Lila turned her attention to Beck. He winced. "There was a rumor of a young woman in Scotland. Her family has made…accusations."

"Oh dear," Lila said. "What sort of accusations?"

"The usual sort." Beck drank his tea.

"Specifically?"

"We don't know," Lady Iddesleigh said abruptly.

"We don't?" Beck asked.

"We don't," his wife said firmly. "We've heard nothing but idle talk, and particularly from one person who we both know will make up a story if she has none to share. We should not cast aspersions on that man, darling. We've heard a rumor, we've no idea if it's true and we'll not say more."

Beck winced. "Yes, but I—"

"I'm very sorry, Lady Aleksander, but that's all we know," Lady Iddesleigh said firmly.

"You didn't give me a chance to speak," Beck complained.

"You don't need one, dearest."

"Very well, my love, but allow me to at least opine the rumor is worth investigating. I could have Donovan inquire—"

"Oh no, no, thank you," Lila said hastily. That was all she needed; Beck's "governor" about town asking indelicate questions. "This is why I came to you first, Beck. You always know what is happening and I trust your discretion. I appreciate your frankness. As you can imagine, these matters require some finesse." She smiled.

"I understand. And I am known for my discretion," Beck said.

Lila nodded. She sipped her tea, her mind racing for a solution. "Does his lordship have, perhaps, a close friend who might know more?" She was fishing, but one never knew what someone might offer when a question was asked.

"Mr. Jonathan Ashley," Lady Iddesleigh said. "He claims to be very well acquainted with Douglas."

Beck gasped. "Blythe, darling, *no*. Of all people, not Ashley."

"But they attended St. Andrew's together!"

"Yes, and now they can hardly abide one another. They had a terrible quarrel some years ago and have never patched things up. Better to leave that one alone."

Lila filed that name away.

"I don't know of anyone else," Lady Iddesleigh said. "Really, my love, it isn't very good of us to speculate." She turned a smile to Lila and shifted forward in her seat. "Tell us, what is the princess really like? I recall her sister being a beauty, and she was…well, honestly, I don't remember."

"She is a remarkable young woman," Lila said. "She will be a wonderful queen." She began to speak about Justine Ivanosen. But in her head she was already thinking of the work she had to do on William Douglas.

CHAPTER EIGHTEEN

WILLIAM'S LATEST TELEGRAPH to Robuchard was met with resistance on the part of Ewan MacDuff. William didn't know how or when they'd crossed the boundary where his valet felt free to read his messages, but here they were.

He'd dashed off his report yesterday, making it short and very much to the point.

> You must remove your matchmaker at once! She has shown herself to be incapable to the task! You will end with a reprobate as a prince consort if you do not heed my advice!

Ewan held the paper in his meaty hand, his lips silently sounding out the words as he read by squinting at the page.

"What is it?" William demanded.

"The telegraph, milord. They'll no' allow the markings."

"The markings?"

He pointed a thick finger at the exclamation points. "The dispatch, he'll no' allow it."

William folded his arms. "Those *markings*, as you call them, are necessary to convey the depth of my feeling on this very important topic. Tell *that* to dispatch."

"Aye, milord." He trundled off, and he and William both knew he would not have a word with dispatch and would remove the marks. William would have to hope that Robu-chard could read the depth of his feeling in his words alone.

He was on his way to Prescott Hall today. He had ar-ranged to share the Duke of Grafton's box at the opera and was feeling rather proud of himself for having thought of it. The entrance for boxholders was different than the en-trance for patrons on the floor, so the princess would not find herself in the midst of an unruly crowd of gawpers. She'd be above them, so to speak.

As William suspected he would be, Grafton was more than delighted to invite the princess to the opera. He had made a bold case for his son, the Earl of Euston, to attend as well, but William had argued against it. They had finally agreed that Lord and Lady Grafton would host William and the two royal princesses, and William could hardly wait to tell Justine what he'd done.

He arrived at Prescott Hall shortly after luncheon to de-liver the invitation.

Lord Bardaline greeted him in the receiving salon. "Ah," he said as if he was expecting someone else, and pulled a face that suggested he was disappointed by finding Wil-liam standing there. "Her Royal Highness is at her exer-cise." He led William down the long hallway—mercifully free of flowers—and onto the back terrace. Once there, he pointed to one of the lower terraces.

Justine, dressed in her fencing attire, was advancing on a man who was twice her size. His footwork was familiar in its sluggishness—the opponent kept stumbling as he tried to parry. "Who is her opponent?"

"Lord Mawbley."

"Again?"

Bardaline shrugged. "He seems to enjoy the sport."

"I'm no' sure that's what he enjoys," William muttered.

Justine forced Mawbley back on his heels again. "She's very good, aye?"

"Mmm," Bardaline said as if unconvinced. When William gave him a look, he shrugged. "I don't consider it appropriate activity for a future queen. Particularly if one is expected to dress in that manner."

William thought dressing in a long skirt with a petticoat would make it a damn sight harder to fence properly. "I would think citizens of Wesloria would like to know that their sovereign can wield a sword and won't wilt at the first sign of trouble. That she can, in fact, lead the charge."

"All very good qualities for a medieval queen," Bardaline said with a slight sniff.

A small dog with a white-and-brown coat suddenly appeared and bounded up the terrace steps, racing for William's feet. He automatically squatted down to greet the dog. Not a pup, but not very old, either. The dog was eager to lick his hand. William indulged him for a moment, and happened to glance up just as Justine pinned Mawbley with the tip of her blade at his throat.

Mawbley dropped his weapon and held out his arms, surrendering. Then he bowed deeply and applauded her. William could hear Justine laugh as she took a bow.

Bardaline set off down the stairs to speak to her, the dog on his heels, leaving William on the terrace alone. He didn't like to be left standing here as if he was the next suitor, so he, too, went down the stairs to the lower level. He watched Justine remove her mask, that long tail of dark braid streaked with the thin strip of white tumbling down her back. He found it exceedingly difficult not to ogle her in her fencing attire. It required what felt like the strength of ten thousand mules. He envied Mawbley his mask.

Justine listened to what Bardaline said, but made a sound

of glee when she saw the dog and bent down to scoop it up. When she stood, she noticed William and smiled, her eyes glittering like panned gold. The effect of that smile on his body was startling. It felt a bit like jumping into a cold lake—all of his senses came alive.

She handed her weapon and mask to Bardaline. "Good afternoon, my lord."

"Your Royal Highness," he said, bowing. "I would ask how you fare but I see that you are very well indeed."

"Thank you, I am." She held up the dog. "You've not yet met Dodi."

He reached out to scratch the dog's ears. "Pleased to make your acquaintance, Dodi."

"She is a gift from Lord Mawbley." She smiled prettily at her opponent.

"How very kind of him," William said.

Mawbley removed his mask and smirked in William's direction. "Her Royal Highness misses her dogs."

William had to swallow down his intense desire to tell the smug bastard that he knew that. He said instead, "Lord Mawbley, how do you do?"

"Very well. If you've come to fence, I should warn you that Her Royal Highness has bested me in every bout."

If he meant to convey that he'd spent much time in Justine's presence to annoy William, he succeeded. "I'm no' surprised. I think we all fully expect to be speared whenever she holds a sword. And your footwork is no' as good as it ought to be."

One of Mawbley's brows rose. His laugh was a little stiff. "Very true, my lord. But at least I will pick up a foil and attempt it. Have you?"

"He has not," Justine chirped as she stroked the dog's fur. "Perhaps he fears being bested."

"I donna fear it. I know it is inevitable. I never learned the sport."

"Didn't you?" Mawbley asked. "I thought all Scots were proficient with a sword and a caber."

"I could teach you, Douglas!" Justine said delightedly. "To fence, that is—I don't know what a caber is. But fencing is exhilarating. Particularly when you win."

William and Mawbley laughed politely. "I would be honored," William said and directed his smile at Mawbley, who certainly had not intended to give the princess a reason to be in William's company.

"My Lord Mawbley, you have my undying gratitude for serving as my opponent today. Thank you." She buried her face in the neck of the dog. "And again, I can't thank you enough for the gift of little Dodi. I have longed for the companionship of a dog. I will see to it that she dines like a queen today. Thank you again for coming."

Mawbley was clearly surprised to be dismissed. "Your Royal Highness. If at any time you need me to stand in—"

"Yes, thank you," she said cheerfully, but William noticed the quick glance she gave Bardaline. Her master of the chamber stepped in between her and Mawbley as she walked across the terrace with the dog.

William didn't hesitate to join her. She glanced at him as he reached her side. "You're here *again*." She sounded... pleased?

"I am." He scratched the dog under the chin. The dog began to pant. "Mawbley again? And where is your matchmaker? I expected to see a queue of gentlemen on the drive."

"I don't know where she is. She's been away for more than a day, which suits me perfectly, as I don't want a queue of gentlemen at my door. My hope is that she has found a rowboat and is, as we speak, rowing Aggiani away from these shores."

"Then we are united in our hopes."

Justine laughed and stopped walking a moment. She used the end of her braid to tease the dog. Dodi tried to bite it. "She did mention that I would meet two potential matches next week." She started up the steps. So did William. "One of them, she said, is a very wealthy prince who is highly regarded. A European, like me."

"That must please you enormously. Did she give a name?"

"Oh, I'm certain she did, but I've forgotten."

She tossed her braid over her shoulder. The tail end of it hit him in the shoulder. "And who is the other gentleman summoned forth to whisper sweet tidings into your ear?"

"I don't recall. Probably another European prince, when you consider all the principalities. Whoever it is, he'll be wealthy and important and worthy of my attention." She smiled pertly. "You know the sort."

"I do indeed." Two gentlemen, wealthy and highly regarded, in one week. It seemed to William that Justine should meet no more than one potential suitor a week. Surely, she needed time to assess one before meeting another. He made a mental note to mention that to Lady Aleksander—she should slow down the progression of suitors. "You must not be terribly enthused if you canna remember their names."

"I am *very* enthused. I happen to like surprises."

"Surprises have a way of rebounding in uncomfortable ways."

They had reached the top terrace and she stopped. A sunny smile illuminated her face. "Nonsense, William. Surprises can be quite fun. Look at *this* one. You're a perfect surprise, aren't you, Dodi?" She buried her face in the dog's fur again, then held her up for William to take.

He couldn't resist the little dog and took her from Justine, petting her, muttering that she looked to be a very fine dog before setting her on the ground. The dog trotted ahead to sniff around some large pots with trees planted in them.

"I only ask because if you knew who the suitors were, I could perhaps offer some insight."

"Should I be amused or bemused that you still seem determined to offer advice when I've plainly said I don't want it?"

"No' advice. Insight. Assistance. For example, if you truly esteem one, I could give you suggestions on how to woo him to you."

Justine's eyes widened. And then she burst into gay laughter. "Do you think I need advice on how to woo a gentleman to my side? I'm going to be queen, William. What more wooing is necessary? Lord save me, but I am *constantly* astounded by your audacity."

"*Och*, I think you like it," he said. "You're to be queen, aye, and you're very alluring, and aye, you could woo the most difficult of men. However..." He paused, thinking how best to say what he was thinking.

"However...?"

"However, when your sister is present, you tend to—" he sought the right word and gestured lamely with his hand "—shrink."

"I shrink?"

"Like a violet."

Her brows dipped. "How is it that just when I think I might possibly call you friend, you say something so preposterous?"

"Am I wrong?" he challenged her.

She folded her arms and looked at the lower terrace. "No."

He smiled.

"Stop smiling like you are some sort of oracle."

"How can I help but smile? Your willingness to admit I am right is one of the things I most admire about you."

"I never said you were right. Don't smile like that. It displeases me. It's entirely too self-satisfied. Is this all you've come to say, William? That my sister outshines me at every turn? You needn't have bothered. I have known that since we were young girls, when a general in my father's service brought Amelia a pony as a gift, even though it was *my seventh* birthday. He could hardly look away from her and remarked to my parents several times that she was a beautiful child. That was just the beginning. So no, you don't have to tell me Amelia outshines me."

William was taken aback. "I never said your sister outshines you, Justine. I said you shrink. To be clear, you outshine her in every way. And the general, whoever he was, was a fool. A bloody damn fool."

She eyed him dubiously.

"What is this look? Can a man no' admire a woman without being suspected of ill will?"

"No."

"Cynical," he said, nodding. He absently traced a finger down her arm. "That will serve you well in your reign." His fingers tangled with hers.

"*I* think so. Better to be cynical than too trusting." She shifted away from him, putting her hand just beyond his reach. "Now, then, what advice have you come to give me today?"

"How disappointed you will be to know that I did no'

come to offer advice so that you can dismiss it. I've come to invite you to the opera."

She gasped. "The opera? I *love* the opera." The dog had scampered back to them, and Justine stooped to pick her up again.

"What a fortuitous coincidence. It is a new production. *Il Trovatore* by Verdi."

Her eyes brightened. "I *adore* Verdi operas. His company performed *Rigoletto* at the palace in St. Edys for my parents."

"Then you're in luck. The opera will be performed at the Royal Italian Opera in Covent Garden. I thought perhaps you would do me the honor of accompanying me?"

She tilted her head to one side, considering him. "Is there someone I am to meet?"

"I'm no' the matchmaker. For your pleasure only."

"Will there be a crowd?"

"Aye, of course. But you will be the guest of the Duke and Duchess of Grafton and view the opera from a box. Above the crowd, so to speak. There is a private entrance into the theater."

"Who else will come?"

William thought about it. "Lord and Lady Bardaline?"

She wrinkled her nose.

"Lady Aleksander?"

She clucked her tongue disapprovingly. "When?"

"Sunday evening. Does that suit?"

Her eyes shone with pleasure. She kissed the dog's nose. "It suits us well, doesn't it, Dodi? Thank you."

"Should you no' inquire of your master of the chamber?" He looked at the lower terrace. Bardaline was ushering Mawbley off and away from Justine.

"Him?" She rolled her eyes.

"Shall I inquire if Princess Amelia is available?"

"Amelia will be in the country this weekend with Lady Holland."

William hesitated. He'd assumed he would take both princesses. He thought about how it would look to the world if she was to accompany him without her sister. "Should we no' ask someone to accompany you?"

"A chaperone?" She giggled. "Isn't that what *you* are? Handpicked by the prime minister of Wesloria himself."

He was about to explain to her with all due certainty that he was most certainly not a chaperone, but Lady Bardaline was hurrying across the terrace to them, a silk garment draped over her arm.

"Someone must accompany you," he said. "Tongues wag in this town, and not kindly."

"Mmm."

"Your Royal Highness." Lady Bardaline curtsied and held out a dressing gown to Justine.

"Thank you." Justine handed Dodi to William. He took the pup. The pup licked his face. Justine put one arm through a sleeve and then the other, and belted it around her waist. "If you think I should have a chaperone, sir, then by all means, I shall have one." She looked at him in a way that could have made him mad with lust if he didn't have that newfound strength of a thousand mules inside him.

"A chaperone?" Lady Bardaline glanced at William. "Whatever for?"

"Lord Douglas has invited me to attend the opera." She was still looking him directly in the eye. "He must think I won't be able to resist his charms as he has suggested a chaperone."

"No, that was no'—I never said anything of the like."

She laughed at him. "You mustn't fret, my lord! I will

arrange it so that all appears proper. Thank you for the invitation. Lady Bardaline will delight to convey to my mother and Prime Minister Robuchard that you are very good at your task. I look forward to the evening."

She turned and walked away, and Lady Bardaline, with a look of mortification, quickly followed her.

William stood rooted to his spot for a few moments, confused by the feeling of having lost his bearings.

And then he realized he was still holding the dog.

Justine realized it, too. She paused at the door and turned back. "Dodi!"

He put the dog down and she raced in the general direction of Justine, veering off halfway to inspect the pots once more.

The little dog was just as confused as William.

CHAPTER NINETEEN

DANTE ROBUCHARD RECEIVED two telegraphs in one day from London. The first was from Lady Aleksander. The second was from the Marquess of Hamilton.

A third telegraph had also arrived, but this one had been directed to the queen. It was, of course, from Lady Bardaline, and was a lengthy one, judging by how much time the queen sat with her head bent over the message, her brow furrowed. Dante tried not to think of the expense of so many telegraphs being sent hither and yon, both in terms of money and in the mood around the palace, because the queen generally became quite agitated when she received them.

He was with the king and queen on the palace terrace, directly outside the private living quarters of the royal family. The royal physicians had advised that direct sunlight was very beneficial to the king, and he was to spend as much time in the sun as was possible. The king was on a chaise longue, buried in furs to keep warm. The queen sat beside him on the chaise, reading. Below them, in the family's private garden, where the bowling games were usually played, eight dancers moved through sets while three string musicians played. It was for the king's entertainment.

The queen suddenly stood and began to pace, blocking the king's view of the dancers.

Dante stood back, his hands clasped behind him. He was among some of the royal family's most faithful servants, including the king's valet, a nurse, a lady-in-waiting and an underbutler. The queen's private secretary was also present, all of them careful to stand back and out of the queen's path.

"We should never have sent Amelia to London," the queen said to her husband. "I said all along it was a mistake."

She'd never said any such thing, at least not to Dante, but he wasn't fool enough to point that out, and neither was the king.

"One must keep a very close eye on her, Maksim. She's so beautiful! It's little wonder that trouble courts her."

Beauty, Dante thought idly, was in the eye of the beholder. Certainly, Princess Amelia was an attractive young woman, but he thought Princess Justine was just as handsome as her sister. She had a certain grace about her. And yet, the queen did not seem to have the same charitable perspective when trouble courted Princess Justine. She often said her older daughter was irresponsible and naive. She would never forgive the princess the affair with Aldabert Gustav.

The queen stopped pacing and with hands on hips, stood before her husband and studied him. Below them, the conductor of the dance recital tried to move the dancers to the right, so that the king might see around his wife. Unfortunately, that put one couple into the hedgerow. The lady's hair caught in the branches and her partner tried to untangle her as the rest of the dancers carried on.

Neither the king nor the queen seemed to notice. The king looked very gray. Dante had consulted the royal physician on his prognosis, and it was not favorable. "He is weakening by the day," the physician had said, and then had added, sotto voce, "He will be gone within the year, barring a miracle."

"We must call her back," the queen said.

"I don't think that is wise, *liebchen*," the king responded.

The queen ignored him, as she was apt to do. "Drakkia? Drakkia, take note," she said, summoning her private secretary.

The gentleman stepped forward with his pencil and small, leather-bound notebook. The king coughed into a bloodied handkerchief.

"Send this directly to my daughters—*Amelia, you are to come home at once. Your behavior with Principe di Aggiani is disappointing and troublesome. Do you intend to follow in your sister's footsteps?*"

"Strike the last sentence," the king said. "It is unduly harsh and I thought we agreed we'd not speak of what happened."

"Very well. Write instead—*what could you have been thinking? The gentleman was there to determine if he was a proper match for you sister. Not you.*" She glanced at the king. He nodded.

"Next sentence—*Justine, you have failed your parents by allowing Amelia to conduct herself in such a manner. You must show responsibility! Your people must know you are competent and not easily swayed by whatever Amelia puts in your head!*"

"I hardly think it Justine's fault that Amelia is impetuous," the king said.

"It's not her fault, but if she doesn't make it her responsibility then what hope will Wesloria have when we are gone?"

"Our daughters will have the wise counsel and steady hand of their husbands," the king said. "Agnes, my love, you must do nothing to disrupt the matchmaking. It is imperative that Justine find a match and marry before the inevitable."

The queen softened. "Don't say that, Maksim." She squatted down beside him.

"Would you have me pretend?" he asked weakly. "The sooner she is matched, the sooner she is home and the abdication may be arranged. Isn't that so, Robuchard?"

"*Je*, Your Majesty," Dante said quietly. He didn't like to think of it any more than the king.

"I should like to be of as much help to Justine as I can before the end. Allow the lady to do what we have engaged her to do."

The queen did not respond to that. She slowly rose and nodded to Drakkia. Her secretary took his pen and paper and left the terrace.

Later, Dante dashed off his own notes. The first to Lady Aleksander—she had written that Principe Gaetano di Aggiani had not been a good match. He didn't know Lady Aleksander as well as he would have liked, but if she thought what had happened was merely "not a good match," he was a bit concerned. He wrote that the news they'd received in St. Edys was concerning and he hoped that she would find a more appropriate contender. He reminded her that she had assured them she was highly skilled at royal matches, and once again expressed his sincere wish that his personal pick—Prince Michel of Miraval—would be looked upon favorably. Dante had a personal relationship with the prince and thought a union with the small Mediterranean seafaring nation would be a boon for Wesloria for many economic reasons.

To William Douglas, he sent a curt reply: *She stays.*

CHAPTER TWENTY

AFTER THREE DAYS away from Prescott Hall, Lila returned late. She'd shooed away the maid who so desperately wanted to attend her, and then had flung herself into her bed, dress and corset and all, exhausted.

She awoke in the very same spot hours later, her legs tangled in her skirt and petticoats.

She'd accomplished quite a lot in the three days away, beginning with arranging an introduction to Mr. Jonathan Ashley. That had been easy enough—friends of her disgraced father were still willing to help his poor daughter, even though it had been several years since her humiliation. And, frankly, introductions were easy to get when one was pursuing a match for a future queen. News of her current commission had already traveled into the countryside.

It was amusing to her that ambitious young men the world over thought highly of themselves and were easily flattered. Sometimes with good reason. And sometimes not.

Mr. Ashley was easily flattered.

She found him to be charming and affable, handsome enough as those things went. He had gold hair and brown eyes, was tall and fit. He would make any woman a good husband, she had no doubt.

But she didn't want him as a husband for the princess. She needed him for another reason.

Before she had contacted Mr. Ashley, she had called on

an old acquaintance of her mother's who could always be depended upon to know the details of any scandal. Rose Maugham, Lady Radcliff, was a fixture in Mayfair. Years ago she'd tried to marry her daughter, Katherine, to an Alucian prince who was now a king. She had failed, of course, because those things required some finesse, and, well, the prince had been caught up in a murder scandal and Lady Radcliff was quite out of her depth.

Lady Radcliff had never recovered from her failure to marry her daughter to a prince and kept close watch on the goings-on in and around Mayfair, and in particular, the bachelors. Over tea, she was not the least bit hesitant to tell Lila what she knew—that the bad blood between Douglas and Ashley had to do with a woman. Lila found the reason tiresome—it always had to do with a woman. Why couldn't gentlemen be more interesting? Lady Radcliff hadn't known the details, other than it had been an age, and she wasn't sure which of them had held the young lady in high regard and which one had swooped in and ruined any chance of happiness. And then she said something curious—that it hardly mattered because of what had happened in Scotland recently.

"What happened in Scotland?" Lila had asked curiously.

"I don't know precisely, but I have heard that the scandal around the marquess is *bad*."

"Very bad?"

Lady Radcliff's ringlets bounced around her face with her nod.

"But surely, if it's as bad as that, someone must know. Scandals always travel so quickly, don't they?"

"The only person I know in all of London who knows more than I do about some things is the Earl of Iddesleigh.

But he has all those children now, so..." She shrugged and sipped her tea.

Beck. Of course he knew. She thought back to how insistent his wife had been that they not say a word. "It hardly matters at all, really. I was merely curious. My interest is in Mr. Ashley."

"Now *there* is an honorable young man," Lady Radcliff said. Although she couldn't remember if he'd been the bad sport or not.

The other thing Lila had learned through the years was that people—women in particular—tended not to believe the worst of a man if he was handsome and rich. No matter what had happened between Ashley and Douglas, no matter the source of the animosity, Lila was confident that Douglas would not take kindly to Ashley as a suitor for Princess Justine.

She had explained it all in a letter to Valentin.

Sometimes absence makes the heart grow fonder.
And sometimes the desire to see an old nemesis lose above all else will make the heart grow fonder still.

It was the unspoken scandal about William Douglas that had her puzzled. As soon as she could, she would call on Beck again.

After meeting with Lady Radcliff, Lila had arranged to meet Mr. Ashley, and ascertained from his mother that he did indeed have the means and connections to marry a woman like Princess Justine. His mother's eyes had sparkled like stars when she realized what Lila was after. When Lila inquired of Mr. Ashley about his feelings for Lord Douglas—she was justified, as he was an acquaintance of Robuchard's—Mr. Ashley had blinked and then said he couldn't possibly know, as his only dealing with him had been years ago, and it had been a small disagreement.

Lila didn't believe that. Men did not hold grudges over some slight at the hands of someone they hardly knew. But Mr. Ashley was a gentleman and would not ruin this opportunity for himself.

He claimed to be quite content with his life and felt certain a royal princess would find nothing to recommend *him*, but nevertheless, he would be happy to make the royal princess's acquaintance. He said he had not been afforded the opportunity the last time she was in London and had heard that she was sweet and unassuming.

Lila hoped her face didn't reveal how his description of Princess Justine's supposed attributes annoyed her. Why would anyone believe that *sweet* and *unassuming* were virtues?

Ah, well. She'd realized years ago that she could not change the attributes by which women in society were judged.

Now, to set things into motion.

THE DAY AFTER Lady Aleksander's return, Justine and Amelia spent the better part of the morning and luncheon at Windsor Castle in the company of Queen Victoria. They had knitted their socks for the soldiers, and afterward, the queen said she enjoyed drawing. Amelia had gone off with Princess Victoria to do something entertaining, and Justine had remained with the queen and attempted to draw the tableau that the butler set before them: a teapot and a teacup and saucer, artistically arranged before a vase with garden flowers, some of the blooms drooping onto the teapot. Queen Victoria had gifted Justine with a leatherbound sketchbook. "You will find that if you draw every day, your skills will improve. But you must apply yourself to the task."

"*Je*, Your Majesty." She tried with all due diligence to improve her skill while the queen instructed her on any number of subjects.

Lady Aleksander was in the salon when the sisters returned to Prescott Hall. She stood up and curtsied and said with much delight, "A sketchbook!"

Justine looked down at her hand. *"Je."*

"I didn't know you were an artist."

"Perhaps because I am not." She opened the sketchbook and showed Lady Aleksander what she'd drawn. Lady Aleksander frowned slightly as she studied it, even tilting her head to one side. "Is it a…?"

"Teacup."

"Oh!" she said, brightening. "So it is."

"Her Majesty is fond of drawing."

"And talking," Amelia added.

Justine shot her a look. Amelia sighed. "I didn't say it to Lady Bardaline. Lady Aleksander doesn't care what I say."

"You don't know that," Justine said. What did they know about the lady, really, other than Robuchard had recommended her?

Amelia gave an impatient sigh. She did not like to be corrected.

Lady Aleksander graciously turned the subject, probably fearing an argument would break out between them, and Justine wasn't certain that it wouldn't—her sister could vex her like no other. On the other hand, she trusted no one like she did Amelia.

"Do you find your meetings with the queen useful?" Lady Aleksander asked.

"Of course," Justine said automatically. Unlike Amelia,

who seemed to have less regard for decorum every day, she knew how to answer so as not to invite questions.

"What did you talk about?"

Justine looked at Lady Aleksander. She also seemed to have far less regard for decorum than Justine. How could she possibly think it appropriate to inquire of Justine anything? In Wesloria, no one spoke to her unless invited to speak. Certainly, no one but her parents and their closest advisers ever questioned her.

Then again, she didn't know why she bristled, other than from habit.

"She was very curious to know how the matchmaking was proceeding, actually. She thinks it has gone on far too long, and the more days I am allowed to languish in this body without a proper prospect, the more difficult potential suitors will think I must be, as there is nothing apparently wrong with my looks."

Lady Aleksander's eyes widened with surprise. And then she laughed. "What rubbish!"

Both sisters looked at her in amazement.

"Well?" she said to their startled looks. "It *is* rubbish. After you're married, no one will ever recall how many gentlemen you considered. Just because Queen Victoria fell in love so readily doesn't mean you must."

"Did she?" Amelia asked.

"Oh, she'll have you believe differently," Lady Aleksander said and took a seat, crossing her legs beneath her gown and letting her arms rest on the arms of the chair. "She will say she had no interest in him, and thought he was too quiet or some such. But she was smitten with him the first time she laid eyes on Prince Albert. What else did she say?"

Justine tossed the sketchbook aside. "She said I ought to

develop the habit of giving alms. That as queen, I must be among my people—*all* people—and not just the handsome and rich ones. She said that my subjects must see me caring for the less fortunate or they would grow to resent me."

"That's sound advice," Lady Aleksander said.

"I thought so, too." Justine perched on the edge of a chair and studied the matchmaker. "I really do wish I could do more."

"But you're so nervous, Jussie. You'd probably die of fright among the poor."

"It's not that they are poor, Amelia. It's merely that they are people." She smiled sheepishly at Lady Aleksander. "I am uncomfortable in large crowds. But enough of that—*you* seem to be in fine spirits."

Lady Aleksander's smile brightened. "I have news that I hope will please you. I've arranged for you to meet Mr. Jonathan Ashley of Kent this evening."

Justine grimaced, but Amelia gasped with delight, clasping her hands together like a young girl.

"He is attractive."

"Really? Very?" Amelia asked.

"Darling, when do you depart for the country with Lady Holland?" Princess Justine asked her sister.

"Four o'clock. Why?"

"Shouldn't you be packing your things?"

"Seviana has done it. You sound as if you want to be rid of me."

Amelia could be so obtuse at times. "I never want to be rid of you. But I think that after the last visit from a gentleman caller, I should see you away from Prescott Hall before anyone arrives. Don't you?"

Amelia gaped at her. "Are you going to hold that over

my head every time there is a caller? Why does no one in this family care about me?"

"I don't think you can say no one cares. Clearly, Mama does." She arched a brow at Amelia, silently reminding her of the telegraph they'd received yesterday.

Amelia looked as if she was about to speak, but as the telegraph had included the very real threat of being yanked back to St. Edys, she wisely, for once, thought the better of it. She stood up and said stiffly, "Good day, Lady Aleksander. *Justine*," she added darkly, then swept out of the room without a word.

Justine glanced at Lady Aleksander. "My apologies."

"None needed. Princess Amelia has her own burdens to bear. With a little experience in a place where she is not the spare heir, she will see she is a princess in her own right. She's like a fine wine—her complexities will be better with age."

"Then perhaps we ought to tuck her away in a barrel for a few years."

Lady Aleksander laughed.

Justine smiled a little, too. "All right, you have me on tenterhooks. Who is Mr. Ashley?"

"I think you will very much enjoy his company. He attended St. Andrew's in Scotland."

Justine hardly cared what school he'd attended, and if Lady Aleksander was going to begin a list with that, this match was already tedious.

"His father is a wealthy industrialist. A steel magnate."

Justine snorted. "That should make Robuchard weep with joy."

"Wouldn't it?" Lady Aleksander chuckled. "The prime minister has his interests. But I have mine. Mr. Ashley is very agreeable. A true gentleman."

Justine was not impressed with that. "You said the same about the last one." She shifted her gaze to the window.

Lady Aleksander was not put off by Justine's lack of enthusiasm. "I understand your trust has been diminished, and with good reason. If you won't take my word for it, perhaps you will trust the opinion of your friend, Lord Douglas."

She'd not expected to hear mention of William and turned her gaze from the window to Lady Aleksander. "He's not my *friend*—"

"No? The two of you seem quite friendly."

She wasn't going to deny that for fear of having to speak of just how friendly they were. "Why should I ask him?"

"He and Mr. Ashley both attended St. Andrew's. I think their acquaintance is longstanding."

Justine blinked. Was there *anyone* he didn't know?

Lady Aleksander smiled, as if reading her thoughts. "Lord Douglas has many acquaintances, doesn't he?"

"Perhaps too many." Still, something about this seemed a bit off to Justine. She began to worry the gold bracelet on her wrist. She had the sense that Lady Aleksander was not telling her everything. "Lady Aleksander—"

"Please, ma'am. I would like it very much if you would call me Lila."

Justine almost rolled her eyes. "So that you might consider us friends?"

"So that I may consider us united in a common goal. I think our association would be easier if we could be less formal with one another." She smiled serenely.

This woman was completely unflappable, and Justine grudgingly admired that about her. "All right, then. Lila. How do you know Lord Douglas has many acquaintances? Did he give you a list?"

Lila laughed. "No, ma'am. My occupation requires that I know who is well connected and who is not, and he is, for better or worse, well connected. Mr. Ashley is also well connected and eager to make your acquaintance. He was disappointed he didn't have the opportunity when you were in London eight years ago."

Eight years ago she'd been besotted with William. She could hardly remember anyone else she'd met.

"Mr. Ashley claims to not have met a member of the fairer sex he truly esteems beyond measure, but is ready to be swept off his feet. He knows quite a lot about you, as he's followed the news through the years."

Justine blanched. "*What* news?"

Lila quickly amended, "Not *that* news." She leaned forward, gave a quick glance at the footman standing at the wall and said softly, "If I may, Your Royal Highness, that incident does not define you. There is much more dimension to you than that."

The bitter laugh that escaped Justine sounded more like a bark. "It was more than an incident, madam. And there is no more dimension to me—I'm not blind. I've been sheltered all my life, confined by crowns and corsets and palace walls. I know nothing of the world, as Aldabert very clearly demonstrated to me and everyone else. I scarcely know myself at times." Much less how to rule. But that, Justine kept to herself.

She glanced at the footman, astounded she had voiced those thoughts aloud. Her father had impressed on her to never show weakness. Weakness, he said, was an invitation to corruption.

"You know more than you think," Lila said. "You've not been allowed to see for yourself just how much you know. No ordinary woman learns to fence when everyone is against it. You are well-read, a highly educated woman. You're accomplished and thoughtful and kind and if you ask me, there is more to be gained from being kind than not. You fell in love. What woman has not fallen in love? It's not a fault or a flaw, ma'am. It is the essence of humanity."

Justine smiled a little. "You sound like my old governess."

"She must have been a wise woman."

Carlotta had indeed been a wise woman. But when Justine turned ten, she was dismissed. That was as long as any governess had ever been allowed to stay with a royal princess, and it was unthinkable that tradition be challenged, no matter how much Justine had begged. To this day the memory of watching Carlotta leave was unpleasant.

Justine kept her gaze on the bracelet she moved around her wrist. "You were saying why you consider Mr. Ashley a good match for me."

"He's rich, he's educated and he is kind. I think he would like your drawing of a teacup very much."

Justine laughed outright.

"He is a man in search of a woman who will share his view of the world. He does not want to be valued only for his name, any more than you want to be valued only for yours."

Justine had never said that. It was uncomfortable that someone could read her so clearly. "If he is such a fine catch, why have I not heard of him?"

"You mean why hasn't he appeared on your mother's list?" Lila asked with a wry smile.

"I mean exactly that."

"My list of names extends beyond those who have curried favor from your parents. The world of a sovereign can sometimes be a bit small. Isn't it at least a little exciting that you've not heard of him?"

"Perhaps a little. He means to call today?"

"I've invited him to dine. With Lord Bardaline's blessing, of course."

"Then you will excuse me. I must see Amelia off for the weekend. And I've not seen my dog."

"Of course."

"And by the bye, I am attending the opera Sunday evening with Lord Douglas and his friends, Lord and Lady Grafton. Please do not think to introduce me to anyone then."

"The opera. How lovely." Lila was smiling like a fat little cat, obviously pleased that she had surprised Justine. Well, the feeling was mutual—Justine was pleased that she'd surprised her, too. But as she walked out of the room, her thoughts were not on what she would wear, but how disappointed she was William Douglas would not be here to see her newest, handsome and kind prospect. How disappointed she was that he'd not be able to find anything wrong with him, and therefore, would not have reason to bet her.

She would, of course, be delighted to tell him how wrong he was when she saw him in a few days for the opera.

CHAPTER TWENTY-ONE

MACDUFF WAS LOSING his touch. He'd selected three neck cloths and none of them complemented the pale blue-and-black-checked silk waistcoat William wore. He held up a dark green neck cloth to his collar and turned to his valet. "Are you blind, then, Ewan?"

"No." He squinted at it. "What color is it?"

William dropped his hand and stared at his old companion. "You're color-blind? How has that escaped my attention all these years?"

"Och," the big man said. "You donna care for things like colors. And I'm no' blind to *all* of them."

"This explains so much," William said. He walked to his bureau and pulled open a drawer. He rummaged around until he found a plain black silk neck cloth and put it on. When he was finished dressing for the opera, he examined himself in the mirror. His waist was still fairly trim, but not as trim as it once had been. He was taller than most, a fact that had always pleased him…but not as tall as MacDuff. His dark hair could stand a bit of a trim, as well as his sideburns. He'd have MacDuff tend to that on the morrow.

He put out his hand, palm up. MacDuff put a top hat into it. The brim was felt, the crown black silk. It was an expensive hat. William donned it and turned to face Ewan.

"You look well indeed, milord."

"No' too long in the tooth?"

MacDuff grunted. "You're a young man yet."

"Still attractive to the fairer sex?"

MacDuff waved his thick hand. "Aye, milord, what your purse doesna catch, your face surely will."

William grinned and clapped him on the shoulder. "That's why you've remained in my employ all these years. Remind me to increase your wages, aye?"

"Aye, that I will."

He wouldn't. He once complained that he had more than enough, and any more would be an embarrassment. One had to admire a man who said such things.

William started for the door. "Donna wait up for me. In fact..." He paused and reached into his pocket for his purse. He withdrew a few bills and handed them to Ewan. "Have a pleasant evening."

Ewan stared at the bills in his hand. "Doing what?"

"I donna know, lad. Supper. A pub. A brothel."

The big man blanched at the mention of a brothel. "I'd *never.*"

William couldn't help a fond smile for this man who was more like an uncle to him than a valet. It was yet another reason he held him in such high esteem. "Then do something interesting, aye?"

"Aye," Ewan said. But he looked perplexed.

ON THE WAY to Prescott Hall, William fussed with the chain of his pocket watch, which had caught on a button of his waistcoat, reminding him why he never liked to carry this particular watch. He was in fine spirits otherwise. He would not admit it to a living soul, but he'd been looking quite forward to this evening. He wasn't an opera aficionado, although he did enjoy it on occasion. What he was looking forward to was Justine. He wanted to know how she would react to the opera. He wanted to see her smile, or to give him that look of exasperation tinged with amusement.

He most especially wanted to kiss her again.

Och, but he'd thought of that kiss too many times to feel completely sane about it. It had kicked some spark into a stalled life, had set the wings of his imagination flapping, had made him feel a wee bit crazed.

When he arrived at Prescott Hall, and the problem of the chain to his pocket watch had been resolved, he sprung from his father's coach with a lightness he'd not felt in an age. He strode up the steps. The door opened before he reached the landing, and the butler bowed.

"Good evening," William said and doffed his hat. "William Douglas. I've come for Her Royal Highness Princess Justine."

The butler drew the door open for him. "If you would be so kind as to wait just here." He gestured to the grand foyer. When William stepped across the threshold, he invited him to put his hat on the console, then briskly walked away.

William stood. He could hear laughter coming from somewhere deep in the house. He inched a few steps deeper into the foyer and cocked his head, listening. Aye, more laughter. Justine's laugh, light and tinkling. Another female. More than one male.

A door opened, then closed, and the *click click click* of the butler's heels on the tiled floors moved toward him. He strode into the foyer and bowed. "Her Royal Highness will see you."

He should certainly hope so, as he was expected. He had a sudden inclination to make this butler understand that he knew the man's princess better than he did. But he walked agreeably along behind the man and was shown into a small salon he'd not seen before. The first thing he saw was Dodi, who came racing for him as if they were old friends. She put her paws on his leg, and he leaned to one side to scratch her behind the ears. He was prepared to make a quip about passing a gauntlet to reach her, but when he turned his head and saw Justine, he was not expecting her to look so...*queenly*, and it took him a beat or two to remember not to gape.

She looked like a dream. She was wearing a gown of gold silk, embroidered and appliquéd with fine gold-and-silver thread. The sleeves sat just below her smooth shoulders, and a garland of silk flowers decorated the form-fitting bodice. Between her breasts she wore a royal badge of some sort. A diamond choker graced her slender neck, the pattern and design of which matched the diamond tiara she wore on her head. Her hair had been styled with a cascade of soft curls framing her face.

He bowed. "Your Royal Highness."

"My Lord Douglas," she said and put out her gloved hand to him. He bent over it, his lips touching her knuckles, his finger finding the small buttonhole at her wrist and touching her skin. He lifted his head. "If I may, you are a vision this evening."

"How kind." She looked gay and happy and beautiful, and he had never been so pleased in his life to be accompanying someone to the opera. Or anywhere, for that matter.

"May I introduce you to my chaperone?"

"Pardon?"

She laughed.

William turned his head, and when he did, his gaze fell on the smug, punchable face of Jonathan Ashley.

Jonathan Ashley.

The man who had tried to debauch the one woman William had ever loved and had very nearly succeeded. He couldn't understand what he was doing here. A feeling of alarm—because he was certain Ashley was here by some terrible mistake—mixed sourly in his gut.

Dodi pawed his leg. Justine bent down and picked her up.

"Lord Douglas. How long has it been?" Ashley asked and casually strode forward to greet him. "What a pleasure it is to see you after all this time."

William could only stare at him. He noticed then that Ashley was dressed in formal attire. The sour mix turned bilious, and he turned to Justine. She was beaming. "I understand you two are old friends!"

"Pardon?"

"I told you I'd find a chaperone." She laughed. So did Ashley. Loudly. "Lord and Lady Bardaline mean to join us as well. They insisted, of course. They can't let a princess into the world all on her own."

That was the first that William noticed the Bardalines in the room.

"If I may, Your Royal Highness," Bardaline said, stepping forward. William noticed then that the master of the chamber was dressed formally. To William, he said, "Lord Grafton kindly extended an invitation for my wife and me to join you and Her Highness. I hope you don't find it too much of an imposition."

How the hell did Bardaline know Grafton? "Pardon? You are acquainted with Lord Grafton?"

Bardaline smiled thinly. "Lady Aleksander introduced us."

Of course she did. William felt like he'd had too much to drink, a wee bit dizzy and possibly seeing things. He'd had a vision of this night, and it had not included the Bardalines, and it *certainly* hadn't included Ashley.

"And once he heard Mr. Ashley was in London, he invited him to attend as well."

William looked at Justine. She avoided his gaze by playing with the dog.

"Now that Douglas has arrived, shall we proceed?" Ashley asked. He held out his arm to Justine. And Justine put the dog down and *took it.*

William looked around for that blasted matchmaker to register his strong complaint, but naturally, she was nowhere to be found. Oh, but he'd have a word just as soon as he found that conniving woman.

There was a kerfuffle over coaches and who would ride with whom to the opera house. It was finally decided—not by William—that the princess would ride with the Bardalines for the sake of propriety. This pronouncement made William even more cross, as he was the one to have issued the invitation, and he ought to at least be afforded some say in the arrangements. But he grudgingly agreed to carry on with the despicable Jonathan Ashley.

He climbed into the coach after his old nemesis, sat across from him, adjusted the increasingly vexing watch chain, then looked up and said, "You bloody wee bastard."

Ashley laughed. He fished a flask out of his boot and took a sip, then offered it to William. William shook his head; Ashley shrugged and pushed the flask back into the boot. "Come now, Douglas. You don't really think you're the only one who can find his way into a princess's salon?"

"She is my friend. And you are a blackguard. Those two things are no' compatible."

"Her friend!" Ashley howled. "Do you truly expect me to believe that?"

Of course he didn't expect Ashley to believe that, because friendship was beyond the realm of what Jonathan Ashley was capable of.

"I think you're envious, Douglas."

William snorted.

"You ought to be. She esteems me."

"Donna be so sure of that, lad," he scoffed.

Ashley smoothed the tail of his neck cloth. "We'll see how friendly you remain with her once I'm king."

He was obviously trying to goad William, and under any other circumstance he would have laughed it off. But Ashley made him irrationally angry and always had. "You'd no' be king, you dimwit, but a prince consort."

Ashley's smile faltered a wee bit, as if he thought perhaps William was teasing him but wasn't entirely certain.

William leaned forward. "Do you think, then, that perhaps you could look at her as a woman and no' a means to an end?"

Ashley rolled his eyes. "High and mighty talk, isn't it, coming from someone at the center of so many rumors having to do with *women*. As if she is not a means to an end for you, too."

William stilled. He couldn't be certain what rumors Ashley was referring to, and he wasn't fool enough to ask. But he feared it had to do with the trouble he'd had in Scotland a few months ago. He hadn't given that situation much thought since coming to London. *No.* It was impossible. There was no way Ashley could have heard anything about it.

Nevertheless, William leaned back and shifted his gaze to the window and ignored Ashley's bitter laugh.

He'd known Jonathan Ashley for many years. He was affable and desired. William had discovered just how desired he was a little more than ten years ago. William had been courting a woman he intended to offer marriage. Then Ashley had come along and she'd fallen under his spell. William never knew exactly what went on between the two of them, but Clara had abruptly gone cold on William. Where she had hinted at her feelings for him, she suddenly thought perhaps he called too often. Bastard that he was, Ashley had tried to coax Clara's virtue from her. Or, at least, that was what William's mother had told him. She'd heard it from Clara's mother.

William didn't hear it from Clara because by then, she'd ended their courtship and had left him completely broken.

In the end Ashley disappeared from Clara's life. He'd broken her heart, and William's in the process, and then William had tried to break Ashley's heart with his fist. That was what young bucks did, of course—they fought. He'd confronted Ashley, he'd prevailed and he'd even broken Ashley's nose.

But...it solved nothing. Clara's heart was still broken, and popular opinion turned solidly against William. It was said *he* was the blackguard, that his abuse of poor Jonathan Ashley was the start of his rough years.

Maybe that had been the start. He'd found it very hard to trust his heart after that, and had gone on to test his heart in the worst possible ways while Ashley had continued blithely to charm his way into the salons of unmarried young women, taking as many liberties as he might before someone stopped him.

Well. William wouldn't allow Ashley to do the same to Justine, even if it ruined the growing esteem between him and the future queen.

CHAPTER TWENTY-TWO

THE DUKE AND DUCHESS of Grafton were already in their patronage box, along with the dowager duchess, so stooped with age that Justine thought she ought to curtsy to her just to look her in the eye.

After the introductions were made, Lady Grafton suggested that the ladies occupy the seats in the front row, and the gentlemen behind them. Lady Bardaline said she thought that was an excellent plan. Justine wanted desperately to tell her lady-in-waiting to stop suffocating her—the woman was always present and forever offering opinions when no one had asked. If Justine had her way, she'd have William on one side, Mr. Ashley on the other. For once in her life she was in the presence of two handsome gentlemen without Amelia to distract them, and she would very much like to enjoy it.

Unfortunately, Lady Grafton had other ideas.

Justine was seated between Lady Bardaline and the dowager duchess. When she was settled, she happened to glance down, and when she did, her chest tightened immediately. Every pair of eyes in that opera house was pointed up, directly at her.

She absently twisted the thin gold bracelet around her wrist.

Of course she'd anticipated the attention. She *always* expected the attention. But the reality was always much worse than the imagining. She shifted back in her chair as a heat crept up the back of her neck. She was thankful her curls fell to her back, because Amelia said her neck looked so splotchy when she was nervous.

She twisted the bracelet faster and tried to keep her countenance serene, her gaze fixed on the stage and its velvet curtains. She became aware of someone at her back, so close that she could feel his breath. And then, a low whisper. "They might as well be miles below you, aye? Nothing but ants, they are."

She gave a tiny nod of acknowledgment. She was grateful to William for saying it, for reminding her that she had nothing to fear all the way up here.

He leaned closer and said, "Lady Grafton, it is good to see you looking so well."

The dowager turned her head in his direction. "Hmm?"

But William had already slipped back into his seat, drawn away by a question from Lord Grafton.

The dowager looked curiously at Justine.

"I am so pleased to have come," Justine said.

"Pardon?"

Justine leaned closer. "I am very pleased to have come."

"Eh?" the old woman asked, cupping her hand around her ear.

"Very pleased to have come!" Justine said loudly.

The old woman gave a start. "Oh. Yes."

Justine smiled and nodded, then glanced the other way, and when she did, she almost collided with Lady Bardaline's face. "Lord!" she exclaimed, surprised by how close the woman was leaning in.

Lady Bardaline was all smiles and excitement. She whispered to Justine, "Mr. Ashley is handsome, isn't he? What do you think of him?"

Every question the woman asked was for the benefit of Queen Agnes. "I think of him in the same way I think of all of them." She left it at that and turned her attention to the stage. If her mother wanted to know what she thought of any suitor, she could simply *ask* her.

She was saved from having to think about the complications of her mother and her spies by the opening curtain.

The first notes gave her heart a start. And then she was gone, her heart and mind swept into the magic of the performance. Her head filled with music and story, and she forgot about the sea of people below, watching her watch the opera behind their opera glasses. She forgot about Lady Bardaline, and the dowager duchess, who fell asleep in the opening act and began to snore. She laughed when Mr. Ashley leaned forward and asked if she feared as much as he did that the glass windows would shatter if the soprano sustained another high note. Justine's Italian was rudimentary, but she understood enough that tears came to her eyes in Act II when Count di Luna sang an aria to the object of his love—*Her smile shines more than a star.* She was the first one to applaud at the conclusion of the second act and kept applauding as the curtain was lowered. She stopped when she noticed the attention of the patrons on the floor began to turn back to her, their interest in her renewed with intermission.

Justine leaned back in her chair, out of view of the curious eyes. Lady Grafton asked if she would like to step out of the box for a bit of respite. Justine glanced behind Lady Grafton to see that the gentlemen had departed the box, with the exception of William, who sat with legs crossed, his hands folded on his lap, his gaze on the stage. Even Lady Bardaline was making her way out of the box. Through the door Justine could see several people were gathered. She imagined the narrow hall, the swaths of wealthy box owners greeting each other and hoping to be introduced to her. She glanced to her right, where the dowager continued to nap, her chin on her chest.

"No, thank you," she said to Lady Grafton. "I'll stay with her ladyship."

Lady Grafton nodded and made her way from the box. Justine glanced at the dowager, who was leaning in her direction, and very carefully, so as not to disturb the old woman, moved over one seat.

She felt William move before she actually saw him slide into the seat between her and the dowager. He stared at the old woman a moment, then lifted the dowager's chin. The old woman tilted to her right until her head met William's shoulder, but she continued to doze.

He looked at Justine, his gray eyes sparkling.

"That is kind of you."

"I acted out of fear that she'll curl into a ball and roll over the railing at any moment."

Justine smiled. She glanced over her shoulder at the door, expecting Mr. Ashley to appear. Surely, he would come and inquire if she needed anything.

"Are you enjoying the opera?"

She turned her attention to William and settled back in her chair. "Enormously. I must thank you again for inviting me."

He cocked his head to one side. "Again? Have you thanked me?"

She gave him wry smile. "Perhaps not. I'm not accustomed to thanking my keeper."

"Ah, I'm still your keeper, then. I thought perhaps your chaperone might have taken my place."

"Impossible! He could never vex me as you do."

He looked pleased by that. "I am delighted my service to you is being noted."

"You don't mind that he has come, do you?" she asked curiously. Lila had intimated that he and Mr. Ashley were friends.

"Aye, I do," he said, his smile lopsided.

"Really?"

"He is the worst for you."

Justine clucked her tongue. "You said that very thing of Principe di Aggiani."

"Aye, well, I was wrong about Aggiani, as now, someone even worse has come along."

Justine laughed at him. "He's been very kind to me! And he's not once asked for praise."

William's lovely gray eyes narrowed. "Has he gifted you with a dog? A horse? Perhaps something more practical, like a goat?"

"How delighted I would be if he had."

"Mmm," he said. "How many times has he been in your company?"

"Tonight is the third time. The first time I hardly had time to make his acquaintance, it was so brief." He'd come to speak to Lady Aleksander, actually, but Justine had been on her way to the garden and had seen him at the door and Lord Bardaline had introduced them. "The second time… he was the guest of Lady Aleksander at tea." Where *was* Mr. Ashley? She glanced over her shoulder, wondering when he thought to return. "And then, of course, tonight."

"Thrice! And to think that when I saw you last, no' four days ago, there was no mention of him."

"I didn't know myself at the time. You know how these things are." These *things*, she was discovering, were at the whim of Lady Aleksander. "There's another gentleman to come later this week. I've not mentioned him, either, but I will now."

William looked away for a moment. He turned back to her. "Justine—" He sat up abruptly, but had apparently forgotten the duchess on his shoulder. She was startled awake when her pillow disappeared, and blinked at the two of them. "What?"

"It is intermission!" William practically shouted at her.

"Ah." She picked up her fan and began to fan herself.

William turned back to Justine. "Ashley is a…" His brows sank, and he looked as if he was searching for a word. "Bastard is too good for him. Degenerate? Aye, that's it. He's a degenerate."

"For heaven's sake, William! Really, are you going to find fault with every gentleman who calls? You could pen your report to Robuchard tonight and simply tell him none of them will do."

"I give you my word that is no' my intent. I donna mean to find fault with them all, but if your matchmaker doesna improve her services, I might. You donna know the man like I do."

"I can't imagine you'd have anything but glowing things to say about him. He's been a perfect gentleman."

William winced.

She was antagonized by his wince and sat up, too. "Do you know he brought me flowers the first time he came? Not like Aggiani, but a handpicked bouquet tied with a lovely ribbon. We've talked about books and music. He sang while I played the piano. He has a beautiful singing voice."

William looked confused. "Is that what you want? Someone who will pick flowers and sing to you?"

Was that what she wanted? It at least seemed like a start. "Of course that is what I want. Doesn't everyone want that?

Doesn't it sound lovely even to your jaded ears to be tied for the rest of your life to someone with like interests? Or perhaps you have something against flowers and singing?"

"I happen to enjoy both greatly. I am very much in favor of flowers and art and dogs. Those are interests I sincerely share with you. I even like books, Justine."

"His interests are sincere, too!" she insisted. Mr. Ashley had been a model of civility and chivalry. And if he'd just come back to the box, he could prove it himself to William. "What is the matter with you? I thought you wanted nothing more than to see me happily affianced so that you could be done with the loathsome task of being my friend."

"You know very well it is no' a loathsome task, and quite honestly, I've come to enjoy it very much. I do indeed want to see you happy, Justine, more than you know. Which is why I am telling you you'll no' be happy with him. I speak from personal experience."

Justine felt a presence beside her. She turned, all smiles, certain it was Mr. Ashley. But it was Lady Bardaline, her eyes bright and her ears pointed in Justine's direction. The others were beginning to filter back into the box, too, still talking, standing about before it was time to take their seats.

Justine leaned closer to William so that she could whisper. "Do you think that perhaps you are jealous?"

He stared at her. Then he leaned closer, too, and whispered, "I will never, to my dying breath, be jealous of a reprobate. Mark my words. He will attempt to take liberties with you, and if you still marry him, he will have a string of mistresses that reach a mile long."

She sincerely wished his breath wasn't so warm against her skin, didn't tickle her. "You're wretched." And then she laughed. Loudly. So that Lady Bardaline would hear her. Even the dowager duchess heard her. They would not see how perturbed she was with William at this moment.

William laughed heartily, too, then leaned in again. "I see you donna believe me. Again."

"I do *not*," she whispered fiercely. "The first time you were lucky. The second time you are jealous."

He shifted in his seat, coming very close, practically facing her. "Allow me to hazard a guess of his attention to you. He flatters you endlessly. Your eyes are like polished gold," he said, his lashes fluttering when he looked directly in her eyes.

Justine clucked her tongue. But Mr. Ashley had said something like that. He said her gown this evening was the only thing that could possibly do justice to the golden color of her eyes.

"You are so well-read he feels inferior in his education."

She stared hard at William. Mr. Ashley hadn't said those *precise* words, but he had wondered aloud how any gentleman could compete with the education of a crown princess.

William's gaze shifted to her mouth. "You are a woman who would inspire a man to love you."

A thread of vibration began to make its way up her spine. Mr. Ashley had said he couldn't fathom how lucky a gentleman would be to wed someone as elegant and poised as she, how proud he would be to have her on his arm.

William saw her hesitation and arched a brow. "That your beauty is beyond compare?"

She snorted. "He never said *that*."

"Then he's a bigger fool than I thought."

"It is obvious he admires me."

"Is it? Because I admire those things in you and more. But I donna say them to gain your favor, Justine. I say them because I believe them."

The flutter in her belly moved to her heart. She was aware that people were taking their seats in anticipation of the third act, but William didn't seem to notice. He held her gaze and said softly, "He may truly esteem you, but he will never be faithful."

That galled her. Why would he never be faithful? Was she not worth fidelity? William's assured belief angered her. "He genuinely esteems me. Would you like to bet that is not so?"

A slow, sultry smile returned to his lips and he looked at her in that way he'd looked at her when they'd kissed, and the blood began to sizzle in her veins.

"Your Royal Highness, the third act is about to begin," Lady Bardaline warned.

William put his hands on his knees. "Aye, Your Royal Highness, I want to bet. I very *much* want to bet."

"Then we are agreed."

He was still smiling as he stood and moved to the back row.

Justine sat back, her heart galloping in her chest. She very much wanted to bet, too.

"What is the bet?" Lady Bardaline asked with a lightness that didn't fit the flare in Justine.

"About the opera," she lied and glanced over her shoulder.

Mr. Ashley had still not returned to the box.

William winked at her.

She turned around. That man thought he knew everything, and really, he knew nothing at all. She was determined to prove it. She would win this ridiculous bet and make him grovel, and if not, well…she wouldn't mind another kiss.

The third act began. Her heart was still racing in her chest, and this time it wasn't because of the music.

CHAPTER TWENTY-THREE

MR. ASHLEY, WHO HAD claimed to be a great lover of opera, and that he saw her affinity for it a sign of her superior intellect, did not return to the box until the fourth—and final—act. Justine had glanced back once or twice, wondering where he was, ignoring William's smirk, and quickly turned her attention to the music. The opera was too good to let anything else occupy her.

Mr. Ashley returned in the middle of the death scene, at the point when Leonora takes the poison so that she dies with her lover. *Rather than live as another's, I wanted to die as yours!*

Mr. Ashley's return necessitated a lot of shuffling about behind her, as Lord Grafton and Lord Bardaline had to allow him to pass, and then forcing William to move one seat over so that he might sit as quickly as possible. And then the man had the audacity to whisper loudly to one of the gentlemen.

His behavior perturbed her. How could he miss the finale? Worse, how could he cause others to miss even a moment of it? How dare he not give these performers his complete attention?

At the conclusion of the opera Justine was on her feet. She still had tears in her eyes from the moving death scene, and was applauding as hard as one might in gloves. She turned about, expecting to see him, but her gaze met William's.

She was surprised to see that he looked a little misty eyed and guessed he, too, had been moved by the final scene. "Wasn't it wonderful?"

"Superb," he said and looked as if he intended to say more, but Mr. Ashley swayed into view.

He was all smiles, solicitous of her opinion of the performance and eager to carry on to the Grafton house. "They've invited us all to come round," he said eagerly. A bit *too* eagerly—Justine could detect the scent of whisky and understood he'd slid a bit into his cups.

Lord Grafton presented the invitation to Justine to return to his house for refreshments. She found it hard to refuse after his kindness of lending his box. But she felt the swell of nerves in her chest as they all bustled out and she was swept into a waiting coach along with the Bardalines. She was at least grateful that the Graftons had not invited hordes to ogle her in their home. Just those who had been guests in their box.

Their home was as grand as all of them seemed to be in and around Mayfair, with a large salon and furniture upholstered in silk chintz. There were at least three cats strutting among them, tails high, rubbing against the ladies' skirts. It should have been the perfect social setting for Justine—there were new faces, but not too many—and perhaps she might have enjoyed it had Lady Bardaline not been so suffocating in her attentions. She hardly left Justine's side, as if she feared a private conversation with Mr. Ashley would result in an elopement.

Justine couldn't believe what she was thinking, but she really wished Amelia was here to take center stage so that she might step aside and breathe. Unfortunately, she was at the very center. When refreshments were served, the Graftons were full of questions for her—what was St. Edys like? When did she expect to return to Wesloria? Did she find the prospect of being queen terribly challenging?

Somehow, she managed through it, and sounded, at least to herself, perfectly collected. Twice, she tried to steer the conversation to the opera, to the breadth of talent the soprano, in particular, seemed to possess. William said, "Aye, her performance was exceptional," but Lord Grafton said he'd heard that Wesloria would be building more rail lines, and was that so?

Eventually, wine and whisky were served along with cake, and everyone seemed in good spirits, the talk lively, the attention on others, and Justine relaxed. Mr. Ashley had assumed the role of Amelia and commanded attention by his laugh and his charming asides to everyone in the room. He was swaying a bit on his feet, and when the butler offered to refresh his glass, he sloshed a bit of the liquid onto the carpet in his haste to agree.

Justine was explaining to Lady Grafton the bit of green she wore on her gown that was the symbol of Wesloria when Mr. Ashley interrupted her. "Will your husband be forced to wear the green?" he asked jovially. "Will he be required to renounce his country?"

Forced? "Not at all," Justine said. She touched the bit of green on her bodice. "It's a mark of national pride, that's all."

"What elegant hands you have, ma'am," he said as if he hadn't heard her. "It is little wonder that your skill at the piano is so advanced."

"They are very ordinary hands, sir, and my skill is average. My mother, on the other hand, is quite adept at the piano." She avoided William's gaze, knowing that he was marking the number of useless compliments Mr. Ashley was giving her.

"There is nothing ordinary about you, Your Royal Highness. I would wager you're a fine dancer as well. Are you? Lady Grafton, we must have music."

"Oh, no, thank you," Justine said quickly. She would rather be tossed out the window than made to stand up and dance in this setting.

"That's a splendid idea," Lord Grafton said. "We might all have a turn about the salon, eh? Madam?" he said, indicating with his head that his wife should seat herself at the piano. "Lady Bardaline, if you will do me the honor?"

Justine wanted to crawl under the settee, but Lady Grafton was quickly on her way to take her seat at the piano. She began to play a lively tune.

Mr. Ashley held out his hand to Justine. She hesitated. "Come on, then," he said gaily.

Justine took his hand and stood up. He immediately twirled her around and began to dance.

She knew the steps to the polka, knew how to follow, but he kept missing steps, then laughing loudly, his breath heaving the fumes of a distillery on her. A near collision with Lord Grafton and Lady Bardaline didn't seem to disturb him in the slightest—he just spun her sharply another way. And again. And again, faster and faster. He spun her so fast that she felt her tiara tumble off her head, and she cried out. That tiara was a gift from the Russian Empress Katherine to her great-great-aunt, Queen Elena. That he had spun it right off her head seemed almost prophetic.

Suddenly, the twirling stopped. Somehow, William stood between her and Mr. Ashley. "That's enough, Ashley," he said softly. He turned to Justine and handed her the tiara.

"Thank you." Her hair had come partially out of its pins.

"What are you doing?" Mr. Ashley demanded of William between gasps for breath. "The princess was enjoying herself. Did you not see her smile? It brightens even the darkest of rooms." He bowed, swirling his wrist in a flourish.

Lord, he was embarrassingly drunk.

When no one answered him, he rose up and looked around the room, then pinned his gaze on William. "What is it, Douglas? Do you not agree? Do you think Her Royal Highness's smile is…dim?"

"Please, Mr. Ashley," Justine said.

"I beg your pardon, ma'am, but I cannot imagine a more charming combination of traits to sit upon a throne—a queen with a winsome smile and an intellect far superior to any I've known."

She turned away, embarrassed now. Lady Bardaline looked mortified.

"Tell her I'm right, Douglas."

"I can think of no other princess more perfectly suited, no."

"You're *both* very charming, sirs," Lady Grafton said, clearly trying to fix whatever had happened here.

Mr. Ashley did not seem to understand that everyone in this room was trying to save him from embarrassing himself more. And he seemed oddly fixated on William. "Still traveling on the continent, Douglas? Or have recent events kept you closer to home?"

Justine didn't know what he meant, but she noted William's dark frown. She also noted that Lady Grafton's face had drained of blood. "What recent events?" she asked.

Mr. Ashley laughed. "Boys are boys and do childish things. It's an adage here, Your Royal Highness. Do you know what that means? It's like…a proverb."

Yes, she knew what it meant, as she was fluent in English, and she had a brain in her head, and there was a similar saying in Wesloria. A boy is a boy even when he's a man, or something like it. She didn't care for his need to explain the word to her, or the insinuation that William had done something childish. Or the way he seemed so determined to find fault with William. She looked at Lady Bardaline, hoping for once her lady-in-waiting could read her expression and they could escape.

"Perhaps you'd like a turn with the princess, Douglas?" Mr. Ashley said as he walked to the sideboard and picked up a clean glass. "You know the ballroom dances, do you? Or is it only country dances in Scotland?"

"It's both," William said. "In Scotland, we appreciate more than one type of entertainment."

"*You* certainly seem to," Mr. Ashley muttered.

In the awkward silence that followed, Justine tried again to relay her desire to Lady Bardaline, but that one clearly didn't understand.

"I have indeed, sir," William said. "I'm a fortunate man to have enjoyed life as I have."

Mr. Ashley laughed again, but it was not a light laugh. It sounded dark, and Justine didn't like it. She didn't like anything about him now. She stared at her lady-in-waiting.

It was Lord Bardaline who understood her. "Your Royal Highness," he said, "the hour grows late."

She could have kissed the old sod. "Indeed it does! Thank you, Lord Grafton, Lady Grafton, for your hospitality. Lord Douglas, thank you for the invitation. I thought the opera divine."

He bowed.

She glanced at Mr. Ashley. "Good evening, Mr. Ashley."

"So soon? But we've not yet had a waltz."

"Another time," she said curtly, and with her tiara tightly

in hand, she began to walk from the room as a butler and
one of the cats hurried ahead of her. She stepped out into
the hallway without looking back, and could only hope the
Bardalines were behind her. She wanted nothing more than
to quit this place, to hie herself to Prescott Hall and burrow
herself under her covers.

She'd had hopes for Jonathan Ashley, but he had dashed
them all to pieces with his drunken antics.

As the coach pulled away, she glanced out the window,
almost fearing that Mr. Ashley would come running after
them. But it wasn't Mr. Ashley who was silhouetted in the
open door of the Grafton House. It was William.

Her heart pattered anxiously in her chest, and she forced
her attention to the Bardalines, both of them complaining
of Mr. Ashley's drink.

It wasn't until they had reached Prescott Hall that Justine realized the bracelet her father had given her was gone
from her wrist.

CHAPTER TWENTY-FOUR

LILA FOUND THE crown princess in the garden the next day, wearing a large straw hat and carrying a wicker basket on her arm. Her little dog, Dodi, was chasing butterflies around her. The princess was snipping dahlias in full bloom and tossing them haphazardly into her basket, then leaning down and grabbing handfuls of candytuft to toss in, too.

"Good afternoon, Your Royal Highness! I didn't expect to see you up and about so early today." She didn't expect to see her cutting her own flowers, either. There were scores of Weslorians about to do that sort of thing.

"It's hardly early. It's half past three." The princess did not look at her, but continued on with her study of the blooms, choosing those she wanted. One bush was all but bare.

The princess's hair hung in one long tail down her back, which suggested to Lila that she'd not had Seviana attend her today. It suggested to Lila she'd come out here to be alone.

"Well, yes, but I heard you and the Bardalines return from the opera at nearly two o'clock in the morning. How did you find it?"

"The opera? It was astonishingly good." She snipped a bloom and tossed it into her basket.

"Wonderful!" She paused a moment to pet the dog, who had scampered away from a butterfly to greet Lila.

"Is it, really, Lila?" The princess glanced at Lila from beneath the broad brim of her hat. "You don't care what I thought of the opera. You want to know what I thought of Mr. Ashley."

The princess was in a foul mood. Lila could hardly blame her, having heard all the details of last night from Lady Bardaline. She shooed the dog away, and Dodi raced back to the hedge and began to dig. "I do care what you thought about the opera, as I have always found it to be such a lovely experience. But if you'd like to talk about Mr. Ashley, I'd be delighted to hear what you have to say. Did he enjoy the opera? Is that an interest the two of you share?"

Princess Justine dropped her shears. She shoved the basket aside and slowly rose to her full height. She faced Lila, hands on hips in a manner that reminded Lila of the stance her mother used to take before scolding her. She knew then that the evening with Mr. Ashley had gone worse than she'd expected.

She was unhappy that the gentleman had turned out to be a drunkard. How could she have possibly known it? Sometimes these things revealed themselves after she'd done her best to uncover the worst about a person. And still, she was a teeny bit thrilled, especially since only a few days ago she'd fretted that perhaps she had chosen unwisely, and that Mr. Ashley was far more appealing to the princess than Lila wanted.

"I don't know if Mr. Ashley enjoyed the opera," the princess said coolly. "I did. Lord Douglas did. But I don't know if Mr. Ashley did. Would you like to know why?"

"Yes."

"He was absent from Lord and Lady Grafton's box for half of it. And he crooked his elbow so many times that I am certain his arm is in a sling today."

"Pardon?"

"He showed himself to be a tosspot."

"Oh dear." Lila wrinkled her nose to show that she was distressed by this news.

"Lord Douglas warned me. He said that Ashley was a horrible person and I didn't believe him. But he was right."

"Lord Douglas warned you?"

"He did! He's been right about both of your matches, Lila. And *you* have been woefully wrong about both of them."

Lila shrugged. *"Balloon d'essai."*

Princess Justine stared at her. "Did you just say…balloon test?"

"I did! Have you heard of them? They send balloons up to test the direction of the wind, and that's what I am doing with you. Testing which way the wind is blowing, so to speak." She smiled, pretending that the princess would understand and accept this immediately. "It's a process."

The princess gaped at her. "It's a flawed process! I never want to see Mr. Ashley again. He was unkind to Lord Douglas, he was so careless in his dancing that a *priceless* tiara came off my head and I lost the bracelet my father gave me!"

"If you don't want to see him again, you won't. It's as simple as that. I'm so very sorry about your tiara. Shall I send Bardaline to search for your bracelet?"

The princess didn't answer. She was staring at Lila, as if she were looking at a distorted painting she couldn't make out.

"We will put Mr. Ashley firmly behind us, Your Royal Highness."

"Thank you." She dipped down for her shears and turned back to the dahlia bush.

"But…"

The princess's head snapped round. *"But?"*

"But…if there was anything about him that you liked or appreciated, it would be helpful to know."

"What? *Why?*"

"So that I might continue to assess your likes and dislikes. For example, you liked the flowers Aggiani arrived with."

"I like flowers. I don't like wagons full of them. It's a waste."

"And you did seem to enjoy speaking of books and playing music with Mr. Ashley."

The princess's unusual eyes narrowed. "I like books and I like music. I would think you would know that. If nothing else, I am sure my mother gave you a list of things she wished I would like and those she wished I didn't."

This young woman was astute. Lila had discarded that list long ago. "Well. The good news is, we've a new caller arriving later today."

The princess's mouth dropped open. "Have you lost your senses? Whoever it is, send him away. I don't want to meet him."

"I think, given your feelings on the first two, that this gentleman just might be the one for you."

"Lady Aleksander, you have not inspired my confidence."

Oh, she was angry—she had reverted to addressing Lila formally.

"He is Prince Michel of Miraval, a lovely Mediterranean principality that I think you would enjoy in the summer."

Princess Justine made a sound of alarm and anguish. She dipped down, picked up the dog and tucked her under her arm. With her free hand she picked up the basket, and with a sharp look at Lila, began marching toward the hall.

Lila hurried to keep up with her. The princess was taller, and her stride was longer and she was forced to jog alongside her. "He is a gentleman. He is kind, and he loves animals—he has quite a menagerie. Goats, chickens, dogs and cats. Do you love animals, or do you prefer only dogs?"

"Of course I love animals. What sort of monster would I be if I didn't love animals? But I cannot be persuaded to affection by a *chicken*."

"He likes to read, too. The last I saw him, we discussed the writing of Voltaire."

"Not another word!" the princess insisted.

Behind them, one of her ever-present guards shouted, *"Cessez!"*

"Sorry, I don't speak Weslorian!" Lila called over her shoulder.

"Weslorian! He's speaking to you in French and commanding you to stop."

"Prince Michel has younger siblings and he is most considerate of them. He will make an excellent father. And while he is…agreeable in looks and stature, he is not so handsome that one must worry about ladies throwing themselves at his feet, as you might have worried with Mr. Ashley."

The princess picked up her pace. So did Lila. "He is a year older than you and is heir to a vast fortune in the sea trade."

Princess Justine paused only to put Dodi on her feet, then began to jog up the terrace steps, Dodi trotting beside her. Lila could not keep pace. She called after her, "He should arrive in time for tea!" And then dragged in a deep breath.

Princess Justine shrieked with agitation as she disappeared out of view. The dog paused at the top of the stairs and looked back at Lila, her tail wagging. When Lila didn't call her, she scampered after the princess.

Lila sat heavily on the steps to catch her breath. She couldn't wait to tell Valentin about this. She had every hope he would be here soon.

When she'd caught her breath, she stood and began to walk, taking the time to feel the sun in her hair and on her face. She followed a path she knew well now. It led around the hall and into the woods. As she came to the corner of the hall, she could see the drive, and noticed someone had just come up on horseback.

Lila paused, shielding her eyes from the sun with one hand. A smile slowly lit her face when she realized who it was. "Well, well, well, my lord. You can't stay away, can you?"

She watched William Douglas hand his reins to a groom. He had something in his hand, which he dropped. He quickly bent to retrieve it. It was a book. He was bringing the princess a *book*. He dusted it off and held it firmly as he strode to the door, taking the steps two at a time.

Lila smiled. How she loved it when all her plans came together.

Now it was time to begin to prepare Robuchard for a match that would not come from his list of names. She began to compose that letter in her head as she strolled into the woods.

BEFORE WILLIAM HAD arrived at Prescott Hall, he'd been very busy.

The first thing he did was send a telegraph to Robuchard.

Your matchmaker is deplorably bad at her occupation! It is good for all involved that I am here to keep a complete catastrophe at bay! I suggest you recall her immediately!

Ewan nervously pointed to the exclamation marks. "They donna like them, milord. The wee fellow, his face gets as red as an apple when he sees them."

"Those marks, as you call them, are a necessary part of the written language, Ewan. Give him this—" He fished a crown out of his purse and handed it to MacDuff. "Tell him it's important the marks stay, as they assist in explaining the urgency of the situation."

Ewan sighed. Off he'd toddled, mumbling under his breath.

The next thing William had done was go to Beck's house. Quite unannounced, which was rude, but he didn't care, as his situation, both internally and externally, had reached a crisis. He was shown to the house garden, where he found the Hawke family quite at their leisure. Frankly, that was the way he found them every time he'd ever called at this house. Beck's wife was seated, flipping through the pages of a fashion magazine. Her belly swelled under her gown—she looked like she would burst forth with another child at any moment.

Beck was lying flat on his back in the grass. Three little lassies climbed over him and moved his limbs about to suit whatever it was they were doing. The fourth girl, the smallest of them, lay next to Beck in the grass, sucking her thumb.

And Donovan, the mysterious governor—and friend, he supposed?—was sitting under a tree, a book in his lap.

William greeted them all and shifted his weight impatiently from one hip to the other.

"Douglas," Beck said jovially. "To what do we owe the extraordinary pleasure of your visit?"

"I need advice."

"Advice! He needs advice, my love," Beck said as if his wife hadn't heard.

"We all need advice from time to time," she said. "I need advice on what gown I should like to commission. There are so many designs from which to choose."

"I beg your pardon. I very kindly offered you advice and you refused it," Donovan said.

Lady Iddesleigh put down her magazine. "I told you, Donovan, I will not wear yellow. With my ginger hair?"

"That's precisely why you *ought* to wear yellow," Donovan insisted.

William was on a mission, and he didn't want to be distracted...but who *was* this man?

"Douglas, is the question that weighs on you appropriate for four sets of enormous ears?" Beck asked.

The oldest one—Mathilda, William thought he recalled—looked up. "Who has enormous ears, Papa?"

"You do. Ears as big as an elephant's. Look at them now, flapping in the breeze."

"I don't have elephant ears!" the lass cried, and together with her sisters, they attacked their father at once, bouncing onto his stomach and his legs while Beck made suitable sounds of distress and pretended to flail his arms.

It was a lovely tableau, this family, and had he not been in such a rush, William might have admired it and marveled at how Beckett Hawke was the very last man in the world he would have pictured in this way. "Ah...no," William said.

Beck ignored him—he was tickling the girls now. At

least Lady Iddesleigh took pity on him. "All right, my little darlings. The gentleman needs your papa. Katy! Katy,
where are you? Why do you always disappear?" she called,
obviously looking for a servant.

Donovan snorted. "If the lass is smart, she's tidying
a room as far from these four as possible." He closed his
book and hopped to his feet, striding to where the girls were
pummeling their father. Lady Iddesleigh hoisted herself out
of her chair and held out her hands for her daughters. "All
right, then. Come, darlings."

At the sound of their mother's voice, three of them abandoned their father without so much as a kiss. Donovan
stepped over Beck and picked up the baby, then followed
the girls, putting his hand on the head of one of the younger
ones who tried to veer off toward a table laden with fruit
and water, and pointing her back in the direction of her
mother.

William bowed as Lady Iddesleigh waddled by, her hand
to the small of her back.

"I hope you receive better advice than what my husband
gave me the time I wondered aloud why we'd not been
blessed with a boy." She moved her hand over her belly.

"So do I," Donovan said as he passed, now carrying the
baby and the next youngest girl.

Beck sat up, his legs straight in front of him. He watched
his family and Donovan climb the stairs and said, "The
next had better be a boy, by God. Am I to live out the rest
of my life with all these girls underfoot?"

William offered him a hand up. Beck was in shirtsleeves,
rolled up to his elbows. He hopped to his feet, straightened
his waistcoat, dragged his fingers through his hair—which
made it stand up on end—and flicked grass from his trousers. He walked to the table and filled a glass with water.

"They'll be the death of me, all of them," he said. "And to think I used to fear death at the hands of Caro, Eliza and Hollis. They were ducklings compared to my brood." He drank the water and looked at William. He dragged the back of his hand across his mouth. "Now, then. What sort of advice do you seek, my friend?"

"I need to know how to get rid of a matchmaker."

Beck laughed. William did not. Donovan, he noticed, had wandered back onto the terrace. He didn't want an audience for this conversation, but he wanted to be at Prescott Hall before it was too late. "She has brought the worst possible candidates to the princess. Principe di Aggiani. Jonathan Ashley."

"Ashley! Dirty little bastard, that one. He called once on my sister Caro. I wouldn't let him in the door."

"There must be something that can be done," William insisted.

Beck cocked his head to one side. "What can be done? And why do you care who the princess marries?"

"I…I *donna* care," he said, stammering a little. He could kick himself—he'd been so intent on enlisting Beck to come up with a plan that he hadn't considered the most obvious question. "That is, I *do* care, as she is my friend. But only for that reason."

"Mmm-hmm," Donovan said.

William rubbed his nape. "Beck. Help me."

"Yes, of course, I will, as you clearly need my help." Beck put down his glass. "All right, then, here it is. I give this advice to you as a friend, Douglas. Do you understand?"

William nodded and indicated with his hand that Beck should get on with it.

"My advice is that you step out of the way and allow

Lady Aleksander to find the princess someone to marry. She must marry, and soon, if rumors of her father's demise are to be believed. And you will be removed from her circle soon enough, as the rumor of a scandal in Scotland has begun to reach London."

William's heart stilled. "What rumor?"

Beck smiled. "You really don't know? Would you like me to repeat all that I've ever heard about you? Because there's quite a lot. Perhaps just the salacious parts."

Donovan laughed.

William had feared the worst after the drunk babbling of Ashley, but hope was such a potent thing, and had managed to cloak his fear. "A rumor…about my father, then?"

Beck shook his head. "About you and a country girl."

He could feel the blood drain from his face. All that money his father had paid to keep it quiet. William had warned him it would never work. "I did nothing, on my word, my hand to God. Nothing happened, other than I tried to help her."

Beck put up his hand, saving William the embarrassment of babbling on. "You needn't say more. It's not me you need convince."

William was suddenly struck with the terrifying thought of those rumors reaching Justine. His heart squeezed with the despair and the injustice of it all. He would rather die than have her think ill of him. He wanted her to esteem him. He wanted her to…to *love* him.

Much like he esteemed her. More every day.

He couldn't stomach even the thought of being removed from her circle, but he knew aristocrats well enough to know it would happen in the blink of an eye. He enjoyed her company. He found her interesting and refreshing and he couldn't bear this, none of it.

"You look ill, my lord," Donovan said.

"I think my heart is failing," William admitted.

"I've an idea," Donovan said.

William looked at him. "Aye, good. But who *are* you? Besides the children's tutor."

Beck burst into laughter. "He's not a *tutor*, Douglas," Beck said jovially.

"Let's just say I'm an old family friend," Donovan said. "Do you want the idea, or not?"

William would take any help at the moment. He gestured for him to speak.

"Invite the matchmaker to tea. Tell her what you know of her picks and offer to assist her. Handsome bloke like you, she'll accept."

"A splendid idea, Donovan," Beck said. "Of course that's what he must do. He'll not win if he challenges her." He looked at William. "So woo her."

CHAPTER TWENTY-FIVE

LATER THAT DAY, when William arrived at Prescott Hall, he was feeling a little down. It was not like him to be sullen—if there was one thing that could be said for him, it was that he maintained an even keel. Even his father couldn't drag him completely into the depths of despair, because as the firstborn and heir, William had learned at a very early age it was best to keep his feelings to himself, lest they be brought out at the supper table to be reviewed by the entire family. His mother in particular didn't care to have a son who was either mopey or excitable.

But it was more than that—he'd always known exactly how he felt about people and things and situations. He never had cause to question his feelings—whatever they were, they generally seemed straightforward to him. This, however, was one time he couldn't rightly sort them out. He was a practical man, and yet, he was feeling entirely too hopeful. He was prepared for the worst, and yet, he felt a peculiar ache.

He didn't like feeling uncertain, and yet, uncertainty was crawling over him like an army of ants.

He got off his mount and promptly dropped the gift he'd brought Justine. He quickly swooped it up and brushed the dust and gravel from it, then strode purposefully to the door before he lost his nerve. Look at him, bringing a gift to a woman who was not his lover.

The butler met him at the door and held out his hand for his hat. "Her Royal Highness is cutting flowers," he said. "She is in the flower beds on the eastern side." He pointed down a long path to the end of the east wing. "The guard will announce you." At the point where the path turned the corner, a guard stood with his back against the wall. He looked bored. Half-asleep.

William put his hat in the butler's hands. "Thank you." He walked in that direction. As he neared the corner, the guard came to attention. *"Stat."*

William didn't know what that meant, but he was going to guess it meant stop. "The butler sent me this way, lad."

"Las ta lebi!" he heard a woman call.

He leaned to his left to see around the guard. Justine was only a few feet beyond. Her face was obscured by the enormous brim of her sun hat. She wore her hair in a long tail down her back, and a gardening apron over her blue dress.

The guard stepped aside and allowed William to pass, but he gave him a dark look, as if he disagreed with the command given. William strode toward the princess.

Justine set down her empty basket and removed her gardening gloves. She brushed a strand of her hair from her eyes. "Why is it everyone insists on finding me in the garden?"

"Perhaps because you're here?" She looked very appealing dressed like a country gardener. He liked it. "Where is Dodi?" he asked, looking around.

"Poor thing is exhausted. I left her with Lady Bardaline." She looked him over. "I suppose you came to gloat."

"Your Royal Highness. I would *never* gloat—that would be rude, aye? I came to give you this." He reached in his pocket and pulled out a bracelet.

Justine's countenance instantly changed. She gasped,

then looked at him with surprise and gratitude, a warm smile suddenly lighting her face. "You *found* it."

"Aye."

"Thank you!" She stepped forward and put out her hand, palm up. "I *despaired* for it. My father gave it to me at my investiture as crown princess. Look, do you see? Our initials, entwined. The king and his heir."

"I did see."

She moved the thin gold chain with the entwined M and J around. "Wherever did you find it?"

"In the Grafton salon, near where your tiara fell. Here, allow me." He stuffed the book under his arm and took the bracelet from her palm. He wrapped it around her wrist, fastening the hook. And then he stroked her wrist with his thumb. He did it because he wanted to feel her skin, to know if it was as smooth and silken as it appeared to him.

She slowly lifted her gaze to his. "What was that?"

He kept his gaze on hers and shrugged. He stroked her skin again, willing his thumb to memorize the feel of it. "Nothing." He reluctantly dropped her hand and took the book from under his arm.

She stared at him for a moment, one eye covered by the brim of her hat, and then glanced down. "What's that?"

"Pardon?"

She pointed at the book.

"Oh, ah…" He suddenly felt ridiculous. Why had he brought it? "It's… I thought you might…" How mortifying— he didn't know how to be this man.

Justine spared him the humiliation of having to choke out the admission that it was a gift and took it from his hand.

"You like books, and I… I thought…" He cleared his throat. "William Thackeray is an English novelist—"

"Yes, I know." She was squinting at the book's spine.

"The title is *The History of Henry Esmond.* I thought it quite English in its story. I enjoyed it."

She glanced up with a dubious expression. "You read it?"

"I think I ought to be offended. I do know how to read, ma'am. Like you, I enjoy it."

"But I've never known a gentleman to enjoy works of fiction."

"All written works are works of fiction. They vary only in degree."

She laughed. She reached into her pocket and withdrew a pair of eyeglasses and fumbled with them, trying to set them on her face while holding the book, and when William tried to reach for the book to help her, she pulled it from his grasp. She managed to set the eyeglasses on her face and opened the book.

William blinked. He wasn't expecting this, but she looked so...so bloody *charming* in her eyeglasses. Without them, she was elegant, refined, pretty. Every inch a queen. But with them, she looked—and he couldn't believe that he was thinking this—adorable.

She happened to glance up and frowned curiously. "What's that look? Have you never seen anyone wear eyeglasses? I may look silly, but they are entirely necessary for me to read. It's not as if I can help it."

"You donna look silly. You wear eyeglasses better than anyone I've ever seen."

"Don't tease me," she said, her eyes on the first page of the book.

"I'm no', Justine. You look..." He had to pause and swallow. This was so unlike him. "Winsome."

She glanced up. *"Winsome?"* Her amber eyes sparkled with amusement behind the lenses. She laughed. And when she did, William couldn't help himself—he cupped her face in his hands and kissed her, catching half of her brim between their cheeks.

Justine instantly squealed against his mouth and put a hand to his chest, pushing him back. "You've lost your mind!" She looked to where the guard was standing.

"Aye, maybe," he answered truthfully.

"I thought *I* was supposed to pay my debt."

"That was no' about a bet," he said, annoyed with himself.

"Then what was it? I know you must be terribly pleased with yourself, having guessed right again."

"I'm no' pleased, I'm angry that he was ever presented to you."

"I should have listened to you." She turned away and moved deeper into the garden. "It would appear you'll have another opportunity to prove your incomparable skill and report to Robuchard. Another suitor is due to arrive this evening. Prince Michel of Miraval. Have you met him? Do you want to warn me now about why he is utterly the wrong pick?"

"I've no' heard of Miraval, much less this…prince," he said with a flick of his hand. He could, in fact, warn her why this prince was utterly the wrong pick, but not for the reasons she expected. Thankfully, she didn't seem to really want him to say, which meant he wouldn't have to put his complicated feelings into words.

"Miraval is a small principality on the Mediterranean Sea. My ancestors once ruled it before they were pushed out by the Spaniards."

"A small principality? That seems reason enough to dismiss him."

Justine laughed and walked to the end of a line of shrubs

sculpted to resemble a giant butterfly. She glanced at the guard, then at William and stepped behind the butterfly.

The guard was leaning with one shoulder against the wall, his back to them. In two strides, William was also behind the butterfly.

Behind it was a bench. There was a small break in the shrubs through which one could see to the other side. And the guard. Justine collapsed onto the bench, pushing her straw hat from her head and letting it tumble down behind her. "That guard is the laziest of them all. He won't even notice."

"You're certain?"

She nodded, then clutched the book to her chest. "This was so very kind of you, William. I *do* like to read, and I've read some remarkable works, not just fiction. I—"

He sat beside her, reached up and took the eyeglasses from her face, folding them carefully.

"Now what are you doing?"

"You mentioned the bet you lost."

"Of course I did. I honor my word."

"Good," he said. He touched her jaw and kissed her cheek. She sighed softly.

"I am going to be a queen. It is imperative that I honor my word. Once the people's good opinion of me is lost, the more perilous my rule becomes."

"Did you read that, then?" He kissed the other cheek, then moved to her neck.

She tilted her head to one side to allow it. "No, my father said it. He's taught me everything I know, really."

"And did he perhaps advise you never to bet what you are afraid to lose?" He put his hand on her knee, then slid down, to the hem of her skirt, finding her ankle beneath the yards of fabric. He kept his gaze on her face, noticing the smattering of tiny little freckles across the bridge of her nose, how the arch of one brow was a bit higher than the other. How the sun shone in her golden eyes.

"I'm not afraid to lose," she said. "I'm afraid of life passing me by."

He paused for a moment. "Life will no' pass you by. No' if you refuse to let it." He leaned forward to kiss the hollow of her throat. She tipped her head back. He slowly slid his hand up her calf, over silk stockings, until he reached her bare knee. He heard her intake of breath and sealed it in her chest with a kiss to her lips.

"You are very free with my person," she murmured and kissed him back, her fingers touching his face, then sliding into his hair.

"Because I canna resist you. Would you like me to stop?"

She gave him a sultry smile. "I didn't say that."

He slid his hand up, past the lace of her knickers, between her legs, to her inner thigh. He expected her to stop him, to slap his hand away, to warn him of the guard. But she didn't do any of that—she parted her legs slightly.

The spin of desire in him was instant, that terrible ratcheting that made it impossible to contain a thought. She shivered when he stroked her thigh, gasping into his mouth and then biting his lower lip. He moved his hand higher.

"We can't do this," she whispered into his ear.

"I'll stop—"

"No!" She caught his hand. "I mean—never mind what I meant. I don't want you to stop."

She might as well have ripped her gown and stood naked before him. He kissed her with all the lust and want and regard that was billowing through him, the wind to his prurient sail. He slipped his fingers through the gap in her knickers and into the folds of her flesh.

She gasped, the sound of it audible, and he again thought he should stop, that he had misunderstood her, and his mind began to reel—how could he be so stupid?

It was almost as if she could read his thoughts because she kissed him. She kissed him hard, her tongue in his mouth, her breath mingling with his. She caressed his shoulders, and she was pressing against him, her back arching.

He had a single thought, small and weak, that they were in a garden, that anyone could walk up and find him debauching the future queen of Wesloria. That could be disastrous for them both. But Justine urged him on and he was no hero, no saint—he wanted this just as much as she did.

It was impossible to fathom how mad he was for her, and he was alarmed by it. He would give up all of the Hamilton estate just to touch her and feel the response she evoked in him. It had been a lifetime since he'd felt so aroused—his blood rushed through his veins, his body strained against his clothes, his heart beat like a bloody Highland drum. He stroked her, his finger swirling and sliding inside and around over and over again and again. Justine pressed against his hand, moving against him, in rhythm with him.

It was not supposed to be like this; she was not supposed to want the seduction; she was supposed to think of other things, to be above his desire for her. But instead, she had sparked this furious, anxious heat in him that was inextinguishable. He didn't know what to do with it.

When his thumb touched the core of her and his fingers performed their dance, she gasped again, lifting against him until she made a muffled cry of release against his shoulder. He could feel her body melting around him, and he caught her with his arm to keep her from sliding off the bench. When she was completely motionless, he withdrew his hand, and put down her skirt and withdrew a handkerchief from his pocket.

Justine opened her eyes and looked directly at him. Her eyes were as golden and warm as the sun. She pressed her palm against his cheek. He felt a current of emotion between them, something that felt very much like mutual affection.

He picked up her eyeglasses and put them back on her face. He smiled tenderly. Justine leaned forward and kissed him so softly that he felt a bit weightless. She sat back and reached for her sun hat. She put it on her head, folded her hands in her lap and turned to face him. "If I were to inquire what we are doing, you and I, what would you say?"

"A fair question." He shook his head. "I...esteem you, Justine. I very much enjoy your company. I find you unbearably attractive."

Her smile widened. "And I find the same about you against all my better judgment! This is *folly*, William. I am in England to settle on a fiancé, not to engage in an affair that will make everything worse. And I can't keep making these *bets*." She directed the remark heavenward, almost as if she was beseeching a higher power.

"It's my fault. I'm no' able to help myself where you're concerned."

"It's not your fault—I've been just as eager to...bet." He saw the gold of her eyes spark at her admission.

"Justine, I—"

"Princia! Princia!"

The guard had noticed her missing, after all. Justine hopped to her feet. "They're looking for me." She leaned over to fetch the book he'd given her, and with one last look at him, a look of dissatisfaction, of a conversation not finished, she walked away, arranging her sun hat on her head as she went.

William was dissatisfied, too. He wasn't sure what he'd been about to say. *Don't meet any more suitors. Look at me. There is something about me I have to tell you, that will ruin all my hope, but I want you. I love you.*

He remained on the bench a moment longer, more at odds with himself and the world than he'd ever been in his life.

CHAPTER TWENTY-SIX

THE GUARD LOOKED panicked when Justine appeared from behind the giant butterfly shrub, and well he ought to have been. Justine could have been kidnapped by now, decapitated and her head piked. Not that she was going to say a word, because none of that had happened, and obviously, she would have perished had he stumbled around the butterfly only moments before.

Thinking about it made her blush. She picked up her basket. She wondered if her expression revealed anything about what had really happened behind the shrub.

"Your Royal Highness, you are wanted," he said, anxiously. He gave a sharp bow.

"I'm always wanted." She would very much like to go somewhere private until the fizz in her blood had faded away, to sit by herself and think about what had happened, and how she hadn't had the least hesitation. How she'd actually *hoped* something like that might happen and had encouraged it.

And when the fizz had died, she would think about who she was becoming. She was not the same person she was when she'd met Aldabert. She couldn't even remember any longer who she had been then.

But who she was now wanted to be with William, to know if he felt the fizz in his blood like she felt in hers.

She glanced over her shoulder. William was there, having followed her out of the shrubbery.

"My lord—"

"Your Royal Highness, we found you!"

Justine groaned softly at the sound of Lila's voice. She smiled sorrowfully at William and turned as Lila sailed into the garden area with Lady Bardaline close on her heels.

"I wasn't hiding, of course you found me." *Oh dear.* She could tell by the slight lift in Lila's brows that she'd spoken too quickly—Lila's curiosity had been piqued.

"I beg your pardon for the interruption, but Prince Michel has arrived."

"Already?" Justine asked at the same moment William said, "Here?"

"I beg your pardon, my lord." Lady Bardaline stepped forward. "The princess has an engagement—"

"Yes, and isn't this fortuitous to find his lordship here! My lord, you *must* stay for supper. The kitchen has prepared a delectable meal in honor of our special guest. The menu, I understand, is *French*."

Justine didn't know which she liked better—that Lila was inviting William to stay, or that Lady Bardaline looked so sour suddenly.

"Thank you, but I should no' interfere—"

"It's no interference!" Lila insisted. She looked to Justine to confirm it was no interference.

William looked uncomfortable, as if he didn't know what to say. It was so unlike the man who had previously relished the opportunity to tell her what to do that it emboldened Justine. "Please, my lord, do stay. It will be livelier with you there. And I've no doubt you'll have useful advice for me."

William's gaze bored right through her eyes and somehow bent toward her heart. "As I've no doubt you'll benefit from it." He smiled.

So did Justine.

"Aye, very well. If Her Royal Highness desires my presence, I would be delighted to join you."

"But is it not better to…" Lady Bardaline looked as if she might cry. She glanced at Justine's basket. "What's that?"

Justine glanced down. It was very obviously a book. But now Lila had noticed it, too.

What was *that* look? What did she suspect? It was a book, for heaven's sake. Why was Lila smiling at her in that way? Had she given something away? She felt suddenly anxious, just as she'd felt the moment she realized her mother had discovered the truth about Aldabert Gustav. She did not like to anticipate a repeat of *that* scene, so she straightened her shoulders and said, "Lady Bardaline, will you be so kind as to see that Lord Douglas is engaged for a time?" And with that, she walked on, as she was allowed to do as the ruling member of this little clique, no apology or explanation necessary, a truth that she still had to remind herself of frequently.

She was not going to answer any questions or entertain any sly looks. She was going to bathe and read her book and pet her dog and think about the extraordinary thing that had happened in the garden.

SEVIANA CONVINCED HER to wear the pink-and-white-striped gown that reminded Justine of the china doll she'd had as a girl. She wore a pearl choker around her throat and a gold-and-pearl comb in her hair, both of them a gift from the Sultan of Oman during a state visit. On the outside she looked like someone who took things very seriously. A woman ready to rule. A descendant of Queen Elena.

But on the inside she felt like a girl, all warm and fluttery. On the inside she didn't care about decorum or morals. She was a woman who would allow a man to do what William had done to her behind a giant butterfly shrub as if she hadn't a care in the world.

She really wished she had the courage to *be* that woman, inside and out. Someone who enjoyed life, who didn't care what people would say of her.

She picked Dodi up and ruffled her fur. "You would never think ill of me, would you, Dodi?" she whispered to her dog.

Dodi responded with some enthusiastic tail wagging.

She put the dog down and made her way to the salon, Dodi prancing alongside her, afraid to be left out.

When Justine entered the salon, everyone in the room bowed or curtsied. Dodi raced ahead, desperate to be acknowledged, and following her little black button nose to the most interesting scents. Justine plastered a smile on her face and moved through, holding her hands at her waist, wishing one person after the next a good evening, all the while biting back any hint of nerves.

Lila was the first to reach her, barely beating Lord Bardaline, who clearly wanted to be the one to make introductions. "Your Royal Highness, please allow me to introduce His Royal Highness, Prince Michel of Miraval," Lila said, then cast out her arm as if on a stage.

Prince Michel came forward and bowed low. "Your Royal Highness, I cannot begin to express what true pleasure it is to make your vaulted acquaintance."

He spoke English without an accent. "Thank you."

He smiled warmly and had very kind eyes. He was trim, hardly an inch or two taller than she was. His skin was dark, his eyes brown with thick lashes and his smile so inviting that it instantly soothed her.

"Have you been in London long, Your Highness?" she asked.

"Only a week. My grandmother resides in Belgravia."

"She's English?"

"She is indeed," he said, clasping his hands at his back. "I was educated here under her watch."

He wasn't the most handsome man Justine had ever seen, but neither was he plain, and frankly, Justine preferred kind eyes and an inviting smile to a handsome face. She glanced at William, who stood behind everyone else. But a chirping sound caught her attention, and she turned to the window.

"You have heard my gift, I think," Prince Michel said sheepishly.

"Pardon?"

"If I may?" He moved as if he meant to get whatever he'd brought, but Lila was furiously conducting the footmen to bring forward the gift, a rather large thing covered in blue silk. Dodi began to bark at all the activity, and Bardaline quickly removed her while the footmen rolled the gift across the room.

Prince Michel pulled the cloth free to reveal a gold birdcage and two beautiful birds sitting side by side on a swing. They had green bodies and orange faces and were the most colorful birds Justine had ever seen. She gasped with delight. "They are beautiful!"

"I feared they wouldn't survive the voyage when we hit rough seas. I fretted over them as if I'd hatched them myself."

"Did the voyage make them ill?"

"Not at all. I seemed to be the only one who very nearly met my demise. When at last the water was calm again, I opened my eyes and these two lovelies were staring at me, surely curious if I had lived."

Justine laughed. "What sort of birds are they?"

"Lovebirds." The moment he said it, Prince Michel blushed. "I beg your pardon, ma'am, but that is what they are called. I didn't mean to imply... I chose them for their beauty, not for their name."

His fluster was charming. "It's quite all right, Prince Michel. I understood you completely."

He laughed self-consciously. "One does desire to make a good impression."

"As my friend Lord Douglas has said on many occasions. Have you met him?"

Prince Michel turned and smiled at William. "I have, indeed. We discovered we have a mutual friend."

"You *do*?" She looked at William.

"Count Jurgen of Bavaria," William said.

"Really? And how are you both acquainted with Count Jurgen?"

"He travels frequently between Miraval and Paris," Prince Michel said.

"I knew him the summer I lived in Paris," William added.

Justine shook her head in wonder. "On my word, Lord Douglas, I wonder if there is anyone of consequence on the continent you've not met."

"Well," said Prince Michel, "it is our first meeting."

"But I think it will no' be our last, Your Highness," William added.

Lord Bardaline interrupted, announcing that wine would be served in the solarium before supper. They repaired to that room and a pair of footmen began to serve. Prince Michel noted the bit of green Justine wore pinned to her shoulder, and the green the footmen wore. He said he thought the wearing of green a delightful Weslorian custom. He said he wished Miraval had such a custom.

He said he'd read the complete history of Wesloria and found it remarkable that so many queens had ruled by right well before they had in other European kingdoms. He said he thought that women brought the steady hand of justice to the throne, and remarked on the rule of his own great-great-grandmother in Miraval, and how she had been the one to see that so many necessary reforms were brought to their small principality.

He was a lovely companion, asking her questions about herself and showing his interest in her country. Justine kept stealing looks at William, trying to read his expression. She wondered if he was thinking of this afternoon, if the same glittering feeling was coursing through his blood. She wondered what he thought of Prince Michel, who, at first blush seemed…perfect.

When Lord Bardaline stepped in to speak to Prince Michel, Justine glanced to where William was speaking to Lila. Her gaze happened to fall to his hand. She recalled how he'd pressed the breadth of his palm against her. She and Aldabert had explored each other beyond the bounds of what was proper, but he'd always been in such a rush. It hadn't been the same with William. It had been—

"Ma'am?"

Justine started. Lord Bardaline was bowing, excusing himself, informing her supper was served.

She smiled apologetically at Prince Michel. If he noticed her ogling William's hand, he was too much of a gentleman to show it.

Lord Bardaline assembled them in a promenade, and she took the arm of the Miravalian prince and allowed him to escort her into the dining room. He was seated on her right, Lila on her left. William was seated at the far end of the table where she could hardly see him. She suspected that Lady Bardaline had not been able to banish him from this supper, so she'd sat him as far from Justine as possible.

Still, as there were only a few of them, everyone was included in the conversation. Prince Michel said he'd heard that the mountain flowers of Wesloria were extraordinary.

"They are beautiful, but I think not as beautiful as any flower from Italy...or so I've heard," Justine said. At the far end of the table, she heard William choke on a sip of his wine.

Prince Michel said that Miraval was known for its wine, and he hoped she was enjoying the glass of it, as he understood it had been served with dinner this evening. William said it was delicious, which gave Prince Michel the opportunity to point out that Miraval hoped to become to wine what Scotland was to Scotch whisky. That prompted a spirited discussion between the gentlemen as to the best whisky distilled in Scotland.

At the conclusion of the meal, the party returned to the salon. Lady Aleksander took the opportunity to show the prince one of the prize paintings of the hall.

William took the opportunity to speak to Justine.

"Well?" she whispered. "What warnings do you have for me?"

He looked slightly exasperated. "To my consternation, no' a one. He is a true gentleman and a delight when compared to your other dinner guests. What do *you* think?"

"I think there is nothing suspicious about him."

They both watched him laugh with Lady Bardaline.

"Is he the one?" Justine asked softly.

"Too soon!" William warned her. "Give it time, aye? The truth will come out. He's on his best behavior this evening."

"But I haven't got time."

William considered this a moment. "Then perhaps we ought to test him."

She glanced at him from the corner of her eye. "How?"

"Give him different circumstances to see how he behaves. For example, he does well enough with birds, but he hardly spared Dodi a passing glance. Does he like dogs?"

Justine snorted. "That's too easy. Everyone likes dogs."

"No' everyone. Would you want to be married to someone for all eternity who did no' care for dogs?"

"No," she said, truly horrified by the thought. "There are dogs in every room at St. Edys."

"We might ascertain what diversions he enjoys. It is entirely possible the pair of you have nothing in common when it comes to hobbies. He might abhor fencing."

Justine gave William an indulgent smile. "It's not necessary for him to enjoy fencing," she said. "*You* don't enjoy fencing."

"Aye, but I enjoy watching you fell men twice your size."

"Perhaps archery?"

This caused William to turn his head and look at her. "Are you an archer?"

Justine lifted her chin. "I don't like to boast, but I happen to be very good."

His brows rose. "Remarkable."

"Is it? Women can take aim, William."

"Aye, that they can. And no' just with an arrow."

"You're not an archer, either, are you?"

"You sound as if you think I could no' hit a house if my life depended on it."

"But you're a very good shepherd." She put her hand to her mouth and giggled behind it.

"Another talent we might add to your very long list—you're a wit."

She swallowed down a full-throated laugh. "I look forward to challenging you to a match."

"Of wits?"

Her laughter was hard to contain. "Of *archery*."

"I will never turn from a challenge. But the goal is to challenge *him*."

She looked back across the room to Prince Michel. "So it is. Shall I invite him to come round again tomorrow?"

"I think so."

"And you'll be here, won't you?" she asked without looking at him. She didn't want to sound too eager.

"If you'd like."

"I can't possibly assess him on my own."

"No, you certainly can no'."

She couldn't help herself—she looked up at him. William smiled affectionately. "I shudder to imagine what you might think acceptable if I were no' here to guide you."

"Imagine," she murmured.

A movement behind William distracted her, and she leaned slightly to her left. It was Lady Bardaline, frowning with disapproval. "Ah. Duty calls." She smiled at William then glided away to join Prince Michel.

"Your Royal Highness, Prince Michel was saying that he would return to Miraval in a fortnight," Lila said.

"So soon? But that gives you very little time in England."

"Alas, I am needed at home. Frankly, I should like to cross before the season of storms arrives. The ship's captain informed me that what I experienced on my crossing was hardly a drop of rain compared to what comes late in summer. I suffer from the affliction of seasickness." He laughed. "That hardly recommends me, does it? A prince of a seafaring nation who suffers from seasickness."

The Bardalines and William, close enough to have heard the exchange, laughed politely.

Prince Michel turned to Justine and bowed. "Your Royal Highness, the evening has been truly delightful, but I must take my leave. My grandmother is expecting me."

"What a good son you are," Lady Bardaline said with cloying sweetness.

"Then you must come round tomorrow," Justine said. "Will you?"

Prince Michel's face lit. "I should like that very much indeed."

"The weather has been so warm," she added. "Perhaps a picnic?"

"What a wonderful idea!" Lila said. "I shall see to it that all is arranged."

"Thank you, madam, but I shall see to it," Lord Bardaline sniffed.

"It might rain," Lady Bardaline said. "It often does this time of year."

Justine fought the urge to roll her eyes. "We will risk it, shall we, Your Highness?"

"We shall!" he said with enthusiasm. "A good rain has not yet made me seasick on land. Thank you. I should like that very much." He bowed and started for the door.

"I shall also take my leave," William said.

"And you must come to our picnic, Lord Douglas," Justine said quickly. "It's all the merrier with more people."

"But…" Lady Bardaline looked at William. "Lord Douglas, are you not expected—"

"Nowhere," William said quickly. "I am expected nowhere and I would be delighted to attend."

"Yes, my lord, we must have you," Prince Michel said and appeared to be genuine in his wish to have William join.

Justine did not miss the look that traveled from Lady Bardaline to Lord Bardaline to Lila, who blithely ignored them both.

"Shall I see you out, gentlemen?" Lila asked and began walking toward them, her arms outstretched as if she meant to scoop them along and carry them to the door. William stole a look at Justine as he passed, and she tried not to let her smile show.

When the gentlemen had gone out, Justine could feel the Bardalines staring all their daggers at her. She slowly turned around. "What is it?"

"Your Royal Highness," Lady Bardaline said. "Perhaps your picnic would be better suited for you without Lord Douglas?"

"It will be better suited with friends."

The woman opened her mouth, but Justine was already moving. "Can it wait, madam? I'm very tired." She was out the door before they could form a protest, much less a lecture.

She went upstairs to her rooms. She dismissed Seviana and readied for bed alone. She crawled under the coverlet with the book William had given her. She ran her fingers down the spine before opening it.

She was smiling. She couldn't wait to see him again tomorrow.

She was even looking forward to seeing Prince Michel, too.

CHAPTER TWENTY-SEVEN

WHEN WILLIAM TOLD Ewan he wanted a clean waistcoat for a picnic, and rejected the first three his valet showed him, the big man looked at him as if he was unquestionably mad.

Well, maybe he was—he wouldn't rule out anything at this point. He had never doubted Ewan's sartorial selections, donning whatever he brought out, even when the colors seemed a little off. He had never worried that he should look as handsome or virile as any other man. He never lay awake at night, thinking of a single woman, recalling every bloody word she said.

Ewan was standing before him, his mouth agape, a waistcoat in each hand. "I donna mean to offend you, Ewan. But these—" William gestured vaguely to the two waistcoats "—will no' suit today's occasion."

"And the occasion, milord, is a…*picnic*?"

He didn't have to make it sound preposterous. "Aye, MacDuff. A picnic. Is there something wrong with attending a picnic?"

"No, milord, no' at all. I want only to clarify so that I might find the right waistcoat." He turned around and stomped off to the dressing room.

It was true that a picnic was something William would never have concerned himself with before now. When he was younger and the lassies wanted picnics, yes, of course, he went, along with all the young gentlemen in and around

Hamilton. That was different—they were like hounds after the skirts, would have done anything for a touch of a hand or a bat of an eye.

But this? He'd not been on a proper picnic with a woman in ages, as he, like MacDuff, viewed them a complete waste of time. He wasn't so far gone that he didn't think this one would be, too—but someone had to keep an eye on this Prince Michel bloke, and he certainly couldn't trust Lady Aleksander to do it. One had only to look at who she'd presented to the princess thus far to know she could not be trusted. While Prince Michel might *seem* a perfect candidate, and presented himself to be quite the gentleman, William refused to trust him after one meeting. He wouldn't trust himself after only one meeting.

He could have done a better job of it, which is precisely what he'd written Robuchard only yesterday.

The candidates are abysmal! You have paid too much for this service! A trained dog might have made better selections on smell alone!

Ewan had refused to carry the note to the telegraph office, insisting that comparing a lady to a trained dog was not the best approach, and complaining once again about William's punctuation. So William had begrudgingly amended.

The candidates are abysmal. You have paid too much for this service. I could have made better selections based on smell alone.

His full opinion, which he would very much like to offer

to *someone*, was that Lady Aleksander's selections for the crown princess were not good enough.

Ewan returned with a pale yellow-and-green-plaid waistcoat that went perfectly with his dark green coat. "That will do, Ewan," William said, pleased. "I knew you'd come round to a picnic."

Ewan frowned and helped William into it. And he kept frowning as William went through a selection of hats, finally settling on a bowler, which seemed to him the most appropriate for a day in the sun. He understood that Ewan didn't recognize him, and frankly, he didn't recognize himself.

He couldn't seem to stop thinking about her. He couldn't keep himself from contemplating the many ways he might end this wretched matchmaking. That was not what he was here to do, quite obviously, but he couldn't help but think of himself as the perfect match for her, knowing full well that he would *never* be considered for many reasons having to do with family and the wee mess he'd gotten himself into in Scotland.

But that didn't stop him from thinking. Imagining. Dreaming.

In his eagerness, he set off a half hour early, and was, therefore, the first to arrive. He handed his horse off to a groom, and as he was walking up the steps, the front door swung open and the butler emerged. He was relieved to see Lady Aleksander behind the butler, and not a wall of Bardalines. He found that couple's presence to be oppressive in more ways than one.

"My Lord Douglas!" Lady Aleksander said cheerfully, then looked at the watch pinned to her breast. "You've arrived earlier than we expected."

Self-consciousness began to finger-crawl its way up the

back of his neck. "Aye, the weather is so fine, I thought I'd get an early start."

Her smile suggested she did not believe his flimsy weather excuse. "Isn't it? A perfect day for a picnic. Do come in, my lord."

He handed his crop and hat to the butler, straightened his yellow-and-green-plaid waistcoat and followed her into the salon. Once inside he said, "I was expecting the Bardalines to meet me at the door and attempt to turn me around."

She laughed. "Are you disappointed?"

"No."

"I'm afraid you won't see them today. They've gone to the country to fetch Princess Amelia."

William tried to read her expression but found nothing there to read. "Nothing serious, I hope?"

"That would depend upon your perspective. The princess sent word that she intended to stay with Lady Holland for a week, and Lady Bardaline thought that was a disastrous idea." Her smile turned wry. "She believes the princess lacks awareness."

On that, he and Lady Bardaline somewhat agreed. But never mind that—William saw his opening. He shot a look at the two footmen who were always in this salon and raised a finger. "Actually." He took a step closer to Lady Aleksander so he might speak in confidence. "I've been meaning to speak to you about that very thing."

One brow rose. "You mean to speak to me about Princess Amelia's lack of awareness?"

"No, no. Princess Amelia is young and randy. It is to be expected."

"Oh *dear*." Lady Aleksander laughed.

"If I may offer a suggestion?"

"Please," she said and gestured for him to continue as

she took a seat on the settee, settling in as though this might take some time.

"It is my observation that it might be more prudent of you to put your efforts to Princess Amelia rather than Her Royal Highness."

"Really?"

He couldn't tell if she was surprised or amused. "Princess Amelia is more likely to bring scandal to the royal family, aye? But her sister is…sensible."

"Sensible." She said it as if she'd never heard the word before and was testing it out. She looked thoughtfully toward the window a moment. "Princess Justine is quite sensible, I agree."

He hadn't expected that, and now he didn't know what more to say without sounding like the meddling old crone who lived near Hamilton Palace. He pressed his lips together and finding nothing more he could possibly say that was acceptable, shrugged as if it was nothing. "I speak only as a friend of Her Royal Highness."

"Naturally. As a friend." She looked like she was on the verge of laughing.

"Have I said something amusing?"

She shook her head.

He nodded, unsure what more to say.

"It's just that I find it interesting that you've come round to this friendship," she said. "I heard you would have debauched the princess given the opportunity when she was the tender age of seventeen."

William felt the blood drain from his face. "I beg your pardon?"

She gave a halfhearted shrug. "Just some old rumors. Nevertheless, you're right."

"I am?"

"You are right to be concerned with Princess Amelia. I should probably pen a letter to Robuchard and tell him so. That is…unless you'd care to have the honor?"

"Me?" He laughed far too loudly. "No, thank you. I scarcely speak to him."

"No?" she said, a wee bit slyly. "Well, you've put me to thinking, my lord. Perhaps I should put off the next gentleman to call and give Her Royal Highness a few days to get her bearings."

William was astonished. "There's *another* one?"

Lady Aleksander laughed as if he were a precocious child. "There is always another one until the matter is sorted and settled. The next is an American industrialist, in London for the summer."

"Eww," William said unthinkingly.

"I beg your pardon?"

He blinked. "What? Nothing, really… I've heard it said that Americans eat with their hands." He shuddered at the thought. "A wee bit toward the uncivilized side of things."

"You don't say. Well, this one seems rather civilized. Henry Thompson is his name. Very well-to-do and well traveled. Do you know him?"

"No." She might as well have asked him if he knew a pirate or a highwayman. He felt a little panicked at the thought of an American and Justine, a brash heathen with fingers where his fork and knife ought to have been. Granted, William had never actually met an American, save an American poet in Paris. But that one was quite old and hard of hearing.

The sound of a carriage on the drive caused them both to glance at the open window; Lady Aleksander stood. William's moment was slipping away. "Lady Aleksander…my intentions are good and heartfelt, aye?"

"Oh, I've absolutely no doubt of it. Thank you for your advice and concern, my lord. It is important that you gave it, even in spite of the scandal swirling about you. I imagine those circumstances must not be easy for you."

The floor suddenly felt as if it was falling out from under him. "I beg your pardon?"

She smiled as she walked past him on her way to the door. "Word spreads so *quickly* in London. I think Prince Michel has come. If you will excuse me?"

He had a sudden and very unpleasant thought of Justine hearing the rumors about him. How had those rumors escaped Scotland? If Justine believed them, she would put him out on his arse. He didn't want that. He couldn't *bear* that.

He was a fool. He should have been prepared for this. He'd known that the rumors would eventually reach London, but he hadn't thought it would happen so *soon*. Before he'd had a chance to...

To what?

He sat heavily on the settee.

To nothing. He was in an impossible situation. He was thirty-three years old, unmarried, a man who had spent the early years of his life hobnobbing around European royalty and playing rather loose with his morals. At the time, it had been preferable to being at Hamilton Palace. But in the past few years he'd mostly spent his time cleaning up the debris his father left in his wake, trying to keep the old man from running all of the family wealth into the ground.

He loved his impetuous father, his excitable mother, his practical sister. And it was his greatest desire to be useful to the Hamilton name and heritage. But it was bloody well difficult when his father made a mess of things and then someone accused *him* of a reprehensible act.

Hand to God, he'd only meant to help.

Several months ago, when William happened to be in London, a local landowner, Mr. Simpson, had gone to his father and accused William of impregnating his daughter when he'd been home for a few weeks over Christmas. When William returned home and heard the news, he swore to his father that absolutely did not happen—William was not particularly careful with his own virtue, but he would never compromise a woman's.

"But do you know her?" his father had asked, suspicious.

Yes, William knew her. And he swore again on his grandfather's grave he'd never touched her. "I mind myself, Father. I understand the consequences to me and our family if I were to be involved in something like that, and I *mind myself.*"

"Then why on earth would he say it?" his father had asked, appearing genuinely confused.

William had tried to explain. He had helped Miss Althea Simpson with money and a horse, but nothing else.

"A *horse?*" his father had asked, scratching his head.

William had started at the beginning. He knew Althea, but only well enough to greet her, really. They were around the same age and had attended some of the same country house parties as young adults. But one day, when in the village of Hamilton, he'd run across her on the central green, clutching the back of a bench, bent over, a hand pressed to her belly. She was ill, he told his father, and looked as if she would wretch at any moment. He helped her to a seat and got her some water from the well.

"What was the matter with her?" his father asked.

"She was carrying a child. A child out of wedlock, which her father was threatening to kill her for. She confessed to me that she meant to meet her lover, the father of the child, and elope."

The duke had pondered this. "Might have been the most sensible thing to do in that situation, aye?"

"I thought so," William agreed.

He'd paid for a room at the inn for the night so she'd have someplace to sleep. He'd given her some money once he discovered she had only a few pounds to her name, and then had hired a horse to take her to the meeting place at dawn the next morning.

And then, William had left her, because he really was a gentleman in spite of what was often said about him, and Althea had assured him she would be quite all right. But she wasn't quite all right—sometime after William left, her father found his daughter and forced her home and, apparently, had kept her locked away since.

After hearing William's explanation, the duke had sighed wearily. "That's a bit of a botch, aye?"

"It's the truth."

"Aye, but it doesna matter if that's truth, does it, now? When you're a wealthy, titled man, the world will find a way to extort you, will it no'?"

To this day William didn't know if his father believed him or not. He had wanted to confront Mr. Simpson, but his father had refused, insisting William would make a bad situation worse. He told William he'd paid the man, and he'd gone off, the extortion done, and if William was to involve himself now, it would only raise more questions. So William had left for the continent.

Then a few weeks ago, when his father had summoned him home, he'd reminded William that since he'd taken care of his problem—William still maintained it was not *his problem*, as he'd done nothing wrong—he felt easy about sending William to do his bidding.

There it was, the reason his father had been able to wheedle him into this royal assignment.

William wanted to tell Justine the horrible thing that happened to him and Miss Simpson. He had no hope she'd believe him, and he couldn't bring himself to ruin the growing regard between them. He thought it perhaps best to keep it to himself and pray to heaven above that she not hear a single ill word said against him before she'd settled on a match and returned to St. Edys.

All he could do was pray.

CHAPTER TWENTY-EIGHT

LILA'S AFTERNOON WAS not unfolding as she had envisioned it when she'd so eagerly jumped at the chance to arrange this picnic. A few complications had cropped up.

The first complication was a mildly surprising one, what with Lord Douglas "suggesting" she turn her attention to Princess Amelia. It was nearly all she could do to keep from laughing at him—the poor man could not have been more obvious had he tried! And she could not have been more pleased. Naturally, she'd allowed him to believe he was persuading her. It was always better to allow a man to think he was winning the game. They were easier to bend to one's will when they thought they were in charge.

But she did feel bad for Prince Michel. He was such a gentleman and would make the most excellent of husbands one day, perhaps even as good of a husband as Valentin. Lila was still of the opinion that Lord Douglas was a perfect match for the princess…but she hadn't yet synthesized the information she'd made Beck give her when she'd called on him yesterday.

She'd gone to see him again to insist on the truth about William Douglas. She'd found Beck alone, save one young daughter who was lying facedown on the floor, kicking her feet and sobbing inconsolably.

She and Beck stood together and stared down at her. "Is she all right?" Lila had asked.

"Quite all right. She's being punished for naughtiness, and the punishment, it seems, is to be locked in a study with me."

"Should we do something?"

"What would we do?" he asked, almost as if he hoped Lila might have an answer.

Lila didn't. So she and Beck had retreated to the other end of his study, and she'd whispered her question to Beck, conscious of the little girl in their presence.

"Oh dear, Lila. You don't want to hear about that," he'd said with a wince. "Blythe doesn't like me to talk."

"I understand. But it's imperative that I know."

He'd eyed her suspiciously. "Why?"

Lila had refused to answer, but she'd returned a look that said he really ought to have guessed.

Beck groaned up at the ceiling. "I don't like to repeat rumors."

"That's not true."

"I mean, not this sort of rumor."

"Fair enough. But please repeat it before I wrap my hands around your throat and squeeze it from you."

"All right, but you are forcing my hand." He leaned forward. "They say he impregnated a girl. Left her there in Scotland with no hope or help. That's the rumor, anyway."

Lila had been so stunned she'd sat back and stared at him. "That doesn't sound at all like the marquess. He may very well be a rake, but he is *not* a degenerate."

"I don't believe it, either, Lila, I truly don't…but something happened. I have known Douglas a very long time. He said he didn't do anything except to try and help the lass, and I believe him. But you know as well as I, darling, that no one ever really cares for the truth."

The little girl, Lila noticed, had stopped wailing. She

had a thumb in her mouth, and her eyes were closed. She'd fallen asleep on the carpet. She turned back to Beck. "Do you think him entirely innocent?"

"Innocent?" He paused, rubbed his temple. "William has a terrible predilection for flirting…at least he did. In the last few years, he's been rather quiet. But I have never known him to be anything but honorable when it mattered most."

That was the impression of him Lila held, too.

"I'm very fond of him, actually. I always found his approach to life rather practical."

Lila nodded. She agreed with Beck; the truth of what had happened was hidden by the salaciousness of the rumor. But what was the truth? She stood up and walked around the sleeping girl on the carpet, thinking. "Do you think his reputation can be salvaged?"

Beck laughed. "Who can say? Whatever the truth of the situation, it remains mostly in Scotland. And as I said, no one cares about the truth."

"On the contrary, in this case, I know someone who might care very much."

Lila needed to know the truth before she went much further, but how on earth would she discover it? She had schemed her way into making this match between two people who were clearly in love, and now she had to make it work, or she would never be hired again. And if no one ever hired her again, where would that leave the impossible Princess Amelia? Lila was very confident the services of a matchmaker would be required for that one.

The second complication was that today, the day of the picnic, Lila had received word that Valentin would be arriving. Her excitement about seeing her husband again was dividing her thoughts between her charge and all she needed to do to prepare for Valentin. So she was a bit distracted when the third complication occurred—Her Royal Highness came bouncing out of Prescott Hall with her dog, Dodi.

The princess greeted both men warmly then asked Prince Michel if he liked dogs.

"I do, yes." He ran his hand over the dog's head.

"This is my companion, Dodi. She rather likes men. You don't mind, do you?" she asked as she handed the dog to the prince.

"Not at all." And he didn't seem to mind, readily taking the dog and scratching her under her chin.

Lila watched as the three of them strolled along the path, Prince Michel with a mound of white fluff under his arm. She followed behind them at a distance into the garden maze, at which point the prince grew tired of carrying the dog and set her down. Dodi caught scent of something under a hedge and began to sniff around it. As the trio moved on, Lila noticed the dog trying to burrow into the hedgerow, clearly after something. She thought perhaps she ought to bring it to the princess's attention, but she and her companions had moved ahead, toward the lake. They were two men trying to capture the attention of one woman, and one woman eager to receive them both. All that attention required their concentration.

Lila thought to turn back to the house herself—they didn't need her to watch over them—but the day was warm, and the three of them started back up the path.

Lila walked ahead of them to make sure the picnic was ready. Just at the end of the gardens was an old yew tree, and underneath the boughs, she'd seen to it that a luxurious picnic had been set up for the princess and her guests. A quilt covered the ground and Turkish pillows had been placed around the perimeter for their comfort. Lawn umbrellas had been placed over two corners and champagne would be served with cold chicken, brambleberries and summer fruits.

The three of them made their way there, the two gentlemen jockeyed to help the princess down before they settled in. Lila had begun to walk away when she heard the princess gasp. When she turned back, the princess had gained her feet and was looking all around them. "Where is Dodi?" she asked. *"Dodi!"* she called.

Lila glanced over her shoulder, half expecting to see the dog trotting up the path.

The two gentlemen gained their feet. Lord Douglas looked at Prince Michel. Prince Michel said, "I think I know where she might have gone. Allow me to fetch her, Your Royal Highness."

"I'll go with you—"

"Please, stay in the shade. I'll fetch her. I'll be but a few minutes."

"Thank you," the princess said. And then she and Lord Douglas…and, well, Lila herself, watched Prince Michel lope down the path to fetch her dog.

And then Lila watched as the princess looked at Douglas, and he looked at her. Lila could almost feel the bolt of lightning between them. They obviously could, too, because they did not look away from each other. It was as if everything else but the two of them had ceased to exist.

She stood at a short distance, trying to be inconspicuous, her thoughts racing, trying to think her way through this. The princess and the marquess took their seats. They sat with their heads together, whispering and laughing, forgetting even the passage of time.

Where Prince Michel had to go to fetch the dog, who could say, but when at last he returned, the bottom of his trousers were wet, the knees muddied and a trail of sweat ran down one temple. But he had the dog tucked securely under his arm. Dodi's white coat was matted on one side and muddied and tangled underneath. Princess Justine didn't notice the prince and the dog at all until he was upon them.

When Princess Justine did see him, she scrambled to her feet as if she'd been caught at something. "Dodi, you naughty little girl. Where did you go?"

"I believe she was attempting to play a game with a rabbit," Prince Michel said. "Under the hedgerow."

"Dodi!" She tried to sound stern, but ended up laughing. "Thank you so much, sir—I hope it wasn't terribly inconvenient."

"No," he said, although it was clear that it was.

The princess asked a footman to take the muddied dog and dispatch her to a bath. Prince Michel brushed the dirt from the knees of his trousers, and then joined the conversation as the three of them dined on. Lila lingered, feeling slightly voyeuristic, standing apart as she was, pretending to admire some roses.

The princess made certain to ask the prince questions and listened to his answers. Which was more than Lila could say for Douglas, who never seemed to take his eyes from the princess.

Douglas mentioned the princess's prowess in fencing. Prince Michel said he was really very poor at it, and thought his talents extended more to archery. He asked how it was that the princess had come to be so proficient at the sport.

"I took it up at an early age," she said. "I learned the history of one of my ancestors, a warrior queen, and I very much wanted to be like her. She seemed so...confident. Fencing was the closest I could come to leading battles. And as I learned it, I realized when I held a foil, it was one of the only times I felt in complete control of my surroundings." She gave a nonchalant shrug. "I find I like that feeling very much." She laughed, as if that was a silly thing, but Lila felt a bit sorry for her.

"You may no' be aware, Your Highness," Douglas said, "that the princess claims to be as accomplished at archery as she is at fencing. I've no' seen it myself, but there you are, a future queen who can take up a sword or a bow."

"You sound as if you don't believe me, Lord Douglas. Perhaps we should have a go of it," the princess chirped. "I asked that some field archery be set up today as a diversion. I could teach you to shoot, if you like."

Douglas chuckled. "I donna think so."

"You don't think I could?" she challenged him. "Would you like to place a wager?"

That brought Douglas's head up. "Are you willing to lose, ma'am?"

"Goodness," said Prince Michel. "Perhaps we ought to have a round as a diversion and—"

"I'm always willing to lose," Princess Justine interjected. "But I hardly ever do." She turned away from Douglas and smiled at Prince Michel. "*Je*, let's have a round, shall we? As a diversion. It will be fun!" She hopped up before either man could offer to help her to her feet.

There was something about this archery business that seemed to be sliding off the path Lila had carefully constructed. She had, at the princess's request, seen that the archery field was set up. But now seeing how keen Princess Justine was for it, she suspected the true reason the princess had wanted it.

Lila had meant to leave them, to prepare for her husband, but instead she followed the three of them and two footmen down to where an archery field had been set up.

Prince Michel pleaded with Princess Justine to go first, but she refused, challenging him to start things off. Prince Michel was such a gentleman that he couldn't bear the thought of preceding a lady, so Lord Douglas stepped in and volunteered, asking them both to step back lest they be hit by a stray arrow. It was a good thing he did, too, as his shots went so wild that Lila thought he must be trying to lose.

The princess laughed gaily. "You're to *hit* the boss, sir," she said. "The target!"

Prince Michel was convinced to go second, and he was fairly good, not hitting the smallest circle painted on the boss, but racking up a few points nonetheless.

Princess Justine was obviously eager to show her skill. She was elegant in her stance, and her arrows seemed to fly like birds off her bow, easily piercing the target. When she'd shot her last of three arrows, everyone politely applauded. She turned a beaming smile to them.

"It's your turn, my lord," she said to Douglas. "Shall we wager this round?"

"That seems hardly fair," Prince Michel said with a laugh.

"Aye, but I'm the sporting type," Douglas said. "What would you wager, Your Royal Highness?"

"What shall I bet him?" she asked Prince Michel. "My kingdom?"

Prince Michel gave a nervous bit of laughter. "Perhaps a pound or two?"

"Mmm. Too small. I will bet you my kingdom, my lord. And if *I* win, I will have your Scottish palace."

"Alas, the palace is no' mine to give."

"Then what will you offer?"

He bowed low. "My liege and limb in service to the

queen. Will that suit? At your beck and call until you beck and call no more."

Princess Justine laughed with delight. "I had hoped for something a bit larger, but I accept."

Lord Douglas stepped up to the shooting line, withdrew an arrow from the stand beside him, took aim…and hit the center ring. Princess Justine cried out with amazement. Prince Michel applauded vigorously.

"What a lucky shot, my lord," Princess Justine said.

"Aye." He drew another arrow and did it again. No one applauded him then. When he did it a third time, Princess Justine cried out, but this time, in protest. She ran to the boss and he followed, and the two of them argued over whether he had earned the highest number of points.

Prince Michel did not follow them. Lila moved to stand beside him, and the two of them watched as the princess and the marquess playfully argued. The princess accused Douglas of tricking her. He didn't deny it and said it was the oldest betting trick there was, and how could she not have suspected it? He said he had no idea what he might do with an entire kingdom. She asked to examine the arrows to see if there was some trickery involved, but he held them out of her reach, teasing her.

Dear God, these two lovebirds were terribly smitten, much more than Lila had believed. "Well," she murmured, thinking what to say.

Prince Michel frowned. "The game has turned serious."

"Oh no, I think not," Lila hastened to assure him. "They are friends. You understand how friends can be with one another."

He looked at Lila and smiled sadly. "I do understand," he said. "Quite well, actually."

"Your Highness," Lila started, but was interrupted by a footman.

"Lady Aleksander. Lord Aleksander has come."

She gasped with delight. "He's come early! Please show him to my suite of rooms and tell him I will be there as soon as possible." She turned back to Prince Michel. "My husband has come from Denmark."

"Then you must go, madam."

"Thank you, but he'll be perfectly fine—"

"I insist," he said. "That is, if the princess agrees. I would much rather you greet your husband than watch us argue over points in a game." He smiled warmly.

He was a good man, Prince Michel. One day she would find him the perfect match, whether he wanted it or not. "Thank you." She watched him walk down to where the princess and the marquess were now examining arrows, then started for the house and Valentin.

One thing was clear to her—the match had been made. She would ask Valentin's advice on how to address the rumor around William Douglas, as it really was rather awful.

CHAPTER TWENTY-NINE

"How could this have happened?" Justine asked frantically. "How the devil did we lose a *prince*?"

"*When* did we lose him?" William asked, frowning with confusion. "He was present for the last round."

"He was present for all *four* rounds, William. He joined us for the discussion of the book afterward. Do you think he's in the maze?"

They both looked at the entrance to the maze from where they stood on the path.

"Where else could he be? We've searched the garden and the park."

They walked to the entrance of the maze, the guards trailing behind them. "I don't understand it," Justine said as they walked into the maze.

"Aye," William agreed. "I've never known anyone to simply disappear."

"I mean that he didn't seem to care for the story of Henry Esmond. He said he was an avid reader and that he'd enjoyed Thackeray's works. Didn't he?" She looked curiously at William, wondering if she had imagined that he'd said it.

"I...think so?" William said uncertainly. He glanced at her, looking a bit remorseful. "Perhaps we might have saved the discussion for another time."

Justine felt remorseful, too. She hadn't paid Prince Michel the attention she ought to have paid him today. She'd been so intent on besting William at archery, and then talking about the book, she had almost forgotten the prince was there. And now he was missing. She tried to think of a way to make her crime seem less of one. "But the question of whether or not Henry Esmond should have told the truth about his bloodlines was a question *anyone* might discuss without having read the book, wouldn't you agree?"

William suddenly caught her hand, forcing her to stop walking. The feel of his hand on hers brought to mind the memory of his hands on her body. Again. It was a memory that kept flooding back to her at the least opportune moments.

Oh, but she'd been thinking about this man all day, and therein lay the problem. She'd watched the way his body had moved when they'd played at archery. She'd tried not to stare at his shoulders when he removed his coat. She'd had to glance away from ogling his thighs. She'd brushed past him twice, deliberately making contact with his arm, like a girl in a ballroom trying to gain a man's attention. What could she say for herself? She couldn't bear to be this close to him and not touch him. And she had treated Prince Michel poorly because of it.

She looked up to see what had captured William's attention. Lila was striding toward them, arms swinging, stride long, as if she had something terribly important to impart. Justine and William exchanged a worried look. Lila stopped directly before them and put her hands on her waist.

"Lila, thank heaven," Justine said. "I'm afraid we've lost the prince. We can't find him anywhere! We think he might have gone into the maze. We're just about to have a look."

"Well, Your Royal Highness, he's gone all right, but not into the maze. He is in Belgravia by now and will be boarding a ship very soon."

"Pardon?"

"He's leaving England! He's returning to Miraval! I dare say he almost took the lovebirds with him."

Alarmed, Justine looked at William. William looked at her and looked just as baffled as she was. "But…but *why*? We'd invited him to dine. He left without a word? Not even a farewell? I don't understand!"

Lila frowned darkly at her. "I think, ma'am, if you consider it carefully, you will understand. As for supper, the two of you will have to share it. Such a waste."

"What do you mean, the two of us? What about you?"

"My husband has arrived from Denmark and I have ordered a private supper for my rooms."

Justine wasn't allowed to dine alone with a gentleman who was not her relative. Her parents were ridiculously strict about presenting even a whiff of impropriety. "But the Bardalines are—"

"Not back until tomorrow, I know," Lila said curtly. "My deepest apologies, ma'am, but the prince did not feel particularly welcome. Therefore, that leaves the two of you." She didn't give Justine a chance to argue that she *had* made him welcome, and thank goodness for it, because Justine hadn't. She felt awful and contrite. He was a good man, and he'd come so far to meet her. He'd brought the gift of the most beautiful birds! She hadn't meant to be so careless with his feelings, but Lila had already turned and was stalking away, leaving her and William.

They stood in silence until Lila had disappeared from view. Justine said sheepishly, "I feel a bit queasy, I think. We've been…*rude*." She could hardly believe it of herself.

"We were no' *intentionally* rude," William said, sounding more hopeful than convinced. But he suddenly smiled. "*Och*, it hardly matters, aye? He wasna right for you."

"I think my queasiness just got worse. You're going to offer another opinion, aren't you? Go on, then—tell me why he wasn't right for me. Tell me why the kindest and most gentlemanly suitor I have ever had was all wrong for me."

"Aye, you said it yourself. He was too kind."

With a snort, she started walking toward the hall. "There is no such thing as too kind. A person is kind or they are not."

"Donna misunderstand me—the prince was a good man. I should very much have liked to call him friend. He was suited for me, but he was no' suited for *you*."

"Then pray tell, wise one, who is suited for me?"

He took her hand in his and brought it to his lips as they walked. "No' just anyone with a title, *leannan*. You are unique. You need a certain sort of man at your side. Someone who is sincere and truthful and no' easily intimidated by your crown. Someone who will respect your throne and the fact that you are the one seated on it, but is no' afraid to tell you the good and the bad."

"And you thought Prince Michel would not respect my throne?"

"Oh aye, he would have respected it. I think he would have been a wee bit daunted by it."

"He didn't seem daunted."

"No? If he wasna daunted, he'd be here now, aye?"

She laughed. "I don't think the dear man left because he was intimidated by my looming throne."

"It's one of many theories," he said.

He was still holding her hand. She liked it. "Now what?"

"On to the next, I suppose."

"If there is a next." She picked up her skirts to walk up the terrace steps. "I've surely depleted all the eligible bachelors who could possibly be considered for prince consort. How many can there be?"

"According to you, princes abound. But there is at least one more." William caught her elbow to help her up the steps. "Lady Aleksander mentioned him."

Justine was surprised by this. "She mentioned someone to you? Who?"

"An American industrialist."

"Eww," she said, wincing.

He nodded. "Exactly what I said. They eat with their hands, the Americans. No' entirely civilized."

She gasped. *"Do* they?"

"I've heard it said."

"I've heard it said they are too proud. Vexingly so. Really, William, why am I so bloody hard to match?"

"You're easy to match. It's the privileged men of the world who are so bloody difficult to match."

Justine laughed. She appreciated his sense of humor— there was always a ring of truth to it. They had reached the terrace and he dropped his hand from her elbow. She paused. "Will you stay to dine?" she asked.

"Do you want me to stay?"

"I do. Remarkably, I have come to enjoy your company."

A slow smile lifted one corner of his mouth. "I'm no' surprised. I warned you fairly that I could be charming under the right circumstances. And I should very much like to dine with you, Your Royal Highness, for the same can be said of you. And if I may, there is the matter of a bet poorly made."

"Do you mean the bet you made under false pretense?"

"I mean the bet we made about the archery." His gaze had taken on a sheen that matched the heat in her skin, melting her from the inside. "And we both know you are a woman who is no' afraid to lose." He smiled seductively.

Fire, Justine was learning, ran quite deep where William was concerned.

SUPPER WAS SERVED in a small drawing room just as a soft, steady rain had begun to fall. A fire blazed in the hearth, and two windows had been opened to allow the air to circulate.

Justine had changed into a simple dark blue gown and sapphire-and-pearl choker. When she rejoined William, his eyes swept over her, and she felt the bees in her chest begin to buzz again. They were a hive now, distracting her.

They took their seats as a footman quickly whisked the third place setting out of sight. They stared at the empty chair. "I can't believe he left without a single word," Justine said, reminded of his disappearance again.

"I have another theory, if you'd like," William offered.

"*Je*, tell me."

"I think it is perhaps because of the way you sucked the lemon like a little heathen at the picnic. I canna imagine how tart it was."

Justine laughed. "My theory is that he left because you kicked over the honey pot and some spilled onto his shoe."

"I apologized, did I no'? The bees were swarming the pot and I discovered then and there that I am afraid of them."

Justine laughed. "I thought your trousers were on fire, you scrambled to your feet so quickly."

They laughed, recalling that moment.

But now William frowned slightly. "Prince Michel laughed about the bees, aye? He said he had no love for bees, or something similar."

"I think he did." She dipped her spoon into the soup. "I

am terribly sorry for what happened. I should have been... kinder."

"I'm the guilty party. I should have allowed you to receive him on your own."

She dipped her spoon in her soup again, but left it there. "But do you think—" she glanced up "—that he was suitable for a prince consort? I mean, imagine if he disappeared while we entertained a state visitor."

William cocked his head to one side. "Did I hear something?" he asked, cupping his ear. "I canna be certain but it sounded a wee bit as if you said that I was right. *Again.*"

She smiled. "Do you recall when I insisted that you not offer even a *hint* of advice?"

"I think of it every day."

"What would I have done if you hadn't?"

"What indeed," he mused. "I donna mean to disparage Lady Aleksander, but Robuchard could no' possibly have engaged a worse matchmaker."

"I must agree." She picked up her spoon. "I suppose you've said as much to your old friend."

William's spoon froze halfway to his mouth. "My old friend, is he?"

"Isn't he?"

He slowly put down his spoon. "May I be completely honest with you?"

She nodded.

"No' politely honest, Justine. *Completely* honest."

"Oh dear. *Completely* honest." She put down her spoon, too. Her stomach gurgled uncomfortably and she steeled herself for bad news. "Has my mother said something to you?"

"Your..." He looked momentarily confused. "No. I've no' had the pleasure of her acquaintance. What I want to tell you is that my father has had some...difficulties."

Difficulties. She didn't know what that meant, but she didn't like the sound of it. She waited for him to continue.

"Of his own making."

She nodded.

"Financial."

She had no call to feel so disappointed in this revelation, but strangely, she did. Financial difficulties were often the cause behind people doing terrible things.

"It was he who arranged this with Robuchard," he said, making a gesture to the two of them. "Some time ago, he found himself in significant debt and has entered into some business dealings in Wesloria, at the behest of your prime minister. But I was coerced into this role by him—no' as a favor to Robuchard."

"I knew it!" she cried. "*Ha.* You are a spy, and for once, *I* was right." But just as quickly as she'd declared triumph, she sobered. He hadn't been entirely truthful with her, after all.

"Aye, you were right."

What else had he been less than truthful about? Justine swallowed hard. "Does that mean that your companionship these last few—"

"God, no," he said quickly and reached for her hand. "No, Justine. *No.* I've cherished every moment, more than I can say. More than I can fathom, really."

She desperately wanted to believe him because the same was true for her. "Why didn't you tell me the truth in the beginning? I asked you."

"I didna expect to be long at the task. And…shame, I suppose. Will you allow me to explain?"

She nodded. He let go of her hand and settled in to tell her about his father's money troubles and bad spending decisions. How the choices he'd made to add to the palace had cost them dearly, and could mean an impoverished Hamilton duchy down the road. He told her about the questionable business ventures his father had entered into over the years for no other reason than he was friendly with the person proposing it. He told her what the losses had meant for the Hamilton estate, and how he'd tried, as best he could, to keep the estate from hemorrhaging everything.

Justine grew increasingly anxious as he spoke, as if these matters of the Hamilton finances were somehow hers. "Are you…are you *poor*?"

William looked startled. "No. Personally, I'm solvent, thanks in part to an inheritance of my own from my grandfather. My father, however, has engaged in a troubling pattern over the years. It's no' well-known outside our family and our duchy's closest agents. Most people assume what they know of me, when really, they know very little."

She nodded. "The same is true for me. Once, I heard that I was an imbecile, and the palace kept me out of sight of the public, lest anyone discover the truth about me."

"Good God." He laughed with disbelief. "It will be the greatest surprise for them all to discover you are clever and astute, aye?" He gazed at her a moment. "If you could have your people know anything about you at all, what would it be?"

"Besides the fact that I need eyeglasses to read?"

"Besides that."

She thought about it a moment. "That I'm afraid."

Her answer clearly surprised him—his eyes moved curiously over her face. Then he slowly leaned forward to put his hand on her knee and give it a light squeeze. "Donna be afraid, Justine. You will make an excellent queen. One who will be written about in decades to come."

She smiled sheepishly. "I can hardly imagine that is true."

"I can and I do. I've no doubt of it. None."

Her smile turned grateful. "You really are a good friend, William. How I misjudged you."

Curiously, he pressed his lips together and glanced down, and she wondered if that had displeased him in some way.

"Why do they no' trust you?" he asked.

She didn't have to ask what he meant. That was the thing about the two of them—they seemed to understand each other in many ways. "My parents?"

He nodded. "And the way the Bardalines watch you, and Robuchard's desire to know what you're about...it all suggests an uncertainty."

It did. She would never be forgiven her transgression. "It's a long story." She moved the soup aside, having lost any interest in eating. A footman was there at once to remove her bowl and William's, even though he was clearly still eating. Once the sovereign or heir had finished, the course was considered over. "No, wait—"

"It's all right," William said, and held up a hand to the footman, indicating he didn't want the soup back. "Tell me."

She waited until the butler had set plates of beef before them, picked up her knife and asked, as casually as she might, "You really haven't heard?"

"I've heard quite a lot about you...and perhaps in particular about a love affair."

Justine snorted. "It was not a love affair. I was cruelly deceived by a liar and a cheat."

His brows dipped as if he couldn't determine if what she said was true. Justine nodded.

"His name—" she looked sidelong at the attendants, then whispered "—was Aldabert Gustav." And then she began to talk softly. She told William how they'd met at the palace during one of her mother's garden parties. About the promises he'd made her, how he would never love another, that he'd sooner die than be without her.

"I was young and inexperienced, and oh, how my heart sang with those declarations of his love." She was no longer that girl—she'd been hardened by scandal and her father's illness and so much more. "I told him how he'd made me feel, as if he could sense how long I'd waited to feel love and be loved." She shuddered now, thinking of her naivety.

William didn't smile or laugh, but sat quietly while she talked.

She told him how she'd discovered how powerful desire was, but that a different sort of power drove Aldabert. It had all been a lie, a scheme drawn up by Aldabert and his ambitious father to compromise her and take his place at her side.

William paled. "The stuff of nightmares."

"*Je*, the very stuff. It taught me a painful lesson. No one looks at me as a woman or a wife, but as a means to an end."

"Justine. That's no' true."

"It is."

"Then what a sad understanding you have, lass. There are users in the world...but there are many more who would love you as a woman or a wife."

Justine wasn't so certain of it. She eyed him curiously. "Why haven't you ever married? The truth."

"I came very near, once. I was entirely smitten with a young woman, ready to offer her all of Hamilton Palace and the future role of duchess."

The idea that William had loved someone so was surprisingly uncomfortable. "Why didn't you?"

"I never had the chance. Jonathan Ashley, who I believed to be my friend, wooed her away from me. And it was regrettably easy to do."

Justine blinked. "Mr. Ashley did that? To intentionally cause you harm?"

"Aye, he did. He seemed to think it was rather a lark."

"Oh, my God, William. Why did you not tell me everything about him?"

"I didna know if you'd believe me. And I suppose a wee bit of my pride prevented me from speaking. A man never wants to be a cuckold." He gave her a sheepish smile. "I think I hoped you'd see him for what he was."

She had, eventually, but only because William had warned her to begin with. "That must have been so painful for you."

"Aye, that it was." He ate some beef, his gaze on his plate.

"And since then?"

"Since then?" He glanced up and smiled devilishly. "I've been a bad boy. I've traveled the continent to escape a broken heart, drank my sorrows, fed my lusts and kept to myself."

"You said you were no longer a scoundrel," she reminded him.

"I'm no'. I finally realized there was only so long I could mourn something that was never meant to be."

She wondered if she had mourned Aldabert long after she should have. "She was a fool, William. You are kind and considerate and clever. You are *much* more desirable than Mr. Ashley in every way."

He looked, she thought, a little hopeful. "I think you've had too much wine," he said.

She'd hardly touched her wine. She picked up her glass. "And then again, not enough."

He picked up his glass and touched it to hers. They drank. "Now tell me a secret about you. Something that no one knows. No' even your sister."

Justine laughed. "There is hardly a thing she doesn't know about me."

"*Och*, there must be something. Come on, then. Friends share secrets."

She felt the bees in her chest again as she thought of the few secrets she harbored. "Would you like to hear my deepest secret?"

"Oh. Aye, I would. The deepest."

She leaned forward. "All right, here it is, my deepest, darkest secret. I very much esteem you. I..." She tried to think of a word that would convey what she felt, but the only word that came to mind was *love*. Nothing else seemed to fit. "*Esteem* you," she said again. "I didn't think I would. I sincerely thought I'd hate you, but I don't at all. Quite the opposite. I so hope we remain friends. I hope you will come to Wesloria. I hope..." Well, she hoped for so much more than that, it was true. "That you will," she finished weakly.

"That is a remarkable secret, Your Royal Highness. Would you like to hear mine?"

"I command it."

He smiled softly. "I esteem you, too. Perhaps above all else. I esteem you in a manner that suggests that I've been waiting for you a very long time. This waistcoat was the fourth one I tried today. I have never in my life felt compelled to think too much about waistcoats, but there you have it. I wanted you to like it."

The light in his eyes matched the sparkle in her blood. The room felt warm suddenly, and she drew a shallow breath. "I love it, William. I've never seen a finer waistcoat."

He twined his fingers with hers. "What has happened to us?"

The sparkle in her began to crackle. She squeezed his fingers. *"William?"*

"Justine."

"Why did it have to be this way?"

He shook his head. He understood that she asked why they had to be so full of esteem for each other when she was here to make a match that would carry her for the rest of her days. "I donna know. But let it be this way for as long as possible."

Yes, let it be this way for as long as they could. She let go of his hand and stood. William looked confused. She walked to the door and opened it. *"Lassan nus,"* she said to the footmen. *Leave us.*

They moved at once. The butler attempted to pick up plates, but she shook her head. He reluctantly followed the footmen out. Justine shut the door behind them and locked it. She could imagine how quickly word would spread in the house that she'd kicked them out while in the company of a gentleman. The Bardalines would hear of this straight-away. But she had tonight, and whatever came after it, she didn't care.

William sat with one arm draped over the back of his chair, one brow lifted with surprise. "What the devil are you about?"

"There is the matter of that bet."

"Ah, yes." He stood and tossed aside his napkin. "You owe me a kingdom, as I recall." He walked to where she stood, cupped her face in his hands and kissed her. And then he reached down and picked her up in his arms.

Justine gave a tiny shriek of surprised laughter.

William carried her to a divan and put her down, then crawled on top of her.

She gazed into his face and stroked his brow. She hoped

she never forgot how he looked tonight. "How I wish it could be different."

"Donna do your wishing now, *leannan*. Live this moment with me." He kissed her.

"What does it mean? That word?"

"It means…" He looked her in the eye. "My love. My heart."

The bees began to spread into her limbs. She would live this moment with him, all right. She wanted desperately for him to make love to her. The need she felt was a pulsing, living thing, pushing against her ribs. She had waited so long for someone to touch her like this, to love her, only her, and somehow she knew that he did.

His hands moved over her breasts and her body as he kissed her neck, her ears, her throat. He moved lower, his hands sliding up beneath her hem, up her legs. He moved down, his mouth trailing across the mound of her breasts, down the fabric of her gown and down even more.

When he pushed her skirts up over her hips, Justine felt a moment of panic. She could not allow what she thought was about to happen, could not risk betraying her country… but instead of his body moving between her legs, it was his head. When his tongue slipped in between the folds of her sex, Justine choked on her breath. The sensation was so exquisite, so incredibly pleasurable, that she felt as if she were floating away, being carried off on a cloud with no care for where she might land. The sounds she heard in a foggy distance were coming from her own throat.

He held her tight, was painstaking in his consideration of her, exploring every crevice, every recess of her body, then flicking delicately across the core of her desire, and deeper into her body.

The pressure in her built—she was careening toward

something explosive, her groans of pleasure turning to pants. He stroked her, sucked her, nibbled until she shattered into euphoria.

She was still gasping for breath as she raked her fingers through his hair. She pulled him up, smothering him with as deep a kiss as she knew how to give. She wanted to cry, or maybe she wanted to laugh, or maybe she wanted to eat a cake with both her hands. She wanted to never be without this, to never be without *him*. She could feel his body hard against her and wanted more than anything she'd ever wanted to carry on, to finish what they'd started. "I'm so sorry," she said.

"No apologies."

"But it hardly seems—"

"No' a word, lass. You've a greater responsibility than any mortal man." He kissed her forehead.

She caressed his face. "Are you the same man who pushed me from the chair all those years ago?"

"I'm the same man who beat you to the chair. Are you the same woman who cried foul?"

"I'm the same woman who declared my victory."

They laughed. He kissed her again, his lips soft on hers now, his fingers gentle against her face.

This was happiness. This was what contentment must feel like, and Justine was amazed to realize she'd never really felt it before now.

He stroked her face, admiring her. "I thought I'd see you once or twice and be done with my charge. But when I was with you, I kept discovering things about myself I didna know were missing, aye? Sides of me I didna know existed. Now I canna imagine no' seeing you."

"I can't imagine it, either. Who will advise me against

my wishes? Who will offer opinions I don't want? Who will give me what I need when I already have everything?"

"No one proper, I'm certain of it. I'll be forced to write you long letters."

"I would like that very much. And I will read them as I pace about the throne room incensed that you would have the nerve."

He laughed. He kissed her again.

And again.

And again.

And when they couldn't kiss anymore without risking everything, they talked. About their childhoods, about their hopes for the future. Children. Dogs and horses. Archery and sisters, fathers and strange dreams.

They talked about *everything*.

William finally left the hall at half past two in the morning. Justine stumbled up the stairs, her hair half down, her chest red from all the kissing, her lips bruised and her smile so wide that it had to take up residence in her heart.

SOMETIME IN THE NIGHT Lila got up to air out a room that smelled of sex and smoke from the hearth. She was naked, her hair down her back. She opened the window to the summer night and breathed in.

That was when she saw Lord Douglas walking to the stables.

Valentin, also naked, stepped up behind her and wrapped his arms around her waist, pressing his hardness against her backside, his mouth against her neck. "I've missed you, woman."

"I've missed you, my love," she murmured.

"Marry off the princess and come home."

"I'm very close to doing just that." She watched Douglas disappear into the stables and twisted around in her husband's arms to kiss him.

A TELEGRAPH ARRIVED as Prime Minister Robuchard sat waiting at the palace for his afternoon meeting with the king.

It was from Douglas, informing him that Prince Michel was a good man with absolutely nothing to offer Princess Justine. That was impossible—Prince Michel had an entire bloody principality to offer. Dante would never have guessed that Douglas would be so bloody unhelpful.

As Dante was shown into the king's private rooms, the queen was pacing as she often did. She gasped loudly just as Dante entered.

"What is it?" the king asked hoarsely.

"Amelia!" the queen fairly shouted. She saw Robuchard and shook her own telegraph at him. "They must come home right away. She's gone off to the country with Lady Holland, and the Bardalines had to go and fetch her! I told you she'd be trouble, Robuchard, but you insisted! This is *your* fault. Drakkia! I want to send for them straightaway. They are to come home at *once*."

"Darling, do you think—" The king tried to intervene but his question turned into a wet, phlegmy round of coughing.

Dante stuffed his own telegraph into his pocket. He would be sending a telegraph at once to Douglas, demanding that he convince the princess to marry one of his choices as soon as possible, for God's sake.

CHAPTER THIRTY

JUSTINE FOUND HERSELF with Queen Victoria a day later as the queen was being fitted for a ball gown to be worn during an upcoming trip to the Palace of Versailles. The gown was exquisite, made of white silk and blue trim. The dressmaker was fitting the royal sash Her Majesty would wear diagonally across her chest, assuring a proper fit with the gown.

"You will soon learn, my dear, that all the trappings of a throne are designed for men. The sashes, the crowns, the robes, even the scepter—all of them too big and too heavy for a woman. You would be wise to walk about with them before appearing in public. No one wants the symbolic vision of a crown toppling off a sovereign's head. As we all know, once the crown falls, the head is soon to follow." She chuckled at her jest.

Justine was too horrified by the image to even smile.

The queen began to fuss about the trim on her sleeve and Justine slipped back into the dreamy wonderland of her memory—the same place she'd been residing for the past day. She kept thinking of William, of the things they'd done, of the way he made her feel. They'd lain together on the divan, talking deep into the night until she began to worry the servants were listening at the door.

They'd talked about so much, and yet it felt as if they'd scarcely even scratched the surface before he told her he had to leave.

She hadn't wanted him to go; she'd wanted him to stay. She'd wanted everything, all of it—his body, his heart, his mind. She wanted to make love to him, to talk to him, to laugh with him, to play with him, to be silent with him.

"Now, then, my dear, what sort of progress have you made in finding a husband?" the queen asked, startling her back to the present.

"Ah…it has not as yet been successful."

"But I've heard there have been squads of suitors."

Justine winced inwardly. All of London was talking about it, then. "There have hardly been squads. Only a few, and none of them right."

"And how are they not right?"

"One was kind, but…" She hesitated. She didn't know what to say about Prince Michel since that had been entirely her fault. "He was kind. Another was a bit of a drunkard."

"Steer clear of *that*. When a man's wealth is completely dependent on you, he will believe himself to be useless. Spirits will make his grievances seem larger than they are, and he will blame you for all of them."

"Oh my," Justine said, taken aback.

"I'm surprised your mother hasn't told you so. Who else?"

"There was another that needed quite a lot of reassuring. And I am to meet an American."

"No," the queen said flatly to that. "Who else?"

Justine desperately wanted to say there was another. One who was not on Lady Aleksander's list, but who perfectly suited her. The only one on her list. "I am aware of no one else."

"Mmm." The queen stepped up onto a box so the dressmaker and her assistant could mark the hem. The queen was so small that from the look of it, they were going to have to cut off a foot of fabric.

Justine had just picked up a glass to drink some water when the queen said, "My advice is to find someone with whom you will enjoy your marital bed. All the rest will follow."

Justine was so startled that she choked on her water and began to cough.

Not that the queen noticed. "It can make the longest days rather pleasant in the end."

"Umm…" She ran her thumb over her bottom lip to catch any water spilling down her chin.

"Don't be fussy, dear. It's a fact of life—the more compatible you are in the privacy of your chamber, the more compatible you are in life."

Both the dressmaker and her assistant shot a look at Justine.

"But how…that is, there is no way to know—"

"You're quite right. There is no way to know. I was very lucky." She lifted her chin as she gazed at herself in the mirror. "*Very* lucky. But do have a care. Too great a compatibility leads to many pregnancies."

Justine felt far less buoyant when she left the queen than before she'd gone in. Just thinking of a marital bed with someone other than William sobered her. She would certainly enjoy his bed…but when she thought of the others, the vaulted candidates, the gentlemen deemed suitable for the role of prince consort, she couldn't imagine it.

Her head was filled with William, only William. His soft gray eyes, his lopsided smile, his thick, dark hair… Why couldn't it be him?

Could it be him?

A thought unfurled in her head.

She had assumed it couldn't be because of the trouble with the Hamilton duchy. Otherwise, wouldn't he have been on Lila's list? But...*could* it be him?

She brooded all the way to Prescott Hall, and would have continued to brood, but Amelia had returned in something of a snit. She was lying on the chaise longue in Justine's sitting room, waiting for her older sister, one arm thrown dramatically over her eyes.

"What is the matter?" Justine asked.

"Everything. The Bardalines might as well be our jailers. Why did they come to get me, Jussie? I was having a wonderful time. I love England and I don't want to go back to Wesloria."

Sometimes it was better not to acknowledge Amelia's wishes and change the subject. "How was the country?"

"Astonishing." Amelia suddenly propped herself up on one elbow and craned her neck around to see Justine. "I met someone."

Of course she had.

"He's wonderful. A considerate man, and so interested in *me*—not you. We had a walkabout."

Justine didn't like the sound of that. She slowly lowered into her seat. "A walkabout."

"Yes, Jussie, a *walkabout*. Deep into a wooded path."

"And what did you do on this wooded path?"

Amelia giggled. "Kissed!" She sat up and leaned toward Justine to whisper, "He kisses magnificently. I think I love him."

"You think you love every gentleman you meet. Amelia! What is the matter with you? You can't do that, not here."

"Why not? What's the harm?"

Sometimes Justine couldn't believe they'd had the same parents, the same training, the same education—Amelia interpreted everything so vastly different than she did. "The harm is your reputation, darling—do I really need to say it?"

Amelia waved a hand at her and fell back against the chaise. "We are in England. No one will know. You're only saying that because of what happened to you."

"*Je*, Amelia, I am saying it precisely because of what happened to me. My reputation suffered. And you are a fool if you believe being in England will somehow shield you."

Amelia clucked her tongue and turned her head to the window. "Trust me, no one pays the slightest attention to me. It's all you and it will always be you. What is there left to me, I ask you? Why shouldn't I be diverted and enjoy my life?"

"There is much left to you, Amelia. I've always said so. I will rely on your counsel, but I can't rely on it if you are banished to the mountains for bad conduct."

"No, you'd have me waste away, a spinster at your side."

"Firstly, I happen to know a spinster or two, and none of them are wasting away. And secondly, that is not true!"

Amelia groaned. She reached into her pocket and withdrew a yellow paper and thrust it in Justine's general direction. Justine took it.

It was a telegraph from their mother.

My daughters, you are commanded to return to St. Edys at once. Amelia, you have proven yourself incapable of behaving properly without my supervision, and Justine, you have proven yourself incapable of settling on a match or supervising your sister. You will end your meetings with Her Majesty the Queen and return home posthaste.

"Good Lord," Justine muttered. "Has Lady Bardaline seen this?"

Amelia snorted. "She delivered it." She sat up and swung her legs over the side of the chaise. "I heard something rather interesting in the country about your friend."

"What friend?"

"Have you any other friend besides the Marquess of Hamilton?"

"Fair point," Justine said drily. "What did you hear?"

Amelia's eyes sparked. "The rumor is that he impregnated a country girl and left her."

The words her sister spoke did not at first take root in Justine's head. She frowned. Then she laughed. "That's absurd! Where did you hear this?"

"There was some talk at supper, and that's the rumor."

The world seemed to shift slightly to the left.

"I, for one, don't believe it's true," Amelia continued blithely. "He's rather sure of himself, and quite free with his words. And he doesn't strike me as a blackguard. Does he you? I should think if he impregnated a country girl, he'd happily let it be known. He'd probably marry her, just to spite society." She paused and looked at Justine curiously. "What's the matter? You don't believe it, do you?"

"No!" she said at once. She didn't believe it. It was impossible. So why, then, was her head spinning? It couldn't possibly be true; she couldn't *possibly* have been so wrong about him! The news was stunning, and she didn't know what to make of it, but she would stake her crown on it being a lie. That was how strongly she believed in him.

But oh, God, what if she was falling for another lie?

"Jussie? You're so pale."

Justine stood up and walked to the window. She pushed it open, then leaned out, taking a deep breath, dragging as much air as she could into her lungs. Somewhere behind her a door opened. And then she heard Lila's voice.

"Oh splendid! You're both here. I am delighted to inform you we've been invited to a supper party."

"A supper party!" Amelia proclaimed, perking up. "Where? No one boring, is it? No old man who used to be an admiral or a minister with stories to tell."

"We'll be dining at the home of Lord Iddesleigh."

Justine slowly turned away from the window and assumed a neutral expression. But Amelia gasped. "We've been there! We attended the most extraordinary soiree when we were here before."

"I expect it will be again," Lila said.

"When?"

"In two days' time."

Amelia came up off the chaise longue. "What have I got to wear?"

"I should think from all the shopping you've done, there would be something in your wardrobe," Justine said tightly.

"*Je*, I'm going to have a look." Amelia fairly skipped out of the room to have her look, excited about the prospect of another social occasion.

When she'd gone, Lila looked curiously at Justine. "How do you feel about the invitation?"

"I've no desire to attend if you want to know the truth."

"I always want to know the truth. Perhaps you'll be more interested when I tell you that your next suitor will attend?"

The woman looked absolutely pleased as punch and it annoyed Justine. "No, I am not more interested. I don't want another suitor, Lila. The first ones have been…lacking."

Lila frowned slightly. "Is everything all right?"

Everything was not all right. Everything felt ridiculous and wrong. "Fine."

Lila took a few steps closer. "Your Royal Highness, if I may—"

"Lila, really...you may not," she said wearily. She meant to turn back to the window but Lila shook her head.

"That's not going to work, I'm afraid."

"Pardon?"

"The petulance."

"Excuse me?" Justine was astounded that Lila would accuse her of it.

"The pet—"

"I heard you, Lady Aleksander. But I can't believe you're speaking to me in that manner."

"Hmm. Neither can I, really, but I think someone has to. You're very good at glowering at me, ma'am, but you rarely say what you feel."

Justine was astonished that someone would speak to her like this, astonished that Lila had pointed out what she knew was true about herself. So astonished she could not think of what to say.

"When will you learn to speak? To say what you want?"

Justine was even more flabbergasted—Lila Aleksander had no right to speak to her like this. "I *have* said what I want, but perhaps you weren't listening, madam. I have very clearly said I don't want any of the gentlemen you've subjected me to."

"Yes, you have been very clear about what you don't want. But you won't tell me what or who you *do* want. What you *truly* want."

What Justine truly wanted was on the tip of her tongue, and yet, she couldn't say it. She needed to think, to sort things out in her mind.

"I have an entire ledger full of young gentlemen. If only you'd give me some indication of what you would like, I could help you."

Oh, but she didn't need Lila's ledger. She knew precisely

who. But even if there wasn't the awful rumor, there was the matter of the Hamilton debts. She could hear her mother now, rejecting the idea for that reason alone before Justine could even voice it.

"I am sure you know you can't return to St. Edys without choosing *someone*. Because if you don't decide, it will be decided for you the moment you set foot in the palace. No one will wait for the right gentleman to come along, ma'am. Their interests will be driven by the throne."

"You don't have to tell me," she said stiffly. "I am fully aware of my fate."

"Are you?" Lila pressed. "Are you aware of what it's like to spend all of eternity with someone you don't love, much less like? Are you aware of how hard it will be to rule while you are having to tiptoe around a disgruntled husband? Or how terribly difficult it will be to bear children when you cannot stand for him to touch you? You are going to be in a position that very few women have been in, and right now, at this moment in your life, you have the opportunity to find a helpmate, and not a hindrance. But you must speak up, Your Royal Highness, and when you do, I will help you with everything I have. But if you don't, well... I wouldn't be the least bit surprised if Robuchard has already convinced your parents of his choice for you."

Justine sat heavily on the chaise Amelia had vacated. Lila held her ground, staring at Justine. "Will you not *speak*?"

Justine bristled. "I have much to think about. Will you please leave me now?"

Lila looked as if she wanted to argue. But she clamped her jaw tightly and turned away, walking out of the room and leaving Justine to wrestle with her private demons.

CHAPTER THIRTY-ONE

WILLIAM RECEIVED A LETTER, a message and a telegraph all in one day.

"It would appear the world conspires against me, Ewan."

"Pardon, milord?" Ewan dumped more hot water into William's bath.

"Never mind." The message looked the least ominous, so he started there. It was from Beck.

Come round tomorrow evening and have a look at the American. We've invited him to dine. Half past seven for wine.

Of course he was going to get a look at the American. He already distrusted the fellow on principle alone and when he met him, he'd find all the reasons to despise him. "Reply to Lord Iddesleigh that I should be happy to dine tomorrow evening. What have I to wear to supper to meet an American?"

"Shall I present you some options, milord?" Ewan asked with the slightest twinge of mockery as he went out.

He was left a letter from his father, sealed with red wax and the imprinted signet of the Hamilton seat, and a telegraph. He had a strong foreboding about the letter and put it aside, lest he sob into his bath and Ewan see it.

He unfolded the telegraph.

The princess must make a selection. Your father and
I are depending on you. DR

"Well, that one lacks all subtlety," William muttered. He
tossed it over the lip of the tub, drew a breath and picked
up the letter from his father.

He read it three times.

And then he sat in his bath until the water turned cold,
staring at rivulets of rain on his window.

Eventually, Ewan returned, carrying a selection of formal waistcoats. He held up a silver one with white em-
broidery.

"No."

Ewan looked at it. "Is it the color, then? Blue is fashionable."

"Aye, but that is silver."

Ewan tossed it aside and held up a dark red one.

William cocked his head to one side. "Do you ever think
of marriage, Ewan?"

All the blood drained from Ewan's big face. "What?"

"Marriage. How is it I donna know if you have or no'?"

Ewan stared at him.

William sighed and sank lower. He was getting cold now.
"Put that aside. I'll wear a black waistcoat and black neck
cloth. You can pick out black from the rest of them, can you
no'? Tell me—did you ever think to marry?"

Ewan put aside the waistcoats. His face, just pale, was
now ruddy with color. He rubbed his palms on his trousers.
"Aye," he said at last.

William would have guessed not, so the admission surprised him. "Why did you no', then?"

"I had no money. No house of me own. I had no' a thing
of value to offer, and I...I let her get away, I did."

William sat up and folded his arms on the edge of the tub. "But eventually, you had a house and coin."

"Aye. But I never met another one quite like her. No one else would do, I suppose."

William understood completely. He'd never met anyone quite like Justine Ivanosen, either. He didn't need anyone to tell him he never would meet anyone like her again. "Did you ever consider going back to her?"

"Aye, many times." He rubbed a finger under his nose, scrunching up his face like he meant to sneeze.

"And?"

"Couldna find the courage. When at last I did, I was too late. She was married with four bairn."

"Bloody hell."

"Aye, bloody hell, milord."

William leaned back again. He swirled the water around with his finger. "Do you regret it?"

The question apparently struck a chord. Ewan began to gather the waistcoats in a hurry. "If I had it to do again, I'd no' let her get away. If you're asking my advice, milord, I'd do whatever it took. Life is too long and lonely to let an opportunity pass, aye? If that is all?"

"Aye, it's all. Thank you, Ewan."

He watched his valet lumber out of the bathing room then stood up, picked up a towel and dried his body. He donned a dressing robe and went into his adjoining bedroom.

This experience with Justine truly had forced him to see another side of himself. He'd never really considered marriage because of the mess that was his family. And, he would freely admit, it had been quite pleasant to flit about the continent in search of the next party.

That was until he met Justine again as an adult and

watched the men parade before her. She deserved better than them. She deserved someone who saw her for who she was—a funny, smart, arresting woman who, as it happened, would one day be queen. He enjoyed her company. He felt he was at his best when he was with her, challenged to be a different sort of man than he normally was in the company of women.

He liked seeing her every day. They were shocked by the same things, liked the same things. They laughed together. When had they become friends? What day, what place, what moment, had they turned to friendship? When had it become even more?

He groaned, rubbed his face with his hands. He couldn't bear the thought of anyone touching her. He wanted that woman all to himself.

God in heaven...he really had gone and fallen in love. That was what this was, right down to the pit in his stomach. He was in *love*. He must be—because he knew without the slightest hesitation, he'd go with her to Wesloria. He would revel in her taking the throne. He would enjoy watching her from the sidelines, being there to help her in any way that he could.

But that would never happen. How could it possibly when the news from Scotland was so grim? He had to tell her the truth.

He had to tell her everything, no matter the consequence. Because that was what she deserved.

CHAPTER THIRTY-TWO

WILLIAM WAS THE first to arrive at the Iddesleigh house on Upper Brook Street. He was clearly early, as the drawing room had not been cleared of the four devilettes and their keeper. Two of the girls were racing around the perimeter, screeching at each other. The next youngest one was on the floor, her face a hideous shade of red, her little mouth a gaping maw as she sobbed inconsolably. The baby was trying to eat the tail of a cat.

Donovan was on the settee with a book, one leg lazily crossed over the other. He seemed not to notice the girls at all.

"Douglas! You're a saint for coming early," Beck said, rising from his spot at the desk and hurrying forward. "I can't possibly take another moment of this." He turned around, as if he'd just remembered Donovan was there. "How long must we endure this?"

Donovan glanced at the clock. "Half hour ought to do it." He put his book aside. "Or I could put a spot of brandy in their milk before bed."

"How dare you even mention it," Beck said and glanced out of the corner of his eye at Douglas. "We employ that method only in the most dire of circumstances."

"The most dire of circumstances being every weekend," added Donovan. He yawned, stretched his arms overhead and stood. "Here's what, milord. I'll take them around to the Tricklebank house for the night. The cat has given birth to kittens."

The oldest girl, Mathilda, stopped running so suddenly that her younger sister plowed into her. "Kiki had kittens?"

"Five of them," Donovan said as he studied the back of his hand. "I wanted to tell you, but you wouldn't stop screaming."

"Papa! May we spend the night at the Tricklebank house?"

"Yes, yes, all of you, but the baby. That one needs her mother's milk. Perhaps a spot of brandy will return her to good humor."

The youngest one had already crawled away and had pulled a book off a footstool.

"All right, then, come along, you little heathens. You'll need your nightgowns, your sleeping caps and a cross to keep away the ghosts."

That didn't seem like the sort of thing one wanted to say to a young child, but the girls shrieked with delight and raced across the room for the door.

Donovan stooped down and swept up the baby with one arm and followed the other three out of the room. "I'll have them back to you at the crack of dawn."

"No need to rush. Take all the time you need," Beck said and kissed each one of them on the top of their head before sending them from the room.

The silence that descended after their departure was quite heavy. William looked at Beck. "You said half past seven."

"Did I? Ah, my fault. I told the rest of them half past eight." He smiled. "Shall we repair to my study for a bit of brandy to calm our nerves?"

"Please."

In Beck's study William moved aside a doll missing its head, a rag puppy and a single shoe to take a seat in a chair near the hearth. Beck handed him a brandy and sat in the other chair after discarding a tiny petticoat, a bonnet and the head of the doll.

William couldn't help but smile. "How your life has changed, my old friend."

"Hasn't it indeed?" Beck said with a weary sigh. "I never thought this sort of life was for me, and I was very firm with Blythe. One child, no more. But I find I enjoy the babies almost as much as I enjoy making them. And it helps to have a wife like mine. She is the rock in this family." He glanced around at the detritus his daughters had left behind. "What about you, Douglas? Do you ever think of domesticity? I should think it well past time." Beck looked at him directly. "Isn't there anyone who has caught your eye?"

William studied his friend. He took a sip of his drink and put it aside. "I've known you quite a long time, Beck. If you have something to say, then by all means, say it."

Beck smiled slyly. "Blythe says I am horrible with secrets. There has been some...ah, talk...of your interest in the Weslorian crown princess."

"And?"

"There has been almost as much talk of that as there has been about a young woman in Scotland in whom you left your seed."

William considered denying the rumor. But he didn't have the strength to deny his feelings anymore. He simply nodded. "I am aware."

Beck blinked with surprise. "My God. Is it true?"

"No," William said firmly. "Do you think so ill of me?"

"I don't think ill of you at all, Will. So what, then, is this about?"

"Extortion." He shrugged. "I tried to help her." He told Beck the story of encountering Althea Simpson, of trying to help her escape to her lover. He said perhaps he shouldn't have done it, but she was distraught and he couldn't bear it. But that her father had caught up with her, and as far as he knew, had kept her locked away in his house. That he didn't learn of the attempt to extort his family until weeks later.

"Good Lord," Beck said. "What did the duke do?"

"Paid him."

Beck winced.

"The worst thing he might have done," William said darkly. "I received a letter from the duke today informing me that Mr. Simpson made a return visit to Hamilton Palace and is demanding more money to keep his silence. My father refused him, and true to his word, Mr. Simpson has begun to spread the word that I am the father of the child and have abandoned her."

"Goodness," Beck said. "This is a dilemma. Your reputation can't withstand any more tarnishing."

William couldn't disagree.

"Especially given the position you're in."

"What? What position is that?"

"I'm going to have to think this through," Beck said absently.

"What are you talking about?"

The door behind them suddenly flew open with such force that Beck spilled a bit of his brandy on his trousers.

"Good *evening*, Lord Douglas!"

Lady Iddesleigh barreled into the room, her pregnant belly seeming to reach them a minute before she did. "We are so happy to have you this evening! What a grand thing, this supper we are having. You won't mind if I steal my husband away for just a moment, will you? Garrett, our persnickety butler, and I have had a bit of row where to seat everyone. I swear, he and I never see eye to eye on these things, do we, darling? We can't agree about where to seat the princesses."

"The princesses?" William said, coming to his feet.

"Oh, didn't I mention it?" Beck asked as he stood. "The princesses will dine with us this evening. Lord and Lady Aleksander as well."

"Is there anything else I should know?" William called after him as his wife dragged him from the room.

Predictably, Beck didn't answer.

WILLIAM FELT ABSURDLY anxious when the butler announced the guests had arrived and showed them into the grand salon for wine. First came Lord and Lady Aleksander. And then the princesses.

However, the moment William laid eyes on Justine, all of his anxiety evaporated. She looked so dignified and fashionable. Her gown had splashes of dark red flowers across its flounces, and she wore a royal badge and ribbon at her breast. Rubies dangled from her ears, and the gold bracelet she always wore was on her wrist. Her hair had been styled very simply in the back and was covered with lace and red ribbons. And the white streak in her hair—he thought again how it looked as if it had been intentionally painted there.

He couldn't imagine ever looking at her and not feeling awed by her. Her beauty was apparent. She didn't have the flawless good looks like her sister, but the sort that radiated from within. It attracted him more every time he looked at her.

Good God, he was lovesick.

He bowed. "Your Royal Highness," he said.

"Lord Douglas. I didn't know to expect you this evening." She smiled with delight.

"Life is full of surprises, aye?"

"And what of me?" Princess Amelia asked.

He made himself look at the younger princess. "Your Royal Highness, how good it is to see you returned to your sister's side."

"I've been in the country," she said. "All the travel has exhausted me." She held out her hand for a glass of wine. A footman put one in it.

"May I introduce my husband, Lord Aleksander?" Lady Aleksander asked and introduced him to William. Her husband had a welcoming face and bright, interested green eyes. William liked him instantly.

The wine was served all around, and small talk was made, mostly Beck and his wife rattling on about the child who had stuffed her coat into the garden fountain. William hardly heard the story—he kept looking at Justine, who sat serenely on the edge of her seat, her gloved hands folded on her lap, smiling and laughing politely as Beck embellished his tale.

He wished he could have a moment alone with her. To say hello, to see how she fared. Unfortunately, he could not divine an opportunity before the arrival of the highly desirable American, Mr. Henry Thompson.

The butler announced him as if he was announcing the President of the United States, complete with the tone of a town crier and the bow of a supplicant. Mr. Henry Thompson strode into the room with an air of confidence that even William did not possess. He paused, one long leg extended, one hand on his hip. He was tall and sturdy, his hair blond, his skin tanned by the sun. "Is this the party?" he asked, and his face broke into a grin.

"Mr. Thompson," Beck said, coming forward. "Welcome to my home. My wife, Lady Iddesleigh."

"A pleasure to meet you, Lady Iddesleigh. And congratulations on the new addition to your family," he said and bowed to her belly.

Justine and her sister exchanged a look.

"Lord and Lady Aleksander, whom I believe you know," Beck said, going around the room.

He did, and the three of them exchanged pleasantries.

"The Marquess of Hamilton and Clydesdale," Beck said.

Mr. Henry Thompson turned to William and sized him up, his eyes narrowing just slightly. He nodded. "I like a good-size man. You know he is capable of hard work."

William didn't know what to say to that. "Aye."

"Do I detect a bit of an accent?"

"I'm from Scotland."

"Well, I like you even better now. I've known a few Scotsmen. As tough as they come."

"We are a hardy lot," William agreed.

"A hardy lot," Mr. Thompson repeated and laughed.

"And if I may," Beck said, drawing his attention. "Your Royal Highnesses, may I present Mr. Henry Thompson of America?"

He bowed, then asked, "Now, which one is which?"

The American was brash, that much was certain. William thought Lady Aleksander might have at least described them to the man before now.

"Her Royal Highness, Princess Justine," Beck said, and nodded to Justine. "And Her Royal Highness, Princess Amelia."

To William's eyes, the man's gaze lingered a moment too

long on Princess Amelia. But he quickly proclaimed himself honored to meet them and that he'd never been in the presence of so many princesses, then turned away, taking in the room. "Nice place," he said to Beck. "Reminds me a little of my father's home on the shore of Lake Michigan. The rooms in his house are bigger, and the furniture a little newer, but about the same."

For once, Beck was speechless. Even Lady Aleksander seemed taken aback. She actually laughed.

William caught Justine's eye. One of her brows rose. He knew what she was thinking without having to hear it from her—she was skeptical at best. Princess Amelia, on the other hand, seemed delighted by this strange man with the flat accent.

The butler offered Mr. Thompson a glass of wine, but he declined. "You haven't got any whisky here, have you?"

"Yes, of course," Lady Iddesleigh said, nodding at Garrett.

When Garrett returned with it, Mr. Thompson took it from the tray and sipped. "Now, that's a man's drink," he said, looking around at the gentlemen holding wineglasses. He grinned at them, then turned his attention to the princesses. "I noticed you both have the white in your hair," he said, gesturing at his own hair. "Not so noticeable in Princess Amelia's hair, but definitely noticeable in Princess Justine's hair. What is that? A royal thing?" He laughed at what presumably he meant as a joke.

No one else did. Everyone else stared at him, expressions ranging from appalled to confused.

"It's a trait of our family," Princess Amelia said. "My father has it, and his mother before him."

"Interesting."

"Perhaps we might come through to the dining room," Lady Iddesleigh said suddenly.

"Yes, let's go through," Beck quickly added, seeming relieved by the suggestion.

They arranged themselves to promenade, Lady Iddesleigh taking Mr. Thompson's arm and pointing out some of the portraits as they passed. Beck took in Justine, and William offered his arm to Princess Amelia.

"What are you doing here?" she asked.

"I might ask the same of you. The better question is what is Mr. Thompson doing here?"

"I like him," Princess Amelia whispered.

"I am no' surprised," he whispered back.

In the dining room, over the first course of soup, Beck asked Mr. Thompson what had brought him to London.

Mr. Thompson—who used a spoon and not his fingers for the soup, thank God—seemed to be waiting for the question to be asked. He began with a short history of himself, how his family had built the biggest steel factory in the Great Lakes region of the United States and how he was here to "make some deals."

There could be nothing more crass than admitting to wanting to make some deals in the home of an English earl. Lord Aleksander stared with fascination at the American. William glanced at Lady Aleksander. Scowled at her, really. She gave him a halfhearted shrug.

When the soup was cleared and the fish was served, William watched Mr. Thompson pick up a fork with his right hand, a knife in his left, the opposite of the way everyone else at the table held their utensils. Princess Amelia asked him about America—what did it look like? Were there a lot of people? Was it very cold there?

Mr. Thompson switched his knife and fork back and forth, depending on whether he was eating or cutting, and said that the scenery was beautiful, far prettier than England, but that Michigan could be as cold as a devil's teat.

"Pardon?" Princess Amelia said. "Isn't it hot where the devil is?"

"I mean that it's damnably cold, miss."

Beck's hand curled into a fist on the table, probably fighting the urge to correct the American's address of the royal princess. "It must be cold in Wesloria, eh? You've got some of those ermine furs, don't you?" He switched his fork and knife to cut a piece of fish, then put the knife down and placed his fork in his right hand again. It seemed to William a lot of work for a bite of food.

"We do have furs, but they are fox. It gets very cold in Wesloria. I prefer the weather in England."

William caught Justine's eye. She subtly glanced heavenward.

Beck shifted around to the topic of American politics, about which, surprisingly, he appeared well-read. All talk fell away, because Mr. Thompson liked having the floor.

After dinner they all retired to the salon. If Mr. Thompson had any desire to court Justine, he didn't show it. He seemed only to want to talk of himself. Even when Lady Iddesleigh sat at the piano and began to pound away at the keys, he kept talking to Lord Aleksander, raising his voice to be heard over the piano. The man was a boor and so unsuitable for Justine that William wanted to put his fist through the wall.

At some point Beck determined the room was too warm and instructed the footmen to open the doors onto the garden. One by one the party began to drift outside. First went Lady Aleksander and her husband, obviously escaping. Mr. Thompson, having found a friend in Lord Aleksander, went after them. Princess Amelia, having found an interest in

Mr. Thompson, scurried after him. And as Beck offered his arm to his wife, William watched Justine go the opposite direction, out into the hall.

He looked at the rest of the party wandering about in the garden and followed Justine. He paused just before the door and took a single rose from a vase of them.

CHAPTER THIRTY-THREE

THE FRONT HALL of the Iddesleigh house had two window alcoves. Justine stepped into the first one and pressed her hands to her belly. She couldn't breathe. All evening, as the reality of her situation had settled into her membranes and her heart, it had become increasingly difficult to breathe. Her skin felt clammy; her scalp tingled. She wanted to tear her hair down from its pins, release the laces of her corset.

Mr. Thompson was the worst of them all. A self-satisfied braggadocio with the manners of a sailor. And then there was William, seated across and down the table from her, so perfect in every way, yet so impossibly distant from her.

What would become of her? Would she be married away to a man who made her long every day for someone else? How wretched, how *lonely*, that existence! That was to be the state of her reign? Why had she been born into this family? Why couldn't she have been born to a simpler life?

She heard a noise and whirled around, expecting to find Mr. Thompson. It was William. Thank God, *William*.

He held out a single rose.

She couldn't help her smile. "You took that from the vase."

"Aye. I wanted to bring you something and it was the only thing available. What are you doing here? Your suitor is on the terrace."

"My suitor," she scoffed. She was hiding; she was escaping that so-called suitor. She was doing everything she was not supposed to do, and it was because of William. "What *am* I doing? You want to know what I am doing, William? I'm falling in love, that's what."

He looked stricken. His hand dropped, still clutching the rose. "With Mr. Thompson?"

"No! With *you*!"

His expression shifted from horror to shock to torment. "*Diah*, Justine, I—"

"But I *can't* fall in love with you, William! You're poor and I've heard the most distressing rumor."

The rose fell to the floor. "I'm no' poor, for God's sake. Far from it. But never mind that. How did you hear it?"

He knew what she was referring to and didn't attempt to deny it. Justine began to quake inside. She felt like she might explode. "Then it's true?"

"No, *leannan*. Nothing you've heard about me is true. But that's the trouble with rumors, aye? I canna prove it to you. You have only my word. The lass, she is indeed carrying a bairn, or perhaps has now been delivered of a bairn, I donna rightly know. But the child is no' mine. My crime was attempting to help her escape to her lover, to marry the father of her child. But that man, whoever he is, was no' acceptable to her father. He caught her and hid her away and tried to extort my father with lies. *That* is the truth, on my honor."

Justine wanted to believe him more than she'd ever wanted anything in her life. But her father's words were whispering through her, warning her to trust no one. Was she as foolish as her mother had accused her of being? Believing yet another man and his lies? But William was so different from any man she'd ever met. She couldn't imagine him abandoning a woman, particularly if she had his child. He was unfailingly honest. Why would he lie to her about this when he'd told her everything else? "How do I know you're not lying to me?"

He winced, as if her question had physically struck him. "You donna know, lass. You have to trust me, but moreover, you have to trust your instincts. I'm no' lying to you now because I would no'. I am no' lying to you now because I have fallen in love with you, too." He took her hand and drew her closer to him. His gray eyes locked on hers. "I would give up everything for you and I would no' risk it with a lie. I canna help that this thing has been said of me, but it's no' true. I would never treat a woman so abominably. And I have always been faithful to my family's legacy, just as you are to yours. Much can be said about me, but no' living up to my word is no' one." He paused and drew a deep breath. "But more than that, *much* more than that... I'd sooner die than have you believe I am the sort of man who would abandon that poor lass. If the child was mine I would marry her because of my own conscience."

He gripped her hand as if he feared she would pull it free.

Justine believed him. Completely. Things had been said about her that weren't true, and there was never anything she could do about it. It was possible she might be the one person who could understand how some man in Scotland had used him ill. How people attempted to use others if there was something to be gained.

"I believe you, William. I do."

He released a breath of relief and glanced down. "*Thank* you." He pulled her closer. "You canna know how much it means to me. For you to have heard such an ugly thing is terrifying. To believe it—"

"But it doesn't matter what I think," she said desperately. "Under these circumstances, my parents would never accept an association with you. I have to live above such rumors. I must be untarnished in everything I do or lose the trust of the people. You know it's true, William. You know the burden I bear. On my word, I wish I could give the throne to Amelia. I want—"

"There you two are!" Lila trilled somewhere behind William.

William closed his eyes in anguish.

"Your Royal Highness, Mr. Thompson is looking for you."

William turned and moved aside, and Justine watched Mr. Thompson saunter forward with a knowing grin, looking back and forth between the two of them. "Well, then. What are the two of you cooking up?"

Justine lifted her chin. She'd had enough of him, of the whole business of matchmaking. "Mr. Thompson, I will be a queen soon, and it is not considered acceptable to question a queen on her actions."

He laughed. When she didn't, his smile faded. "Are you serious?"

"Quite."

"Mr. Thompson," Lila said quickly, "might I have a word with you?" She stepped in front of him, gesturing to the study. Mr. Thompson didn't seem to notice her—he was staring at Justine with an expression that said he meant to challenge her. But he conceded to the pressure on his arm and allowed Lila to lead him into the study.

William smiled. "You hit him right in the gullet with your crown."

"Sometimes it is necessary."

Just then, a bell rang, the sound coming from the study. Seconds after that Beck came striding down the hall, passing them and disappearing into the study. Just as quickly as he'd gone in, Lila came out. "Well. You two have certainly made a cake of it, haven't you? Please come back to the salon."

"We were having a private conversation," Justine said.

"Yes, we all see that. But if you could, for a few moments, at least, return to the salon." She glanced over her shoulder to the study door.

"Aye, come," William said and put his hand to the small of Justine's back and guided her into the salon.

Lord Aleksander, Lady Iddesleigh and Amelia were all standing in the salon, all looking anxiously in the direction of the door.

"What has happened?" Amelia asked.

"I don't really know," Justine said.

She could hear the voices of men in the hall, could hear a door opening, then closing. And then Beck strode into the room. "Well, *that's* done."

"What's done?" his wife asked.

"Mr. Thompson has left."

"He's *left*?" Amelia cried. "But why?"

"He had some steel to talk about or some such," Lila said, coming in behind Beck.

Justine and William exchanged a look. This was it, Justine realized. This was the moment. If she was ever going to speak up for what she wanted, now was the time to do it.

She could feel that quake begin at her toes and start to work its way up as she turned to Lila. "You wanted me to speak for myself, madam? I am ready to speak."

Lila slowly smiled. "And I can scarcely wait to hear it." She began to wave her arms, asking everyone to sit.

"What are you doing?" Justine asked.

"Preparing your audience."

"I don't want an audience."

"Unfortunately, you have one and you always will. Consider it good practice for the future. All right, everyone. Be calm. Your Royal Highness?"

Justine looked at William again. He was standing to the side. He looked uncertain as to what she was about, but he gave her a nod of encouragement and touched two fingers to his breast, just where his heart would be.

She didn't know if he was telling her to have heart or that she was in his—whatever he meant, it buoyed her, and she would take all the help she was offered. She was quaking inside, and her breath was short.

But remarkably, she thought she could do this.

She had a sudden image of herself on the battlement at Astasia Castle, pleading for her life. This was obviously not as dramatic as that, but it *was* her life. What she hoped would be a long one, too. And she felt absolutely right in this. She was trusting William, but more importantly, she was trusting her instincts.

She drew a breath. Amelia inched to the edge of her seat, as if she thought she might have to catch Justine should she faint.

"I was sent to England for one reason." Her voice was, to her surprise, strong and clear. "Well, two, really. The first was to put a scandal of my own making to rest. But the second was to make a proper match. A princess cannot be a queen without a man nearby, as the saying goes."

"I don't care for that idea," Lady Aleksander said.

"Neither do I, but when all the ministers of your kingdom are men, sometimes there is very little you can do about it."

All the women in the room nodded.

"For the last two years, as my father has weakened, and I have come closer to assuming the throne..." Her hand started to quiver. She grasped it with her other hand and held tight, pressing them both to her belly. "I have been told what I can or cannot do, or say, or *be*. But in this, I will not be told. I *will* have my say. It's my life, after all."

It felt as if everyone in the room was leaning forward, as if they feared she was about to abdicate. Amelia especially seemed stricken. "Justine," she said softly. "Please don't do whatever you are about to do."

Justine ignored her. She looked at William. "I love him."

There was a moment of silence. Justine wondered if anyone had heard her. William had not moved, and no one had said a word. But then Lady Iddesleigh said, very softly, *"Oh."*

"What?" Amelia cried. "You love *him*?" She pointed at William.

"No' a resounding vote of confidence, but I understand," William said.

"Yes, Amelia. I love him. Moreover, I *trust* him. He is the only person who has ever told me the truth. He is the only person to really see me."

Every head in that room swiveled toward William. He tried to smile. But then he shrugged, palms up, and said, "Aye, and I love her, with all my heart. It would be a damn sight easier if I didna, but I do, and I'd give all that I have and am for her."

"That is *so romantic*," Lady Iddesleigh sighed. She leaned back against the settee, her hand caressing her belly.

"What are you saying?" Amelia demanded. "Do you mean to marry him?"

Justine drew another breath. "I can't."

Amelia looked around at them all with utter confusion. "Will someone kindly explain what is happening?"

"Or rather, *he* can't," Justine amended. "There is a bit of a problem in that a young woman has said her—"

"I beg your pardon, *leannan*, but her father had said it."

"Right, yes. Her father has accused William of fathering her child."

Amelia gasped. She stared at William. And then at Justine. "Oh no. Then it's true? This is…this is so *bad*, Jussie. What are you doing?"

"He didn't do it, Amelia. He is innocent. Even you said you didn't believe the rumors about him."

"*Je*, but you can't believe *him*—"

"Of course he didn't do it," Beck said and stood. He began to pace beside Justine. "Douglas is a scoundrel, but he is an honorable one. If he says he didn't, he didn't."

Everyone looked at William again.

He put his hand on his heart. "On the lives of my future children, I did no'. If I had, I would do the honorable thing."

"The problem here is, we've got to convince the rest of the world that he didn't," Beck said. He stopped pacing and looked around the room. "That is…we're all in agreement that these two young pups deserve their chance at happiness? Show of hands." He raised his hand.

His wife eagerly raised hers. So did Lord and Lady Aleksander. As did Justine and William.

Amelia looked all around her. "Really? But I thought you hated him." She slowly raised her hand.

"I did, but then I didn't," Justine admitted.

"You *hated* me?" William exclaimed.

"I'll explain it later," she said. "Lord Iddesleigh, we are agreed. You were saying?"

"Yes. Well, then. In my estimation, what we need is the father to come forward and admit the truth."

"I believe that to be a problem," William said. "I don't believe the father knows he is a father."

"That's outrageous!" Lady Iddesleigh cried.

"I believe that's why Mr. Simpson has kept the lass locked away. He had set his sights higher for his daughter."

Everyone's brows furrowed.

"Perhaps there is a way to expose Mr. Simpson's lie," Lord Aleksander said.

Lila gasped. "Yes, of course, darling, you're absolutely right."

"But how?" Lady Iddesleigh asked.

"If someone else said they were the father of the child, Mr. Simpson would have to put his accusations in the open," Lila suggested. "He'd have to prove it was Lord Douglas."

"Wouldn't he just accuse him again?" Lady Iddesleigh asked.

"Probably. But with another man swearing that he is the father, who would believe Mr. Simpson?"

"Especially if the other man was someone from whom Mr. Simpson had nothing to gain," Lord Aleksander said.

"Like the father," Lila added.

"I don't understand!" Amelia said crossly.

"What about this?" Lila said. "We find a gentleman of mean circumstances to declare himself father of the child. Mr. Simpson will have two choices. He can accept it, or declare it is not true and prove that it is not. Which, of course, he can't do."

"And in the meantime, if we can discover the true identity of the father, Douglas can bring him forward," Beck said excitedly.

"Yes!" Lila cried triumphantly. "He will save the poor girl and her child, unite her with her lover, expose Mr. Simpson for the swindler that he is and be proclaimed a hero!"

"Wait," William said, throwing up a hand. "I appreciate the imagination and enthusiasm. But it seems a wee bit far-fetched to me. Might we no' ask Ms. Simpson who is the father and bring him forward?"

"No," Lila said, shaking her head. "Her father will say you are attempting to wash your hands of your responsibility. The real father must be brought forward independent of the Simpsons so that Mr. Simpson can be exposed as the swindler he is."

This was ridiculous. How could something like this ever work? But then Justine realized everyone was looking at her, waiting for her to agree to this plan. "This makes no sense. Who would pretend to be the father?"

"Leave that to me," Lila said.

"And what about the real father?" she pressed.

"We'll find him," Lila said confidently.

"How?" Justine insisted. "This all seems rather fantastic."

Lila gained her feet and crossed the room to Justine. She took her hands. "Ma'am. This is the thing I do quite well. I am not going to allow some wretched father in Scotland ruin a love I have worked so hard to put together."

"*Excuse* me?"

"And I certainly won't allow Robuchard to name one of his associates to be your husband."

"Oh!" Amelia said. "Not Robuchard!"

Justine locked her gaze on Lila. She wanted desperately to believe she could do this.

"I told you in the beginning I would find you who you need and deserve. I never said it would be easy," Lila said.

"You'd be advised to listen to my wife, Your Royal Highness," Lord Aleksander interjected. "She is never wrong."

Lila smiled. "See how good a husband can be?"

But William suddenly appeared at her side and put his hand on Lila's arm. "Donna pressure her into foolishness,

Lady Aleksander," he said. "I donna know if we can find the father of the child. I donna know if any of this will work." He put his arm around Justine's shoulders and drew her aside. "You have your country and your throne to think about."

"But how can I think of it without someone I love and trust at my side, William? How can I possibly be queen without someone I know who loves me? I love you. I want you to be with me. I *need* you to be with me."

He took her hand and brought it to his lips. "I love you. I love you enough to step aside—I'll no' bring more scandal to you."

She winced. "But this is our only hope."

He frowned, and she could see him trying to think of an answer, a solution that would work. But at last, he nodded. "As absurd as it is, aye. It's our only hope."

She pressed her palm to his cheek. "This time I ask that you trust *me*. I believe in Lila."

He sighed. "God help us both, then."

Justine turned and faced the room. She wasn't shaking anymore. "*Je*, all right. We haven't very long. My mother is attempting to force Amelia and me to return to St. Edys as we speak."

"Then let's get started," Lila said.

"This is so very *exciting*," Lady Iddesleigh gushed.

"I think I may be ill," Amelia muttered.

"Why do these things always happen in *my* house?" Beck demanded of no one.

Justine looked at William. He tried to give her an encouraging smile. She tried to return one.

CHAPTER THIRTY-FOUR

LILA TOLD VALENTIN she needed fifty pounds.

"Why?" He was lying in their bed, his feet crossed at the ankles, one arm behind his head to pillow it.

"An actor needs a proper suit of clothing."

Valentin frowned. "What actor?"

"He is a friend of Lord Iddesleigh's governess, Mr. Donovan."

Valentin's brow crinkled. "My English is not what it once was, but I thought a governess was female."

"She is. I mean, a governess is. He's not exactly a…" She waved her hand. "Let me start from the beginning."

She explained to Valentin that she'd had a long talk with the Earl of Iddesleigh, and Mr. Donovan, the tutor, governor, manservant—whatever he was—had been present. He'd suggested he knew someone who could play the part of the frantic father, and rather convincingly at that. Lord Douglas would pay him a good wage for the work, but Lila had realized she needed to have him properly outfitted when in Scotland.

Valentin listened, then rolled off the bed, went to his things, rummaged through a leather bag and produced the fifty pounds. "You are the most clever of them all, my darling…but are you certain this scheme will work?"

"No," she said honestly. "I rather think it's doomed to fail. But it's my only chance. And if I can't make it work,

I fear Dante Robuchard will see to it that there is no work for me in Europe. And…I really hate to lose."

Valentin wrapped his hands around her waist. "Tell me the plan again."

"The actor will go to the village of Hamilton and make a show of searching for Miss Althea Simpson. He will proclaim her to be his love, will announce that he's been told there is a child, *his* child. When word reaches Mr. Simpson, he will deny it. He is obviously trying to profit from his daughter's mistake."

"His daughter may well deny it, too. What would possibly entice her to agree that this stranger is the one?"

"That's the tricky part, isn't it? She won't deny it if we reach her first. When Mr. Simpson trots her out to deny that this poor stranger is the father of her bastard child, we hope to be there with the true father. She won't deny *him*. After all, she was trying to reach him."

"How do you propose to find the true father?"

Lila hadn't worked all that out. "We need her to tell us who he is. We bring the true father forward, the truth is known and Lord Douglas is free to marry the princess. That is, if Robuchard can be convinced."

Valentin nuzzled her neck. "My darling Lila…you do realize this sounds like a poorly written play in some run-down theater, don't you?"

She laughed. "I knew you'd understand."

"I understand well enough that I'm going with you. I don't want you caught up in any bad dealings."

"I was hoping you'd say that," she said and kissed him. "We leave in the morning."

WILLIAM ARRIVED AT Prescott Hall the next morning to meet Lord and Lady Aleksander. Ewan had come, too, and thank

God for it—William was so discombobulated that he'd almost left without his things.

He'd never in his life been such a tangled mess of anxiety. It felt as if his whole life had been building up to this moment, and his life going forward was resting on a house of cards.

The footmen were loading the Aleksanders' bags onto the carriage. Lord and Lady Bardaline had come out and were buzzing around them like flies, eager to see the lot of them dispatched away from Prescott Hall. The pair had no notion of what was underfoot, and Lady Bardaline seemed on the verge of hysterical laughter. "We've enjoyed your time with us, Lady Aleksander. Safe journey!"

Princess Amelia had come to watch the dispatch, too, and said, "For heaven's sake, they'll be back in a week or so."

Lady Aleksander ignored the Bardalines altogether. "My lord, will you come inside for a moment?" she asked, gesturing William forward.

When he stepped into the foyer, he was relieved to see Justine coming down the stairs with Dodi tucked under her arm. She had on her gardening apron, her hair loose down her back. She looked so beautiful that he wanted to stand there a moment and quietly take her in, in case this was the last—

"Five minutes," Lady Aleksander said. "I can't hold them off any longer."

She meant the Bardalines. William looked at Justine. She indicated with her head the receiving room and went in ahead of him.

William glanced at Lila. "Go," she said.

So he did. He followed Justine into a room empty of footmen and butlers and matchmakers and jailers. He quickly shut the door in case any of the aforementioned thought to join them.

Justine put down the dog, then rushed into his arms. She pressed her face to his chest. "This will never work! How could I have agreed to this?"

"Justine. *Leannan.*" He caught her face between his hands and lifted it. "Keep faith. Say your prayers. This is the only hope we have."

She looked on the verge of tears and wrapped her hands around his wrists. "What if it fails? You must come back to me, William. Do you hear me? You *must.* I will be lost without you. I can't stop thinking—I can't be queen without you."

He kissed her softly. "You donna need me to be queen. But I *will* come back to you." He kissed her again. "I will walk if I must. I will climb through brambles and swim rivers and beg for my supper—nothing will keep me away." He kissed her once more. "Have faith."

A single tear slipped from the corner of her eye. "This is madness."

"Aye, it is. But think of the stories we will tell our children." He wrapped his arms around her and kissed her again. A long, deep kiss. He tried to infuse her with as much hope as he could, to give her an unspoken promise that he would find a way.

He didn't know how in God's name they would find a way, but he was willing to die trying.

He finally let her go, stroked her cheek and pressed his hand to her neck before he walked out.

WHEN HE'D GONE Justine moved restlessly about the receiving room, Dodi following her every step, and finally came to stand behind the settee. She gripped the back of it and sank down, crouching, trying not to vomit. As it was, she could hardly breathe. She had a terrible sense of doom, as if this was the last time she would ever see him. No one ever removed a scandal from their name—she knew that better than most. She would not be allowed to marry him. She would be forced instead to marry a man she could not bear to touch and would think of William always. *Always*.

She heard someone come in and tried to swallow down her grief and her nausea.

"Jussie? What are you doing?"

Amelia's feet appeared beside her. "I am trying desperately not to wail."

"Oh, darling," Amelia said. She slid down to the floor beside her and wrapped her arms around her. "You really *do* love him."

She really did.

They remained like that, Amelia holding Justine and Dodi until Justine could breathe again.

CHAPTER THIRTY-FIVE

MR. PAUL BARTHOLOMEW insisted on learning his role in this caper on the long, twelve-hour trip to Glasgow. William had put them all in the first-class car on the train, which Mr. Bartholomew had inspected, and had declared, in spite of its small size and hard seating, was appropriate for his rehearsal.

He spent the first hour peppering William with questions about Miss Althea Simpson. He began with the obvious questions, such as her height, the color of her hair and eyes. He asked about her disposition, whether or not she was demur or if she commanded a room. And then proceeded to ask head-scratching questions about the sound of her laugh, and the size of her feet.

William tried to explain that he really didn't know her well at all, had only met her a few times before the day in question. But he gave Mr. Bartholomew as much information as he could.

Had she borne the child? Mr. Bartholomew had asked.

William didn't know. He had encountered her around the Yuletide, and now it was summer. It was entirely possible she had given birth. It was also entirely possible she hadn't.

Then Mr. Bartholomew began to rehearse. For his performance he'd selected the moment he would enter the village's largest public house to inquire after his lost love. He took the small step to the head of the train car and then pretended, by walking between the seats, to enter the common room of the public house, look around him and then ask if anyone could direct him to the home of the woman he would marry, *Miss Althea Simpson*!

William thought that was a rather theatrical entrance. But it was nothing compared to what followed.

Mr. Bartholomew played all the parts.

"Who's asking?" he asked in a surprisingly good Scottish brogue, playing the part of the proprietor.

"It is I, the father of her child, the love of her life. How could I have known that our love bore fruit? How could I have understood that she needed me? She did not send word. She simply…disappeared!" He paused here and looked at the rest of them. "I'll work on the exact wording, of course."

Lord Aleksander took an interest and sat up. "Who are you, man?" he asked, playing the part of a patron.

"Robert Barstow, at your service." With a flourish of his hand, Mr. Bartholomew bowed.

"Who is that, then?" William asked.

"A fictional character, obviously. I shan't have a mob of angry country folk searching for me when this is all said and done." He cleared his throat and lifted his chin. "Robert Barstow, at your service. Where is she? Where is my love? *'Who could refrain that had a heart to love and in that heart courage to make love known?'*"

Lord Aleksander smiled. "Shakespeare, eh? A nice touch, Mr. Bartholomew."

"Thank you."

Lady Aleksander took part, too. "We won't tell you, sir. How can we know if what you say is true? How can we know if you mean harm to the poor girl?"

Mr. Bartholomew considered this. "What harm could I

possibly cause her, other than to provide for her, care for her and my child and cherish her all my days? If you won't tell me, I shall remain at this table until Althea Simpson is brought to me. With her golden hair, her gentle laugh, her large feet and manlike hands..." He paused here and glanced around at them. "They will need to understand that I indeed know who she is, you see." He resumed his character again. "I will not rest until I have her. How could this secret be kept from me? How could she have kept my child from me?" He clapped his hand to his heart and grimaced. "Does she not understand my love for her? How could she have slayed me in this way?"

Lady Aleksander looked at her husband. "That ought to get tongues wagging, don't you think?"

"It ought to get him killed," Ewan muttered.

William had to agree. This was looking more and more ridiculous with each passing mile, and he despaired of anything working.

"How do we find the true father?" he asked of no one in particular, his desperation spilling out of him.

"Molly McGuire," Ewan said.

"Pardon?"

"Kitchen lass. Goes to market every day. She could pass a message to the kitchen lass at the Simpson house, aye?"

Now everyone looked at Ewan, startling him.

"That's really rather perfect," Lady Aleksander said. "My lord, you must write a letter to Miss Simpson and tell her what we're about."

"Is it really perfect?" William groused. He gestured at Mr. Bartholomew. "All of this seems absurd."

"I said I'd work on the wording," Mr. Bartholomew said, clearly wounded.

"You must have faith, my lord," Lady Aleksander said. "Nothing ever happens without faith."

Well, that was a problem, then, because William was leaking faith all over the car.

IT SEEMED A week instead of one very long and interminable day by the time they arrived in Glasgow. William hired two carriages, one for the short ride to the village of Hamilton, where tomorrow Mr. Bartholomew would launch his performance—hopefully an improved one. The second carriage was for the longer ride to Hamilton Palace, where the Aleksanders would be the guests of the duke and William for a night or two.

On the way William toyed with the idea of warning the couple about his family, but in the end decided there was nothing he could say that would prepare them for a palace in a perpetual state of construction, an overabundance of antiques and a father with some very wild ideas.

They arrived at Hamilton Palace just behind William's sister, Lady Fraser, and her two lads. "William! We weren't expecting you!" Susan threw her arms around him, hugging him tight. "Thank God you've come. Mama is purchasing new rugs from Belgium."

"I'll have a word with her." He introduced his sister to the Aleksanders, and together they all went in, the lads running ahead, shouting for Grandpapa.

The duke and duchess were clearly surprised to see their prodigal son and fussed over him, his mother concerned about the length of his hair, his father concerned that he wasn't in London doing what he was supposed to be doing, and why hadn't he sent a messenger to inform them he was coming? "What in blazes is this about?" his father demanded once the introductions were made.

William considered his family, all gathered—well, Susan's husband, Lord Fraser, was not there, but then again, he rarely was—and decided that there was no time like the present to make his announcement. He had always subscribed to the theory that if one was to be shot, it was better to get the shooting over with rather than prolong the agony with a flowery speech. "Your Grace," he said to his father.

His father's eyes widened and he looked at his wife. "Must be rather serious, then, aye?"

"Papa, then," William said. "I've an announcement. I've come to tell you that I…"

He hesitated, uncertain how to say this, exactly.

"Darling?" his mother asked.

"I am…" What was the matter with him? He couldn't find the words to convey how he felt about Justine.

"Oh no. Will! Are you *dying*?" Susan whispered.

"No! Well, no' that I am aware. I'm…in love. Aye, that's it. I've fallen in love. There you have it." He gave a jaunty little swing of his arm for emphasis.

He expected something in return. What he got was stunned silence.

Susan looked at their parents. They looked at her. "Who?" Susan asked for them all.

"Aye, that's the problem. I have fallen in love with Her Royal Highness, Princess Justine Ivanosen."

That was met with more stunned silence. And then Susan broke into peals of laughter. "Oh my! Donna tease us so, Will! You gave our hearts a fright!"

William stared at his sister, waiting for her to get hold of herself. She at last looked from him to the Aleksanders and back to him. *"No,"* she said gravely. "Will…you've no', have you?"

"I have."

"And she loves him," Lady Aleksander chimed in. "It's truly a love match. But there is the matter of this terrible rumor about him that could very well remove him from consideration. As you can imagine, the Weslorian king and queen are quite keen to have the princess marry someone with an impeccable reputation. We've come up with a plan to repair this, but we'll need your help."

"My son is in love?" William's mother said dreamily. "I have prayed for this moment. But I do beg your pardon, madam—my son's reputation doesna need *repair*."

"Mama," Susan said and looked at her mother pointedly.

"I mean, not a lot," the duchess amended.

"If I may explain," Lady Aleksander said and stepped forward and began to talk.

When she'd finished, the Douglas family sat silently, all of them staring at the floor for a very long moment.

"Your plan, madam, is laughable," William's father said at last. "But it is true we have no more money to pay Mr. Simpson for his silence."

Susan shrugged. "It's at least as reasonable as accusing you of fathering that bairn. I've known Althea all my life and she would curl into a ball and die of fright if you came near her."

"Beg your pardon?" William asked.

"Well, I donna know what else we might do," his mother said. "Will, darling, are you certain you want to marry a princess? Might there be some…considerations? That is—"

"Mama," William said. "I am certain. Whatever the considerations, I am certain."

"Well, then. I suppose we must give this…plan…a go."

"We need to get a message to Miss Simpson," Lady Aleksander said.

William nodded. "Ewan said Molly McGuire can deliver a note to the kitchen lass in the Simpson house."

William's father gestured to a footman. "Go and fetch Molly, then. Tell her no' to be a mouse about it. It will all be over soon."

"Papa, that sounds as if you mean to sack her," Susan said. "Tell her to come and say no more," she instructed the footman.

"I'm no' wrong," the duke said as the footman strode from the room. "The girl shivers like a leaf every time she's out of the kitchen."

They all discovered this was true minutes later, when Molly stood before them, shivering. But Lady Aleksander, with her reassuring smile and kind voice, convinced her that she was not in any sort of trouble, and, in fact, the family needed her desperately.

"They need me, ma'am?"

"They do. Do you think you could get a very important message to the kitchen girl at the Simpson house?"

The girl looked around the room at all of them, wide-eyed. "Aye. My cousin Janie, she's the scullery maid."

Of course. If William had been able to think a moment, he would have realized that everyone around here was related to everyone else.

"Well, then, my lord, I think you should write the letter," Lady Aleksander said to him.

"Aye, that he should," his father agreed and looked at a footman. "Robert, bring up some of the cellar whisky, aye? We'll make a right proper celebration of it."

And that, William's parents did. As he struggled to write a letter to Miss Simpson that conveyed he was trying to help her, but would need to know the name of the father of her child in order to do that, his father regaled the rest of them with the time-honored classic tale of how he had come to the conclusion that he was the direct descendent of the Scottish kings.

When William had written the letter, he gave it to Molly. Molly put on her cloak, and away she went to deliver it.

For the rest of the night, William could hardly sit. He kept getting up and going to the window to look for any sign of the girl. He imagined that everything had gone wrong, that the girl had lost the letter, or Miss Simpson was gone from Hamilton now, or her father intercepted the letter and knew what they were about. He imagined that Mr. Bartholomew would fail and would be run out of the village.

He imagined that he would not see Justine again. It felt like a burr in his heart. Every movement sent a sharp pain through him.

The girl did not come back to Hamilton Palace that night. William slept not at all.

The next morning Ewan was dispatched to the village to watch Mr. Bartholomew's performance and report the outcome of it. William paced, waiting for Molly McGuire to return. He sent a groomsman out to look for her. He didn't see her along the road.

It was afternoon before Molly finally returned, ambling up the road. William strode out to meet her on the drive. "Where have you been, lass?"

"I beg your pardon, milord!" she said and started to shiver. "But the hour was late and my cousin insisted I stay for the night. The cook gave me the day today. I had some things to do in the village."

William drew a long breath so that he wouldn't snap at her. Perhaps they hadn't made it clear that time was of the essence.

He heard someone behind him and turned to see Lady Aleksander walking quickly to them. She looked as anxious as he felt. Apparently, he was not the only one who hadn't slept last night.

"Well? Did she give the letter to her cousin?" she asked.

"We're just getting to that. Well, lass?"

"No, milord."

"No?" William thought his heart would stop beating. His heart was going to fail him, right here, in front of Hamilton Palace. Maybe he ought to hope for it—it was surely less painful than this.

"No," Molly said softly. "Miss Simpson, she come down from her rooms. She had the bairn, and he's such a fine-looking lad."

"A boy!" Lady Aleksander said.

"Aye, ma'am. Still in swaddling, but has a bit of ginger hair—"

"Molly." William spoke as quietly and evenly as he could. "What did Miss Simpson say?"

"She opened the letter," she said, mimicking it, "and read the letter, and she folded it and put it in her pocket. And then she said, 'Please tell the marquess that the name he seeks is Graeme Ross.'"

"Graeme *Ross*!"

William hadn't heard his sister come out onto the drive, but here she came, her gown billowing out behind her, one of his nephews running after.

"Do you know him, then, Susan?"

"Aye, Will! You know him, too. He has the farm down by the river, remember? We used to buy apples there when we were young."

William suddenly remembered it. A modest farm, a good farm.

"He's a good man, a hardworking man, aye?" Susan said. "But I'd wager no' good enough for Mr. Simpson, is he? He wants Althea to marry above their lot, always has. He was forever sending the poor lass off to soirees and country house parties where she didna know a soul."

Molly was staring wide-eyed at Susan, listening to this. William thought it better if they continued the conversation privately. "Thank you, lass. You may go." He waited until Molly had hurried on, then motioned for Lady Aleksander and his sister to follow him inside.

They retreated to the dining room, where the duke and duchess were enjoying a leisurely luncheon—they'd been at it for two hours.

"Well?" his father demanded. "Did the silly lass return to us?"

"Aye. She brought us a name—Graeme Ross. And Miss Simpson has been delivered of a lad."

"Ah, Ross! Good man, honest man. Hardworking, just like his old pa. Aye, he'll be a good father, I'd wager. Happy to have a son, I'd say. He'll do right by Miss Simpson, that he will."

Just then, they heard the sound of voices at the door. A moment later the butler entered the dining room, and Ewan was behind him. The big man looked disheveled. He looked as if—and this was hard to fathom—he had run from the village.

"Ewan! Has something happened?" William exclaimed. "Are you all right?"

"Aye, milord. Been quite the dust up in the village, that it has."

"Oh no," Lady Aleksander said. "What happened?"

Ewan held up a finger and put his hand to the small of

his back, wincing dramatically as he drew a breath. Everyone in the room waited, watching him closely.

"Mr. Bartholomew," he said. "Now, that's an actor for you, aye? Had me convinced."

"Ewan, what *happened*?" Susan demanded.

"He said…" Ewan paused to draw another breath.

The rest of them leaned forward a bit more.

"That he'd come to claim his woman and his bairn, that sort of thing. Better than he said it on the train, I'll give him that."

"And?" William asked, trying to hurry him along.

"Well… Mr. Simpson's brother was present, having a pint, he was. Might have had more than the one, if you want me honest opinion. Or perhaps he's got a bad back, I donna know, but he was doing a bit of swaying on his feet."

"Aye, Ewan, *and*?"

"He said the bloke was a fraud, milord. Then, the McFee brothers—you've seen them, have you no'? About the size of the cairns on old Bessie's land, the two of them—well, they meant to toss him out. But then Mrs. Palley asked them all why the bloke would say it if it weren't true, for it was surely trouble, and should they no' ask the lass if what he said was true?"

"Oh dear," William's mother said. "This doesn't sound good, does it? Does anyone think this sounds good?"

"Aye, Your Grace, there did indeed follow quite the heated debate, it did." Ewan paused to wipe his brow.

William thought he might explode before Ewan ever got around to the reason he'd raced back here. *"Ewan!"*

"Aye, milord. It was decided then and there that the only way to solve it was to call Mr. Simpson to the public house."

"What of Miss Simpson?" Lady Aleksander asked.

"Why didn't they think to call her? I think *she'd* know better than her father."

"No, madam, no—Mr. Simpson, he's the one to speak for the family, aye? They wanted to hear from him, and then decided they ought to hold Mr. Bartholomew till they did. They'd no' allow him to leave."

"Will, there's no time," Susan said breathlessly. "By the time you bring a carriage around to the Ross farm on these terrible roads, Mr. Simpson will have come and gone, and Lord knows what they will have done to your friend."

William's head was spinning. Everything was spinning, right out of any shred of control they might have fooled themselves into thinking they'd had when they'd stepped off the train yesterday.

It was decided he would ride to the Ross farms. In the meantime, his father, Susan and the Aleksanders would head for the public house to stave off any harm to Mr. Bartholomew.

A half hour later William was pushing his mount down the river road to reach the Ross farm. Once there he leaped off the back of the horse and ran to the house, knocking hard on the roughhewn door.

No one answered.

He pounded again, only harder and, growing impatient, stalked around the house, trying to peer into the windows. He couldn't see anything.

He went to the barn next, but no one was there, either. He returned to the door of the house and banged again. But with every strike, he could feel all hope slipping away from him. He'd been a fool to ever wish for it, to believe that he could find a woman like Justine and actually marry her.

He'd been a bigger fool to ever hope this ridiculous,

harebrained scheme could work. His throat felt raw, and his eyes burned with the unshed tears of frustration and loss.

What would he be after this? How would he carry on, feeling half the man he'd been before he'd ever gone to Prescott Hall? He felt more defeated than he ever had in his life. He felt detached, like his life was floating away from his body.

He turned away from the door and began to walk toward his horse. But something made him look up, and a swell of joy surged through him. Mr. Ross was walking up a path from the river, carrying a pail and a fishing pole. "Mr. Ross!" he called, waving his hand high overhead.

When Mr. Ross saw him, he stopped. He put down his pail and rod. "My lord?"

"Praise God, you're here, lad. For a moment I thought all was lost." He laughed like a madman.

Mr. Ross eyed him warily.

"Ah, aye, you've no idea why I've come," he said. "I donna mean to be blunt, sir, but we havena much time. I've come to speak to you about Miss Althea Simpson."

Mr. Ross paled. "I donna know Miss Simpson."

Another mistake—William should have spent a bit of time preparing to break this news to Mr. Ross, but in the midst of everything, he hadn't thought of it. He walked down the path to stand before the man. "I beg your pardon, Mr. Ross, but there is something you must know. Perhaps you already know and donna care to admit it."

"I donna know anything," he said.

"Miss Simpson…" He rubbed his nape. "She has delivered a bairn. A boy. Ginger hair."

Mr. Ross's body visibly tensed. His eyes turned hard. "I've heard the talk."

But his reaction confused William. He'd heard the talk?

"Then why…?" William paused. He understood. Mr. Ross had heard the rumors about *him*. "The child is no' mine, if that's what you think. *You* are the father. Ginger hair!" he all but shouted, gesturing to Mr. Ross's healthy crop of ginger hair.

But Mr. Ross snorted and bent down to pick up his pail and rod, and started walking, brushing past William as he went up the hill.

William whirled around "Where are you going? You must believe me, man. The bairn is *yours*. There was never anyone but you, and certainly no' me, aye?"

Mr. Ross stopped walking and turned around, looked him square in the eye. "If it were mine, she would have met me as we agreed. But the last anyone saw her, she was with you, milord." He continued up the path.

"Why did we no' anticipate this?" William shouted heavenward, then strode after him. "You've got it all wrong, man. I tried to help her. I tried to make it possible for her to reach you, do you understand? At least hear me out. Give me that. Give *her* that."

Mr. Ross paused and looked back. "You think I donna understand? You got a child in her, and you donna want it. You are here to saddle me with your by-blow." He started walking again.

William wanted to put a fist in his mouth or through a tree, but he was running out of time. He kept talking. "I got her a horse and a room in the inn. I told her how to get to the place you'd agreed to meet." He frantically dug through his memory of that day. "Go out the old fort road and at the fork, go right!"

Mr. Ross paused.

"I saw her to her room, that I did, for I did no' want any-one to bother her. But then I left, because in spite of what you might think you know about me, I am a gentleman. I assumed she would leave at first light. Unfortunately, and unbeknownst to me, her father found her before that could happen."

Mr. Ross shook his head.

William felt desperation climb up his throat. His hand had developed a curious shake, and he could feel his scalp perspiring. "Mr. Ross. *Graeme*." He stretched out his hand, as if to put it on the man's shoulder, but Mr. Ross was too far away. "I understand. Your pride has taken a beating. You've heard things, aye? They're no' true, on my honor, but the rumors have put a dagger in your heart. You've had a love that made you ache, and when that love disappeared, it put fire in your veins. How can a man live with that fire? But I'm here to help you. I'm here to give you the chance to make things right. You can still be with the woman you love. You can still hold your child in your arms. A ginger-haired lad."

Mr. Ross lifted his gaze to William.

"But if you donna come with me now, *right* now, she will be lost to you forever. Can you bear that? Can you get up tomorrow and the day after that and the day after that knowing you did no' do everything in your power to have her?"

Mr. Ross didn't move. He just glared at William in silence.

William dropped his hand, resigned. "Well, then. I suppose that's that, aye?" It was clear that Graeme Ross would never believe him. Susan should have come. But he'd come, the man Mr. Ross believed had ruined his love and his woman, and he'd just made a bad situation worse.

He felt his life float far away from him, and felt almost serene in his despair.

CHAPTER THIRTY-SIX

THE TELEGRAPH FROM Queen Agnes was delivered by a contingent of six Weslorian soldiers. "What does it say?" Amelia asked, her voice high-pitched with her nerves.

Justine read the telegraph again as she stroked Dodi on her lap. "We are commanded home. We are to sail as early as Friday."

"Oh!" Lady Bardaline clapped her hands. "This is wonderful news. I think it for the best, Your Royal Highness. Queen Victoria will be on her way to France, and Lady Aleksander is...well, she is perhaps not as well connected as your parents had hoped. But you mustn't fret." She smiled slyly.

She mustn't *fret*? Justine stared at her lady-in-waiting in disbelief. "Go," she said simply.

Lady Bardaline gave a nervous little laugh.

"Leave my sitting room, madam."

Amelia's eyes widened. She stared at Justine, then at Lady Bardaline.

Lady Bardaline rose slowly from her seat. She looked as if she was struggling with the urge to speak as she walked to the door. She even turned back, but instead of speaking, she gave both sisters a dour look before she went out.

Seviana quietly went to the door and locked it.

"Thank you, Sevie," Justine said. She held out Dodi. "Will you take her out for a walk?"

Amelia looked at Justine with wonder. She waited until Seviana had taken Dodi and quit the room before she squealed. "At *last*! You were wonderful, darling! I can hardly abide the woman. But never mind her. What are we going to do, Jussie? We won't board the ship. We'll ask Lady Holland to help us."

Justine shook her head. "Did you see the small cavalry Mama sent? They are here to make sure we board the ship, darling."

"But I don't want to leave. I *like* it here. And what about Douglas?"

Yes, what about William? Every day Justine waited for word. Every day she held Dodi and paced in front of the window to see if they'd come. It had been four full days. She went over it and over it—a full day of train travel to Scotland, another one back to London. One day to confront Mr. Simpson. One day to…

Well, she couldn't imagine it, and now she had only two days left before someone would force her to depart. If he didn't come back in two days, her life was over as far as she was concerned. She would be a queen without a heart. A heartless queen. A heartless, mourning queen.

William didn't come back that day, no matter how often she looked out the window and willed him to. Justine was furious with her lack of foresight—she didn't even know where to send a letter to him.

The next day Justine and Amelia were forcing themselves to pack when a footman came to tell them that Justine had a caller. "Lord Iddesleigh, ma'am."

Justine and Amelia looked at each other, thinking the same thing—he had news. They raced downstairs, and he turned to the door when they burst into the receiving room.

He was smiling…but his expression turned a little panicky when they both rushed forward, eager for his news.

"Lord Iddesleigh, so good of you to come," Justine said breathlessly. "Any news?"

"Your Royal Highnesses," he said, bowing. "Alas, no. I had rather hoped you might be able to share some?"

Justine's body sagged along with her hope. Her body felt so heavy suddenly. "No. Not a word."

"Ah."

Amelia collapsed onto the settee. "It isn't fair," she murmured.

"They've failed, haven't they?" Justine asked the earl. "If they had been successful, we would know, wouldn't we?"

"Darling! Don't say it," Amelia begged her.

But Lord Iddesleigh winced. "My advice to you, ma'am, is not to give up hope. I learned long ago that it is better not to assume the worst until there is proof. It only makes for sleepless nights, and despair tends to feed on itself. Think good thoughts." He smiled.

She smiled sadly. "It's too late for that, I'm afraid."

Lord Iddesleigh sighed. "I have come to bid you adieu. My wife desires to spend her confinement in the country at our seat. Unfortunately, there are times in an earl's life when he must be about the business of earling, and at the same time, make his wife happy." He wrinkled his nose. "I can't imagine why she wants it, as there is hardly a thing there but a crumbling old castle."

"Thank you for your hospitality, my lord," Justine said. "We are sailing for home on Friday."

"Oh." Iddesleigh frowned. "So soon? We will all of us be sorry to see you go. I wish only the best for you and your sister."

It was too late for that, too. The best had come and gone.

After Lord Iddesleigh left, Amelia resumed the packing. She seemed to understand that Justine didn't want to talk. It wasn't until much later that afternoon that Justine managed to pull herself together.

Her father had once told her that disappointments are like waves—they carry you down to the lowest of lows, but at the end of the wave is another peak, and that she should always look forward. Head up, chin up, do not let disappointment sink her.

Justine had no choice. She would be queen soon enough and would always have the good of Wesloria to tend to before herself. That was the devil's bargain for a life of privilege.

There was much to do before they left. She would pack her love for William in the softest of silk and tuck it in a corner of her heart. But she did not have the luxury of time to mourn him.

It was dusk, and she had refused tea and asked them not to make her supper. She would do her duty, but she would not force herself to eat when her appetite had been smashed. She was lost in thought, carefully wrapping her books, when she heard a commotion on the drive below.

Her heart quickened. She slowly got up and went to the window, afraid of more disappointment, another hope soundly dashed. But a dusty carriage with the Duke of Hamilton's crest had pulled into the drive. As she watched, Lady Aleksander emerged.

"Who is it?" Amelia asked, bursting into the room. She crowded into the window beside Justine.

Justine held her breath. Lord Aleksander came next. And then a man Justine did not recognize. He stood back and looked into the interior of the coach.

One long, booted leg appeared. And then another. "Oh, dear God," she said and grabbed Amelia's hand.

"It's him, Jussie," Amelia whispered. "It's really him."

Justine whirled around and ran, leaping over the piles of things to be packed. She flung open the door and picked up her skirts, running down the stairs, nearly colliding with Lord Bardaline below when he wandered out of the study. "What the devil?"

She pushed past him and raced onto the drive and to William. She didn't stop running, didn't take a moment to collect herself and greet the travelers. She threw herself into his arms and he caught her, his arms going tightly around her, squeezing her to him. He kissed her cheek, her neck.

And then everyone was talking at once.

"What took you so long?" she asked him.

"An unplanned trip to Gretna Green."

"Where?"

William laughed. His face was free of worry, his eyes dancing in the low light of a sinking sun. "Let's go in and I'll tell you everything."

"Wait, William…is it over?"

"Aye. It's over, lass."

IN THE GRAND SALON, as the footmen bustled around serving wine and whisky, Justine learned that the scheme, as ridiculous as it had been, had actually *worked*. She was giddy with disbelief and happiness, and laughed louder than anyone. "But how?" she demanded to know.

"It was remarkable," Lord Aleksander said. "My wife has performed a bit of a miracle. Not only has Lord Douglas shed the rumor, he somehow emerged the hero of this tale. I thought the entire village of Hamilton would lift him to their shoulders and carry him off."

"Tell us, tell us!" Amelia cried, bouncing in her seat.

"If I may be allowed," drawled Mr. Bartholomew.

"Please," said Lila.

Mr. Bartholomew walked to the center of the room, spread his arms wide as if testing the space, then began the reenactment of his performance at the public house. He acted all the different characters, pausing to explain to his audience who was who. He paused for a dramatic setting of the scene for when Mr. Simpson arrived, explaining he was as red-faced as if he'd been burned, and accusing him, Mr. Bartholomew, in the role of Robert Barstow—Justine was never really very clear on who, exactly, Robert Barstow was meant to be—of being a fraudster and a cheat. He further accused Mr. Barstow of wanting to extort money from the Duke of Hamilton in exchange for covering the sins of the duke's son, the marquess.

"And there, it very nearly fell apart," Lila said. "Douglas's father, the Duke of Hamilton, said Mr. Simpson had done the very same. Mr. Simpson first denied it, then said it was owed to him, as the marquess was the father of his grandchild, and then, who should arrive like a knight come to save the village, but the marquess himself, in the company of Mr. Ross." She laughed and looked at William. "I thought you'd never come!"

"I thought I'd never come. We'd no' considered that Mr. Ross would have heard the rumor about me and no' believe me innocent of the charges. Why would he, aye? The last he heard from Miss Simpson was that she would meet him. She never did, and the last person who saw her was me. What was the man to think?"

"How did you convince him?" Amelia asked.

"I donna rightly know. I'm no' ashamed to say I begged him, cajoled him, nearly hit him." He chuckled. "And then

I asked him if he could bear to live another day knowing he hadn't done everything to be with the woman he loved." He looked at Justine and smiled. "Because if it were me, I could no' bear it."

Her heart very nearly fluttered out of her chest.

"Ahem," Mr. Bartholomew said, not wishing to relinquish his stage.

"Please," William said, gesturing for him to continue.

Mr. Bartholomew resumed his dramatic reenactment of the moment William told the crowd—which had grown by the hour, Lord Aleksander interjected, everyone coming from near and far to watch the scene unfolding at the Cock and Sparrow—that he never intended but to help Miss Simpson reach the man she loved. And then, to vouch for him, his sister arrived with Miss Simpson and her newborn son, Graeme.

"Named for the father, of course," said Lila, beaming. "The moment Mr. Ross saw her and his son, he very nearly fell to his knees. He asked her then and there to marry him."

"I beg your pardon. *I* meant to tell that," Mr. Bartholomew said.

"Oh. Do go on."

"She said yes, or aye, or something like it, and her father tried to intervene but was put off from it by the crowd," he said and acted out the brawl that followed the dramatic ending of his play.

Mr. Simpson then showed his true colors by banishing his daughter and her new son from his house. It was clear to all assembled that she and Mr. Ross were very much in love and had been made to suffer by the selfishness and greediness of her father.

"There was nothing to be done for it," William said. "There we were, with two unmarried people very much in love, with a bairn. We took them posthaste to Gretna Green to see them married as they ought to have been. Althea Simpson will never be forced into her father's house again."

"But…but is the scandal done and dusted? Is it well and truly over?" Justine asked.

"Oh no," Lila said. "The story is everywhere. I've no doubt it has already reached London. But the scandal has taken a turn and now the marquess has emerged as a veritable saint, and I daresay for the first time in his life."

William laughed. "I've no doubt of it."

"He is hailed for the kindness shown Miss Simpson when he could have easily turned a blind eye," Lila continued. "He is applauded for devising a scheme to trick the truth from Mr. Simpson before he could extort the duke again, and then finding the father of Miss Simpson's child and putting him with the woman he loves. There will not be a word said against him now."

"Good Lord, it's a miracle," Amelia mused.

"And your performance, Mr. Bartholomew! It couldn't have happened without you," Lila said.

The gentleman smiled coquettishly. "I should like it to be mentioned in the London papers, if at all possible."

"I think we can arrange it," Lila said.

"I'd just like to be entirely clear," Justine said, before someone began pouring champagne. "There is no longer a scandal involving the marquess?"

"That's right." Lila said.

It was true, then. Justine's heart quickened. Her palms were damp. She was suddenly reminded of the time she had gone to Astasia Castle and had stood on a parapet, looking out at the valley. She had felt the pull of her ancestry, of her destiny that day. She felt it now. She was about to do something terribly bold, but she could feel the destiny in it. This was right.

She stood up and turned to face William. "Will you rise?" Her voice cracked slightly, and she noticed that Amelia looked a bit alarmed. Well, Justine was a bit alarmed, too. She could feel that internal quake, but she swallowed it down.

This was perhaps the most important moment of her life.

She kept her gaze on William, saw the hint of a smile on his lips. He stood and bowed. "I think a knighthood is no' necessary, Your Royal Highness."

Lord Aleksander laughed.

Justine swallowed again. Her nerves, her blasted nerves, were trying to strangle her. But she wouldn't have it. Not this time. She was a bit wobbly, but she sank down onto one knee. She heard the gasps behind her but she kept her gaze on William. "Lord William Douglas, Marquess of Hamilton and…and…"

"Clydesdale," he said.

"Clydesdale," she echoed. "Will you do me the honor of marrying me, of being my husband, and my prince consort, my helpmate, my love?"

Lady Bardaline, who had remained silent, suddenly cried out. "Your Royal Highness, you can't!"

"Madam, please," Amelia said. "You are ruining the moment!"

"This will *never* be allowed," Lady Bardaline protested. "Your mother will not allow it!"

"Keep calm, madam. I've already sent a telegraph to Prime Minister Robuchard, informing him a match has been made," Lila said.

"You've *what*?" Lord Bardaline shouted.

"I beg your pardon!" Justine said loudly.

Everyone stilled.

"I'm in the middle of something here, and his lordship has not yet answered."

William laughed. He came down on one knee, too, and took her hands in his. "Aye, ma'am, I will marry you. I will love you, adore you, protect you, advise you, defend you, and above all, I will serve you as my queen. That is, assuming Wesloria allows my citizenship."

"Your Royal Highness," Lord Bardaline said softly, trying a different tack than his wife. "Surely, you understand that the king must agree to any proposal of marriage."

"Yes, I understand." She smiled at William. "He will."

William grinned. He stood up, took her hand and pulled her to her feet. And then he wrapped his arms around her and kissed her fully on the lips.

The room erupted into chaos behind her. Amelia was crying, someone was cheering and the Bardalines were shouting at Lila.

Justine didn't care. She felt buoyant with love and gratitude and wonder and eagerness for the future. She felt as proud and as confident as she ever had in her life, her chest bursting with it. She'd made a decision for herself as the future ruler of Wesloria, and she was certain it was the best decision she would ever make.

The future suddenly looked bright.

She felt like a queen.

She was a queen.

THE SAILING WAS put off for another five days, so that the Marquess of Hamilton could have his things packed and readied for the voyage. A flurry of telegraphs went back and forth between London and St. Edys, and there was still much negotiating to do, but the princess had been right—

her heartfelt telegraph to her father had done the trick. No matter how much Queen Agnes and Prime Minister Robuchard might have objected—and Lila didn't know that they had, but if they had—King Maksim was still king and approved of his daughter's happiness.

Lila watched as carriages arrived at Prescott Hall to whisk Justine and William, Amelia and Dodi and all their trunks to the ship. "They are so much in love," she said wistfully.

Valentin put on his long coat. "Are you coming?"

"I am." She had just put the finishing touches on her note to be telegraphed to Robuchard, explaining to him that Princess Amelia needed a little time to mature, that was all.

Valentin bent over her at the desk and kissed the top of her head. "Do you know who else is in love?"

"I do," she said and sealed the note, then stood up to hug her husband.

EPILOGUE

One month later

JUSTINE AND WILLIAM were in bed, their bare legs and arms wrapped around each other in lazy, post-coital satisfaction. She stared up at the embroidered canopy above them, feeling dreamy and sated. "Why is it that no one ever tells you how wonderful intercourse is?"

William laughed and kissed her shoulder. "You're no' supposed to like it, *leannan*. You're to bear it as your duty."

"But I *love* it."

"Aye, you're an insatiable little beast."

"*Je*, I am, and thank the saints I have an insatiable husband." Her fingers trailed down his chest, to his groin and below.

"What are you doing?"

"I don't have to be dressed for another hour."

"Your servants will tear down the door if you donna come out soon."

She giggled. "Let them." She kissed his mouth, then his chest and then moved down.

William had taught her about pleasure, how to give it, how to receive it. She often thought of what Queen Victoria had said about finding compatibility in the marriage bed. That was the best advice the English queen had given her.

She and William were so in love, and confirmed it almost every day in this bed.

The transition for William had gone easier than Justine had anticipated. He loved Wesloria, he'd said, because *she* was Wesloria. He'd made acquaintances, of course he had, because he was a personable man. And, naturally, he advised her, even when she didn't want to hear it.

She'd returned to Wesloria to find her father gravely ill. The change in him after a summer away was profound. The royal physician had informed her that he likely wouldn't live another month. Because of his deteriorating condition, her marriage had been a private affair. Everything had happened so quickly, before she'd had time to think.

At the end of the week her father intended to formally abdicate in favor of his heir. She would be coronated as sovereign immediately. William would swear his fealty and be made prince consort. And Seviana had made a delightful new collar for Dodi to mark the occasion.

It was all so fast and so dreadful…but Justine was at peace with it. She knew within a week of taking her wedding vows in the palace chapel that she'd made the right decision. She couldn't imagine being queen for a moment without William. Not a single moment.

Later, when she finally emerged from her private chambers, Seviana winced at the state of her hair and immediately set about readying her. She was to open the new city library this afternoon.

She arrived with no time to spare, thanks to her reluctance to leave her bed and her husband. The distinguished guests were seated, and Justine was hurried up onto the platform to make her remarks. Her breath was short, and her scalp tingled uncomfortably, but she took a deep breath, pulled out her eyeglasses and put them on. She glanced at her mother to her right, who gave her a slight roll of her eyes. She glanced to William on her left. He smiled and gave her a subtle wink.

And then she looked at the sea of people before her. This would always be the hardest part for her, but she felt more confident than she ever had. She could practically feel William's strength around her, and in that strength she'd discovered a part of herself she hadn't known existed. It was astonishing—all it really took was for someone to believe in her to give her permission to believe in herself. That was what William had done for her.

She could do this. She could be a queen.

She could be anything.

She smiled at the people gathered. *"Ledia et harrad,"* she said clearly. *"Bon mowen."*

* * * * *

Get 4 FREE REWARDS!

We'll send you 2 FREE Books plus 2 FREE Mystery Gifts.

FREE
Value Over
$20

Both the **Romance** and **Suspense** collections feature compelling novels written by many of today's bestselling authors.